CONTROLLING INTEREST

Books by Elizabeth White

Off the Record

Fair Game

Fireworks

Prairie Christmas

Sweet Delights

The Texas Gatekeepers

1 | *Under Cover of Darkness*

2 | *Sounds of Silence*

3 | *On Wings of Deliverance*

CONTROLLING INTEREST

ELIZABETH WHITE

ZONDERVAN.com/
AUTHORTRACKER
follow your favorite authors

Controlling Interest
Copyright © 2008 by Elizabeth White

Requests for information should be addressed to:
Zondervan, *Grand Rapids, Michigan* 49530

Library of Congress Cataloging-in-Publication Data

White, Elizabeth.
    Controlling interest / Elizabeth White.
       p. cm.
     ISBN 978-0-310-27305-9 (pbk.)
     I. Title.
   PS3623.H574C66 2008
   813'.6 — dc22

2007047706

Interior design by Michelle Espinoza

Printed in the United States of America

08 09 10 11 12 13 • 23 22 21 20 19 18 17 16 15 14 13 12 11 10 9 8 7 6 5 4 3 2 1

*This book is dedicated in loving memory of my friend,
Tammy Jayne Litton, who loved to read.
And for Nicole: Welcome to the family.*

ACKNOWLEDGMENTS

For what started out as a fairly straightforward detective caper, this story turned out to require quite a bit of research. For the details involving Yasmine's Pakistani-Muslim family, I'm indebted to an Internet blog maintained by a charming Pakistani-American gentleman who willingly answered my questions about language, names, and religious customs, but who wishes to remain anonymous. Any lingering mistakes, I take full responsibility for.

As usual, I owe a debt of gratitude to Scott, Ryan, and Tammy — who brainstormed story ideas and read drafts of the manuscript along the way — and to my agent, Beth Jusino, who is a constant source of encouragement. Huge thanks to editors Leslie Peterson and Becky Shingledecker for making suggestions, correcting errors, and smoothing prose. Couldn't do it without y'all.

FOREWORD BY TERRI BLACKSTOCK

Dear Reader,

Elizabeth White is my sister from the South, as well as my sister in Christ. I was introduced to her years ago when we shared space in an anthology called *Sweet Delights*. It was one of her first published books, and I knew I was going to be seeing a lot more of her. Since that time, I've gotten to know Beth as a kindred spirit. When we go to writers' retreats and conferences, she's always one of the few people who speaks my language—southern! She's also an excellent writer. I love her humor and wish I could come up with her descriptive verbs and funny phrases. As for her Christianity, she's the real deal. And her writing proves it.

I was recently working on a first draft of a new book—the part of writing I hate the most—when I took a break to read *Controlling Interest*. I was reminded of some of my earlier novels that had a strong romantic relationship as part of their plots. I could tell in the first few pages that it was just what I needed. Natalie, the heroine, made me giggle, and I was instantly caught up in the intrigue of the missing young Pakistani woman, Yasmine. The romance in this book is such a treasure. Natalie and Matt's bumbling relationship as they partner together to solve this missing person case is . . . well, fun. Before I knew it, I was caught up in the story and had forgotten my own book!

But the faith message gives this book the depth I love. Elizabeth White doesn't write about perfect Christians who have it all together. She writes about flawed Christians who are works-in-progress, navigating their way through their faith and learning what it means to be more like Christ. If you've been a Christian for a long time, you'll find it refreshing to see Christ through eyes that are brand new to Christianity, as some of her characters are. If you're new to it yourself, you'll be able to relate strongly to the fits and starts of living in faith.

So curl up and relax, and enjoy Elizabeth White's southern style! I think you'll come away with a new favorite writer.

Terri Blackstock

A NOTE FROM THE AUTHOR

I grew up in a Mississippi suburb of Memphis. I've always loved the river, the bridge, Beale Street, Graceland, and all the other funky southern things that went into the writing of this story. My very first published novella was set in Memphis, and I've always wanted to go back there. So here's Matt's love story, which begins next to an Elvis-themed clock shop (a product of my imagination) on Beale Street, just around the corner from the Peabody Hotel—where the ducks still parade every afternoon at five on the dot.

The riverboat as I've described it is not any particular one, but is instead an amalgam of several cruises that I've experienced over the years. You can go to just about any Mississippi River port and catch a sleepy, relaxing dinner cruise. Most of the restaurants and hotels Matt and Natalie patronize on their adventure are made-up; however, the Memphis Rendezvous is legendary for its ribs, Silky O'Sullivan's on Beale boasts a beer-drinking goat, and Chamoun's Rest Haven Restaurant is a landmark outside Clarksdale, Mississippi.

The Beale Street Waterfront Mission was inspired by the Beautiful Feet Ministries of Fort Worth, Texas, founded and run by my friends Mike and Sarah Myers. A mission that serves the physical and spiritual needs of the residents of low-income east side neighborhoods, including homeless individuals and families, the "Feet" is a functioning church with Sunday and weekday ministries. In addition to church services and Bible studies, Beautiful Feet offers a clothing and food ministry, mission trips, and outreach projects to local shelters, prisons, and halfway houses. For more information, contact Mike Myers at (817) 536-0505.

As always, I pray that Christian readers will take this story as a challenge to hands-on faith and to finding the source of truth in the Bible. I pray that readers who aren't sure of their relationship with Jesus will meet him face-to-face. He loves you!

Comments about the story are welcome via my website, www.elizabethwhite.net.

CONTROLLING INTEREST

ONE

Natalie Tubberville had one thing on her mind as she whipped her ice-blue Miata up the ramp to the Memphis International Airport terminal. Well, three things. A Big Mac, supersize fries, and a chocolate shake. Chasing down details for one of Dad's oil-rich clients since five a.m., she hadn't stopped to breathe, much less satisfy her howling stomach.

Screeching into a parking space, she shoved the gearshift into park and hopped out of the car. She glanced at her wrist. Tweetie Bird pointed to ten minutes of five. Ouch. She had to book it. Yasmine Patel, having come all the way from Pakistan, deserved a warm welcome, and Natalie hated to make her wait. It wasn't Yasmine's fault her dad had put a twist on Eddie Tubberville's arm—thereby hijacking a good chunk of Natalie's vacation.

She had no idea what a Pakistani girl would look like. Did they wear the hookahs you always saw in the movies? Wait, *hookah* didn't sound right. Come to think of it, that was a pipe. The caterpillar in *Alice in Wonderland* smoked a hookah. *Bookah*, then.

No, *burka*. Something like that. She should have asked Daddy for a picture. Yasmine would be dark-haired, no doubt, and small. Maybe with one of those red paint splotches between her eyes. If more than one Middle Eastern young woman had arrived on this flight, Natalie was going to be in big trouble.

She hauled it across the lobby toward baggage claim. These platform clogs made it hard to run, but she couldn't stand to leave them in the closet this morning. When you got new shoes, you were supposed to wear them. It was a rule somewhere. Besides, at five-foot-four she needed the extra inches.

She should have made a sign. Wait. Good idea. She dug in her purse—a little red-beaded wrist bag, barely big enough to carry a credit card—until she found a folded-up Orpheum program from *Annie* and a Crimson Tide lip pencil. By the time she reached baggage claim, she had the program covered in crooked red letters: YASMINE P. Smiling, holding the program above her head, she took up a station facing the hallway where deplaning passengers entered the baggage claim area. Tourists and home folks began to stream by like minnows in a creek.

She caught the eye of a businessman in a tired-looking suit. "Excuse me. Were you on Flight 57 from Amsterdam?"

"Huh?" The man glanced at her over his shoulder. "Yeah. First one off the plane."

Considering the Patel fortune, Yasmine had probably flown first class, too, and shouldn't be far behind. Natalie could spring for a late lunch at Mickey-D's. Or maybe Ruby Tuesday. Daddy wouldn't mind paying.

A couple of old women in polyester pants outfits shuffled by. Then a cluster of teenagers, apparently home for spring break. Natalie waited, dancing with impatience—and aching insoles—on her cork platforms. Maybe she'd take them off and pretend she was a model some other time.

One clog in hand, she spied a dark young woman hesitating behind a middle-aged couple in matching "I Love Holland" T-shirts. The girl wore a long, silky apple-green tunic over loose-fitting matching leggings. Shiny black hair peeked out from under a diaphanous embroidered shawl, and intricate beaded earrings swung against her fragile jawline. A series of thin gold bangles jingled on one wrist, and a diamond pendant sparkled at her throat. Wow. Exquisite.

But the big black eyes were shadowed with fatigue, the full mouth turned down at the corners. The twelve-hour flight must've been a killer.

"Yasmine!" Natalie waved the program. She dropped her shoe and tried to shove her foot in it before Yasmine disappeared. "Yasmine Patel!"

The young woman stopped, passengers swarming around her like bees around a particularly exotic orchid. She stood on her toes and caught Natalie's gaze. Her eyes flicked up to the improvised sign, then widened. She looked over her shoulder and bolted around the Holland tourists.

Away from Natalie.

Natalie got her shoe on without twisting her ankle. "Yasmine! Hey, it's me, Natalie Tubberville. I'm your ride!" She dodged a mom pushing a baby stroller and caught up to her passenger. "Aren't you Yasmine?" She swung around in front of the Pakistani girl, forcing her to stop. Good grief, she was a little thing. Natalie felt positively gargantuan.

Yasmine's shoulders slumped. "I am Yasmine Patel." A hesitant smile showed small, perfect white teeth. "You are sent for me?"

"Sure am." Natalie held out a hand.

Yasmine offered her slim, elegant fingers. "So happy. Thank you for coming." Extravagant black lashes swept downward. "I am feeling . . . some lost."

Natalie tried to peg the accent. A bit sing-song, infused with a British twang. Sophisticated, compared to her own Tennessee drawl, but definitely wobbly. Natalie's heart softened. Maybe the girl was acting weird because she'd expected her fiancé to meet her.

"Well, come on, let's snag your luggage and I'll buy you some lunch. You hungry?" She took off toward baggage claim.

Yasmine tip-tapped along beside Natalie on jeweled sandals. "Thank you, I am not hungry, just—please, could you slow down?"

"Good grief, I'm sorry." Natalie slowed, looking down at her diminutive companion, who was panting like a Pekeapoo on a leash. "Wasn't thinking."

"It is no worry. But I would like a drink of ..." Yasmine took a deep breath, as if coming to a monumental decision. "Starbucks. Yes, caramel vanilla macchiato, if you please. Whole milk with a packet of Splenda. Whipped cream on top."

Natalie blinked. Yasmine hadn't seemed to be the demanding type. "Starbucks?" That was going to add fifteen minutes onto her wait for lunch. She switched the mental list around and decided she'd eat at Carrabba's. Big juicy steak with Caesar salad on the side. Daddy owed her big-time for this.

Yasmine looked up at her with huge, limpid near-black eyes. "I did not see a Starbucks sign somewhere? I thought all American airports—"

"Of course there's a Starbucks. No problem. This way." Natalie made a U-turn.

"No, no. Please." Yasmine clutched Natalie's arm. "You get it while I find my luggage. We shall save time." She linked her fingers under her chin. There was a solitaire rock the size of Baghdad on her engagement finger. "Please? I am anxious to see my ... my fiancé, but I am sooo thirsty."

Okay, kinda different, but what do I know? Natalie sighed. "Alright. You go on to baggage claim, get a skycap to help you, and

I'll be right back." Natalie backed toward the refreshment center. "No problem."

"Whipped cream," she muttered as she limped into Starbucks and stood in line for what seemed like an hour. Tweetie was pointing to five-thirty by the time she'd ordered, recklessly adding a double mocha espresso for herself. She'd be awake all night, but then she was half the time anyway. Life was too interesting to waste it sleeping. *Carpe diem*.

She sat down at a little round table to contemplate her guest's odd behavior. Maybe she'd been raised in a harem. No, that was Mesopotamia.

Ten minutes later, she had laid a trail of Splenda packets in the form of a giant yellow *N* when she noticed the counter clerk craning his neck. "Caramel vanilla macchiato and a double-mocha espresso?"

Natalie jumped up and snatched the drinks along with a handful of the yellow packets. Surely Yasmine had her luggage in hand by now. Coming from that far away, planning to stay and get married, the Pakistani girl probably had a ton of clothes. Unless she planned to do some serious trousseau shopping. Natalie brightened. She could offer to help with the shopping.

She walked fast, sipping the espresso and wincing at the pain in her feet. The clogs were staying in the closet tomorrow, new or not.

There was the carousel for Yasmine's flight, a few pieces of luggage still going round and round. She scanned the crowd. No bright-green tunic and shawl. Just plain everyday American T-shirts, suits, and baseball caps.

Natalie could've sworn she told Yasmine to wait in baggage claim, but maybe she'd gone outside.

She circled the area one more time, then, sipping espresso for fortitude, stomped toward the exit. Chasing the girl all over the airport hadn't been part of the agreement. Daddy owed her dinner at the country club and a movie. Nothing less.

A line of taxis waited outside. People were stowing luggage in trunks, paying off drivers. "Yasmine?" Natalie called uncertainly.

Her eye caught a flash of apple-green disappearing into a white van parked at the Northwest Airlines entrance. The van's side door slammed from the inside, the end of a gauzy scarf catching in the crack.

Holy schmoly. Yasmine had gotten into a complete stranger's van. What was she thinking? Panic shot through Natalie, from the soles of her feet all the way up to her chest.

"Yasmine!" She took off running, heedless of whipped cream and hot coffee sloshing out of the tops of the two cups. "Ow!" Her purse dangled on her wrist, swaying wildly. Her feet screamed with pain. If she fell and broke her neck it would serve her right. She should've worn jeans and sneakers today. A denim mini-skirt was completely inappropriate apparel for chasing heiresses.

The van pulled out into the drive and headed for the exit. Natalie chugged faster, beginning to pray. *Oh, Lord, what's going on?* She kicked off the shoes, tossed aside the coffee, and bore down. Her final Little League baseball all-star game flashed through her brain.

Pitcher Natalie Tubberville rounds third and heads for home. The centerfielder makes the throw. She slides to avoid the catcher's mitt. Her hand swipes at the corner of the plate and misses. She's out!

The van wheeled out of sight, pouring diesel smoke into the sweet Memphis-in-May air.

When Daddy found out she'd misplaced the heiress-bride, he was going to write her out of his will.

Lovely.

Matt Hogan was giving fasting a whirl. Test-driving it around the block to see what happened.

Dad would probably say he was being sacrilegious at worst, flippant at best, but a guy couldn't be too careful. Even with God.

After all, he reasoned as he loitered by the hostess station, there was some verse or other about trying God and proving him faithful. He didn't have a clue where that was, or what it actually said, but Dad would tell him if he asked.

The wood smoke smell of the place made him glad he'd chosen to swear off women instead of food. The Rendezvous was world famous for its ribs. His new business partner definitely had taste—in more ways than one, judging by the blonde seated across from him.

Eddie Tubberville was a piece of work alright. Granted, the guy was single—divorced, to be precise—but the girl looked young enough to be his daughter, cute in a clean-scrubbed kind of way. Not exactly the type Matt would've picked for a high roller like Tubberville. The cornsilk hair was chopped off chin length, tucked behind one ear. Little black glasses perched on a button nose, and a dimple flashed beside her mouth when she talked. Which was a lot.

He checked the hang of his old blue sport coat, worn with khakis and a faded yellow polo. A good impression was critical.

Deep breath, Hogan. Swagger over like you own the place.

As he approached Tubberville's table, the blonde's hands circled. "Daddy, I'm telling you she just disappeared! The van was gone before I could take a breath. What was I supposed to do?"

Daddy? So Tubberville wasn't such a sleazeball after all.

"I'll tell you what you were supposed to do," Tubberville barked. "You were supposed to go to the airport, hold up a sign, and take her to her hotel. How can you possibly lose a woman in a lime-green harem costume?"

"She wanted coffee, and I was trying to be hospitable! How would I guess she'd abscond with a couple of yahoos in an electrical van?"

Matt cleared his throat.

Tubberville turned around. "Hogan! There you are." He stood up and offered a handshake. "I'm afraid you've walked in on a situation here. Meet my daughter Natalie. Natalie, this is Matthew Hogan. He runs the PI agency I was telling you about."

Matt nodded.

Natalie sort of grimaced, as if she wasn't sure whether she should smile or not, then gave her attention back to her dad. "Anyway, she *knew* I was there to pick her up. I mean, there was the Orpheum playbill and everything!"

Matt had no idea what a theater program had to do with a missing harem princess. He was more interested in the fact that this girl had ignored him. Women did not ignore him—at least, not unless he wanted them to. He stuck his hand in front of her face. "Pleased to meet you, Miss Trouble—uh, Tubberville."

She looked down at his hand, then up at his face. Behind the glasses her eyes were a pale, black-shot green, with black lashes and dark eyebrows. Cat eyes. Reluctantly she shook his hand, a glint of humor tugging the corner of her mouth. "Me too. Have a seat and join the fray."

"You don't know how true that is," Tubberville growled. "The trouble part, I mean. This girl's been making chaos out of order since she rode her bicycle into the school building in kindergarten."

"Daddy!" Natalie's bottom lip stuck out.

Matt grinned. "Catch me up. Who's gone missing?"

"Daughter of a business connection of mine, Abid Patel. The girl's name is Yasmine. She was set to marry a young man she's been engaged to since birth. Guy named Jarrar Haq."

"I take it these people are Middle Eastern." Matt looked up as a waitress brought him a glass of water and a menu. "Thanks."

"No problem," said the waitress, giving him a gratifying once-over. "I'll give you a few minutes to look at the menu."

"Just bring me the ribs special with a Coke." He looked at Tubberville. "You guys order yet?"

"We were about to. Triple that order, little lady." Tubberville dismissed the waitress with a wave.

Natalie bristled. "But, Daddy—"

"You know you always order ribs, so don't get all snotty on me." Tubberville glanced at Matt, a twinkle lurking in his eyes. "Girl eats like a football team and still has to run around in the shower to get wet. Burns a thousand calories a day flapping her mouth."

Natalie's face flamed. "If I could get a word in edgewise, I'd remind you I haven't had a bite since dawn. I was going to take Yasmine to dinner."

Matt, who considered himself a connoisseur, could see little to complain about in Natalie's figure, even if she was a little on the skinny side. She had on a modest red knit top that complemented her pale, shiny hair and clear English-rose complexion. For some reason he felt like coming to her defense.

"Everybody loses a bride occasionally," he said mildly. "What's the big deal?"

"The big deal is Abid Patel's honor, not to mention a three-million-dollar oil account." Tubberville glowered. "We don't find her, we're all going to be on the skids. Including you, Hogan."

"Me? What's it got to do with me?"

"If I take a hit on this thing, I'll have to fold the agency. Can't afford a losing investment." Tubberville folded his arms.

"Huh? Tubberville, you can't fold my agency!"

"Since I own fifty-five percent of the company, I certainly can."

"Whoa. Just hold the bus right now!" Matt's stomach did a three-sixty flip. He glanced at Natalie, who was staring at her dad open-mouthed. "I let you buy in to help me get back on my feet—not to blow me down like a tornado."

"Daddy!" Natalie's voice rose on an excited squeak. "You didn't tell me you own a detective agency!"

"That's because it's none of your business," Matt said, frowning. "It's my company. I started it, and I run it. Your dad's just the—the CFO."

"I have legal controlling interest, which means I hold the purse strings. And here's what you're going to do if you want River City Investigations to stay in the Yellow Pages. You're going to find Yasmine Patel and bring her back for her wedding."

Matt considered himself a fairly phlegmatic sort of guy. And then there was the whole giving-his-life-to-God thing. He gripped the edge of the table. "You're not my boss, Tubberville," he said quietly. "You can't tell me what to do."

Tubberville leaned back, flicking his napkin open as the waitress appeared with a loaded tray. "I just did."

"Daddy, let me!" Natalie's eyes were wide, hands clasped under her chin.

"Let you what?" Tubberville's gaze slid to Matt. The tension in the atmosphere was as thick as the odor of barbecue pork and onion rings.

"Let me find her. I'm a trained detective. For goodness' sake, I have a degree!"

Matt snorted. "In what? Cosmetology?"

Natalie's translucent skin flushed from her collarbone to her hairline. "I'll have you know," she said through gritted teeth, "I graduated *magna cum laude* from the University of Memphis with a degree in criminal justice. I've been working for the sheriff's department down in Tunica for the past two years, and I passed the detective's exam last week."

"Is that right?" Matt grinned. "Well, maybe you *should* go looking for the sultan's daughter—especially since you're the one who lost her!"

"Now wait just a minute—"

"Hold on, you two." Tubberville patted his daughter's wrist. "Take a deep breath, honey."

Matt looked from one to the other. Signing over a major portion of his agency to Tubberville had seemed like a good idea at the time. Now—not so much. "Suppose I do go looking for this girl. Are you going to pay my expenses?"

"I won't have to. Abid Patel will pay a chunk of change to get his daughter back. From what Natalie says, we don't know if Yasmine left on her own or if she was kidnapped."

"Kidnapped?" Matt frowned. "Why don't you just bring in the police?"

"Because it's a touchy situation. Abid has enemies and allies all over the Middle East. We alert the authorities, and we risk getting the feds involved with what could be just a family scandal. Until we know why Yasmine left, Abid wants to keep it a private search."

"You mean the guy already knows his daughter's missing?" Matt shook his head. This ball of yarn just kept getting more snarled.

Tubberville nodded grimly. "He knows. And he's not happy."

Natalie shook her father's hand off her wrist. "It *is* my fault. I'm going to find her." She set her chin, and the soft lips quivered.

Playing the femininity card. Matt's sympathy dissolved. "This is a professional investigation. I don't think the Tunica Sheriff's Department is going to want to let go of their secretary."

"You are an insufferable pig." Her eyes blazed like peridots under a jeweler's lamp. "But I'm going to assume you're upset and ignore you." She turned to her father. "Dad, look, I know I can find her. I'm a woman, and I can figure out how she'll think. Besides—" she glared at Matt—"I actually care."

Tubberville leaned back as the waitress put a plate of ribs in front of him. "Maybe you're right. It might be effective to have a woman working on the case too. What do you think, Hogan?"

"I think—what—what do you mean, what do I think? I think you're crazy." Matt wanted to howl with laughter. He was supposed to work with a little girl who looked like Gidget and—*magna cum laude* or not—seemed to have the attention span of an ADHD flea?

Tubberville picked up a slab of ribs dripping with sauce. "Well, it doesn't matter what you think after all. It's my company. Or rather, mine and Natalie's. I bought it with the intention of setting her up to be your partner and giving her twenty-five percent if she decides she likes it. So work with her or take your agency into bankruptcy—and I'll hire another PI to find Yasmine."

Natalie felt her mouth drop open. "Daddy, are you serious?"

Matt Hogan put his hands in his hair. "Tubberville, you can't give away my company to a *girl*!"

But the jail door had just swung open, and Natalie wasn't about to let it clang shut in her face again. After two years in the Tunica County Sheriff's Department, she was profoundly aware of the triple strikes of youth, femininity, and blonde hair—and bulldog determined to overcome all three.

Who did this guy Matt Hogan think he was? Maybe she'd experienced a light-headed moment at that big flashing grin, but she knew better than to trust her hormones. Forrest Gump's mama had it right. You could count on every box of chocolates hiding at least one slimy cherry-surprise center, no matter how delectable the outside might look.

"Girl?" she said politely, staring into Matt Hogan's incredulous hazel eyes. "There are no girls here. There's only me—a woman who now owns twenty-five percent of your agency. I suggest you play nice."

"Play nice?" he echoed. "Play *nice?*" He pressed his lips together, revealing a couple of deep dimples. She could see the cogs spinning in his brain. This was not a stupid man. Finally he shrugged and stood up, dropping his napkin onto the sticky pile of ribs in front of him. "My best friend just married the chief justice of the Alabama Supreme Court, so we'll see how long this cockeyed deal holds up. I suggest *you* take your Barbies back to Tunica, or wherever you came from, and let me take care of my agency."

"My Barbies—"

"Thanks for dinner, Eddie—" Hogan nodded at Natalie's dad—"but I'm not hungry anymore. I'll start interviewing people at the airport tomorrow and see if I can find your girl." He smirked at Natalie. "The *other* girl."

Daddy calmly wiped barbecue sauce off his chin. "Hate to tell you this, bud, but you don't have the case without my 'other' girl."

"Then I don't need it. I'm outta here."

By the time Natalie found her tongue, Hogan was halfway across the restaurant, headed for the door.

Daddy chuckled. "I like that boy."

"How can you say that? Did you hear that condescending, chauvinistic tone of voice? Did you see the way he looked at me?"

"He looked at you the same way every male outside the family has looked at you since you turned twelve."

"That's what I mean. Nobody takes me seriously."

Daddy didn't look the least sympathetic. "Then you'll just have to prove him wrong. Beat him to the punch."

"You mean find Yasmine first?" Natalie sat up straight.

"There's a pretty good incentive. Abid is offering a finder's fee of fifty grand."

"Fifty-*thousand*? Dollars? Holy schmoly. I could buy out your part of the agency with that!"

"Not quite," Daddy said dryly. "But at least you could afford the insurance on your car."

"I told you I'd pay you back—"

"Never mind, I'm just kiddin' you, sweetheart. Use the money for whatever you want. Now are you going to quit that dead-end job in Casino Royale, Mississippi? Move home and quit burning up the road?"

Despite her irritation with a certain pig-brained private investigator, Natalie felt like dancing around the room. "I'll go home and type up my resignation as soon as we finish eating. Just wait 'til I tell Mom." She cut a piece of meat off a bone with her knife and fork.

"How's your mama doing these days?" Daddy casually picked up his glass and slurped.

Natalie gave him a sharp look. "Busy as ever. Why?"

"I just happened to remember it's her birthday this weekend. You might tell her I wish her a happy fiftieth."

Her parents had been divorced for fifteen years, but neither of them forgot birthdays or anniversaries. Natalie had no basis for comparison, of course, but that always struck her as a little abnormal.

"Why don't you tell her yourself? She'd be glad to hear from you."

"Oh, I don't know." Daddy's florid complexion turned even redder. "She never had time for me, even when we were married."

"She asked about you the other day." What her mother had said was, "Tell your dad if he can't pay Nick and Nina's tuition next semester, I'm going to pull them out and send them to UT Knoxville, where they can get my alumni scholarship." Natalie saw no need to stir up bad blood.

Daddy took the bait. "Did she now?" He looked pleased. "Think I'll give her a call tonight."

Natalie's romantic heart melted into a puddle. Her father was still in love with her mother. *Aw. Lord, you could work that thing out, if you had a mind to.*

Too bad her own love life stunk like week-old cabbage.

The attractive crooked smile of Matt Hogan flashed through her brain. *Oh, no you don't,* she told herself sternly. *We are not going there.*

He was Some Pig.

Oink.

⌒

"Matthew Hogan, you are a certified pig," said Tootie Shee-han. His landlady stood in his kitchen door, holding an apple pie in one hand and a mop in the other. Ethel Mertz on steroids.

Matt, sitting at the table inhaling a bowl of Special K, glanced at the pile of dishes overflowing the sink and at the trash can stuffed with empty TV dinner boxes and discarded junk mail. He hadn't been home for nearly three months except to eat and sleep. And he'd been out of town a good chunk of that time, hanging out with his parents in northern Illinois.

"If it bothers you, Tootie, you can stay downstairs." Matt punched a button on the laptop in front of him to launch his email program. He pretended to ignore the domestic diva's glare.

Nostrils flared and mop brandished, she advanced into the room and set the pie on the counter. "I should take this pie back downstairs and feed it to the dog."

"Don't you dare." Matt turned in alarm. "He already waddles like a pregnant hippo."

"Now there's a visual to keep you awake at night." Tootie looked over Matt's shoulder. "Speaking of pregnant, have you written to your sister since she had the baby?"

"I called her last night." Matt closed the email program and shut the laptop. "How did you know she had a baby?"

"I saw the sack from Babies 'R' Us in the backseat of your car. Unless there's something you're not telling me, I figured it had to be for Cicely."

"Why don't you come to work for me? You're a better snoop than any PI I ever met."

"Is that a compliment?" Tootie grinned at him, throwing a web of wrinkles into play at the corners of her shoe-button brown eyes. "Retired school teachers are the most observant folks on the planet."

"I suppose you'd have to be." Matt got up to hunt through the dishes in the sink for a fork. "I ate all my cereal. Can I have this for dessert?" The smell of cinnamon and fruit and sugar steamed through the pie's beautiful lattice-work crust. There definitely was a God.

"Baby, you can do whatever you want to with it." Tootie pointed the mop. "But first you better shovel out this mess before that pretty girl downstairs gets to your office. Otherwise she might never come back."

"What pretty girl?"

"Little blonde with one of those funky choppy haircuts? I didn't know you had a partner. You've lived and worked in my building for six months now. You'd think something like that would come up in conversation."

Matt froze in the act of scooping pie into a marginally clean saucer. He'd considered just eating it out of the tin, but Tootie's gimlet eye was on him. "I don't have a partner. Well, Natalie's dad is technically my partner, and he's got some crazy idea about giving her twenty-five percent of his share, but—" He stopped himself. Tootie had a way of eliciting information he never intended to part with. "She's not my partner, and she's never going to see the inside of my apartment."

"Natalie, huh? Suits her."

"I'll tell you what her name ought to be." Matt stuffed a bite of flaky, gooey crust into his mouth. "T-R-O-U-B-L-E. I can't believe she had the nerve to show up here. Guess she told you she's got a degree in criminal justice. Like that's supposed to make her Magnum P.I." He glanced at the clock on the microwave. Definitely should have started with his quiet time this morning, instead of email. Not even eight o'clock, and already he was in a tailspin.

"I'm sure she's a lot smarter than you give her credit for." Tootie backed toward the door. "I've got to get to mass. Just wanted to tell you to put on a clean tie for your partner—visitor, whatever she is. Don't forget to put that pie in the fridge, if you want it to last."

"I'll have it eaten before it can go bad." But Matt opened the refrigerator and set his prize on top of a pizza box. Twelve years of church school as a kid had left an ingrained respect for teachers, retired or not.

Put on a clean tie. As if that would impress a girl like Natalie Tubberville. As if he *wanted* to impress her.

Matt picked his way through an explosion of clothes, investigative journals, and weapons and tech catalogs. One day he was going to have to get a backhoe in here and start over. The thought of his mother seeing the way he lived made the hair on his arms stand up.

The bedroom wasn't much better than the kitchen or the living room. His bed didn't even have sheets on it. He'd gotten tired of washing them and putting them back on, so every night he just stripped to his underwear, cranked down the air conditioner, and rolled himself up in the comforter.

By moving a set of thirty-pound dumbbells and yanking hard, he managed to get his closet door open. He poked through the array of ties on a rack he and his grandfather had made when Matt was in the eighth grade. It was one of his prized possessions. He'd been collecting vintage ties almost as long as he'd been collecting baseball cards.

Choice made, he retraced his steps to the kitchen and took another bite of the pie. Then he located his keys beside the dead ivy plant on the windowsill. He looked down at his tie with a grin. Natalie Tubberville had better have on sunglasses.

⁓

Natalie looked out Matt Hogan's office window. Beale Street below was quiet this morning, with a muted, dusty light sifting through the storefronts. A wino slouched against the lamppost on the corner, and a police squad car had a radar trap in an alley—the only signs of life.

Weird place for a young guy like Hogan to live. Matt. Her business partner. That was a weird thought too.

The lady with the mop said Matt lived above her in a studio apartment behind his office. The old building, probably built around the turn of the century, also housed an Elvis souvenir shop, a café, and a law office.

Natalie wandered around the office, inspecting the laptop computer, the neat stack of papers on the corner of a functional metal desk, and a couple of file cabinets in one corner. She pulled a drawer open and found the files labeled in dark masculine print, all caps, like a draftsman's hand. The floor was swept clean and shone with a recent coat of wax. Matt must be an organized person. Boded well for their relationship, because Natalie herself was ... well, Dad always teased her that she'd leave her head behind if it weren't attached.

Her IQ was around 140, but that didn't necessarily translate to practical things like filing and scheduling. Which was one problem she'd had at the sheriff's department. She couldn't wait to show up on Monday and hand in her resignation.

Plopping herself into the only comfortable chair in the room, which was behind Matt's desk, she leaned back and contemplated the antique fan whirring in the nine-foot ceiling. The landlady—what was her name? Tootie?—had turned it on before darting off to alert Matt that he had a visitor. Nice lady, reminiscent of her senior English teacher. Slightly severe mien relieved by a twinkle in the eyes.

Natalie had counted about a hundred and twenty rotations of the fan when the doorknob rattled. Matt Hogan burst in, crackling energy like an electrical storm. Even his hair stood on end.

And look at that tie. The Golden Gate Bridge arched across aqua water, with Alcatraz like a lump of coal in the background. His blue-and-white striped shirt did little to tone down the virulent effect.

He stopped in the middle of the room and folded his arms. "What are you doing in my chair?"

"I ate your porridge too." She uncrossed her legs and stood up. "If you'd invest in something besides folding chairs for your guests, you wouldn't have this problem."

"You're not a guest. Nobody invited you. Besides, office hours are from nine to five. I was eating breakfast."

"If you're this rude to everybody who comes to see you, no wonder Daddy had to bail you out." He flinched and Natalie clapped a hand across her mouth. "Oh, I'm *sorry*. That was uncalled-for." She sighed. "Forgive me for sitting in your chair and interrupting your Cocoa Puffs and pointing out the fact that you're a failure."

Matt's mouth dropped open. He stared at her a moment before that appealing grin slid into place. "Come on, Natalie. Tell me what you really think."

She backed toward the window, crashing into the blinds. "I didn't mean—"

"Yes, you did. But I'll overlook it for now." He moved one of the metal chairs away from the wall and sat down. "Have a seat, Goldilocks—no, no, you take the comfortable chair—and tell me what brought you down here at the crack of dawn."

Natalie gave him an uncertain look. Typically she could read men like a comic book; the pictures were right there on the surface, with thought balloons parading over their heads. But Matt Hogan's expression was perfectly bland. A slight quirk curled his fine lips, the only indication of irony.

Squirming in the padded leather ergonomic desk chair, she studied a framed portrait of a handsome middle-aged couple stuck on top of the file cabinet. Three different wedding pictures flanked it. Matt was in all three, dressed in tux and bowtie.

"Always the best man, never the groom." He grinned.

"You're not married?"

He held up a ringless hand. "No. Which is why I'm nice to Tootie. She feeds me pie, not to mention mopping and waxing my office. Those are my sister and brother and my best buddy."

"Oh." This put a whole new spin on things. Matt looked to be in his late twenties. Most guys that age were married. Unless there was something wrong with them.

"I have commitment issues," he said as if reading her mind.

"I didn't ask—"

"No, but you were thinking it." He propped one ankle on the other knee and folded his arms. "Why is a thirty-year-old man still single, you want to know."

"Are you thirty?"

"Yes. And I'm going to tell you something else you didn't ask, but since you busted in here without making an appointment, you have to listen. I spent nearly three decades running away from who my parents raised me to be. About a year ago, my friend

Cole—in the middle picture there—showed me the way back. Since I'm a new man, I'm not going to insult you or kick you out or make a pass at you. I'm going to tell you as politely as I know how that this is *my* detective agency. I worked like a dog to build it, and I don't need or want a partner, not even your dad. As soon as I make enough money to buy back his shares, I will." He tilted his head. "You get my drift?"

"Oh, yeah, Clint Eastwood, I get your drift." Natalie gripped the edge of the desk. "Now it's my turn to tell you something. I don't believe it's an accident that my dad bought out your agency just when Yasmine Patel disappeared. I prayed about this all night long, and I think we're supposed to work together to find her."

"Supposed to? What's that mean?"

She shrugged. "When God opens a door, I generally walk through it."

"I just told you. This particular door is shut."

She stood up so fast the chair zoomed backward and hit the wall. "And I told *you* I'm not going anywhere."

Matt rose, frustration in every line of his lean, elegant body. "Look, Natalie, I'm sure you're a very nice girl, but you need to pick on somebody your own size. Why don't you find some other agency to work for? Heck, start your own! I did it when I was even younger than you."

"I'm twenty-four! And I know good and well that I don't know enough yet to run my own agency. I have to learn from somebody who knows the business inside and out. Sure, you had to have a financial jump-start, but you've got a stellar reputation in the industry. I checked out all your references and—"

"You did what? Who do you think you—"

"If I were a potential client, of course I'd want to hire the best. You *are* the best. You've got to help me find Yasmine. What if she's in trouble?"

Matt huffed and stared at Natalie. The cord on the fan ticked a few times as it went round and round.

"You a praying woman?" he finally asked.

"Yes. I am." Natalie stuck out her chin.

"What if I'm not hearing God say anything?"

"You've got the radio up too loud."

"Huh?"

"Daddy always gripes at me for cranking up my car radio so loud I don't hear my cell phone."

Matt's dark eyebrows twitched together. "That doesn't make one bit of sense."

"Never mind. What I came here for today is to make you a deal you can't turn down."

"What are you, the Godfather? I can't think of a thing you've got to offer me."

Natalie wished she'd worn her platforms today instead of sandals. Disconcerting to stare up at the man from six inches below. She raised her heels off the ground. "I'm offering to hand over my percentage of the agency—if I don't contribute significantly to finding Yasmine."

"What exactly does 'contribute significantly' mean?"

She circled a hand. "I don't know. We'll figure that out."

He snorted. "Okay. Say the miraculous happens. Say you accomplish this significant contribution. We're right back where we started."

"Oh, no. We're way beyond that. If I find Yasmine, you've got to give me the secret handshake. Make me a real partner, not just Daddy's figurehead."

Matt took a step backward. "You're crazy. I'm not making a promise like that."

"Will you at least think about it? What have you got to lose? I'll work hard, and by the way, the finder's fee is outrageous. We'll both come out smelling like the proverbial rose."

"Finder's fee? How much?"

"Fifty-thousand smackeroos."

"Fifty-thousand—?" His mouth hung open. He blinked. "If you'd back off, I could earn that finder's fee. You'd get your share."

"Yeah, but I can't learn anything that way. I admit I'm inexperienced, but if you'll teach me what you know, I can be a real help. Come on, the Bible says, 'Two are better than one, because they have a good return for their labor.'"

"Are you sure that isn't Shakespeare? Where does it say that?"

"Ecclesiastes. Little book between Proverbs and Song of Solomon."

"The sex book."

Natalie rolled her eyes. "Aren't you the spiritual giant."

He blushed. "I told you I was away from God. Maybe you could help me catch up."

She did a double take. "You're thinking about it, aren't you? Letting me tag along."

"Maybe, but you'll have to keep your distance." He took another step backward.

"Now *you're* not making sense. How'm I supposed to keep my distance if we're working together?"

"Never mind." Matt held up his hands. "I'll take care of that. Your job is to remember who's in charge."

THREE

Yasmine wandered down Beale Street, working hard at invisibility. In a city full of dark-skinned people, this wouldn't have been difficult if her mother hadn't insisted she make the twenty-four-hour flight in the traditional Pakistani *shalwar kameez.* "Jarrar will expect his bride to be properly dressed for the first meeting," Ammi had told her, adjusting the embroidered *dupatta* around her shoulders.

Since what Jarrar expected was no longer an issue—she hoped—Yasmine had every intention of getting rid of the costume. She stuck out like a canary among a flock of sparrows. *Thank you so much, Ammi.*

A cluster of young women came out of a shop to her left and stopped to stare. One of them lifted the camera dangling from a strap around her neck and aimed it at Yasmine.

Lowering her eyes, Yasmine hurried past. But she managed to note the girls' outfits. Tight, low-cut jeans and skimpy knit tank tops in multiple layers that bared an embarrassing amount of flesh.

The young woman who had met her at the airport hadn't been dressed that way. She seemed to be a friendly person whom Yasmine would like to have gotten to know. But she would have taken her to Jarrar's home, so the only course had been to run away.

It was early in the day, but she had to start thinking about a place to stay for the night. Also her stomach ached for food. She hadn't eaten anything since the hamburger she'd had last night. Begging was not an option, but Abbi had raised his daughters to be resourceful, scandalously so. Uncle Rais was always saying Abbi was too westernized, too liberal, regarding the upbringing of his three children.

Unfortunately, Abbi had not been too liberal to arrange a marriage for Yasmine.

Resourceful. Yes, by the grace of God, she was indeed resourceful. He would help her reach her destination before Jarrar could enforce the marriage.

First she had to remove this getup—that was what Zach called it. She unwound the *dupatta* and stuffed it into her backpack. Feeling rebellious, but much less eye-catching, she walked along humming, face lifted to the mild breeze. She'd already run away from the fiancé chosen by her father. What was one more little rebellion?

She stopped. She'd never see Abbi again. Or Ammi or Liba. Or Uncle Rais who treated her like a two-year-old. The staggering import of this truth buckled her knees so that she had to lean against the closest brick wall.

She hoped she was doing the right thing. The Holy Book commanded one to honor mother and father. And she did so in her heart. But how could she marry Jarrar when she didn't know him, let alone love him? How could she align herself with a man who had done the things Jarrar had?

The thought of going back was scarier than going forward.

With a lump in her throat, Yasmine took a step, then another, down the sidewalk. The street was busy, crowded with old buildings lumped together in tawdry fashion, their crumbling bricks forming a messy backdrop to flashing neon. They were nowhere near as ancient as the buildings of Karachi, but they had a tired sort of weight about them, as if they might tumble down if she breathed too hard.

Her sandaled feet ached along the insoles, but she turned around and hurried to catch up to the young woman who had taken her photograph. Perhaps she would be kind as well as tactless enough to photograph a stranger.

"Excuse me," Yasmine said boldly.

One of the three dark-skinned girls, the one with tight braids and a big laugh, looked around to find Yasmine. Her eyes flicked up and down the yellow-green *shalwar kameez*. "Yeah?"

"I am so sorry bothering you, but could you direct me, please, to the closest cheap store?"

"Sheep store? What's that?" The girls looked at one another and giggled.

Yasmine sighed. If anybody needed an interpreter, it was she. "I need clothing." She lifted the filmy side panel of her *shalwar kameez*. "Jeans and a T-shirt?"

The girl with the braids smiled. "You don't want a thrift store. You want the mall."

"No!" She'd seen pictures of American malls. Too many people. "Just send me to the cheap clothes place."

One of the other girls, notable for clownlike makeup, spoke up. "We could show her to the Salvation Army. That's just a block down on Jackson."

Yasmine recognized two words. Salvation and army. Salvation she needed, but she wanted to stay as far away from armies as possible.

Before she could protest, the three young women turned in flank and left Yasmine behind. She hurried to catch up. "Wait! I don't want to—" Then she saw the store's sign. It looked vaguely familiar. A red shield. Oh—*that* kind of salvation. *That* kind of army.

One of the girls opened the door and held it for Yasmine to enter. "Thank you," Yasmine whispered as she slipped through. "So kind."

"You gon' be okay?" asked the braided girl, backing outside. "You got some money?"

Abbi owned several oil wells. Of course she had money, though it happened to be in a form she could not spend. "I have enough for cheap clothes. Thank you. I am fine."

The girl gave her a doubtful look, then disappeared. Yasmine was on her own again.

She looked around the store. She couldn't see where the shield applied. *Salvation Army.* What a peculiar name for a place with so much junk. Rows and rows of clothing were arranged on steel racks—ladies' on one side, men's on the other—apparently sorted by color rather than size. A couple of tired-looking manne-quins sported outfits that Yasmine somehow knew were sadly out of style. Perhaps she should rethink her choice of boutique.

She sidled toward the ladies' section. A woman leaning against the cash register near the door didn't seem to be concerned about Yasmine's appearance. Perhaps Middle Easterners in traditional dress shopped in this store on a regular basis.

After a long, confusing search, she found a pair of jeans that looked like they might fit and a T-shirt with Elvis on the front. The young, handsome Elvis, not the older fat one with enormous sideburns. Yasmine was proud of her knowledge of Memphis his-tory. When she'd thought she would have to live here, she'd decided she might as well learn about the place. The T-shirt would help her blend in, here in the King's hometown.

She took the outfit to the fitting room, hurriedly stripped off the *shalwar kameez*, and put on the American clothes. She'd guessed correctly, but—*oh, my.* The jeans weren't as low-cut as those worn by the girls who had brought her here. Still, she felt *bepardah*—exposed. Her dressy sandals looked funny with the jeans, so she wandered over to the shoe rack. After examining a row of down-at-heels sneakers, she shrugged and returned to the fitting room. For some reason she couldn't bear the thought of wearing used shoes.

Dressed in her own clothes once more, she took her purchases to the register, which was surrounded by a glass case displaying an amalgam of brooches, earrings, bracelets, and necklaces. She fingered the earrings Abbi had brought from a business trip to Morocco. She wasn't going to buy cheap jewelry, even to blend in.

"How much, please?" She laid the jeans and T-shirt on the counter.

A smile lightened the clerk's lined face. "Good choice, dearie. You can't beat Elvis when he was a young buck. That'll be four dollars for the jeans and two-fifty for the shirt. With tax, it's … let's see. Seven-ten."

Yasmine blinked. She could almost afford another outfit with her U.S. dollars. But she'd best be frugal until she could get to a bank and exchange more rupees. She lifted the *shalwar kameez* draped across the counter. It would take up a lot of room in her small backpack. She looked at the lady. "You may do whatever you want with this. I can't take it with me."

The lady's eyes widened. "You gonna donate it? You better let me give you a receipt."

Yasmine frowned. "I get a receipt for giving something away?"

"For your taxes."

Abbi paid plenty of tax in Pakistan, but clothing donations had no effect on it. Yasmine shook her head. "No. But I think I will keep this." She picked up the beautiful *dupatta* Ammi had given her for her birthday last summer and stuffed it into her backpack. Parting with it was impossible. She smiled at the clerk. "Thank you. Good-bye."

Properly dressed—she thought with irony of her mother's comment as she'd put Yasmine on the plane—she walked out of the store into the bright sunshine.

She considered her next move. Across the street was a law office next to a coffee shop whose dark, strong odor brought waves of homesickness. Drawn, she crossed the street and looked in the coffee shop window. People clustered around small tables, intent on conversation or focused on laptop computers. She could treat herself to just one cup of espresso.

But getting to Rafiqah—the one person she knew in this city, the one person from home who would help her escape—was more important. She straightened her shoulders and stepped back from the window. As she walked past the law office, a lady on the inside, cleaning the front window with a blue cloth, peered out. Her stern face and the hidden twinkle in her eye reminded Yasmine of her Aunt Karimah—whose flamboyant turbans and westernized clothing, cigarettes, and expensive perfume everybody tried to hide from Yasmine and Liba.

The lady raised her bottle of cleaning solution in greeting, giving Yasmine a wave with the blue cloth. Yasmine smiled and hurried on.

As she walked toward the smell of the river, she kept thinking about Zach. He'd never explained exactly what his job was, and he would often disappear for days with no explanation other than to apologize when he returned and say he'd missed her. The day he bought her the little silver ring, which she wore on a chain hidden under her blouses, was one of the happiest days of her life. She hadn't taken it off since—even the weekend she went home for holiday and her parents told her about the wedding.

She understood the rules of her culture. One did not flout the wishes of one's parents. Besides, she loved Abbi, who made it clear the connection was one that would benefit him—and that offending the family of the Commerce Minister would create untold awkwardness. So she'd swallowed and said she would think about it, and everybody assumed that meant "yes." Especially Ammi, overjoyed that her elder daughter was finally marrying suitably, indeed brilliantly. Only Uncle Rais watched Yasmine carefully and said she'd better be sensible or she'd break her parents' hearts.

Yasmine faltered. She looked over her shoulder, caught the eye of the lady in the window, and stumbled on. There was more at stake now than her parents' approval.

She had to get to Zach.

⌒

Jarrar Haq was outraged. The moment his private jet landed at Wilson Air Center, attached to Memphis International Airport, he turned on his cell phone and called Yasmine's father.

"You are coming to the U.S., no?" he demanded as he gestured for Feroz to collect the carry-on luggage. "She must be found."

Feroz, scowling, followed with his own duffel bag and Jarrar's briefcase trapped under one muscle-bound arm. In the other hand he carried a pair of thirty-pound dumbbells.

He deserved to be inconvenienced. Because Jarrar had detected something odd in the tone of Yasmine's last couple of emails, he had sent his bodyguard to retrieve the girl from the airport. Despite every precaution, she had given Feroz the slip, as well as Tubberville's brainless daughter.

Ignoring his grumbling subordinate, Jarrar bounded down the steps to the tarmac and headed for the terminal as a crew of mechanics swarmed the plane. They would clean it and go over it thoroughly before parking it in the hangar Jarrar rented by the year. He paid well for good service.

Which was one reason the marriage must be consummated.

"I am making arrangements." Patel sounded offended. "My wife and daughter wish to accompany me."

Jarrar could not have cared less about Patel's feelings. He had bought the man's daughter with his father's good will. Business was business. "How do you propose to find her?"

"I assure you no one cares about my daughter's return more than her mother and me. My colleague Eddie Tubberville has secured a detective who will spare no expense or effort to find Yasmine."

"Tubberville?" Jarrar entered the air-conditioned terminal and, waving away a solicitous airport employee, shoved open the door of the lounge. "Is not this the man whose stupid daughter lost Yasmine in the first place?"

"Do not be so quick to disparage him. Tubberville knows the value of a daughter."

Finding the lounge empty, Jarrar covered the phone with a hand. "Feroz, leave my briefcase on that table and deal with the rest of the luggage." After Feroz had left the room, Jarrar went back to Patel. "I must meet this detective. Make sure he understands the confidential nature of our situation." He paused, considering how his words must sound. "I am very concerned for Yasmine's reputation. And yours."

"I assure you," Patel said quietly, "no one appreciates my honor more than me."

With that Jarrar had to be satisfied.

The airport was buzzing with activity, and out of habit, Matt kept his eyes peeled as he headed across the central lobby. You never knew when you might see something—or somebody—important.

"So when did you decide you wanted to be a private eye?" Natalie trotted behind him, her sandals making slapping noises against her heels.

Like little gun shots. *Pow! Take that, Hogan, right between the eyes.*

Matt got on the down escalator and looked over his shoulder. "It wasn't a conscious decision. I just kind of wandered into it." All morning she'd been lobbing questions at him. He felt like an interviewee on *Larry King Live.*

She caught up to him, despite his best efforts to leave her behind. "Didn't you read the Hardy Boys when you were a kid?"

"Not voluntarily."

"You don't like to read?" She sounded like he'd just told her he ate locusts and honey for breakfast.

"I don't get the point of fiction."

"Wow." There was a moment's blessed silence while she digested his illiteracy. "How do you 'wander' into a career like private investigations? I studied for four years and still don't know everything there is to know."

He shrugged. "The idea never occurred to me until I'd already graduated from Northern Illinois with a business degree." He caught her elbow as she stumbled off the escalator. "I had no idea what I wanted to do, so I followed one of my girlfriends here to Memphis. She's a journalist, works for the *Commercial Appeal* as a food reporter."

"Girlfriend? Are you still dating?"

He shook his head. "We split after a couple of months. But I liked the warm weather down here, so I stayed."

"But I thought—Daddy said your agency used to be based out of Chicago."

"It was. Anyway, I spent a lot of time hanging out with newspaper people. They introduced me to one of their sources, a detective named Sonny Johnson. You sure you want to hear all this?"

"I like to know what makes people tick." She gave him a sunny smile. "Especially when they're surly."

"I'm not surly!" He squinted at her. "Whatever that means."

"Perpetual bad mood. You've hardly cracked a smile since we left your office."

"Don't you think I've had reason to be a little ticked? Getting my business hijacked right out from under my nose?" They reached baggage claim. "Is this the last place you saw Ms. Patel?"

"I told you, I watched her get in a van parked outside." She huffed. "How is it my fault you sold your agency to my dad?"

Matt veered toward the exit. "It may not be your fault, but that doesn't mean I have to like it. The whole reason I'm in this mess is because for once in my life I tried to do what God told me to do. Looks like there should've been some kind of reward. Instead I get kicked in the teeth."

Natalie looked up at him, nose scrunched. "There's nothing in the Bible that says God doles out rewards like a gumball machine. Sometimes you don't see the reason for things until years later. Sometimes not at all. Why don't you tell me what happened?"

"That's another long story." The automatic doors opened and they walked outside. Lord save him from nosy women. "You wanted to know how I got from Memphis to Chicago and back. So anyway, I needed a job, and Sonny gave me a couple of computer-investigation projects. He saw I had a knack for it and taught me some tricks of the trade. I liked it enough to go into business with him. Then my dad had a heart attack."

"Whoa. I'm sorry to hear that." Natalie's animated expression softened.

"Yeah. Well, I went home to help my mom out. After Dad recovered, my sister talked me into staying. I was still pretty much a Good-Time Charlie at that point, and Chicago's got a busy nightlife. Lots of business for a PI, if you know what I mean." He shrugged. "I opened my own agency and stayed there for a while until I took a case in Alabama."

"You mean Judge Kincade? That was all over the news last summer."

Matt nodded. "It was the beginning of the end—both for my client and me. I backed the wrong horse and wound up getting stiffed."

"But you met the Lord because of it. Aren't you glad about that?"

"Sure, I—I guess so. Of course I am." Matt squirmed. "Is this where you were standing? Where was the van parked?"

She pointed. "Down there. Northwest passenger pickup."

"Okay, come on." Matt approached a broadly built skycap notable for a shock of gray hair—J.T., according to his nametag. "'Morning, sir. Could I ask you a couple of questions?"

"Happy to," the skycap boomed. "What can I do you for?"

Natalie smiled. "We need help finding someone who disappeared from the airport yesterday just before six o'clock."

The skycap frowned. "A child?"

"No, a woman—a young lady about my age."

Matt reached into the pocket of his jacket and handed a three-by-five photo of Yasmine to the skycap. "This is the girl we're looking for. She's Pakistani, small and dark, dressed in one of those gauzy tunic-and-pants outfits—lime green. She arrived on a flight through Amsterdam, and Natalie here sent her to pick up her luggage while she went for coffee." A completely female and ridiculous thing to do, in his opinion. "Were you working yesterday?"

"Yeah, but this is a busy airport." J.T. spread his beefy hands. "No tellin' how many Middle Eastern women came through those doors. I can't watch 'em all the time."

"How about the van she got into?" Natalie was all but bouncing on her toes. "It was white with some kind of lightning logo on the side—an electrical company maybe?—parked in front of baggage claim."

J.T. tapped his chin. "We had some trouble with the carousels yesterday. There were a couple of guys from Mojo Electric here working on them."

Natalie lit up. "That's it! That's the logo I saw. Come on, Matt." She grabbed his arm.

Matt shook hands with the skycap. "Thanks, man. You may have saved a woman's life."

"Glad to help."

On the way back across the parking lot, Natalie tugged Matt's sleeve. "Where'd you get Yasmine's photo?"

"Your dad emailed it to me last night."

"Last night? Then you were planning to take the case all along!"

"No, I wasn't. But I save everything. Learned the hard way."

She gave a small, indignant huff. "Daddy could've given me her picture before he sent me to pick her up."

"Baby, nobody said life is fair," Matt said callously. "Get used to it."

"Oh, trust me, I'm used to it. But that's the kind of thing you need to teach me."

"You just learned, right? You'll never forget. Always take a picture with you if you have one."

"Got it," she muttered, tucking the photo into her purse. "Oh, and unless you want a karate chop to the throat, please don't call me 'baby' again."

⁓

Natalie paid for Happy Meals at the Golden Arches. She shouldn't have made the karate chop remark. Nick, the little twerp, told her regularly that her teasing had all the subtlety of Miss Piggy on a tear. She noisily sucked the last of her milkshake down as Matt drove his neat black Volvo to an industrial area in central Memphis. He probably had no idea how chauvinistic he sounded.

She looked out the window, where a row of recently remodeled office-warehouses lined a set of railroad tracks. Trees were scarce and the pavement was crumbly, but the area had a generally hopeful appearance. At least the whitewash on the doorframes was fresh.

Matt parked beside a truck in front of a building emblazoned with the "Mojo Electric" lightning bolt. "Okay, Nancy Drew," he said as Natalie started to get out. "I'm taking the lead."

She sighed. Too bad a karate chop was out of the question.

Slinging the strap of her saddlebag purse over her shoulder, she followed Matt to the office door. She'd left the little spangled wrist-bag at home, since it wasn't big enough to hold a PDA. Pretty soon she was going to have to start carrying a feather-edged tote like Grandma Tubberville.

Matt held the glass door for Natalie to walk through. At least he was a gentlemanly chauvinist.

"Depending on what we find here," he said, "we split up. Divide and conquer."

"Split up?" She halted inside the tiny foyer. "I can't learn from you if I'm not with you. Besides, my Investigative Techniques professor said you should always have one person conduct the interview, and another to take notes."

"I've never had that luxury, so I make a point of remembering what people tell me. Then I write it down when I get back to the car."

"I'm sure you've got a fabulous memory, but what if you have to talk to somebody for more than a few minutes? It's important for court records to have detailed notes. Besides, your partner can observe clues in a room, note body language, all kinds of stuff you can't do if you're by yourself."

Matt looked at her for a moment, frowning. "Guess you have a point. I'm always torn between starting at the last place the person was seen, or with family members who know them. You know, letting the trail get cold versus ascertaining their probable moves."

Natalie's mouth fell open. That had almost sounded like a compliment. "I printed out a list of questions. If you'll take the short version and conduct the interview, I'll take notes. Goodness knows I'm used to clerking." She hesitated. "Then when we finish here we could go see Yasmine's family."

"Your dad says Yasmine's parents are still in Karachi. They hadn't planned to come over until a couple of weeks before the wedding. Now that she's disappeared, her father's gone postal. The Patels will fly in tomorrow."

"That eliminates an interview with them, then—at least for today. What about her fiancé and his family?"

"I get the feeling they know facts about her, like we do. But not so much personally. Yasmine and Haq were hooked up by their parents long-distance."

Natalie made a face. "How could you marry a guy you never met before? What if he was a dork? What if he turned out to be a wife-beater?"

"You know what? I bet there are a lot of American women who marry men like that, guys who've deliberately hidden things. Seeing people socially doesn't let you into all their secrets."

She gave him a speculative look. "I suppose so. What secrets are you hiding?"

"If we ever see each other socially, I'll let you know." He looked amused. "Come on, let's see what gives with these Mojo guys."

Natalie followed Matt into the barren little office and looked around. As expected, wires of every conceivable thickness, length, and color hung on the corkboard walls. A woman of indeterminate age with brassy yellow hair sat reading a travel brochure behind a counter. She looked up when the door opened.

"Read the sign," she said in a raspy smoker's voice. "No solicitors allowed."

"We're not soliciting." Natalie sailed up to the counter. "We just want to talk to the two guys who were fixing luggage carousels at the airport yesterday."

Matt stepped in front of her. "That's right. Do you know where we could find them?"

Second banana wasn't Natalie's favorite gig, but she moved to the background.

The yellow-haired lady leaned around Matt to look at Natalie. "They're out on a job."

Top Banana moved aside with an ironic hand gesture. Natalie grinned at the lady. "Can you give us an address?"

"Maybe. Did Joey win the lottery again? He's the luckiest goober I've ever seen."

"I don't know anything about the lottery." Natalie smothered a laugh. "We think these two guys gave a friend of ours a ride from the airport. She—the friend—has disappeared."

"My stars, those two just can't leave the ladies alone. If it ain't stopping at Hooters between jobs, it's picking up strange women at the airport."

"You mean they've done this before?"

"Done what?"

"Picked up women." Natalie felt like she was in an Abbot and Costello sketch. "Where would they take her?"

"Take who?"

Matt, lips quirked, cut Natalie a look. "May I?" When she shrugged, he leaned on the counter and gave Yellow Hair his charming smile. "Let's start over. What's your name, sweetheart?"

"Peaches."

"Okay, Peaches. Here's the deal. Joey and his buddy—wait, what are their full names?"

"Joey Roberts and Leland Stafford."

"Right. Roberts and Stafford. They took the daughter of a business associate away from the airport after she'd been met by my lovely—uh, partner here." He ignored Natalie's frown. "If you'll tell us where we can find these two guys, we'd like to ask them a few questions."

"Are they in trouble? 'Cause if they are, I'm not saying a word. Joey ain't got the sense to come in out of the rain, but he's a sweet guy. And Leland's our best technician. We can't afford to lose him."

Matt shook his head. "We're not the law, we're just trying to find Yasmine."

Peaches looked at Natalie. "You swear?"

She nodded. "Promise."

"Okay. Well, there's a little pool hall off Airways, over by the airport. They like to hang out there after work. It's called Porky's."

"Porky's?" Matt frowned. "Is that next to Fred's Dollar Store at the Winchester intersection?"

"That's it. You know the place?"

"I've heard of it." Matt glanced at Natalie. "Thanks, Peaches. We've got to be going."

"Guess you heard about the little dust-up down there last year. It was in the paper. Place almost burned down. If the cops hadn't of raided—"

"Hey, look at the time." Matt grabbed Natalie's arm and peered at her wristwatch. "We have another appointment. Will you give my card to Joey and Leland if we miss them?"

"A raid?" Natalie dug in her heels as Matt towed her toward the door. "I wanted to hear about the fire."

"What's the big deal? We gotta go. Besides, Peaches is busy."

Natalie looked over her shoulder. The woman already had her nose buried in a *Star* magazine. In the parking lot, Natalie yanked her elbow out of Matt's grasp. "You are certifiable, you know that? How're we going to learn anything if you decide to leave just when the conversation gets interesting?"

Matt looked harassed. "Alright. Whatever. You go talk to Yasmine's future in-laws, and I'll interview the two Good Samaritans."

"We decided not to split up."

"That was before I knew you were going to be such a—" He raised a hand before she could protest. "Alright. Let's go. But don't say I didn't warn you."

CHAPTER
FOUR

Matt had no intention of spending every waking moment with the blonde baby detective. She was cute and all, but she was driving him crazy with her questions: *How do you pass the time while you're conducting surveillance? What's the best way to get information out of the police? Can you really trust what you find on the Internet?*

He vaguely remembered following Sonny Johnson all over Memphis about a hundred years ago, learning the ropes. But at least he'd had the sense to keep his mouth shut and watch, rather than antagonize his mentor.

While they were waiting for the five o'clock Happy Hour at Porky's, he'd taken Natalie back to his office for a lesson in background searches. He was a man of his word. No purpose would be served by letting her flounder on her own. Besides, he might as well make the most of having somebody to do the office drudgery he tended to put off.

For the last two hours she'd sat at his computer—a two-year-old Mac laptop that he planned to upgrade as soon as he got the funds—running down information on Pakistani groups in Memphis, while he stood at the window making phone calls. The problem was, every time he ended a call, she'd get his attention and ask him something else. Something surprisingly intelligent.

It was almost four o'clock when he finally stuck the phone in his pocket and flung himself into the folding chair around which he'd been pacing like a lion in a cage.

Natalie looked up. "You're a very twitchy person, you know that?"

"I'm not used to company."

Instead of looking offended, she laughed. "Having to watch your language is good for you."

"Sorry." He felt his face heat. He'd caught himself just short of profanity at least three times, but she hadn't let on that she'd noticed.

"I imagine it's difficult to break a habit like that. I appreciate you considering my feelings."

"It's not just you. My mother always winces. I've got to clean up my act before I go home again."

"Where are your parents?"

"Still in Illinois. You sure ask a lot of questions."

She tipped her head. "You make your living asking questions."

"That's different." He shifted his shoulders. "There's a purpose to that."

"You don't think I've got an agenda?"

He sat up straight. "What agenda?"

"I have this new partner that I've got to spend a lot of time with during the next few days. I need to know what makes him go tick-tock-tick." She waggled a finger back and forth, then glanced at the wedding photos on his desk. "Besides, I've been staring at these people for two hours. I'm dying to know who they are."

"The one on the left is my little sister, Cicely, and her husband, Timothy. They just had their first baby. The one on the right is my big brother, Drew, and his wife, Autumn. They have a couple of rug rats named Molly and Spenser."

"The middle one is your friend Cole?" Natalie picked up the frame to peer at it more closely.

"That's right." She'd remembered Cole's name after one mention. Impressive. "I haven't seen Cole since Christmas, because he and the judge live in Montgomery."

"What's her name? Do they have any kids?"

"If I'm twitchy, you're nosy. No, they don't have kids yet, but Laurel's expecting in June."

"Oh, *she's* the Supreme Court chief justice who was in the news last year?" She touched Laurel's glowing face. "Wow, she's gorgeous."

"Yeah. McGaughan's always had good taste." Matt studied Natalie's pert profile. It wasn't as classic as Laurel McGaughan's, but there was something vital there that drew the eye.

Natalie set down the photo. "So you have friends in high places."

Matt shrugged. "I don't think of it that way. They've been real good to me. I even lived with them for a month or so right after … Well, Laurel had this crazy idea it was her fault I lost all that money on the Field case. I went to their church until I decided to come back to Memphis and start over. Probably should have stayed a little longer, to get better grounded, but I didn't want to cramp the honeymoon."

"Where do you go to church here?" Natalie picked up the plastic toy that had come with her lunch and started twirling it around her finger.

"I'm a ship without a port at the moment. Mom and Dad are Lutheran, and Cole and Laurel are Baptist, but I can't find one that suits my lifestyle. The liturgical stuff doesn't feed me enough, but I don't care for rock-n-roll when I worship either. So I sort of ... float around."

Natalie frowned. "I don't know that worship is about lifestyle. Church is a body you get grafted into. It changes you, not the other way around."

"You sound like my mother." Matt grimaced. "I don't know how to explain it. I just want to find some kindred souls and hang out." He could see Natalie preparing to argue. "Let's save this discussion for later. It's time to head for Porky's fine establishment. You got your pepper spray handy?"

Any city as old as Memphis had its seamy parts; having grown up in the area, Natalie knew where they were. But Mom and Dad had kept her fairly sheltered. Running around with Matt Hogan was a revelation.

They took the interstate down to the south side of town, where a jumble of federally subsidized housing alternated with industrial plants, dilapidated shopping strips, and the occasional well-tended old neighborhood. Eventually they passed exit signs for the airport, whose runways and terminals sprawled to their left, then took Winchester toward Airways just before hitting the Mississippi state line.

She looked at Matt, who was driving in comfortable silence, the radio tuned to a political talk show. "You sure you know where you're going?"

"Yep. Been here lots of times."

"Seems like a weird place to hang out—your office being downtown and all."

"I like to play pool."

"I know but—"

He glanced at her and turned down the radio. "What? You're not gonna tell me playing pool is a sin, are you? I've already had to cut out most of my favorite things to do."

"Goodness, you're touchy. It's not that. But this is a really depressed part of the city. Depressing too."

"Natalie, I told you I'm not a rich guy like your dad." Frowning, he kept his eyes on the road. "I can't afford the downtown nightlife. Or fancy dinners and upscale dance clubs and movies and theaters."

Under the irritation she saw hurt. "I didn't mean—"

"Oh, never mind." He flipped on a turn signal. "Here we are." They turned into a paved lot in front of a brick-and-metal-sided little building with a flashing blue neon sign that read "Porky's Pool." Another sign in the window advertised "Happy Hour: half-price beer."

Face expressionless, Matt turned off the ignition and jumped out of the car. Natalie scrambled to follow. And watched him morph in front of her eyes.

His posture became loose-limbed, shoulders carried at a rakish angle. A faint smile tipped his mouth—the kind of cocky smirk she'd have been tempted to slap off if he'd just been introduced to her. He swung open the pool hall door, stuck his head in, and yelled, "Hey, where's the party?" Holding the door for Natalie, who hardly knew where to look as she slid past him, he looked her up and down and whispered, "Pretend you don't know me."

"That shouldn't be hard," she muttered. "Who *are* you?"

He just winked and followed her inside.

Fascinated and just a bit nervous, though aware of Matt's solid presence at her back, Natalie took note of her surroundings. It had been a long time since she'd been in a bar. Bad memories. The liquor counter and bar took up the whole left side of the large open room: bottle after bottle, with a plain mirror fixed in the center of the far wall. Billiard tables flanked the remaining walls, with a few small tables and their chairs in the center of the room. About what she would have expected, except the paneling looked new, gleaming with wax, and the mirror shone.

"I thought you said there was a fire," Natalie said under her breath to Matt.

"They rebuilt. Go on over to the bar and ask for our guys Joey and Leland." Matt gave her a little push in the small of the back, then swaggered toward the closest pool table where a couple of middle-aged guys were chalking their cues.

Get over yourself, Nat, she told herself. *This is your chosen profession.*

Taking a silent breath, she approached the bartender, a twenty-something guy with a short haircut and sideburns, who was squatting to organize something under the bar. She could see a ring and a couple of steel studs along the top edge of one of his ears and a large snake tattooed on the back of his neck.

She smiled. "Hi. I'm Natalie."

He looked up—a square, solid young face—and his eyes widened. He got hastily to his feet. "Hey. Can I help you? Beer's half-price."

"Thanks, but could I just have some soda water? I'm looking for a couple of guys who hang out here."

He grabbed a glass and filled it, the soda fizzing pleasantly. "You know their names?"

"Yeah. Joey Roberts and Leland Stafford. They work for Mojo Electric, and they would've been in here yesterday afternoon around this time. Did you see them?"

The young man set Natalie's water on the counter. "Sure. They're in here nearly every day, even though neither one of 'em plays worth a—"

"Are they here this afternoon?" Natalie snatched up the water and sipped. Matt wasn't the only one with a tendency toward bad language.

"Right over there." The young bartender tipped his head, and Natalie followed his gaze to where several men in work uniforms leaned over a table in the back corner. "Joey's the littlest one, and Leland's the bald dude. Every day he comes in with a new cap and loses it in a bet. You know Joey won five hundred bucks in the lottery last year?"

"I heard." Natalie laid a couple of dollar bills on the bar and smiled. "Thanks." She tried to catch Matt's eye as she walked by him, but he was in vociferous conversation with a hulking young man who towered, arms folded, over everyone else in the room. Wide of shoulder and narrow of hip, he had "bouncer" written all over his thick forehead. Pressing a hand against her quivering stomach, she approached the table in the back. Why had Matt sent her to do this by herself? She didn't know what she was doing.

Something told her not to pull out her notepad and pen. Putting her hands behind her back, she made herself slow her pace, even though every male eye in the room—which was all of them—followed her progress.

She halted a few feet from the table. "Excuse me. Which one of you guys is Joey Roberts?"

The smallest man held his cue to his chest and straightened his posture. "That's me."

Natalie zeroed in on Joey's round face. "I heard you won the lottery last year. I wondered if I could ask you some questions." Not a single lie in that, though she'd implied she was a reporter or something.

Joey reddened. "Sure."

"Can we sit down at a table? I'll buy you a drink." Natalie glanced at Leland, who was googly-eyed. "Your friend too."

"Okay," the two men said in unison.

Natalie smiled and led the way to an empty table. They all sat down. "My name's Natalie Tubberville. I'm interested in what you can tell me about the young lady you transported from the airport yesterday afternoon."

"You mean Jasmine?" asked Leland. "Can I go get our drinks?"

"Yes, but make sure it's nonalcoholic."

Leland looked disappointed. "Okay. If you say so." He stood up, knocking over his chair, and headed for the bar.

"What's Jasmine got to do with the lottery?" Joey sat back, arms folded.

"Nothing," said Natalie blithely. "Did she tell you her name's pronounced 'Jasmine' with a *J*?"

"I don't know. Maybe. Why?" Joey was definitely looking suspicious.

Natalie laid one of Yasmine's photos on the table. "Is this her?"

Joey glanced down. "Maybe," he repeated. "What'd she do? You got a badge or something?"

Ignoring the badge question, Natalie sighed. "We don't know. It's her family who's worried about her. I was supposed to pick her up. Actually, I *did* meet her as she came out of the gate, but she sent me for coffee and disappeared. She's a very rich lady who's supposed to get married in a couple of months, and we're afraid she's been kidnapped."

"Kidnapped!" Joey's thick brows rose in alarm. "Me and Leland wouldn't kidnap a flea. You can ask anybody here. She come running toward the van just as we were leaving the airport and said she wanted to come with us wherever we were going, which was here. She come inside with us and took off to the restroom. Next thing I know she's gone. I swear, that's all we did."

Natalie stared at the little electrician. Beads of moisture were collecting under his thin mustache, and dark splotches spread under his arms. "You didn't see where she went?"

"No! I told you, I got into a game of eight-ball and forgot all about her. I got a wife and a kid at home, and I don't play around with no women, especially foreign ones." The spate of words halted as his buddy returned, plunking a couple of soft drink cans on the table. "Leland, tell this lady we don't know nothing about that Iraqi girl we carried here from the airport."

"She wasn't Iraqi, doofus." Leland picked up the fallen chair, turning it around backward before straddling it. "She was Indian. I think she was from some reservation in South Dakota."

Natalie stifled a smile. "Actually, she's Pakistani. Leland, did you happen to notice her when she came out of the restroom? I need to find her and make sure she's not in any danger."

"You think some terrorists are after her? She did look kind of scared. Breathing hard and all like that."

Natalie blinked. Sounded like Yasmine might be in real danger. "Okay, back up. Did she approach you while you were still inside the terminal? Did you see anybody following her? Apparently she left her luggage."

Leland shook his head. "I told you, she come running after us when we were about to leave. Grabbed the door handle and jumped in the van. Me and Joey couldn't hardly make sense out of her, 'cause her accent was so weird. But she showed us a hundred-dollar bill and said she'd pay us to take her wherever we were going."

Joey butted in. "I might've seen somebody Indian-looking coming out of the terminal right when we took off. I looked back to make sure she had her seat belt on." He blushed. "I got a two-year-old, so it's a habit."

Natalie's lips parted. Was there somebody besides her and Matt following Yasmine? "Did she say *anything* that would give you an idea what she was running from, or where she might be headed?"

Joey and Leland looked at one another, shrugged, and shook their heads. Bubbas they might be, but clearly they were good-hearted men and wanted to help.

"Okay, guys, thanks for your help. Would you mind if I get a phone number where I can reach you if something else turns up?" She pulled out her PDA to take down Joey and Leland's cell numbers.

She hoped she'd handled this interview correctly. Matt sure was taking a long time with—

A crash came from the front of the room. What now? She looked over her shoulder.

Holy schmoly. Bouncer dude had Matt in a head lock and was towing him toward the door.

Natalie screamed and jumped to her feet. "Matt! Let him go! Somebody help!"

Shouts of "Fight! Fight!" went up. A chair flew across Natalie's vision. Glass shattered as a mob of truck drivers ran past, grinning, fists in the air. Somebody yelled, "Call the cops!"

Natalie couldn't see over the mob, heard nothing but the roar of chaos. Heart chugging, she climbed up on a chair and dug out her cell phone. By standing on her toes she got a glimpse of the big man struggling to hold on to Matt, who squirmed like an eel.

Her hands shook as she fumbled for the 911 speed dial. *Poor Matt...*

Then she looked up and realized Matt was in control, with the bouncer held in a firm behind-the-back arm twist. His body, lithe and fierce, looked almost relaxed as he gripped the bigger man as easily as if he had twice the weight.

A shout of appreciation went up from the crowd as Natalie abandoned the call. Better find out what was going on before she got Matt in trouble.

Somebody decided it was time to separate the two men. It took three of them to subdue the big bouncer, who wound up thrust into a chair in the corner, puffing like a locomotive.

Meanwhile, Matt straightened the rolled-up sleeves of his button-down shirt, then smoothed a hand across his tumbled hair. He shrugged off a few congratulatory pats on the back and looked around. Over the crowd, his gaze found Natalie standing on the chair, the cell phone and her purse still clutched in her hands.

She had a sudden illogical urge to burst into tears. Matt seemed perfectly alright, though there was a red splotch across one cheek and his shirt collar flapped under his ear. His expression reminded her of one of those cool, sardonic characters in a Steve McQueen prison break movie.

Looking at him, her weepy feeling translated into outrage. She jumped off the chair and shoved her way through the men still milling around Matt. "Move! Let me through! I said move." Finally she reached him. She whacked him on the arm with a closed fist.

He blinked down at her as if a poodle had suddenly bitten his leg. "Hey! What's the matter with you?"

"What's the matter with *me*?" She glanced at the bouncer, who silently scowled at the men holding him in his chair. "I'm not the one who initiated a bar fight."

"I didn't initiate anything!"

"Then you better start explaining. I never saw such idiotic behavior. You're supposed to be helping me find Yasmine!"

"That's exactly what I was trying to do. I knew this wasn't a good idea to come here." Matt looked around at several interested bystanders. "Would you mind?" They backed away, and he caught Natalie by the elbow. "What'd you find out from the Mojo guys?"

"Not much. They picked her up outside the terminal. Said she looked scared, and there might have been some Indian guy following her out. Neither one of them saw where she went once she got here."

Matt frowned. But before he could respond, the bouncer behind him lunged away from his guards with a growl.

Responding instinctively, Natalie darted between the two men and shrieked, "Stop!"

To her astonishment, Bouncer Boy put on the brakes and skidded to a stop in front of her. Shaking his head, he started to step around her.

"Don't you dare." She put her hands on her hips. "I've had enough of you boys fighting. One of you better tell me what's going on before I send through that 911 call."

"I'll tell you what's going on," the bouncer said grimly. "This is the moron who burned the place down a year ago. He got away with it then, and now he's got the nerve to show up here again." He gently picked Natalie up and set her aside. "So if you'll pardon me, little lady, I'm gonna smash his pretty face into the middle of next week."

FIVE

Big Dean glowered over Natalie's shoulder, clearly poised to take Matt apart piece by piece. Good thing McGaughan had demonstrated a couple of wrestling tricks a few years ago.

"Hey, man, let's take this conversation outside." Matt lifted his hands palms out and backed toward the door. He shot Natalie a look to stay her thumb on the 911 speed dial, not sure how the cops would've interpreted the situation.

Huge mistake to let Natalie come along. Trouble was, he couldn't figure out how to say no to her, which didn't bode well for their (hopefully brief) partnership. Two days, and she'd already learned to look at him with those big green eyes, lashes so long they flirted against her glasses, and smile her way into whatever she wanted. Spooky.

One day life was gonna knock her off her pins. It would be like watching a kitten get run over.

So when he'd seen Dean the Machine, who'd been around back in what McGaughan called "BC days," he'd scrambled to figure out how to handle the situation. Sending Natalie to take the interview, he'd stationed himself between her and Dean—effectively guaranteeing a confrontation with two hundred and fifty pounds of solid muscle married to a serious lack of brain power.

Now, to his relief, Big Dean snarled and turned for the front door. Natalie gave Matt a what's-going-on? look, but followed in merciful silence.

Dean led the way to a corner of the building. Traffic roared down Airways as Matt scanned the parking lot. It was full of vehicles but empty of patrons, as they were all inside guzzling half-price beer. He was on his own. Well, except for Natalie, and she only counted as a liability.

He stuck his hands in his pants pockets and went on the offensive. "So, Big Dean, are you a partner in this venture?"

"No." Dean's fists balled, ham-sized biceps jumping. "But Porky's my brother, and he like to never recovered from that fire."

Natalie folded her arms. "Matt, have you been playing with matches again?"

"Funny." Matt shrugged. "It was totally an accident. Besides, the fire department cleared me. Nobody was hurt, and the place looks better than it ever has."

Dean prized an index finger loose and pointed it at Matt. "That's beside the point, and you know it." He glanced at Natalie. "It was New Year's Eve. This guy and a bunch of other idiots were setting off fireworks out here. Knowing they're *illegal* in the city limits." He glared at Matt.

"Like you weren't right there with us. My Roman candle just happened to be the one that got a little off-target and landed on the roof. Look, man, I paid the fine, and Porky's insurance took care of the repairs. Come on, you didn't want me to go to jail for that!"

"I wanted to push your head down into your intestines. If you didn't have this lady with you, that's exactly what I'd do."

"But Matt's very, very sorry about the accident—right, Matt?" Natalie's dimple appeared beside her mouth, and Matt watched the tic disappear from Dean's jaw. It was downright miraculous. "I'll vouch for the fact that he's a reformed man. No more pyrotechnics."

"Of course I'm sorry." Matt tried to look sincere. Which wouldn't have been so difficult if Natalie hadn't just out-charmed him. "I promise I'll tell all my billiards buddies this is the place to come."

The big man's shoulders relaxed. "I wouldn't have thought you'd have the guts to show your face again."

"We had to talk to a couple of your regulars," Natalie interrupted. "Joey Roberts and Leland Stafford had seen a young woman we're trying to find. Maybe you saw her yesterday evening when they brought her here."

Dean looked marginally interested. "Maybe. What did she look like?"

"Twenty-five years old, Pakistani—never mind, here's her picture." Matt pulled Yasmine's head shot from his pocket. "She had on a lime green outfit, one of those loose, gauzy dress things with pants."

Dean took the picture and nodded. "Yeah, I remember. Tiny little thing, noticed the big brown eyes and funny outfit. Wondered what the heck she was doing with Joey and Leland."

Natalie bounced on her toes. "Joey said she went into the restroom, but he lost track of her after that. Did you see where she went?"

"She asked me if I'd call her a cab, so I did, on my cell. She waited by the bar talking to Jason until it came."

Natalie gasped, and Matt wondered if he'd ever been that ex-cited about doing his job. "Did you notice which cab company?" She pulled out her pad and pencil.

Dean looked up at the sky. "Yellow, I think."

"Yellow." Natalie wrote it down as if the bouncer had narrowed their search beyond three-quarters of the cab service in Memphis. "What time was it when they picked her up?"

"Nearly six — happy hour was just about over."

"Yellow Cab, six o'clock." Matt took Natalie's notepad, scrib-bled, and stuck it in his pocket. "Let's go. Thanks, Deano." Half-way to the car, he looked over his shoulder. Big Dean was stand-ing right where they'd left him, head down. Compunction needled Matt's conscience. Leaving Natalie, he walked back. "Tell your brother I'm really sorry about the fire. I should've already come to him to apologize."

The bouncer looked up, face softened. "Big of you, man. Apol-ogy accepted. Just don't bring no more fireworks to celebrate the holidays, okay?"

"You got it." Matt offered a hand, which Dean took in a crush-ing grip. Then, chuckling, he accompanied Natalie to the car. "Guess I'm lucky I got off with a smashed hand and messed-up hair."

"Um-hm. You're welcome." Natalie waited for him to open her door.

"What? I'd have brought him around eventually."

"Yeah, after he tossed you through the window."

"Porky's doesn't have any windows." Matt sighed. "Alright! Thank you, Condoleezza Rice, for your masterful diplomatic skills. Nobel Peace Prize coming your way."

Natalie grinned and slid in.

As they drove, she was so quiet that Matt glanced at her. "What?"

She bit her lip. "Is there a lot of that kind of stuff in your history?"

"What kind of stuff?"

"Fights. Fires." She circled her hand. "Yada yada."

He hesitated, his mother's voice ringing in his ears: *Be careful where you go and whose company you keep, Matthew. The consequences of your choices will follow you around the rest of your life.*

The ironic thing was the biggest train wreck of his life had occurred after his decision to follow Christ—or, more precisely, because of it. If he'd kept George Field's crimes to himself, he wouldn't be in this fix.

A buried memory of one of his father's favorite sermon topics surfaced. *Then you will know the truth, and the truth will set you free.* So far the truth had brought a hurricane of problems.

And Little Miss Trouble wanted to know about his history.

"I've never been arrested, if that's what you mean," he said with a sidelong look. "I haven't done anything worse than most guys my age."

"Well, there's a ringing endorsement." She rolled her eyes. "I'm trying to figure out exactly what I've gotten myself into."

"You should've thought of that before you weaseled your way into my agency."

She caught her breath, and he immediately regretted his response. Talk about kicking kittens.

"Look, Natalie, my life is what it is. I haven't been a perfect Christian guy all my life. I could rake myself over the coals for all the mistakes I've made, or I can keep going and try to live the rest of my life for a better purpose. Right? Isn't that all anybody can do?" He made a face. "Look at the bright side. If Big Dean hadn't uh … accosted me, we might not've asked him about Yasmine."

Her lips curved. "Yeah, but next time I might not be there to run interference. I thought the guy was going to go after you again. And he's twice as big as you!"

"Size isn't everything." He looked at her sideways. "My frat brothers used to call me Houdini."

"Somehow that doesn't surprise me." Natalie sighed. "Just promise you'll warn me next time we head into one of your old haunts."

⁓

At six o'clock Yasmine slumped on a bench in W. C. Handy Park, contemplating the big gray statue. She'd just walked all around the park, reading every plaque. Mr. Handy, it seemed, was quite a famous composer and trumpet player—though she'd never heard of him before today. Maybe the great blues musician's example of courage and creativity would inspire her to do the brave, perhaps foolhardy, thing she was contemplating.

All day she had wandered the streets of downtown Memphis, trying to summon the nerve to approach Rafiqah Akbar. Her boarding school chum's last letter had relayed her excitement at being chosen as a pre-doctoral intern at the University of Memphis Psychological Testing Center. The PTC was only a few blocks away from here.

Surely Rafiqah, an unmarried young professional, would sympathize with Yasmine and abet her flight. How many nights had they stayed up past curfew, giggling over movie stars?

Still ... Rafiqah was traditional in her faith and family loyalties. She might advise Yasmine to return to her fiancé. What if she called Ammi and Abbi and gave her away? Was it worth the risk? If her parents made her return, she could not tell them why she had fled. The things she had learned about Jarrar after Zach's last letter iced her veins.

Shivering, she watched a couple of pigeons squabbling over a piece of waxed paper with a streak of mustard down the middle. Her mouth watered. Watching people walk by with those big, soft, yeasty-smelling pretzels had been exquisite torture. But until she found Rafiqah, she must be careful with her American money.

Unzipping her backpack, she extracted her leather coin purse and peered inside it. She still had the credit card and a few hundred rupees, plus about ten American dollars. *Why* hadn't she thought to exchange more in customs? Now it was too late. Banks were closed for the day, even if she'd known where to find one with a foreign exchange department. And tomorrow started the weekend. Clearly her gifts lay in languages, not planning.

Grunting in frustration, she replaced the purse and heard the soft papery crackle at the bottom of the backpack. She withdrew a sheet of hotel stationery, worn at the creases from being folded and unfolded, over and over, and scanned the bold masculine print.

Sweetheart,

I'm writing so you'll always know how beautiful you are to me—inside and out. You've changed me so that I'll never be the same. I understand why you had to say no, but you have to know that I don't leave you easily. My job is taking me away from you, and I guess that's for the best. Otherwise I couldn't stand by and watch another man—especially a man like Haq—claim you. I've thought and prayed about what I should do until I can't sleep. I can only tell you to be very careful.

May the Comforter sustain you in what you have to do—as he sustains and keeps me. I release you from your promises, because your heart has to remain whole for your husband. It will be alright. I'll pray for you, and you know where I am if you need me.

Always and forever yours,
Zach

For a moment she stared at the folds of the letter, blinking away tears. It rent her heart in two, just like the first time she'd read it, three weeks ago. At first it had thrilled her aching heart. Then it had made her ponder some of the questions Zach had asked about her relationship to Jarrar. Questions about her fiancé's politics. About his religious faith.

And the letter made her wonder about Zach himself. His job that he never fully explained. A job that seemed to have something to do with the embassy, or maybe the U.S. military, but which sent him to odd places at odd hours so that she never knew when he might call, and the number was always blocked.

Only last week, after Zach was gone, did she put it together that he'd been as interested in Jarrar's movements as in Yasmine herself—and it wasn't simple jealousy.

She'd begun to ask questions herself. And what she'd discovered about Jarrar Haq had sent her running away from Natalie Tubberville at the airport.

Refolding the letter, she slid it into the back pocket of her jeans. She was not going back.

⌒

It was around nine p.m. when Natalie slipped inside Silky O'Sullivan's. Resisting the urge to put her fingers in her ears, she stopped just inside the door. Every table was full, the bar crowded; the walls were painted with neon yellow, red, and cyan blue, but otherwise dim lighting threw shadows in large corner pockets. Dueling pianos, Silky's normal late-night entertainment, competed with the clamor of conversation bouncing off the walls and old wood floors.

If Yasmine was here, she'd chosen a terrific place to hide.

When the dispatcher at the cab company confirmed that their cabbie took Yasmine to the corner of Union and Beale

Streets, Natalie and Matt hotfooted it to historic downtown Memphis—home of blues, booze, and barbecue. As a homegrown Memphis girl, Natalie was quite fond of barbecue and the blues. Booze, not so much anymore.

After a couple of fruitless initial inquiries around the original address, they'd decided to split up to cover more ground. Matt took the north side of the street, Natalie the south. Silky's was about halfway down her side.

Odd to be on her own again. During the course of the long day, she'd gotten used to Matt's merciless teasing. There was a certain pleasure in feeding it back to him too. *Trouble*, ha. Shouldn't be hard to find an equally insulting nickname for him.

Meanwhile, she had a job to do. Interviewing inebriated blues aficionados. Memphis in May brought the oddest combination of pilgrims to the blues Mecca. Elvis freaks of all ages. College students seeking an escape from the pressure of final exams. Artsy Baby Boomers in love with classic American music forms. Bored businessmen from out of town. Young professionals out on dates.

Natalie's last time in a bar had been an awkward celebration of a college roommate's twenty-first birthday. She'd sat there watching everybody else get drunk, wishing she were anywhere else and promising herself she'd never do anything like that again. But this was business. She loved people and figured she could handle a little smoke and noise for another couple of hours. Pushing away from the wall, she skirted the room looking for Yasmine's bright costume.

A thought stopped her. What if Yasmine had changed her clothes? Arriving directly from Pakistan, she might be reluctant to wear American clothes. On the other hand, she'd worked in the embassy for two years. Maybe Yasmine had become more westernized than anybody would expect. After the conversations with Dean the Bouncer and the cab company, one thing was clear:

Yasmine had not been kidnapped. Natalie and Matt were after a runaway.

Natalie approached the bar and smiled at an attractive brunette in a low-cut knit top and tight black pants. She gestured toward the empty stool beside her. "Hi. Is anyone sitting here?"

The woman, perhaps in her mid-thirties, grimaced. "Unfortunately, no. My date didn't show up."

"Uh-oh." Natalie sat down. "Men are pigs sometimes, huh?" She sent mental apologies to her father and brother.

"You got that right." The woman gave Natalie a wan smile. "You meeting somebody?"

"No. I'm looking for a missing person." She opened her purse and took out Yasmine's photo, sliding it onto the polished surface of the bar. "Have you seen her?"

The woman shook her head. "But I've had my head down. Ask Wilson. He knows everybody in downtown Memphis." She clonked her glass against the bar to get the bartender's attention. "Hey, Wilson, come here a sec."

Wilson, stocky and bald, sporting a neat goatee, hurried over. "What can I get for you?" He smiled at Natalie.

"Nothing, thanks. I'm just passing through. I hoped you could tell me if you've seen this young lady today."

Wilson took the photo, peered at it, then looked up at Natalie from under thick brows. "You from out of town?"

"Kind of. I'm moving back to Memphis after being away for a couple of years." Natalie leaned in. "So have you seen her or not? Her name's Yasmine."

"She's pretty. I'd remember her." He gave the picture back to Natalie. "Nope. And I've been here since one this afternoon."

Natalie swallowed disappointment. She'd been hoping to get a lead before Matt did. "Is there somebody else who might've been less … occupied than you? Somebody out in the main part of the restaurant?"

Wilson grinned. "You might ask Killian. He attracts all the ladies."

"Killian? Who's that?"

The woman beside Natalie burst out laughing, slapping her hand against the bar. "Yeah, go talk to Killian. If he hasn't seen your friend, nobody has." She made a sloppy gesture toward the rear of the room.

Natalie twisted to look over her shoulder. Ten or twelve customers had formed a line at a white picket fence running the length of the back wall. "Is that a goat?"

"Yes, ma'am. Killian loves to schmooze with the customers, especially when they give him a beer."

"The goat drinks …" Natalie shook her head. "That's crazy."

"Yeah, well, welcome to Beale Street." Wilson turned when another customer snagged his attention. "If I can't get you a drink, you'll have to excuse me. Feel free to look around for your friend."

Natalie nodded and slid off the bar stool. "Killian," she muttered, heading for the back of the restaurant. It took her about twenty minutes of standing in line to reach the famous Irish goat—by which time she'd interviewed everybody she passed. Every time she showed Yasmine's picture, the universal reaction was "Pretty girl," followed by "Nope, haven't seen her."

Tongue firmly in cheek, she leaned over the fence and flashed the photo in Killian's whiskery face. "Have you seen this woman?" The goat bleated and gave her a sloppy kiss on the cheek. Laughing along with several bystanders, Natalie wiped her face on her sleeve. "Down, boy. I don't pick up strangers." She smiled at the jolly-faced old black man handling the goat's tip jar. "How about you, sir? She look familiar?" Natalie slid a dollar into the jar.

The man took the picture and held it close to his filmy eyes. "Hmm. Maybe. But it was early in the day."

Natalie gasped. "Really? She was here?"

"Pretty sure it was her. She came in here and sat in a corner by herself. Conrad, our cook, felt sorry for her and gave her a bowl of soup, then she left. Not much business then."

"What time was it? What was she wearing?"

"Child, I don't know what time it was. Me and Killian was just taking out the trash and restocking the tables before lunch. Might've been about eleven. Maybe earlier." He scratched the goat under its chin. "Don't know what she was wearing. Eyesight's not so good no more."

Natalie's excitement fizzled. The old man might not have seen Yasmine at all. "Could I talk to the cook? Maybe he'd recognize the picture."

The old man squinted. "Don't see why not." Giving the bearded goat a fond pat, he reached for a battered walnut cane leaning against the wall. "Come on." He heaved himself out of his chair.

Natalie followed as the old man hobbled through the kitchen door. *Please, Lord, let it be Yasmine he saw. She might really be in danger, wandering around this place by herself.*

The kitchen was a noisy hive of activity: platters clattering, steam hissing on the stove, metal spoon clanging on metal pot. The odors of grilled meat, seafood, and grease hung heavy in the air. Hands behind her back, Natalie looked around in fascination. The culinary arts didn't figure into her talents.

Her tour guide stood in the middle of the room and bellowed, "Yo, Conrad! Where you at, brother? Come over here and see can you help this young lady find her friend."

A sweaty, coffee-colored face peered around a steel door. "Ray, can't you see I'm busy?"

Muttering, Ray stumped across the kitchen with Natalie in his wake like a duckling following a particularly grumpy old drake. "Busy, like—" He cut himself off, glancing guiltily over his shoulder. "You remember that little lady come in here this morning, the one that ate a bowl of gumbo and fished all the okra out of it?"

"Yeah-huh. So?" Shutting the steel door, Conrad wiped his face on his apron. "You always bringing some kind of strays in here. If it ain't goats, it's little girls. This one hungry too?"

"No, I already ate." Natalie presented the photo of Yasmine. "I'm looking for this young lady."

Conrad plucked the picture from Natalie's fingers and fumbled for a pair of reading glasses. He put them on while Natalie held her breath. "Mmm. Yep. That's her." He handed the photo back to Natalie. "Only she was wearing jeans and a black Elvis T-shirt. Said she got 'em at the Salvation Army store down the street. Quiet little thing. Ate her gumbo—" he chuckled—"except for the okra, then skedaddled when a couple of cops came in for early lunch."

"Which way did she go when she left?" Natalie put the picture in her purse, barely refraining from jumping up and down. An Elvis T-shirt. That ought to be easy to spot.

Conrad stuck his glasses back in his apron pocket. "Had to see to a truckload of meat just then, so I couldn't say. Looked around and she was gone."

"Likely scooted out the back door and down the alley." Ray pointed. "Thataway."

Natalie's gaze followed the arthritic finger. The open kitchen door revealed a pitch-black, muggy Memphis night. She gulped.

CHAPTER
SIX

Matt looked across the street, hoping Natalie was having better luck on her side of Beale. Two doors down, an outdoor café was lit by a street lamp around which moths fluttered like a waking dream. A big silver moon floated in the east, painting dusky shadows on the broken sidewalk and streaking the old brick walls of ancient storefronts.

Man, he loved this city. Beale was home, and he never tired of the raw musical energy pulsing under its sleepy surface. He'd heard some wailin' good sounds as he scoped out bars, cafés, and clubs like the Blues Hall Juke Joint he'd just left. But right now he could've done without the odd angles and dark alleys. He'd seen neither hide nor hair of one small Pakistani oil princess.

Splitting up from Natalie had seemed like a good idea at the time. But as he showed Yasmine's picture to group after group of increasingly drunk blues enthusiasts, he began to doubt the wisdom of leaving Natalie on her own. Granted, she had charm oozing from every pore and could talk her way out of a straitjacket.

But she was also young and pretty and naïve. The more he thought about it, the stupider his plan to divide and conquer seemed.

Making up his mind, he charged across the street, digging his cell out of his pocket as he went. He must've been out of his mind to agree to this crazy partnership in the first place. Hadn't he just told God, in all caps, "NO MORE WOMEN"? A temporary fast from romantic entanglements. Not that Natalie was in any way likely to be interested in romantic entanglements, particularly with him. *Or me with her, come to think of it.*

But theoretically she was a female, and he was a male who couldn't help looking at a well-made specimen plunked right under his nose.

Oh, yeah, he'd noticed. That cornsilk hair and the perfect little chin and the dimpled mouth. Just what he needed. Distraction.

Shake it off, Hogan. Back to business.

He pushed Natalie's speed dial. It rang four times, then went into a Spanish voice mail message. *"La persona que usted ha llamado . . ."* He listened, impatient. The first time he'd gotten her voice mail, he'd almost hung up, thinking he had a wrong number. Then he heard "Natalie" in the middle of the mumbo-jumbo. When he'd asked her later why the Spanish voice mail message, she laughed and told him she was experimenting to see if she could learn a second language—and then couldn't figure out how to change it back.

Ditz. He smiled. *But cute.*

It wasn't so cute thirty minutes later when he couldn't find her and she still wouldn't answer the phone. He'd told her to put it on vibrate and hold it in her hand, so he could reach her over any loud music. Where was she?

Steaming, he yanked open the doors of Silky O'Sullivan's oyster bar and literally felt liquor and cigarette fumes permeate his skin. Back in the day, this had been one of his favorite haunts. At the moment he was way more interested in locating one green-eyed blonde. When he found her, he was going to—

Something told him to stop. Just stop. She wasn't dilly-dallying; she wasn't lost. A cold, creepy chill walked up both arms and collected at the back of his neck. She was in danger. He stood for a frozen second inside the warm, humid noise of O'Sullivan's and tried to imagine where Natalie might have gone. He'd already been in every club along both sides of the street. This was his last shot.

The knot in his gut tightened as he approached the bartender. "Hey, man." He slid a five across the bar. "A friend was supposed to meet me at nine, and I'm late. Little blonde named Natalie. She may have been looking for a Pakistani girl—"

"Oh, yeah, she came through here about fifteen minutes ago." The barkeep jerked a thumb toward the back of the room. "She went off that way to see the goat."

Okay, that was the last straw. Here he'd been all worried about her, and she was wasting time gawking at the local menagerie.

Stiff with indignation, he headed for the back of the bar. He recognized old Ray, dozing beside the goat pen with his feet propped on a stool. Matt slapped the bottom of the old man's tennis shoe. "Ray! Hey, long time, no see."

Ray awoke with a start and blinked up at Matt. "Hey, boy, where you been?"

"Here, there, and yonder, as they say." Living upstairs from Tootie Sheehan had significantly altered his vocabulary. "How're you feeling these days?"

"Felt any better, they'd put me in jail." Ray grinned.

"That's good. Listen, I'm looking for a friend, blonde girl named Natalie." He measured shoulder-high with his hand. "About this tall, with glasses. Have you seen her?"

Ray nodded. "Um-hm. She came through here looking for the little Pakistani lady we fed this mornin'. You know her too?"

Natalie found Yasmine? And didn't bother to call me? I'm going to kill her. "Yes, sir. Where'd she go?"

"Last time I saw her she was heading out the kitchen door into the alley."

Fear slammed Matt in the chest. "You let her go out there alone?"

"Wasn't no 'let' to it. She just took off without a—hey, where *you* goin'?"

Matt looked over his shoulder. "Thanks, Ray. Check you later."

He ran through the kitchen, which was swarming with activity, moist heat, and a symphony of clanging metal, toward the open back door. He burst out into the sudden dark silence of the alley.

"Natalie!" He stopped and listened. A cat yowled nearby, and a horn honked somewhere over on Union Avenue. The dumpster reeked of shellfish. "Natalie!"

His heart felt like it was pumping tar through a plastic straw. The single bulb stuck in a broken fixture by the door cast a blob of saffron-colored light at his feet; beyond was black dark.

"Natalie?"

"Oh, no!"

Every hair on his body lifted. That was Natalie, and she sounded frightened.

"Where are you?" The voice might have come from the corner of the building to his left. But maybe not. "Natalie?"

"Matt, come help me!"

"Hold on, I'm coming." He ran toward the last place he'd heard her voice, eyes adjusting to the darkness as he skirted dumpsters, cars, and motorcycles parked in the alley. Finally he saw a small shadow, darker than the darkness, crouched against a chain-link fence. He reached Natalie and tried to lift her up. "Are you okay? What happened?"

She wriggled to get away. "I'm fine. But this man needs help."

He glanced down. "What man?" All he saw was a pile of rags at his feet.

"Matthew!" She gave him an indignant look and laid her hand on the rags. "This poor man—I was asking him if he'd seen Yasmine, and he just keeled over and passed out. "

Matt looked down. There was indeed a human torso under the pile of mismatched clothing. "What do you suggest we do about it?"

"We've got to take him to a shelter. We can't leave him here!"

They certainly could. Every minute they wasted, Yasmine was getting farther and farther away. But Matt could tell by the expression on Natalie's face that she wasn't budging unless he played Sir Lancelot. Or Don Quixote. Or one of those clanky dudes in chain mail.

"Alright." He sighed. "Move out of the way."

She did, making sympathetic little noises that for some reason tugged at Matt's heart a lot more than the smelly, undoubtedly lice-ridden specimen he lifted in his arms. *Almighty God*, he thought, trying not to breathe. *Here but for your grace ...*

"Don't drop him!" Natalie cautioned as Matt staggered under the lanky weight of Homeless Harry.

He grunted, shifted his burden, and headed for the alley between Silky's and the cappuccino bar next door. "I think there's a men's shelter over on Jackson Street. Did he have anything useful to say before he passed out?"

"No, but the cook at Silky's saw Yasmine earlier in the day. Ray, the old man with the goat, took her to the kitchen to get her something to eat, and she stayed nearly an hour. They said she had on jeans and an Elvis T-shirt she'd bought at a thrift store. She got scared when some cops came in, and she left."

"Is that what you were doing behind the bar?" He turned down the sidewalk toward the shelter. Fortunately, by this time, the crowds had dwindled. Still, they got some strange looks. Probably not many guys would entertain a date by toting around a street bum.

Natalie didn't look the least embarrassed. She glanced at the man's young-old face as if to make sure he was still alive. "The cook said she went out the back door, and I looked for her all over that alley. But of course it was too dark to see anything. Then this poor guy asked me for money—"

"What if he'd tried to hurt you?" Matt's feelings suddenly boiled, but he wasn't sure who he was mat at.

"Hurt me?" Natalie looked up at him incredulously. "He can't even walk by himself."

"Still, don't you ever wander off in the dark by yourself like that again."

She just snorted.

"You didn't give him money, did you?"

"I didn't have time." She looked guilty.

Matt shook his head and clamped his lips together, not trusting himself to be civil. She was a certifiable airhead. A kind, compassionate one, but an airhead nonetheless. Her father needed to know what kind of danger she'd put herself in.

Fortunately for Natalie—and fortunately for Matt, whose arms were beginning to ache—they reached the shelter and awakened a sleepy attendant, who settled their homeless protégé with little fuss. Matt and Natalie scrounged up twenty bucks between the two of them, handed it to the grateful attendant, and beat it back outside.

Natalie put her hands on her hips. "Now what? We still don't know where Yasmine went."

"Let's go to that cafe next to Silky's and strategize. I'll buy you a cappuccino."

"Okay."

Natalie followed close on his heels. Matt noticed she didn't object when he put a protective hand at the small of her back. The lights had begun to go out along the street. "I'm serious about being more careful around here at night. This isn't the suburbs."

She looked up at him. "You should see some of the places I've patrolled in Tunica. Except for the strip where the casinos are, it's so rural the mailman can't find half the addresses."

"You went out on patrol?"

"Occasionally. Most of the time I worked as dispatcher. I did a lot of the clerical work the 'boys' didn't want to do." She sighed. "It was frustrating."

"Why didn't you interview for the Memphis PD? You could've worked your way up to detective."

"My parents talked me out of it. You've met my dad. He's such a Papa Bear." She said it affectionately.

Matt had to admit if he had a daughter, he wouldn't want her patrolling an inner-city beat.

"But you know what?" Natalie's voice firmed. "I'm a grown-up, and I'm taking charge. Life's too short to spend it moping around, wishing things would change."

"Yeah, but there's that balance between going after what you want and dealing with what happens in spite of your best efforts. I want to know how God's will plays into the mix too."

Natalie nudged his arm. "Why, Matthew, that's a very pro-found question." He looked down and found her smiling up at him, magenta Beale Street neon playing across her face. "Let me know when you get it figured out."

He shrugged, embarrassed. "I'm not a deep thinker. But lately I've been wondering if … if there's more to life than chasing skirts and looking for the nearest party. Where do you go to church?"

The non sequitur didn't seem to faze her. "I joined a little Methodist church in Tunica. My parents aren't churchgoers, so when I move back here, I'll be looking for a home, like you."

"Your parents aren't … Then how did you meet the Lord?" Matt steered Natalie around the corner past Silky's. She was like a little gemstone, facets blinking with new light at every turn.

"My college roommate was a Christian. She was maybe the first one I ever knew well. She didn't even sleep with her boyfriend, and I thought that was so weird, I couldn't help watching the way she lived."

Matt nearly swallowed his gum. "Uh—"

"But I understand it, now—you know what I mean? I keep myself out of trouble, now that I know you're supposed to. Which is the main problem with this jerk-o boyfriend I had up until a week or so ago. I met him at church, and he kept pressuring me to—you know, go further than I wanted to, so I finally got disgusted and told him to take a—" Natalie seemed to realize Matt was gasping for air. "Is this more than you wanted to know? I could shut up now."

"No, I—it's just that I never talked about stuff like this with a woman before." He ran a hand around the back of his neck. "I've probably been guilty of acting like your jerk-o boyfriend in the past."

Natalie laughed. "I can tell you don't have any designs on me. Which is a little hard on the ego, but very comforting too."

Of course he didn't have designs on her. She was like a piece of candy stuck on the bottom of his shoe. But he didn't want to hurt her feelings. "You're one of the prettiest girls I've ever seen. It's just that I'm fasting from women right now. You understand." They had entered the cafe, and he held a chair for her to sit down.

Those fine dark eyebrows pinched together. "I think that was a compliment. I'll take it." Her dimple appeared as she sat down. "I've never fasted before. Are you praying about anything in particular?"

He hesitated. He was praying to get control of his agency back. "Just stuff in general."

"Ah." She was quiet for a moment as she looked at the menu.

Matt watched her. She was not a stupid woman. "It's nothing personal against you, Natalie."

She looked up and sighed. "I know. But if you get what you're praying for, I go down in flames."

He didn't know what to say, so he crooked a finger at the pretty young waitress hovering nearby. He'd flirted with her a time or two in the past. "What do you want to drink?" he asked Natalie.

"Cappuccino's fine."

"Two of those with whipped cream," Matt said, and the waitress backed away—reluctantly, he could tell. *Fasting, Hogan.* He gave Natalie his attention. "So. We've got to make a plan about Yasmine. Did Ray or the cook have any idea where she might have gone?"

Natalie shook her head. "At least we know what she's wearing."

Matt gave her an appraising look. "You got a lead before I did. Good work."

Natalie blushed. "I was in the right place at the right time."

"Yeah, and you asked the right people the right questions." His own record today hadn't been so stellar. *Moving right along.* "I'll go back in the morning and look around some more behind Silky's. Why don't you go to the thrift store? Maybe the folks there noticed something else that'll give us a lead."

"Okay. But I'll be at my mom's until eleven or so—we always have Saturday morning brunch." She looked up when the waitress brought their coffee. "Thanks."

"No problem." The girl gave Matt an assessing once-over that clearly said, *If you get bored with this one, I'm available,* then left the check.

Boy, was it hard for a guy to keep his head on straight. *Lord, help me out here* ... He glanced at Natalie, whipped cream on her upper lip, oblivious to sexual come-ons going on right over her head. "Fine. Do your brunch, check out the thrift store, then call me when you're done. We'll compare notes. The sooner we catch up to Yasmine, the sooner we get our fifty grand."

Money. That was what this was all about. Money and getting his agency back.

⟿

"So how was your first day as my daughter's partner?"

Putting the cell phone on speaker, Matt kicked aside a basketball as he walked to the closet and hung his Alcatraz tie on the rack beside Yosemite Sam. "About what you'd expect."

He'd promised to call Eddie with a report, but at nearly midnight there was no need to go into bar fights, homeless bums, or late-night cappuccinos.

Tubberville chuckled. "Nat has a talent for stirring things up."

"That she does." He paused, then went ahead and admitted it. "She actually found the first lead on our girl."

"Ho! Good for her. So what's your next move?"

"In the morning we'll check the thrift store where Yasmine apparently bought a change of clothes." Matt sat on the bed and pulled off his socks, then flopped onto his back. He was suddenly exhausted from hauling the dead weight of an unconscious drunk guy a block and a half. Maybe his next move should be a workout at the Y.

"Outstanding. But it'll have to wait 'til after the family brunch. My wife—my ex-wife, I mean—told me to invite you along."

"Natalie said something about that." But she hadn't mentioned her father being there. "Are you sure your ex doesn't mind a stranger coming?"

"She wants to meet the guy who talked Natalie into moving home."

"It wasn't—"

"Oh, you and I know that." An undertone snuck into Tubberville's voice that in another man Matt might have called diffident. "But let's keep that our little secret, okay?"

Matt frowned. "Whatever you say, Eddie." Tubberville's matrimonial machinations were none of his business. "What time?"

"I'll pick you up around eight forty-five."

"Okay." Matt yawned. His cappuccino was wearing off. "If I'm going to be coherent, I'd better get some sleep. See you in the morning, Eddie."

He closed the phone and tossed it onto the suitcase he used for a bedside table. Unbuttoning his shirt, he staggered into the bathroom to brush his teeth. He had a feeling he was doomed to spend the next eight hours dreaming about a pair of sparkling green eyes and a smile like sunshine.

⌒

Tinkerbell started barking like a Rottweiler when Natalie opened her mom's front door without ringing the bell.

"Shut up, you dumb little dust bunny." She scooped the Yorkie into her arms and walked through the living room into the kitchen. "Mmm. French toast." With an appreciative sniff she leaned over to kiss her mother's cheek.

"Good ear ... um, nose." Mixing bowl under her arm, Mom vigorously beat eggs, milk, and cinnamon with a wire whip. She did everything vigorously, which was why Smith & Nephew paid her six figures a year to chase down new accounts. "So tell me how the private detective thing is going."

"We're making progress. Last night we found out Yasmine bought some clothes at a thrift store on Beale Street. I'm going there after we eat. Matt's checking out an alley behind a pub where she was seen." Natalie picked up a breadcrumb and fed it to Tink, who gobbled it, then growled when Natalie set her on the floor.

Mom looked over her shoulder. "I told you not to feed her people food, Nat. She'll get spoiled."

Tinkerbell yapped and sat up to beg. She looked so much like an indignant little Ewok, Natalie laughed. "We sure wouldn't want that to happen."

Smiling, Mom plopped some French bread slices into the batter. "There's some fruit in the colander in the sink. Would you arrange it on that glass tray by the fridge?"

"Fruit? Are you still trying to make me healthy?"

"One can always hope." Mom tucked a strand of still-blonde pageboy behind her ear and shot Natalie a peculiar look. "So what do you think about your new partner?"

Natalie fumbled a handful of strawberries. "He's a little overprotective."

"What do you—Oh, goodness, there's the door. And the phone's ringing."

"I'll get the door." Natalie ran, relieved to escape the question about her partner. Matt had seemed as glad to part ways as she. Not that they didn't get along in an *I Love Lucy* kind of way. He was so easy to talk to that she'd found herself blurting out things she had no business telling a virtual stranger. Especially a male stranger. Telling him she wasn't a virgin but had been practicing celibacy—good grief. But he didn't seem to mind; in fact he'd seemed entertained by her chatter. Most of the time he forgot to treat her like a fourth wheel on a tricycle.

But then there would come one of those jarring moments when one or the other of them remembered they were in a competition. Like when he'd admitted he was praying about booting her out of his agency. Boy, was that a conversation killer.

And it had happened again when he dropped her off in the parking lot behind his building. He insisted on unlocking her car door and then waited until she got the engine running. When she rolled down the window to wave on the way to the exit, he stopped her and leaned in the window.

"Don't forget to call me in the morning," he said. "You might make a decent detective after all."

She'd swallowed at the pure masculine glint of appreciation in his eyes. "I hope so, 'cause I've got a pretty tough critic to impress."

And then his expression shifted. Realization. Wariness. He *was* the tough critic, and his goal was to push her back where she came from.

Reminding herself of that, Natalie yanked open the door. "Dad! Mom didn't say you were coming." Her gaze took another startled leap over her father's shoulder. Mom had also failed to mention he'd be dragging Matthew Hogan along. "Matt! What are you doing here?"

Dad grinned at her confusion. "We had a phone conference last night, and I talked him into coming this morning. I knew your mother wouldn't mind."

"I'm sure she—"

"That was Nina on the phone." Mom appeared in the kitchen doorway. "She said she's stuck in traffic and to please wait for her. I was just about to tell you I invited the guys." She walked over and gently prized the door out of Natalie's frozen hand. "But we're not going to feed them on the porch."

Natalie forced down the warmth jangling through her at the sight of a pair of deep dimples and amused hazel eyes. She stepped back. "Come on in. But don't give people food to the Ewok."

"Wouldn't dream of it." Her father barreled through, followed by Matt. "Nick's right behind us."

After her tall, lanky younger brother came in, Natalie shut the door. She glanced uncertainly at Matt, then led the way to the kitchen, where Nick headed straight for the refrigerator and Matt held out a hand to Natalie's mother.

"Hi, Mrs. ... uh ..." He looked at Natalie. "Tubberville?"

Mom laughed. "Yes, but call me Deb. Eddie and I have been divorced for years, but I never bothered to change my name back. Too much trouble."

"Don't try figuring out these two, Matt." Regrouping, Natalie picked up Tinkerbell. "Let me introduce you to the most important member of the family."

"That would be me." Her brother stuck his messy dark-haired head around the refrigerator door, blue eyes dancing. "Right, Pip-squeak?" He ruffled Tink's hairy ears. The dog snarled at him.

"Don't antagonize the cook's roommate." Natalie tilted her head toward Matt. "Nick, this is my new—new—" Matt probably wouldn't appreciate having the partner thing rubbed in his face.

Before she could figure out what to supply, Nick rose to full height, a carton of milk in one large hand. "Boyfriend?" His rubber face shifted into younger-brother mockery. "You mean Fel-schow crashed and burned even faster than the last one? What was his name? Oddity? Oddment?"

"Ozment," Natalie said, annoyed. "Matt's not my boyfriend. We happen to be working together on a missing persons case."

As usual her brother glossed over the most pertinent information. "Then Felschow's still hanging around? When're you going to give that arrogant idiot the boot he deserves?"

Natalie glanced at Matt, who leaned back against the doorframe, eyes alight. Nick never knew when to stop. The only way to avoid being eaten alive was to attack first. "Does Dad know you did that stunt audition for the new Grisham movie?"

"Shhh! Keep your voice down!" Nick glanced at his parents, who had drifted into the living room together. "I'm gonna tell him after grade reports come out."

"You do movie stunts?" Matt looked admiring.

"I've been an extra in a couple of flicks filmed here. Been training for the stunt stuff. I'm into martial arts, and I've done some rock climbing and skateboarding and—"

"You're supposed to be looking for a real job." Natalie gave her brother a reproving frown. "Something safe, like waiting tables."

Nick waved airily. "Dad always comes around. You know it's easier to get forgiveness than permission."

"Nick!"

Her brother laughed. "Come on, Nat, lighten up. You're worse than Mom."

"What's that supposed to mean?" Deb had returned to the kitchen, wiping her hands on an embroidered tea towel tucked into the waistband of her slacks.

"Mind your own business, Natalie," Nick muttered under his breath. "I'll tell 'em in my own time."

Grinning at Natalie's spluttering indignation, Matt addressed Nick. "What year are you in, man?"

"Third-year sophomore at UM." Nick's glare dared Natalie to comment. "I'm not a complete egghead like some people."

The front door opened, and Nina came in without knocking. "*¡Hola, mi familia!*"

"It's my other big sister!" Nick ran to snatch Nina into a bear hug. He rubbed his chin whiskers against her flyaway caramel-colored curls.

She wriggled. "You're squishing me! Let go!"

Nick patted her on the head. "Ten minutes older, and she thinks she can boss me around." He scooped a handful of blueberries off the platter and flung himself onto a kitchen chair.

"You guys are twins?" Matt looked from Nick to Nina.

"Technically. Mom swears we were both in her womb at the same time." Nina gave Matt her shy smile. "I'm Nina."

"I figured." He offered a hand. "I'm Matt. Your dad's my business partner."

Natalie noticed he hadn't mentioned her. Masking her hurt, she checked the bread soaking in its batter. "Mom, should I start a round of toast?"

"Please. Nina, did you bring the orange juice? Good. Who'd like some?" Mom herded the men into the living room.

While Nina poured juice, Natalie adjusted the griddle temperature. She enjoyed cooking, though she'd be the first to admit she wasn't terribly good at it.

She caught Nina looking at her. "What?"

"He's cute," Nina whispered, angling her head toward the living room, where Matt was relaxing on Mom's white love seat. "Does he have a girlfriend?"

"Come to think of it, I don't know." Natalie frowned. "But he's thirty, so he's too old for you."

"I didn't mean for me, silly." Nina rolled her eyes. "Although ten years isn't *that* big a deal."

"Well, I'm sure not interested. Anyway, he's trying to get rid of me. Dad gave me part interest in his agency, and Matt resents the heck out of it. I'm quitting my job in Tunica on Monday, moving back home."

Squealing, Nina set down the juice carton and ran to hug Natalie. "Yea! Are you moving in with Mom? Wait a minute." She pulled back to frown at Natalie. "How come you didn't tell me?"

"No firm plans on housing, and I didn't tell you because it's a recent development." Natalie smiled at her sister. "I've been tied up with our case since Thursday morning."

"Ooh! A real case. What kind?"

"Missing person. One of Dad's Pakistani clients lost his daughter. We think she ran away, but nobody knows why. She was supposed to get married in a couple of months."

"That sounds romantic. Sort of Romeo and Juliet-ish." Nina batted her soft blue eyes.

"Maybe." Natalie frowned. "We're going to interview Yasmine's parents tonight. If she had another boyfriend in Pakistan, that might explain it." Her father's boisterous laughter, booming counterpoint to her mother's infectious chuckle, caught her attention. "What's going on with the parental units? They're spending an awful lot of time together lately."

"You mean in a romantic way?" Nina made a face. "Mom's not about to give up her job to go back to the Suzy Homemaker gig. They're just bickering as usual over child support."

"Doesn't sound like bickering to me." Natalie shook her head and flipped a piece of toast. "But you're right, they both seem perfectly content to be single. Hey, hand me that platter, so I can unload some of this stuff."

As Nina helped her shuffle thick, crisp chunks of toast onto the serving plate, Natalie couldn't resist a glance into the living room. Mom sat on the arm of the chair Dad occupied, though she was smiling at some enthusiastic tale Nick was telling. Dad's gaze was on Mom. He looked happier, more relaxed, than she'd seen him in a long time.

Natalie was about to elbow Nina when she realized Matt was watching *her* watch her parents. As their eyes met, a faint, quizzical smile took the place of the rather sardonic expression she'd gotten used to over the last couple of days.

Suddenly off balance, as if he'd caught her mentally undressed, she averted her eyes and started babbling to Nina about syrup containers. But as she tried to focus on her sister's reply, one thought took center stage in her mind: how could half a smile seem more intimate than anything she'd ever done with the men she used to date in college?

⌐

Haq stood at the plate glass window of his penthouse, looking down on Union Avenue. He kept an apartment in Memphis not only because it was convenient to have a base of operations, but also as a means of assuring U.S. immigration authorities that he intended to continue doing business that would promote good relations between Pakistan and America.

Keeping INS happy was of primary importance.

He had spent the previous day making phone calls, checking the background of the detective hired to find his fiancée. The results were mixed. Matthew Hogan had at one time possessed a stellar reputation for entrapping cheating spouses, but just last year he had been involved in a case with less than successful results. His former client was, in fact, currently serving a long term in prison for campaign fraud.

Haq had no intention of finding himself in a similar embarrassing situation.

At least Yasmine's parents had arrived to help oversee the search. Abid Patel had called the moment he landed at the Memphis airport, and Feroz had driven them to the Peabody. Patel could afford the best—which was, of course, his main attraction as a father-in-law.

Money. One simply had to have it.

His iPhone buzzed quietly against his hip, and he looked at the caller ID before answering. "I have told you repeatedly not to call directly. It is too dangerous."

Faisal Yashir chuckled. "You give the Americans entirely too much credit, my brother. They listen in the wrong places."

"It is you who makes the mistake of underestimating them." Haq wheeled away from the window. The sight of all those cars whizzing up and down the avenue below, symbols of infidel wealth, burned his soul. Wealth could buy any amount of information.

"Ah, Jarrar. Fear brings mistakes. You must act with cold confidence. I have the product for which you have been waiting. I only await your payment."

Haq thought of the desertion of his intended bride, whose wealthy father would have no relationship to him until the marriage contract was signed. "I will have it soon. My marriage is to take place in two weeks."

And, praise be to Allah, he would find Yasmine before then. He would make very sure of it.

SEVEN

Saturday morning Yasmine slipped out the front door of the shelter onto an all but deserted Jackson Street. Stomach hollow with apprehension, she squinted in the bright sunshine. She had to find Rafiqah today.

Last evening she had arrived at the testing center where Rafiqah worked, only to discover that it had closed an hour earlier. With no phone number or address with which to contact her friend, she would be forced to come back tomorrow.

As she'd trudged back in the direction from which she'd come, it finally occurred to her why the red shield on the thrift store window seemed so familiar. During the earthquake of '05 she had been safe in Islamabad, but the aftershocks had affected her work in the embassy. She had been kept busy translating for American relief organizations who sent volunteers into the mountainous areas of northern Pakistan.

When she'd spotted another of the Salvation Army symbols on Beale Street, she'd timidly walked inside. The administrator, a kind but busy man, had said they only housed men and directed her to the women's shelter a few blocks over. The workers there provided a meal and a clean bed, then fed her a hot bowl of oatmeal this morning. She wasn't fond of the gooey stuff, but at least it filled and warmed her. These American Christians were extraordinarily kind.

The roiling of her stomach had nothing to do with lack of food. Indecision. If she hadn't waited so long, perhaps she would already be safe with Rafiqah. The longer she was on her own, the more likely she would be forced to return to Jarrar.

Maybe she should return voluntarily.

Blinking stinging eyes, she faced the Peabody Hotel looming on the corner of Union and Beale. She could check into the room her family had reserved for her and call Abbi and Ammi. Cast herself upon their mercy and ask forgiveness for the unthinkable thing she had done. Tell them she'd returned for her wedding. All would go as planned, and by mid-summer she would be Jarrar Haq's bride.

A wife. To a man who was not Zach.

And she would have to close her eyes to who Jarrar Haq was.

"May it never be," she whispered.

With a shuddering breath, she reversed her direction and headed toward the tall, glass-and-steel building where her friend worked. *My Lord, give me courage, I pray.*

∽

After an hour spent scouring the alleys behind Silky's, Matt called Natalie and asked her to meet him in the lobby of the Peabody. A national historic landmark built in the 1920s, the old hotel boasted Italian Renaissance architecture that played like a *Gone with the Wind* set. It was a thriving tourist attraction, but

Matt had walked past it so many times that now it was just a fixture on the skyline.

He found Natalie sitting in a comfortable chair, one of several clustered near the central bar, staring up at the stained glass skylight in the domed atrium.

"What's the matter? You look like your best friend stole your boyfriend."

Natalie rolled her head to look up at him. "I feel like a failure. I just interviewed the clerk in the thrift store. The lady showed me Yasmine's tunic and pants outfit, but had no idea where she went when she left the store. Yasmine apparently isn't one for chitchat."

"That's more than I found. Yasmine's gone to ground somewhere, but we've got photos out all up and down the street. Somebody will have seen her." He held out a hand. "Let's go talk to the family. Maybe they'll give us a new place to look."

Natalie sighed and let him pull her to her feet. "Alright. Lead on, McDuff."

As he and Natalie headed for the elevator, Matt hooked a thumb at the grand piano near the bar. "This place sure isn't for the underprivileged. It'd cost me a week's salary to stay here one night."

"I know. Mom gave me a high tea party here on my twelfth birthday, but I haven't been back since." Natalie smiled at the sight of a bunch of kids leaning over the sides of the magnificent travertine marble fountain in the center of the lobby. They were watching the famous Peabody ducks paddle in its pool. "Aren't they cute?"

"I like my duck with orange sauce."

Natalie gave him an insouciant grin. "Are you taking the lead on the interview?"

"Depends." Matt punched the elevator button. "If I give you the secret bat-signal—" he closed one eye in elaborate pantomime—"you take over."

Natalie wrinkled her nose. "I'm serious. Where, exactly, are we going with them?"

"Wherever they'll take us. Just remember—Middle Eastern men can be notorious chauvinists." He caught her look and grinned. "Worse than me. So when we're talking to Yasmine's daddy-o or her fiancé, you need to leave it to me." He paused. "You'll handle the women better."

"I'm surprised you'd admit something like that."

"Why?" They got on the elevator, and Matt hit the fifth-floor button. "One of the main strategies of investigation is plain old common sense. You watch how people act, then play on predictable behavior." He waved a hand. "Culturally and gender-wise."

"I guess that's true."

Natalie's admiring expression warmed him. He didn't often have somebody look up to and respect him.

The elevator dinged as the doors opened again. Matt looked at Natalie. "Here we go. You ready?" She nodded and Matt followed her down a hallway paneled in rich dark wood and lit with gleaming brass light fixtures. He turned when Natalie heaved a sigh. "What's the matter?"

"My parents spent their wedding night here in a Romeo and Juliet suite."

"What's a Romeo and Juliet suite?" He watched room numbers. The Patels should be on this hall.

"Two-story suite with these beautiful curved iron stairways and a balcony right inside the living room." Her tone was so odd, Matt stopped with his hand raised to knock on the Patels' door. Natalie was looking down, fiddling with her little handbag. "I was in the seventh grade when Mom and Dad divorced. I couldn't understand why they couldn't get along and live together, and I spent hours locked in my room, mooning over their wedding album."

Matt shook his head. "Girls."

"Are your parents still married?"

"Thirty years."

"Thirty? But you're—"

He laughed. "Yeah. But nothing immoral. I was a honeymoon baby."

Natalie grinned. "I guess you could say I was a pre-honeymoon baby. I used to humiliate my mother by informing random strangers that I was in her tummy when she got married."

He snorted and knocked on the door. "Well, weren't you a little pill?"

After a moment the heavy old door opened to reveal a small woman in traditional Pakistani outfit. Its eye-popping persimmon color emphasized her creamy skin and unlined face.

The woman failed to smile. "Yes?"

Recovering, Matt presented his card. "I'm Matt Hogan with River City Investigations. I called a little while ago. Are you Mrs. Patel?"

"I am Shazia Patel," she said in heavily accented English, stepping back to let Matt and Natalie in. "Please. Come in. I shall get my husband."

Mrs. Patel led the way into the suite, which was richly furnished with antiques, fine paintings, and thick carpets. She gestured toward a sofa across from the mahogany manteled fireplace. "Sit down, please. I shall be right back." She disappeared into a bedroom.

Natalie looked around, wide-eyed, then dropped down beside Matt. "This place is amazing."

"You've never stayed here?"

"No. But one day ..." She glanced at Matt, her cheeks suddenly flaming. "Never mind."

Her mind might as well have been behind a glass display case. The thought of Natalie on a honeymoon should have made him squirm, but he found himself smiling. "It'll happen one day. You'll have some guy wrapped around your finger before he knows what hit him."

"My dad says he'll give me ten grand if I elope. Then I could afford a night here."

Matt grinned at her. "You might want to consider it. Maybe old Oddball will take you up on the offer after all."

"Ozment. And I told you he's out of the picture. There's *nobody* in the picture. So shut up."

"Oh, I'm cowed." He looked around, startled to realized that Mrs. Patel had returned to the room with a short, slender, meticulously groomed man in dark trousers and a crisp white button-down shirt and tie. Matt jumped to his feet. "Mr. Patel."

Obviously pretending not to have heard their unprofessional banter, Abid Patel offered his hand. "You are from the investigative agency of my friend Eddie Tubberville?"

"Yes, sir. And this is my associate, Ms. Tubberville. Eddie's daughter." Having Natalie along with him might be an advantage after all.

Patel nodded and gestured for them both to be seated. "Please. Make yourselves comfortable." He and his wife took the upholstered chairs on either end of the magnificent beveled glass coffee table in front of the sofa. "Thank you for your promptness in coming to see us. We are most disturbed by our daughter's disappearance." He looked at his wife. "Shall we say frantic?"

"I can understand that, sir. We're doing our best to find her." Matt studied the shadows of fatigue under Patel's deep brown eyes, the thin lips clipped together. "We've run across evidence that she was right here on Beale Street, as recently as yesterday noon." He glanced at Natalie. "Show them what you found at the thrift store."

Natalie opened her bag. "These belonged to your daughter, right?"

Shazia snatched up the yellow-green fabric and held it close. "Yasmine's *shalwar kameez*! You found it at a ... I do not know 'thrift store.'" She looked at Natalie, a quirk between her elegant dark brows.

"Resale," said Natalie. "Used clothing and household goods. Inexpensive stuff."

Shazia sucked in a breath. "My daughter will not wear used clothes."

"Well ..." Natalie glanced at Matt. He shrugged, letting her have the floor. "She bought a pair of jeans and a T-shirt there. We nearly caught up with her at a blues bar yesterday."

"A *blue* bar?" Shazia shook her head.

"*Blues* bar," her husband corrected. "A place where they play music of the African American heritage." Frowning, he straightened his already rigid posture. "Yasmine loves American music. I should never have allowed her to go to boarding school."

"The guys we talked to at the bar seemed to think she was perfectly okay." Matt pulled out a notepad and pen. "Yasmine seems to be a pretty independent lady. She managed to find a ride to Beale Street without any trouble. Any idea why she headed this direction? Did she know you'd be staying here at the Peabody?"

Patel shook his head. "She was to have stayed here, but we hadn't planned to come over to the U.S. until closer to time for the wedding. We wanted to let Yasmine settle, get to know her future husband's family."

"I wanted to come with her." A note of censure colored Shazia's soft voice, though her eyes remained properly lowered. "But my husband thought it not necessary."

Patel scowled at his wife. "I do not know why my daughter came to this part of town—unless she was seeking out the music attractions."

"Okay." Matt made a note. "We'll check out some of the other hot spots. Sun Studios, maybe. The Elvis souvenir shops. Seems kind of unlikely, though, that she'd be hitting tourist attractions when she could do that later with her fiancé."

"Ammi."

Matt looked over to find a lovely young woman, probably no more than a teenager, standing in an open bedroom doorway. She was dressed in jeans and a layering of sweaters—undoubtedly in deference to the air conditioning cranked down to sub-zero temperatures. The soft voice continued in a musical flood of Urdu.

Shazia, glancing at Matt, answered rapidly and gestured for the girl to go away.

"Wait." Natalie lifted her hand. "Is this your other daughter? May we talk to her?"

Abid Patel's thick brows drew together above his hooked nose. "For what purpose? Liba is a child. She has been in school in Karachi for the last three years. She is only here because summer term has yet to begin."

Matt assessed the situation quickly. Natalie was right. Yasmine's little sister could be useful, if they could get around Patel's protectiveness and dismissive attitude.

He gave Patel a man-to-man look. "Maybe Miss Tubberville could treat her and your wife to some ice cream while you and I finish our discussion."

"I suppose that would be appropriate." Patel pulled at his lower lip, giving his wife a stern look. "But do not under any circumstances go into any of those blues bars, Shazia. American culture has already corrupted our family."

"Very well." Shazia inclined her head toward her husband, then spoke to her younger daughter in affectionate Urdu.

A spark of exasperation lit Liba's brown eyes. "Ammi, my English is perfect, and I am not a child."

"Liba!" said her father sharply.

Shazia laid a dainty hand on his arm. "I will speak with her, Abid." She looked apologetically at Matt. "May I offer you refreshment before we leave?"

"No, thanks. You ladies go and have a good time on Beale. We'll figure this thing out." He surveyed Patel's glowering expression. *We better figure it out, Lord, or I'm toast.*

⌒

"I just feel so bad," Natalie said, slurping down the last of her root beer float. "If I'd made Yasmine feel more welcome, maybe she wouldn't have run away. I usually don't have any trouble getting people to talk to me—in fact my dad always says I should've been born a parakeet. Do you think I scared her off by being—I don't know—" she waved her hand—"too nosy or something?"

Shazia glanced at Liba. "I am sorry. My English. 'Nosy' means having big nose?"

Liba giggled around a spoonful of Ben and Jerry's Chunky Monkey. "No, Ammi. Nosy means you get in someone else's business. Like . . ." She rattled off a phrase in Urdu that of course Natalie didn't understand.

Shazia's expression cleared. "Ah. But I do not think that would make Yasmine run away. She is friendly parakeet too. This is why she took the job with the embassy. She love to talk to people, make them understand and get along with one another. Since she is a little girl, she makes friends easy."

"Then I don't get it." Natalie sat back, deflated. She watched Liba scrape every last drop of ice cream, banana, and dark chocolate out of the bottom of her cup. "Liba, did your sister write to you at all before she left to come to the States? Did either of you talk to her on the phone?"

Liba set her empty carton on the little round table and twisted her hair around her finger. "When I'm at school, I talk to her on the phone once a week at least. But we email every day." She slanted a glance at her mother. "When Headmistress lets me on the computer."

Shazia bit her lip. "There are many dangers for young women on the Internet." She looked at Natalie. "My daughters are more ... how you say ... innocent than American young women. I have asked that Liba's computer time be strictly chaperoned."

Natalie blinked. "You don't have to explain to me. I certainly wouldn't criticize. So what did Yasmine think about getting married? What's her fiancé like?"

"He has the reputation of a fine man. We have not meet him."

Oh yeah. Mail-order bride, just like you always saw in those TV shows about Alaska and the Old West. She tamped down her instinctive American indignation. "What did Yasmine have to say about it? Getting married sight-unseen, I mean."

"Yasmine is a dutiful daughter. She does what her father wishes. She knows we know best for her future."

"I think my sister had some ... reserves." Liba gave her mother a little lift of the chin. Not defiance, exactly. But just a tad of moxie in the brown eyes.

Natalie scribbled a note in her PDA. "Reservations? A little worry, maybe?"

"Yes, worry." Liba's eyes dared her mother to disagree. "She has always wanted to see America, but moving here forever, to live with a stranger ... You see why that would not be easy."

"I had never met your father until our wedding day," Shazia said firmly. "We have being very happy."

"Yes, Ammi, but you are another age."

Natalie smiled at Shazia's offended expression. "You mean another generation. The world has changed. As they say, it's a global community."

"Yes, maybe, but my daughters are brought up very traditional. They go to school where we send them. They make the highest marks. They never go with bad company. They go to mosque every week." She gave Liba an annoyed look. "They marry the man we choose."

"Ammi—"

Shazia cut Liba off with a wave of her small hand. "We discuss this later in private. The important thing is to find your sister."

"You're right, Mrs. Patel." Natalie put down the notepad and touched Shazia's hand. "Which means I need to ask Liba some questions that might have uncomfortable answers. Can you let her answer without getting upset?"

Shazia sucked in a breath. "I am no upset!"

"Ammi."

"Well, maybe a little." Tears swam in Shazia's soft brown eyes. "I just want my daughter to be safe. I am so afraid for her. She does not know this big country. She does not know anyone. How we will find her?"

"Matt and I are going to keep trying until we do." Natalie rolled her PDA stylus between her hands. "Liba, if I can get you to a computer, will you let us print some of Yasmine's emails? If I can get to know her better, tracing her possible movements might be easier."

"Of course." Liba studiously avoided her mother's gaze.

"Great." Natalie took her phone out of her purse and punched Matt's speed dial.

He answered on the first ring. "Natalie! Where are you?"

"I'm still with Liba and her mother. Hey, can I take them back to your office and use the computer? Liba's got some emails from her sister and said I could print them out. Maybe they'll give us a lead."

Matt was silent for a beat. "That's a good idea. I'll meet you there in ten minutes."

"Wait—how's it going with Mr. Patel?"

"I'll tell you when I get there. Just ring the doorbell and tell Tootie I said to let you in the office." He muttered under his breath. "Guess I'm going to have to get you your own key." He didn't sound happy about it.

"Don't worry, I won't steal your pencils." She clicked the phone off and made a face at Shazia Patel. "My partner. My biggest fan."

EIGHT

As he passed the Jailhouse Rock Clock Shop, Matt glanced over his shoulder at the scowling young businessman dogging his heels. He had escaped from Abid Patel only to find himself caught up in the tide of Jarrar Haq's hot-blooded Middle-Eastern impatience. If he knew what he'd done to get himself trapped in this sitcom, he'd repent right now.

The outer door of his building opened before he could get his key out of his pocket.

"Matthew!" Tootie yanked him inside. "I wish you'd tell me when you've got company coming. I would've waxed the floors."

"I'm busting my butt every time I take my shoes off as it is. This place is like a doggone skating rink. No more wax!" He looked around to make sure Haq had followed him into the foyer.

Of course he had. No getting rid of Prince Ali Baba anytime this century. The Pakistani computer nerd stood next to Tootie's antique coat rack, arms folded, heavy brows hooked together. He eyed Tootie's floral housedress, apron, and fuzzy slippers with patent disdain.

Tootie gave Haq an equally jaundiced glare. "Speaking of taking off your shoes ..."

"Tootie, don't start, okay? This is Jarrar Haq, my client's future son-in-law. Haq, this is my landlady, Mrs. Sheehan. Tootie, have you got any soft drinks handy?"

Of course I do, sweet cheeks." She directed a pointed look at the braided rug before backing into her apartment. "Wipe your feet."

"You allow that woman to talk to you like a servant." Haq followed Matt upstairs to his office. Matt noticed he did not wipe his feet on the rug, rather stepped over it.

"We have an understanding." Matt looked over his shoulder as he reached the landing. "Aren't there women who more or less benevolently run your life?"

Haq's lip curled. "Hardly. Even my mother defers to me. When I marry, I will be master of my household."

"Hmph. Your life's gonna be one heck of a wrestling match." Matt opened his office door. He found Natalie seated at his computer, Mrs. Patel and Liba leaning over her shoulder. The printer was spitting out sheet after sheet of paper. "How's it going, Nancy Drew?"

Natalie looked around, eyes sparkling behind her glasses. "This is so interesting! I found a program that translates Urdu to English. Except some of it's a little ... strange. Liba's going to help me with the idioms that don't work when they're literally translated."

Mrs. Patel looked over Matt's shoulder and gasped. "Jarrar? Jarrar Haq?"

Liba and Natalie looked at one another, then stared at Haq, who drew himself up to his rather impressive six feet.

"I am Haq." He nodded at Mrs. Patel without offering a hand. "I believe you must be Yasmine's mother."

"Yes, I—why are you here?"

"He showed up at the hotel just as I was about to leave." Matt gestured for Haq to follow him into the room and offered one of the folding chairs. He was going to have to work on getting some more comfortable furniture. "Your husband got a business call, said he'd meet you and Liba for dinner at seven."

Haq hesitated, then gingerly sat down. "I am concerned about Yasmine's disappearance. Perhaps she was drugged on the plane." He seemed, Matt thought, outraged as well as bewildered.

"She didn't look drugged," said Natalie thoughtfully. "A little nervous maybe . . ."

"Natural, how do you say, bridal nerves," cut in Mrs. Patel. Clearly she didn't want to offend Haq.

Natalie seemed to have no such compunction. "I can understand why," she said, frowning at Haq. "Are your parents here in the U.S., Mr. Haq?"

"They are still in Islamabad because of my father's governmental responsibilities. They had planned to arrive a few days before the wedding with my sisters and their families."

Matt took out his notebook and leaned a hip on the corner of the desk. He warned Natalie with a look to pay attention and keep her mouth shut. "Remind me what your father does, Haq. I understand he's somebody important in the Pakistani government."

"That is right." Haq's thin, ascetic face unscrewed slightly. "My father is the Federal Minister of Commerce. *Very* important."

"Especially to my father," said Liba.

If Jarrar heard the trace of cynicism coloring the teenager's soft voice, he overlooked it. He gave her a lofty look. "As you say. But my father is not a man to let his daughters run wild. All three of my older sisters are married and living in Karachi with large families." He smiled. "I look forward to the companionship of marriage myself."

Matt suppressed a shudder. Companionship, yes. Marriage, not so much. "Haq, how long have you lived in the States? No offense, but couldn't you find a woman you wanted to marry over here?"

Haq's narrow shoulders lifted. "I have had difficulty finding a woman of suitable parentage and religion here in America. My parents negotiated the marriage contract with the Patels. Our fathers have been associates for many years. Because of her background, Yasmine will understand her role in a wealthy, well-connected family such as mine."

When Natalie's expression clouded, Matt knew he'd better jump in before World War III ignited in his face. "Yeah, I can see that. And of course we'll find her. There's got to be some good explanation for her disappearance. So why don't we examine these emails Liba has pulled up for us?"

Liba already had one in her hands, correcting the translation. Her full lips were pursed with contained laughter. "This electronic translator is ridiculous."

Matt waved a hand. "That's not likely to help us find her anyway. Let's skip that stuff. Did Yasmine ever say if she had friends who could help her when she got to the States? Anybody with family or other connections here?"

"She corresponded with me." Haq looked offended at being ignored. "Twice."

"Two whole letters." Natalie shook her head. "Did you save them?"

"Why would I do that? It was all silly female nonsense about wedding dresses and party favors."

Matt could sort of sympathize with the guy, but Natalie put her hands on her hips. "You pitched your fiancée's mail in the garbage? Some help you are."

"There was a friend Yasmine mentioned." Liba was flipping through the emails. "A young woman she went to boarding school with. It has been quite awhile since she spoke of her, though. I cannot remember her name ... Wait, wait." She triumphantly yanked a page free, letting the other papers scatter to the floor. "Here it is! Rafiqah Akbar—a psychology intern. She lives right here in Memphis."

Matt and Natalie simultaneously snatched at the email just as Tootie barged in. She carried an old-fashioned metal tray loaded with five plastic tumblers and a plate of cookies that smelled like cinnamon and vanilla.

"Lemonade, folks! And my prize-winning snickerdoodles." Tootie set the tray down on Matt's desk and stood back, brushing her hands together. "Come on, everybody eat up."

Reluctantly surrendering the email, Matt took a handful of crisp, cinnamon-dusted cookies and peered over Natalie's shoulder. She was getting awfully big for her britches, as Tootie would say, but he'd give her kudos for persistence.

Natalie's bottom lip pushed out as she read. "It doesn't say where this Rafiqah lives. But maybe she's in the phone book." She frowned at Matt. "Would you quit chewing in my ear?"

"Sorry." He twitched the page out of her hand. "I'll do the search while you take Mrs. Patel and Liba back to the hotel. On the way back, ask around to see if anybody near the thrift store or Silky's has seen Yasmine today. We'll debrief in the morning."

"In the morning?" She gave him a suspicious look. "You're going to take the case away from me, aren't you?"

"Why would I do that?" He grinned and offered a hand to Haq, who stood and shook it with great dignity. "Thanks for your help, man. We'll let you know when we find your girl." He nodded at the two Pakistani women, standing by the window holding un-touched glasses of lemonade. Anxiety drew Mrs. Patel's face together as if Tootie had left out the sugar, and Liba seemed reluctant to leave. "Mrs. Patel, I promise we'll stay in touch. Meet your husband for dinner, get a good night's sleep, and one of us will call you tomorrow."

Natalie headed for the door with her charges in tow, but on the way she skewered Matt with a look. "I'll call you tonight." The door shut behind her with a soft snap.

Tootie started loading tumblers on the tray. "Boy, you have met your match."

Matt was very much afraid she was right.

After leaving Liba and her mother in the lobby, Natalie blew a kiss to the Peabody ducks and walked the two short blocks back to Beale. Three p.m. and on her own again. She looked up at Elvis's statue on the way past.

"Contrary to popular belief, you not only left the building, you're dead," she told him.

He curled his lip.

Natalie curled hers too, then laughed at herself. Trading insults with the King wouldn't help her find Yasmine.

Only a sure-enough God intervention was going to do the job. She'd been learning to pray lately. It still made her stomach flutter a little—the awareness that her every thought was bared before an almighty Presence. But his Spirit walked with her. That was a good thing.

Wonder if Matt prays like I do. Wonder if he gets up in the morning and flings it all out there for God to take care of.

Matt didn't seem like the kind of guy who'd let his spiritual ducks fly wild. From what she'd seen so far, he was more likely to want them paddling in polite circles around a fountain.

So, Lord, how about a little moving of the Holy Spirit right now? I believe you. So would you show me and Matt both what you're up to?

She walked past a pretzel stand set up on the corner of Third and Beale. She'd passed it earlier in the day but didn't stop because of a crowd of tourists surrounding it. On a portable stool behind the wagon sat a wizened little white-haired man wearing a shapeless blue sweater and a Memphis Grizzlies ball cap. The smell of yeast and salt made Natalie's stomach growl. Matt, the turkey, had booted everybody out of his office before she got one of Tootie's cookies.

Making a U-turn, she retraced her steps back to the pretzel wagon.

"Hey," she said to the vendor with a smile. She peered through the window across the front of the cart and pointed at a poppyseed pretzel. "I'll take one of those."

"Yes, ma'am." The old man's words whistled through his scanty collection of teeth. He picked up the pretzel with a sheet of waxed paper. "You visiting from out of town? Don't believe you're one of my regulars."

"No, sir, I live here, but I'm looking for somebody. You wouldn't happen to have seen this young lady in the last day or two?"

The man gave Natalie her treat and took Yasmine's photo. He squinted. "Sourdough with raisins."

"Sir?"

"She wanted sourdough with raisins. Skinny little Indian-looking thing. Tried to give me some foreign money, but I told her no way." The old man tugged his cap and looked down. "She looked like she was gonna cry, so I just gave her a pretzel."

Natalie felt like hugging the skinny, snaggletoothed little man. "When was this? Did you see where she went?"

"Last night, when I was about to close up for the day. Saw her walk toward the Salvation Army shelter." Mr. Grizzly jerked a thumb to the right and squinted. "She a runaway? Should I of told the cops?"

"No, sir—well, she's sort of a runaway, but she's an adult." Natalie thought of her father's admonition not to involve the police until Abid Patel gave the word. "I'll check at the shelter and make sure she's okay." She smiled at him. "Thanks, you've been a big help."

Skipping toward the Salvation Army sign above a door in the middle of the next block, Natalie took a big bite out of her poppyseed pretzel. "Thanks, God," she mumbled around it. "You've been a big help."

Matt had logged just over an hour at the computer, searching for information related to a Pakistani psychology intern named Rafiqah Akbar, when the doorbell rang. He heard the soft clump of Tootie's slippers in the foyer, followed by her clarion voice at the door. Normally he paid no attention to her visitors. Relatives, retired school teachers, and church friends were always dropping by for banana bread or blueberry muffins or just a cup of coffee.

Then a double set of footsteps ascended the stairs.

He didn't even look up at the trademark rat-a-tat knock which always preceded her iron-gray head poking into his office without waiting for a response. "No thanks, Tootie. I've got all the cookies I need for now." He absently reached for another snickerdoodle.

"Well, here's you another one anyway," said Tootie dryly.

Matt's gaze flicked past the computer monitor. His mouth dropped open. Just behind his landlady stood the flame-haired waitress from the coffee shop.

She smiled and twirled her hair. "Hi, Matt. What's up?"

"You're here." He stood up, sending the chair whizzing backward to clonk the windowsill.

Tootie scowled. "You're going to have to repaint in here."

"I told you you've been putting too much wax on the floors." Distracted, he rubbed at the scuff mark on the wall.

"Of course I'm here," said whatever-her-name-was.

Was he supposed to remember it? Had he invited her over and then got amnesia? "Well, hey," he said heartily. "Nice to see you."

Oh, yeah, it was nice to see her. A lot of her. Her neckline dipped to roughly the vicinity of her navel, and a strip of slim, bare belly peeked between her top and her jeans. He stared at it like a cobra under a charmer's spell until Tootie cleared her throat.

"Are you expecting any more clients? It's five o'clock, and I'm ready to sit down and watch *Jeopardy*."

Matt jerked his eyes off the redhead's navel ring. "Uh, no. No more clients. In fact I didn't know—" He looked helplessly at his visitor's cleavage before finding her face.

Her blue eyes held a pleased smile. "I thought I'd surprise you. You left your card at the café, remember?"

"Did I? Oh, yeah, guess I did."

Tootie's stern face swam between him and the redhead. He blinked as Tootie moved the folding chair to the center of the room and patted the seat. "Here you go, dear. I keep telling Matthew he should get some more professional furniture." She retreated to the door and waited until the girl reluctantly sat down. "I'll just leave this open. Y'all call if you need anything."

Matt considered hollering, "Help, I need my mother! Or a bedsheet to drape over this woman." But that would probably be a little overdramatic. He waved Tootie away. Retrieving his desk chair, he sat down. Nice solid chunk of maple between him and temptation.

Not so long ago, he would have feasted his eyes on the bounty before him. After all, she was serving it up on a silver tray.

Unfortunately, huge chunks of Scripture ground into him in junior high chapel also traipsed through his brain. *How can those who are young keep their way pure?*

Well, duh. *Don't look down.*

He fixed his gaze on the girl's face. Lord knew, it was pretty too. He went for honesty. "Hey, I'm sorry, but I don't remember your name. You're gonna have to help me out."

"It's Heather." She pouted a smile. "Heather Hill. When you left your card, I thought you were interested. That girl with you last night wasn't your girlfriend, was she?"

"Heck no! She's my business partner."

"Well, then." Heather crossed one knee over the other and leaned forward a little. "I got off early and was just on my way home, so I thought I'd stop in and see if you had dinner plans."

Matt started to sweat. He could actually feel his armpits getting damp. This girl was really, really hot. And all she wanted was a dinner companion. It would be rude to shove her out of the room.

His gaze drifted downward, then jerked back up. "I didn't have any real plans."

"There's a good blues band down at B. B. King's tonight. Why don't we get a bite to eat and hang out for a while?" She smiled, eyes half closed. "My treat."

He shook his head. Then nodded. Her treat.

I'm toast.

NINE

The Beale Street Women and Children's Shelter at dinnertime on a Saturday night was a babel of laughter, babies crying, and dishes rattling. Having spent several Thanksgivings serving food at shelters on the south side of Memphis, Natalie walked in looking for someone in an apron. It was a given that the person in charge of the place would be too busy to answer questions.

A quick look around revealed a cultural olio of black, white, Hispanic, and Asian faces—all female, except for a young man, probably in his early thirties, who was supervising the chaos at the children's table while feeding a baby in a high chair.

The young man slipped a spoonful of something goopy into the baby's mouth, then smiled across the room at a pretty brown-eyed woman serving rice to the ladies seated around a long, sturdy cafeteria table. The young woman winked at him, and Natalie's heart melted. *Lord, I sure would like for somebody to look at me like that one day.*

Okay, so the young woman wore an apron, but her husband was most likely the man in charge.

Natalie circled the large, open room, dodging a pack of little boys shooting each other with imaginary guns and making appropriate noises. She rounded the children's table and smiled at the baby. "Hi, kiddo, know where I can get some of that good stuff?"

The baby gave her a cereal-smeared grin. "Da!" he shouted.

The young man laughed and wiped the child's chin with his bib. "You're welcome to it, but I recommend the chicken and rice. Go ask my wife over there. She'll get you a plate." He put down the baby's spoon and offered a hand. "I'm David Myers, the pastor and director here. This little squirt is Davey."

"Hi, David, I'm Natalie Tubberville. I'm not hungry, but I'll be glad to lend a hand after I ask you a couple of questions. Would that be okay?" The baby grabbed the spoon and flung it onto the floor. Natalie picked it up and handed it to David. "I'm a great dishwasher."

He peered up at Natalie. "We'll take all the help we can get. What kind of questions? Are you a reporter?" Expression hopeful, he wiped the baby's spoon off on a napkin, then absently stuck it in his shirt pocket.

"Sorry. No, I'm an investigator. Here's my card."

David took the card. "Is this your real name? Funny, you don't look like a Matthew."

She smiled at his teasing. "Matt's my partner. I'm new with the agency, so I don't have a card of my own yet. Anyway, we're looking for a young woman named Yasmine Patel. A pretzel salesman a couple of streets over saw her head for the Salvation Army shelter, but it turns out they just take men. They said to check with you. This is her picture. Have you seen her?"

David studied the photo, holding it out of reach of the baby's flailing hands. "Maybe." He looked over his shoulder. "Alison, come here a sec when you get done over there, okay?"

His wife set the pan of rice down in the middle of the table and brushed her hands off on her apron. "What is it?" She gave Natalie a curious glance as she lifted little Davey out of his high chair. "Come here, snookums. Give Mommy love."

The baby buried his face in his mother's neck, and another little stab of envy pierced Natalie.

"Honey, this is Natalie Tubberville." David showed his wife the picture. "Do you remember seeing this girl in the last day or two?"

Snuggling the baby, Alison sat down on one of the child-sized benches to study Yasmine's photo. The noise level had dropped dramatically after a couple of elderly black women shepherded the children into a side room. Alison's eyes lit with recognition, but she sent Natalie a cautious look. "Why do you ask?"

"Oh, I'm sorry. I'm a private detective hired by her family to find her. She disappeared from the airport a couple of days ago."

Alison met her husband's eyes. "We don't talk about our residents with strangers. Many of them are fleeing abusive husbands."

"I understand." Natalie nodded. "But that's not the case with Yasmine. She had come to the U.S. to get married."

Alison bit her lip. "Getting married? She didn't have a ring on, that I noticed."

Natalie clasped her hands together. "You mean she was here?"

Reluctantly Alison nodded. "She stayed here last night. But she left early this morning. I don't think she was comfortable with all the noise."

"Did you talk to her?"

"I tried." Alison's smooth forehead wrinkled. "She had an accent, but she wouldn't tell us where she came from or where she was going. She wanted to pay for her room and board with money that looked like—I dunno, maybe rupees. Is she Indian?"

"Pakistani. Did you take her money?"

Alison shook her head. "We like to let people pay if they can, but what would we do with rupees? She was very polite, but quiet." She paused, glancing at her husband again.

"She hasn't done anything wrong," Natalie assured her. "Her family is worried about her. She came over from Pakistan to get married this summer. Arrived on a flight day before yesterday. Then she just—*pouf!*" Natalie snapped her fingers. "Disappeared, like that. Did you notice anything else odd or different about her?" The woman paid attention, a rare characteristic. "She was wearing a pair of beaded earrings. Did she still have them on last night?"

Alison looked at the ceiling. "I'm pretty sure she did. No other jewelry. Well, except for her shoes. She had on a pair of fancy little sandals, and they'd rubbed some serious blisters on her feet. I had to give her some Band-Aids."

"Hm." Natalie stared, stumped. Was that important? "Are you sure she didn't mention anything else about what she'd been doing all day? Maybe that'd give us a lead on where she's going."

"I'm sorry. Like I said, she kept to herself." Alison looked at her husband again.

He patted the baby's bottom. The little guy was sound asleep against his mother's shoulder. "What about the bed she slept in? Maybe she dropped something that would be helpful."

"I suppose we could look in the dorm. Let me put Davey in his crib first. Guess he's not getting a bath tonight."

Alison disappeared with the baby, leaving Natalie to chat quietly with David. She discovered the young couple had graduated from a Memphis seminary the previous year and had decided to stay on at the street ministry they'd founded as an extension of their studies.

David rubbed a hand over the table. "We get donations from churches all over the county, and volunteers come in from states as far away as Texas and Georgia and Florida. Next on our wish list is a bus."

"I'll mention it to my mom. She's not a churchgoer, but she's very generous and has a lot of money connections." Natalie smiled. "You never know."

"Wow, that would be great. We'll take whatever help we can get, thanks."

Alison returned without the baby, but she carried a small walkie-talkie-type monitor. "Come this way, Natalie. Since the weather's warm, the dorm isn't very full. I don't think I've assigned anybody to the bed your friend slept in last night."

Natalie followed Alison into a room that connected to the dining room. The spacious dormitory had a clean-swept tile floor and ceiling fans whirring overhead. There was a bathroom visible through another open door, live with the sound of running water and the laughter of children. "This is nice," she said, taking note of six or eight stacked bunk beds lining the walls. Each bed was made with plain white sheets, a pillow, and a beige blanket folded at the foot.

"We're proud of what the Lord is doing here." Alison walked toward a top bunk under a window whose mini blinds were pulled against the approaching darkness. "This is where Yasmine slept. I've already replaced the sheets, but you're welcome to look around if you want."

Natalie stared at the taut white covers on the bunk. What would Matt do if he were here? She wasn't sure of the rules for finding people who didn't want to be found, especially a woman with very little money in a foreign country.

She turned as a woman's smoky voice, husky from years of cigarette consumption, interrupted her thoughts.

"What you lookin' for, Miz Alison? Did the baby lose one of his toys?" A small, stooped woman wearing a pink warm-up suit stood in the doorway of the dorm room. Her hair was pulled back in an ash-gray ponytail tied with a pink ribbon. The faded smile was gentle.

"No. Keturah, this is Natalie, um … Tubberville, right?" Alison glanced at Natalie for confirmation. "Anyway, she's looking for the young Pakistani woman who stayed in the bunk above you last night. I don't suppose she talked to you, did she?"

Keturah's eyes, full of a lifetime's hard experience, took on a guarded expression. "She didn't say hardly nothing. Why?"

Natalie went into her spiel about Yasmine's forthcoming marriage. "Her family's so worried about her that they're offering a reward," she finished. That wasn't strictly true, but Natalie figured even if the Patels didn't come through with individual rewards for people who had helped find Yasmine, she herself would foot the bill. With a fifty-thousand-dollar finder's fee to play with, she could afford it.

"I already got my reward." Keturah folded her arms. "The Lord Jesus done set me free. But if that little girl's in trouble, I don't mind helping. I heard her sniffling, late last night while I was trying to go to sleep. So this morning over breakfast I asked her what was the matter." She shrugged. "Wouldn't say, but she did ask me if I had ever been to the Psychological Testing Center."

Natalie clasped her hands together. "Her friend Rafiqah is a psychology intern of some sort. I bet Yasmine knew she was there." She ran to give Keturah an impulsive hug. "Thank you, thank you!"

Keturah patted her on the arm. "You're welcome. Tell Dr. McWain I'll be by on Thursday for my appointment."

⟶

Yasmine cowered behind a lamp post at the corner of Jackson and Beale, watching as the blonde woman who worked for her father and the Kumars left the shelter. She had a happy, confident sort of walk, like most Americans, as she turned in the direction of the coffee shop Yasmine had passed earlier in the day. Natalie Tubberville had a reason to be happy and confident. She was going to make a lot of money when Yasmine gave herself up and went back to her family.

Which now seemed inevitable. Yasmine pressed the back of her hand against her mouth to stifle a sob. Tears flooded her eyes, blinding her to the lengthening evening shadows. Rafiqah had finished her studies and moved, leaving no forwarding address. Yasmine had only herself to blame. With no idea how to tell her friend that she was now a Christian—as far as her family was concerned, an infidel, unfit to bear the name Patel—she had not answered Rafiqah's last letter. Written on letterhead from the testing center, it had begged Yasmine to stay in touch. Rafiqah was lonely in America, desperately missed her culture. But Yasmine could not answer. She was a coward.

And now, because of Natalie Tubberville, she could not even spend another night in the shelter. What was she going to do? Completely on her own in this enormous foreign country.

She grasped the silver ring resting against her bosom. It grew warm in her hand, comforting her. Maybe Zach didn't really love her. Maybe he'd only been using her to get to Jarrar, and possibly that was the only reason he'd written that letter. But at least he was a Christian. If she went to him he would help her. The ring told her so.

Leaning back against the lamp post, knees weak, she held it out, palm flat. The little fish cut into the metal winked at her in the dying sunlight. Ah, symbol of her Lord and Savior. The one who watched over her and supplied courage when she most needed it.

Help me, Father. Show me where to go now.

B. B. King's on Saturday night was hopping with music, food, and conversation. At first Matt found himself sliding neatly back into a comfortable social round. It turned out Heather was a graduate student in British literature at Christian Brothers, possessed of a fine mind as well as a fine body. The only problem was, she kept returning to a one-sided debate over whether or not William Shakespeare actually wrote all those mind-numbing plays he'd read in high school. Well, technically that Cliff guy—whoever he was—had helped Matt out a lot. In any case, he couldn't have cared less about sixteenth-century ghostwriting.

By seven o'clock he was regretting his decision to abandon his date with Google and patter down the primrose path.

"I kept hoping you'd come back to the café and ask me out." Heather leaned against his shoulder, sipping at a straw stuck in a frozen drink. Its fruity smell barely penetrated the fumes of "Paris Hilton" wafting from her neck. "So when you didn't, I decided to take things into my own hands." She hooked an arm through his and gazed soulfully up at him.

He blinked down at her, trying to breathe.

Hogan, what in the name of Elvis do you think you're doing?

Think? There's no thinking going on here.

Bingo. Business as usual. Is this what you want?

I've been really good since I turned my life over to God. He said it's not good for a man to be alone. What I want is to not be lonely.

In a sudden moment of clarity, Matt's brain took an elevator—along with his conscience—to the ceiling, where he looked

down at the moron letting himself be hit on by a girl with whom
he'd had maybe one and a half conversations and who was practically sitting in his lap. Was she really going to make him less
lonely?

When his cell phone vibrated against his hip, he snatched it
off its clip and flipped it open. "Trouble—um, Natalie—Where
are you?"

"Stop calling me 'Trouble,'" she retorted. "Where are *you*? I've
been trying to call you for nearly an hour."

"Alright, alright. What's going on?" He glanced at Heather,
who moved a hair's breadth away from him. A tiny frown marred
the smooth freckled forehead.

"I've got a lead on Yasmine. I went to this homeless shelter
where she spent the night, and there was a lady there who said
she asked about the Psychological Testing Center, so I went there,
but of course it's closed tonight, so I'm thinking we ought to make
some phone calls and see if we can—"

"Take a breath, okay?" Matt assessed Heather's expression,
which had gone from slightly cloudy to chance of rain. "I'm at
B. B. King's, but I was just about to leave. You want to meet me
back at the office?"

"That's where I am. Well, I'm in Tootie's living room. She said
it would be more comfortable than waiting by myself in your office, especially since there was no telling when you'd get back,
since you went out with that—"

"Okay, okay, chill. I'll be right there." He closed the phone.

"Who was that?" Heather drew back, dark red eyebrows
scrunched. Her nails dug into his arm.

Matt didn't really care. He had been rescued, and he knew it.
"That was my partner. I have to meet her to discuss this case we're
working on." He shrugged. "I'm really sorry."

"I bet you are." She sucked down the rest of her drink, then clunked the empty glass onto the table. "Where's my purse?"

"Here it is. I can walk you home."

"No, thanks. I see a friend of mine over at the bar." She looked up at him and sighed. "You're really cute, Matt, but I know when a guy's not interested. And I'm not into self-flagellation."

"Self what?"

"Never mind. 'Sigh no more, ladies, sigh no more, men were deceivers ever. One foot in sea and one on shore, to one thing constant never.'" She tucked her purse under her arm and headed for the bar.

Matt watched her go with more relief than regret. If men were deceivers, women were just plain weird.

⤿

Natalie jerked open the apartment door to find Matt standing there with his hands in his pockets, trying to look nonchalant. "What's the matter with you? I'm out on the street working my socks off while you're in a blues club, wining and dining some bimbo."

"I'll have you know, I've been listening to Shakespeare quotations for the last hour and a half. I need an Advil." Matt flung himself onto Tootie's green plastic-slip-covered sofa. He eyed the two-by-four-inch piece of knitting in Tootie's hands. "What the heck is that?"

Tootie, wobbling in her rocker with her fat little Boston terrier Ringo snoring in her lap, peered over her glasses. "It's a blanket for the homeless. Natalie told me about the women's shelter she went to this afternoon."

Matt snorted. "Might keep somebody's left toe warm."

"Never mind that." Natalie propped her hands on her hips. "What are we going to do about Yasmine?"

He sat back, one ankle crossed over the other knee, fingers linked across his stomach. In jeans and a plain blue shirt, with a loosely knotted pink-and-red patterned tie, he looked relaxed and ridiculously attractive. "Too late to do anything now. Monday morning we go to the Testing Center."

"Yeah, but that's a long time from now. It's going to be dark soon. She'll have to have a place to stay. Won't she go back to a place she's familiar with, like that shelter?"

"Probably." Matt pinched the bridge of his nose. "But would she stay there once she finds out you were looking for her?"

"Good point." Natalie dropped down beside him and put her head in her hands. "The problem is, we still don't know enough about her. Is she running *away* from something, or *to* something?"

"Hey." Matt laid a hand on top of her head, his touch teasing but somehow comforting. "Don't stress so much. Your brain'll explode."

She caught a curious glance from Tootie and hurriedly sat up. *Thou art not a bimbo,* she told herself.

"Sounds to me like you both need a good night's sleep." Tootie dropped one needle to unsnarl her yarn. "Go to church in the morning and have a day off."

Matt and Natalie looked at each other. "Church," said Natalie.

Tootie held her needles in the shape of a cross. "The place you go once a week to sing hymns and listen to a sermon."

Matt shifted his shoulders. "Yeah, well, the problem is, neither of us exactly has a church at the moment." He leaned a little closer to Natalie, as if for rescue from Tootie's disapproving eye.

Probably her imagination.

Tootie got her knitting back under control. "You should come with me. Father Tim's doing a series on the book of Deuteronomy."

"Deuteronomy." Natalie met Matt's twinkling hazel eyes. "Sounds great, Tootie, but—"

"—but the church that sponsors the shelter has a service on Sunday morning," Matt interrupted smoothly. "I vote we check that out. Maybe Yasmine will show up there."

"She's Muslim. Why would she go to a—" Natalie stopped as Matt's left eyelid flickered. "I mean, that's a great idea. I told Alison I'd help when I could. She said they were looking for somebody to play the piano."

"I didn't know you play the piano." Matt looked downright incredulous.

"There are a lot of things you don't know about me," she said tartly. "I know how to knit too."

Tootie tossed her skein of yarn and needles into Natalie's lap. "Then straighten out this mess before it turns into a toboggan instead of a blanket."

Natalie looked at it dubiously. "I'll see what I can do. Matt, I really am tired. If you think there's nothing else we can accomplish tonight, I'm going over to my mom's for the night."

"Okay. Come on, I'll walk you out to your car."

Natalie gathered up her new project, along with her purse, and followed Matt downstairs and out to the street where her car was parked. She unlocked the Miata and climbed in.

He held the door, looking down at her with a frown. "Be careful driving home. This isn't a safe neighborhood for women."

Sheesh. He was getting to be such a big brother. "I'm always careful."

"Yeah, right. You and your dark alleys."

"Okay, *generally* I'm careful. I'll see you in the morning."

But instead of letting go of the door, he squatted down to her level. "I'm glad you called when you did."

"Why? I got the impression I was interrupting a good time."

He looked down. "Well, it was and it wasn't." The shadow of the car door hid his face, but from his tone of voice, she'd bet he was blushing.

"What do you mean?"

"Let's just say I need somebody to watch my back every now and then."

Natalie hardly knew what to do with this yank in the conversational knot. "You weren't fixin' to do something ... stupid, were you?"

"No. Not really. I don't think so." Matt jiggled the door back and forth. "Never mind. Forget it." He started to rise.

"Wait, Matt." She laid her hand on his shoulder. He'd been mostly kind to her. Maybe they were becoming friends. "I know how hard it is to break bad habits. My language was awful for awhile, and sometimes I still slip."

"Yeah." He seemed relieved that she understood. "That one too. I think I've been lonesome lately. Don't have anybody to talk to but Tootie and Ringo—and you can imagine what *those* conversations are like."

She smiled at his wry tone. "Maybe ..." She hesitated. "Maybe she's right, that church would be the best thing for us both. The Lone Ranger stuff is dangerous."

"I guess. Do you read your Bible every day?"

"I try to. Why?"

"Well, it's just—" He let out a breath. "I know you're supposed to do that, and I've tried, but it seems so boring. Makes me feel guilty, but I don't even like to read the newspaper. How'm I supposed to get into a bunch of thee's and thou's and verily I say unto you's?"

"It helps to think of it as a love letter. Anything impersonal is boring."

Matt sighed. "Part of the problem is, I can hear my dad's voice reading it, like he did at bedtime when I was growing up. Puts me right to sleep."

A pang of envy struck. "Your parents are Christians, then."

"Yeah. Actually, my dad's a retired bivocational minister."

"Really? Then how'd you get so far away?"

"When I got out of high school I hopped on the first spiritual plane and zoomed off as fast as I could. I didn't think the church had anything relevant to say to me. Or if it did, I wasn't listening. Not until I met Cole and Laurel McGaughan."

"The couple in the photo on your desk?"

He nodded. "You know that verse about scales coming off your eyes? That was me. Rude awakening when I got in trouble."

"See? The Bible *is* relevant, when you pay attention."

"Oh, I know. And looking back on it, I'm thankful for all the Scripture my parents and my school teachers stuffed down me. It comes back to me at odd moments." Matt rubbed his forehead. "I just have a hard time making myself choke it down on a daily basis."

Natalie fumbled for the right words. *Lord, please help me here.* "Being a disciple is following the example of your teacher. I guess that's why it's called discipline. It's like food. Has to be consumed daily. If you don't, you get weak, and girls in low-cut tops and tight jeans will be a bigger temptation."

There was a moment of quiet as Matt looked up at her. "You must think I'm a real loser."

She squeezed his shoulder. Surprisingly powerful shoulder. "I think you've got more courage than a lot of men who never ask for help."

The white glint of his teeth flashed. "And I think you're a lot smarter than I first thought. Even if you are trouble waiting to happen." As he stood up, he kissed her forehead. "Meet me at the chapel next to the shelter in the morning. Maybe we'll get lucky and zero in on Yasmine."

Forehead tingling, Natalie started the car and backed out. She'd never had a conversation like that with any man, not even the late unlamented Bradley. Especially not Bradley. Strange, when for the last two days she and Matt had been like a couple of pool balls caroming on a table, crashing against one another and bouncing apart again.

She reached up and brushed a finger across her brow. She was getting dizzy from not knowing what to expect.

CHAPTER
TEN

Sunday morning as Matt passed Tootie's apartment, she poked her head full of curlers out the door. "Don't forget your Bible."

He pulled it out from under his arm. "Got it." With Tootie to nag him, he hardly missed his mother. Women just seemed to be genetically wired to run a man's life—or at least try to. Poor Mom had had little success in that arena. Which was why he had no desire to get married.

"Married?" he muttered out loud as he started down the stairs. "Who said anything about getting married?"

"What's that, Matthew?"

Startled, he looked over his shoulder. "Nothing, Tootie. Just talking to myself." He ducked out the front door.

Out on the street he looked around, enjoying the quiet. Though the sun was well up in the east, the work force hadn't yet arrived in the shops. Street bums were sleeping off liquor binges, either in a back alley or at one of the shelters. Tourists were still abed. The short walk over to Jackson Street would be a good time to pray for guidance for the day.

Last night he'd lain awake past midnight, thinking about what Natalie said about reading his Bible. Asking forgiveness for his lack of discipline and praying for new passion. Maybe the passion wouldn't come all at once. But God wouldn't hide from those who sought him.

Natalie was right about the Lone Ranger thing too. His heart warmed, knowing she'd be praying for him. Never had imagined he'd look forward to sharing his office. But Natalie was such a cheerful little thing, with that pale yellow hair and bright smile.

Life was going to be a little bit lonelier after he finally got rid of her.

Mood deflated, he looked for the little blue Miata and found it parked in a metered space just down from the chapel. He checked to make sure she didn't have a ticket, then remembered the meters didn't run on Sundays. Pulling out his PDA, he made a note to ask Tootie to get Natalie a parking pass for the lot behind the building. Might as well, since she'd be working there for the next few weeks.

He hurried past a patrol car and gave a thumbs-up to the cop reading a Sunday paper spread across the steering wheel. The service was scheduled for nine, and it was about ten 'til. He hated to be late. The ultimate rudeness, his mother always said.

The glass storefront windows, painted with the words "Waterfront Chapel" in black lettering, glistened with a recent cleaning. Matt paused to scan the winos and addicts and ragged-out women lined up in metal folding chairs. The room would be rancid with cigarette smoke and other unmentionable odors. He looked down at his old but clean jeans, the crisp white oxford shirt, and a Mardi Gras tie he'd bought in Mobile last year. He'd known a few lean years himself, trying to get the agency up and running. But he'd never been reduced to sleeping in a city park or under a bridge or in an abandoned building.

He had a lot to thank God for.

What was he going to say to these people? What if he ran into the man he and Nat had carried to the shelter the other night? Maybe going to church with the down-and-out would be good for him. Cole had talked him into helping with a soup kitchen back in Mobile a couple of times. That wasn't so bad.

Taking a breath, he stepped inside. Over the heads of the congregation he saw a plump young woman with a round, pleasant face handing out Bibles. She looked up and smiled as if she recognized him. He looked around to see if someone else had followed him in.

"Matt!" She beckoned, wiggling her fingers. "Come on in. Natalie said you'd be here. She's gone to help David bring the piano in from the truck."

Matt shrugged and skirted the clump of winos, about thirty men and five or six women. He didn't see his friend, Homeless Harry.

"I'm Alison." The brown-eyed woman offered her hand with another smile. "You can do this while I go and check on the children in the other room. We're almost ready to start."

Adding the stack of Bibles to his own, Matt looked down at a woman in the front row. Her smile exposed several missing teeth, and her eyes were bloodshot. But she seemed alert and sober.

"Thank you," she said when he handed her a Bible. She opened it randomly to the middle and hit Proverbs. A dirty finger caressed the fragile page. "Could I keep this?"

"Sure," he said recklessly. He'd buy the chapel another one.

Feeling ridiculously heroic, he continued his task. By the time he got to the back row, empty-handed — he'd given his own Bible away too — he had relaxed enough to begin joking with the clients. Patients. Whatever you called them. Not everybody needed a Bible; some had brought their own, and a few were still in hangover mode. But they were all human beings with souls behind the sunburnt, dirty faces and foggy eyes. He was ashamed of his initial reluctance.

He looked up and found Natalie on the other side of the room, tinkering with the buttons on an electric piano. She had on jeans and a fluttery-sleeved green blouse that made her eyes glow. Or maybe it was her smile that shone. She'd apparently entered through the back door with the tall, dark-haired young man in glasses who was shuffling papers against a music stand.

The young pastor laughed when Natalie took off on a bouncy rendition of "The Addams Family" theme. "I think it's working now," he said, moving his hand in a cutting motion.

Natalie grinned and smoothly slid into "Amazing Grace."

"Morning, everybody." The pastor grinned at his ragtag congregation. "Glad you're here. If you're new, I'm David, and my wife Alison is in the room with the children. We're very blessed this morning to have Natalie playing piano for us. I think y'all know this song, so let's stand and sing."

Matt slid into the back row beside a couple of black men and tried to sing. The old hymn was so familiar, he normally wouldn't have noticed the words. But suddenly the word "wretch" stood out as if pasted on a New York billboard. He'd been just as lost as any of these people. *You found me, God. When I was running just as hard as I could away from you. Let me show you my gratitude. Let my life count for something besides making money and having a good time.*

Natalie thought he had courage. At least she'd said so last night, probably out of kindness. But he knew his own weakness, and he'd need more than a certificate like the one Oz had bestowed on the Cowardly Lion. He was going to need transformation from the inside out. Looking around this room, he saw the damage wrought by a powerful enemy—an enemy who'd like nothing better than to render Matt Hogan null and void.

Make me not afraid, Lord. Make me your warrior.

⌒

Natalie hovered as Matt effortlessly hefted the electric piano and loaded it into David's little Nissan truck. She wasn't surprised that he'd shown up for the service, but his enthusiasm in handing out Bibles and joining in the singing—tone-deaf though he may be—had come as something of a shock.

"Thanks, brother." David swiped his brow with the back of his hand. "I borrowed this thing from one of our sponsor churches, and they need it back for their evening service."

"No problem. Glad to help." Matt pushed up the truck's tailgate. "Now that I know you're here, I'll probably slide on over a little more often. I live about midway down Beale where the Elvis clock shop is."

"Now there's a slice of Americana for you." David put his arm around his wife, who held the baby against her hip. "Alison's anniversary gift came from there, didn't it, honey?"

Alison nodded. "Dear old Elvis's guitar keeps perfect time. Which reminds me—it's nearly noon, so I'd better get Davey home for his nap." She smiled at Natalie. "Why don't you and Matt come back for lunch? We've got plenty of soup and french fries."

Natalie shook her head. "No, thanks. My mom's expecting me home."

Matt looked down at his feet. "I shouldn't impose."

"Impose?" Alison laughed. "We cook for fifty to a hundred folks every single meal. What's one more?"

Matt's mouth fell open. "Who pays for all the groceries?"

"We're sponsored by several local churches, plus restaurants and grocery stores donate food." David looked at Natalie. "You're going to ask your mom to look into getting us a bus, right?"

"Sure." Natalie hesitated. "Are you sure Yasmine didn't come back to the shelter last night? She couldn't have slipped in without you noticing?"

Alison shook her head. "No. If she was there, I'd know. We had our usual crowd of women, with a few kids and babies."

"I guess you're right." Natalie sighed. "I'm parked in front, so I'll go out that way. Enjoyed the service, David. See y'all later."

"Bye, Natalie." Alison hugged her warmly. "Thanks for sharing your talent."

"I'll walk out with you," said Matt. "Oh, I forgot to tell you, I did get a lead on the Akbar woman." He opened the back door to the building. "Got an email early this morning, which is why I was a little late. I'll check it out this afternoon and let you know."

Natalie stopped under his arm as he held the door for her. "Why didn't you tell me?"

"It's an old address from a couple of years ago that turned up on Google white pages. Might be nothing, so don't get excited." He looked down at her, the vivid eyes lazy and humorous.

Natalie made herself walk on. He didn't have to keep her apprised of his every move. Even close partners didn't live in each other's pockets all the time. "I know. I'm just frustrated that this is taking so long."

Matt swung along beside her. "Nothing unusual. I've had cases drag on for months. Aren't you going over to Tunica tomorrow to resign from your job?"

Was he trying to get rid of her again? "I've already taken care of it on the phone. The sheriff said he'd mail all my stuff to me, and not to worry about coming in. Which is a really good thing."

"Why?"

She shrugged. "My old boyfriend's still there. I wasn't looking forward to a confrontation."

Matt frowned. "Was he ugly to you? I could beat the snot out of him for you if you want."

A little bounce of ... something scooted under Natalie's ribs. It was really nice to have a protective male around, even if he was halfway teasing. She could just see herself showing up at the sheriff's office with Matt in tow. Bradley would go berserko.

She shook her head. "Not necessary. But one thing I need to do soon is look for an apartment. Mom and I aren't compatible."

"That surprises me. I liked your mom a lot."

"Oh, she's great. It's just that she's such a neat freak, used to her empty nest. I can't remember to put stuff in the dishwasher, and I leave my clothes everywhere." She opened her purse to dig for her keys, embarrassed. "You probably think I'm terrible. Your office is squeaky clean."

He laughed. "That's because Tootie mows through there on a regular basis. You should see my apartment. I don't let her in there unless she's got a pie in her hand."

Natalie looked up. "Really?"

He held up his hand in a Vulcan salute. "Total slob."

"Wow." She eyed his neat shirt and purple-green-and-gold tie. Bold but clean of line. "I never would've known."

He leaned close. "I'll keep your secret if you'll keep mine."

Something skipped between them. She caught her breath, met his eyes, and let her gaze drop to his mouth just an inch or so away. One beat. Two. He didn't move, and he was looking at her lips now. Ooh. Broad daylight outside a church. On the other hand, privacy was overrated. She closed her eyes.

Nothing happened. She opened her eyes to find Matt gazing over her head. "What's the matter?"

"There's a lady in a pink track suit watching us from across the street. I'm getting a little creeped out."

Natalie turned. "That's Keturah. She's the one who talked to Yasmine Friday night."

"Maybe you should go see what she wants."

"You think she wants to talk to me?"

"I'd bet on it." He stepped away, leaving blank, empty space between them. His expression was wiped clean of any physical tension. "I've got to get back to David and Alison's. Call me if you find out anything new." With a wave he disappeared inside the chapel.

Natalie stared at the closed glass door. Rats. What was that all about? Sighing, she looked over her shoulder. Keturah was crossing the street, heedless of a bus turning the corner.

"Keturah!" Natalie waved. "Watch out!"

In the nick of time the little homeless woman scooted across, outrunning the bus. She grabbed Natalie's arm. "I thought that was you! I saw her again. She's in the park."

"Who? Yasmine? What park?" Natalie shoved the idea of kissing Matt Hogan to the back of her brain. Pure, godly women didn't think about kissing men they'd only known for three days. As far as she knew.

Keturah's arms windmilled. "Riverside Park. I went down there first thing this morning to pick up cans, and there she was, asleep on a bench."

"She slept in the park last night? Oh my gosh! I wonder if she knew I was looking for her at the shelter." Matt had already gone back to the shelter with David and Alison. Natalie could call him. On the other hand, she didn't really need him, just to check this out. "Keturah, can you show me where you saw her last?"

"Yes, ma'am. Come on." Keturah started back across the street.

"No, no, let's take my car." Clutching her keys, Natalie darted toward the Miata. Adrenaline jellified her knees. If she found Yasmine by herself, she'd prove she deserved a full partnership in the agency. *Woo-hoo!*

⌒

Mid-morning Jarrar faced his unhappy father in the living room of his apartment. His parents had arrived late last night, and his mother still lay asleep in the second bedroom, exhausted from the long transatlantic flight. As the Haqs always flew first-class, his father's displeasure had nothing to do with crowded flights. Neither did it relate to the quality of the fine Turkish coffee the two men shared.

"Yasmine must be found, Jarrar." Father's severe face drew tighter as he stared at Jarrar across the top of his cup. "One does not share the bread, but one shares the shame."

Jarrar had heard the proverb many times during the course of his life. If one chose unwisely in matters relating to business or family, the effect reverberated upon all of the *biradari*, one's patrilineal kin. At present he could not reveal the plans that would reflect glory upon them all, but Father would certainly be pleased in the fullness of time when all came to light. Though Father had perhaps developed closer ties with the West than was good for Pakistan, he was a good Muslim. And Jarrar knew how to play the game.

Still—Father was entirely correct that Yasmine must return for the wedding.

He acknowledged his father's wisdom with a nod. "I spoke with the detective who has been hired to find her." Technically, he supposed there were *two* detectives. The woman he dismissed, however, as the Americans would say, as an "airhead." "He believes that Yasmine is still here in Memphis. That she spent the night at a—" he took a breath and blurted it out—"homeless shelter. She has exchanged her Pakistani clothes for American jeans and T-shirt and is apparently on some kind of slumming tour."

Predictably, Father was incredulous. "This cannot be true."

Jarrar felt the rage overtake him. He could still hardly believe Yasmine's shameful behavior himself. "She should be beaten. She *will* be beaten when she is mine. If I had known that she would be so incorrigibly selfish and vulgar, I might never have—"

"The choice was not entirely yours, my son," his father reminded him, frowning. "Yasmine was chosen for her lineage and because her father's money is frankly necessary to everything we hold dear. She is beautiful and educated, and her understanding of American and British ways will be invaluable to us."

"Yes, Father, as you say." Jarrar bowed his head respectfully, though a smirk threatened to break through. Father could not know the potential power Jarrar held in his two hands, ready to explode upon the infidels who strove to conquer the Muslim world.

"In any case," Father continued, pleased by Jarrar's outward deference, "you must spare no expense in locating and reclaiming your bride, but by all means, keep it quiet. If the press discovers she voluntarily left you, they will blow it completely out of proportion. The diplomatic embarrassment would be unbearable."

Jarrar's lip curled. "The American media does enjoy a romantic scandal." Americans loved to gawk at one another, dwell upon minutiae, gamble away their power. They did not deserve the massive wealth that Allah—all praise be to him—allowed them to enjoy for this brief moment. "I assure you, Father," he continued smoothly, "I am doing everything in my power to recover Yasmine. We will use the American detectives, but I have sent Feroz to pursue any leads they are not able to follow."

Jarrar considered himself worthy of earthly glory as well as that which was to come in the afterlife. Therefore Yasmine must be returned to his possession.

⌐

Matt shoved through the Peabody's revolving door and tried to shut out the image of Natalie standing in front of him, reeling him in with tiptilted green eyes and a misplaced dimple. She was such an innocent kitten, she probably had no idea what it did to him when she closed her eyes—an embossed invitation if he'd ever seen one. Oh, yeah, he'd wanted to kiss that dimple and then slide his lips over to find out what she tasted like, and it wasn't just loneliness or lust. It was growing affection, and curiosity about whether or not she was as fine as she seemed.

Then he remembered they were playing a game—the one where he had something she wanted, which was part of his agency. Well, maybe it was the other way around. Whatever—it was a good thing that cuckoo lady in the track suit interrupted his incipient idiocy.

Putting Natalie out of his mind and anticipating a ballgame on TV when he got back to the apartment, he'd sat down to a noisy, carb-heavy lunch with the Myers family. Unfortunately he'd barely filled his plate when the phone rang. Jarrar Haq wanted an update. So he'd gulped his soup down and told himself a walk would be good for him.

Passing through the lobby he looked up and saw a group of ladies enjoying high tea on the mezzanine, cackling like a bunch of elderly hens. Brought Natalie to mind. He could picture her, a bright-eyed preteen dunking a scone into clotted cream, strawberry jam smeared up to her elbows.

Smiling, he took the elevator up to the fifth floor. Haq had an apartment in town, but he'd asked Matt to meet him at the Patels' suite. His parents had arrived in the States last night, and they wanted to meet the American detectives who were searching for their future daughter-in-law.

Matt knew he had little of interest to tell them. After greeting both families, he took the wing chair beside the fireplace and crossed one ankle over the other knee. *Never let 'em see you sweat.*

"Why you are not looking for Yasmine?" Mostafa Haq—Jarrar's big-wheel dad—bore the expression of one accustomed to being instantly obeyed. "It is necessary that we find her."

With the full brunt of six pairs of night-black eyes focused on his face, Matt addressed the Commerce Minister. "Can't be in two places at once. I'm here talking to you." He neglected to mention he'd been planning to spend the afternoon watching the backs of his eyelids while a baseball game played on TV.

"It is the Christian holy day." Deema Haq laid a gentle hand on her husband's wrist. "I'm sure Mr. Hogan was in church."

Matt eyed the woman with respect. Haq could take lessons in diplomacy from his elegant little wife. "Actually, I was, ma'am. But I'm hoping to get a lead from an email I'm expecting this afternoon. I'll follow up on it and keep you informed."

"What kind of email? From who?" Abid Patel sat on the edge of the sofa, hands planted on his knees. His body was taut as a bowstring, his thin face gray with fatigue and worry.

"I think I may have found Rafiqah Akbar, your daughter's friend who has been here in the States for over a year. Thanks to Liba." He nodded at the teenager curled up in a side chair. Matt squinted. She had a book in her hand, *The Secret Life of Beekeepers*, or something like that.

Liba blushed and looked down at her novel. "I worry for my sister," she said quietly. "I want you to find her."

"Do you need money?" Patel reached for his wallet. "I can give you a thousand dollars. Two if you want."

Matt resisted the urge to hold out a hand. "Not at the moment. If we have to travel I'll take you up on it. But right now we have clues that lead us to believe she's never left Memphis."

Jarrar Haq scowled. "Then perhaps we should set a watch at the airport. Do you not think of this? What about the bus stations?"

"Yasmine is a gently reared young woman," said Shazia Patel. "She would no more get on a public bus than she would fly to the moon."

Matt reached for the knot of his tie. "She may be gently reared, but we know for a fact that she stayed at a local homeless shelter Friday night." He ignored the Patels' collective gasp of disbelief. "Matter of fact, I've been asking for her at the bus stations, and I've got some contacts at the airport. But it's more likely she'd just rent a car and go wherever she wanted."

"We do not know how much American money she had." Yasmine's father brushed an agitated hand over his thinning black hair. "If she uses her credit card, can you trace her?"

"Yes, but she hasn't used it yet. Your daughter's a smart woman. If she doesn't want to be found, which looks to be the case …" Matt paused. "Mr. Patel, I have to tell you, that's the strange thing about this. Why would a wealthy young woman like Yasmine be so determined to avoid us? A couple of times we've gotten close, and then she disappears like a puff of smoke. If you have any idea what she's running from, I need you to be straight with me."

The question had been aimed at the Patels, but Mostafa Haq got to his feet, outrage in every line of his tall, dignified body. "Mr. Hogan, do you accuse this good family of some kind of abuse?"

Matt blinked. "Of course not. But there's got to be some reason—"

"I assure you my daughter has no reason to run away." Abid Patel had stiffened in outrage. "If anything, she has been well and truly spoiled, and my wife has been overly lenient in her upbringing. Allowing her to work in the embassy in Islamabad may have been our most critical mistake."

"Abid!" Shazia laid trembling fingers against her lips. "Please, in front of guests—"

"Alright." Matt held up a hand. "Forget I mentioned it. Don't everybody get all in a flap."

Jarrar Haq gave him a cold smile. "We simply want to make sure that you are doing everything possible to bring Yasmine back to us. We worry for her safety."

To Matt's relief, his phone buzzed against his hip. "Excuse me, let me see—" He flipped open the phone. "Natalie! What's the matter?"

"Hey, I'm down at the docks. Get over here right now. Yasmine just got on a riverboat, and it's taking off."

CHAPTER

ELEVEN

Natalie did not swim. Not only did she *not* swim; she *couldn't* swim, because she was *afraid* to swim. A very bad experience in a neighbor's pool when she was in the first grade had left her with something akin to hydrophobia. Even now, taking a shower was only tolerable because the alternative was to smell.

But as the *Delta Queen* pushed away from the dock with a groan of paddlewheels and earsplitting whistle blast, she'd actually entertained an impulse to jump into the muddy black water and dogpaddle after it. One nanosecond later she was ten yards away in the landing area, jumping up and down and screaming, "Come back! Yasmine, don't go!"

But the boat kept chugging downriver on a Mississippi current.

Natalie sat down on the crumbly concrete and dropped her head onto her knees. So close. The only option was to wait for Matt to arrive.

Ten minutes or so later, a shout came from the bluff above and behind her. "Hey, Trouble! Are you alright?"

She looked over her shoulder to find Matt vaulting down the steps like an Olympic athlete.

Halting, he stood over her panting. "What happened? Are you hurt? Where's Yasmine?"

"Headed downriver on the *Delta Queen*. Keturah showed me where she spent the night under one of those tents set up for the barbecue cook-off. I let her get away."

Matt held out a hand. "Natalie, get up off the ground." His voice sounded oddly strangled—undoubtedly what he'd like to do to her.

She looked away and sighed. "Why? I'm a terrible detective."

"Look, you better stand up. There are ants crawling into your shoes."

Natalie shrieked and scrambled to her feet. She yanked off her sandals and brushed at her feet. "If that isn't just par for the course!" She slapped the soles of her sandals together to shake off any remaining ants.

He grinned as he inspected the tail of her skirt "You might want to take a swipe at your posterior too."

"Would you stop laughing? This is not funny."

"I never thought I'd say this, but my life has sure been more entertaining since you busted in." He picked up one of the sandals she'd dropped and handed it to her. "Here, put these on before you blister your feet on the pavement." He tipped his head. "You have pretty feet. The toe ring's a nice touch."

Natalie slid into her sandals. "I almost caught her." She looked for the boat, now a tiny dot against the horizon. The sun glared off the water and bounced against the steely backbone of the Arkansas Bridge, and she lifted a hand to shade her eyes.

"Okay, so you didn't catch her. Let's find some shade and you can fill me in."

Because he was being so calm, she drew herself up. "I need some serious caffeine."

"That's my girl." He grinned at her. "Life goes on, babe. *C'est la vie.* What goes around comes around. If you can't beat 'em—"

She had to laugh. "Shut up, Matthew. Your clichés are getting farther and farther off-base."

"Is that farther or further?" He swung in the direction of the parking lot. "I never can remember."

"Like it matters." Natalie trudged up the ramp behind him.

Matt stopped and faced her. "Listen to me. There are going to be breakthroughs and there are going to be setbacks. This, my dear, is a breakthrough."

"I don't know how you can say that." Natalie twisted her hands together. It was crazy how much she wanted Matt to think well of her. She looked away, acutely aware of his solid presence. She could almost hear his heart pumping, and his tie smelled like baby food. "I never had to study anything in my life. High school or college."

She heard the smile in his voice. "That's sick."

"I know. This is way harder than I thought it would be." She looked up at him and was surprised by an odd, soft expression in his eyes.

He turned and bolted the rest of the way up the hill. "Look, we've got it made," he tossed over his shoulder. "We know exactly where Yasmine is. We'll drive to wherever the first stop is and wait for her. Come on, my dear Watson, we have a case to solve."

❧

"I said I needed caffeine, not pork."

"Protein's good for the soul." Matt pulled Natalie along to the next booth under a red-and-yellow striped awning. He hadn't planned on attending the World Championship Barbecue Cooking Contest, but if Yasmine had spent the night here, it was worth scoping out. He glanced at Natalie's sunburnt face. Besides, safety in crowds seemed like the wise course. "I bet you never made it over to your mom's for lunch, did you?"

"No, but—Matt, come on. We've got to figure out what to do next about Yasmine."

"Relax. We'll get to Helena in plenty of time to meet the boat. All you have to worry about is whether you want ribs or pulled pork." He winked at her. "What happened to your little buddy in the track suit?"

"I don't know. I saw Yasmine running toward the boat and took off after her." Natalie screeched to a halt. "Keturah was helping me ask around, and next thing I knew, she'd disappeared."

"Hey, y'all," boomed a large, sweaty man behind a grill in the shape of a potbellied stove. His wiry brown beard fell onto the bib of a crimson apron, and he brandished a stainless steel fork the size of a backhoe. "What can I do you for?" A banner at the back of the booth read, "Welcome to the College of Pig Knowledge."

"I'm not hungry," said Natalie stubbornly.

"Hogwash, if you'll excuse the pun. Everybody needs a little meat on their bones." Mr. Piggy eyed Natalie's lissome figure and elbowed a woman shoveling baked beans and potato salad onto plates for a family gathered at the other end of the table. "Ain't that right, hon?"

The woman, who was roughly the same size and shape as the grill, winked at Matt and filled another plate.

Matt pulled out his wallet. His meal at the shelter had been interrupted too. "We'll take two pulled pork plates with all the trimmings."

"Sure thing." The grill-master skewered a chunk of meat and plopped it onto a cutting board. "You folks enjoying the concerts?"

"No, we're not here for the festival." Natalie stood on her toes to peer over the counter. "We're detectives working on a case."

"That right? Sounds interesting. I like those *CSI* shows. A little gory, but then I work with meat all the time."

Matt watched the meat fall apart under the onslaught of a massive cleaver. "It's not a murder case. Missing persons." He extracted a photo of Yasmine along with a twenty. "This girl right here."

Their host laid down his fork and took the picture between a sticky thumb and forefinger. "Pretty gal. She came by here right about the time we were shutting down."

"Really?" Natalie's glum expression disappeared. "You saw her?"

"Yep. I offered her some of our leftovers. Acted like she was starving to death, but all she wanted was beans and salad."

Matt nodded. "She's Muslim. They don't eat pork."

The man's wife twitched the photo out of his hand. She examined the picture, her beehive hairdo wobbling as she shook her head. "She ducked out the back of the tent when a Hindu-looking man walked past. Looked scared to death."

Natalie gasped. "Maybe somebody else is chasing her after all!"

"She left her totebag behind. Maybe you can get it back to her. Me and Dewey are clearing out of here first thing in the morning." She reached under the table for a small black canvas backpack with pink trim. "Here ya go."

Matt and Natalie grabbed at it simultaneously, but Natalie was quicker. She backed away with the bag clutched to her stomach. "You can't look in a girl's bag."

"Why not?" Matt demanded.

"There might be something personal in it."

"Well, yeah. That's the whole point."

"You two don't look like you're related to that little girl," said the man in the apron, looking a bit apprehensive. "Betty, I don't think you should've handed it over like that. We ought to've given it to Security."

"No, no, we'll take care of it, I promise." Natalie, fortunately, looked both honest and kind. "We work for her family. Matt, give him your card. Yasmine is a runaway oil heiress, and she's on a riverboat cruise headed to New Orleans. The only way she'll get this back is if we take it to her."

Matt took out a business card and handed it to Dewey. "If you saw the man Yasmine was running away from again, would you recognize him?"

"Maybe." Dewey gave Betty a warning look. "Maybe not. Is there some kind of reward for this girl?"

"As a matter of fact, there is." Matt threw caution to the wind. "Tell you what. We'll stay in touch with you. Do you have a cell phone number where we can reach you?" He pulled his PDA from his pocket.

Dewey and Betty retired behind the table to confer. After a moment, Dewey folded his arms and looked manly while Betty reached into her pocket and produced a business card with barbecue sauce stains and bent corners. She handed it to Natalie. "Here. I don't turn on my cell phone unless I have an emergency, so I don't know how much good that'll do. But you can call our daughter and leave a message. We stay in touch with her. Her number's on the back." Betty's small brown eyes were kind. "I'd like to know when Yasmine gets home safe."

Natalie leaned over the table to give the woman a hug. "Thank you so much! We'll be in touch."

Matt picked up the two Styrofoam to-go boxes and backed out of the booth. "Come on, Trouble. We've wasted enough time."

"Wasted? How can you say that? We got Yasmine's backpack!" Natalie followed, waving at Dewey and Betty over her shoulder.

"Alright. Whatever. Let's sit down at that table over there. We can eat and go through it." He caught her look. "Okay, *you* can go through it."

Matt plunked their food down on a picnic table in a grassy area with a stunning view of the river and the bridge. Behind and to the side, multi-colored tents and awnings exploded in pinwheels of circus colors, with families and couples milling around like the ants that had crawled into Natalie's shoes. Tantalizing odors of charcoal, roasted pork, and tangy sauces drifted on the mild spring breeze.

Natalie looked up as a red, blue, and yellow Superman kite floated overhead. "Too bad we don't have time to enjoy this."

"Might as well." Matt straddled a bench and opened his lunch. "We're about to take a road trip, so we'll be pretty busy for the next few days."

Natalie sat down across from him. Shoving her box of food away, she unzipped the backpack. "This is so weird. I know we have to look in it, but I feel like a criminal anyway. Maybe we should give it to Yasmine's mother first."

"No way." Matt swallowed a bite of potato salad rich with eggs and onions and mayonnaise. Betty was one first-class cook. "There's something funny going on with that family. I don't trust any of them. Except maybe Liba."

"Why not?" Natalie looked up. "They're paying us to find her. They obviously have her best interests at heart."

"Not every family is as close as yours, Natalie. Abid has got some real control issues, and Yasmine's an adult. For her to disappear without a word isn't normal."

"You're right. Well, here goes." Taking a deep breath, Natalie drew the backpack close and pulled it open.

Matt continued to eat while Natalie withdrew a pile of feminine stuff: a package of tissues, gum, and a zippered makeup case, which contained a couple of tubes of lipstick, a small bottle of Tylenol, and a tiny manicure set. A hairbrush came next, followed by an eelskin wallet.

"Uh-oh," Natalie murmured. "She's gonna be in trouble without this."

"How much money's in it?"

"Let's see." Natalie unsnapped the wallet and poked through it. "Three fifty-rupee notes and about five American dollars. Looks like about twenty euros. A Visa ... it's got her name on it. Some bank in Pakistan." She handed it to Matt. "Here. You can take a look."

"Thanks." He laid it on the table, more interested in what else she might pull out of the backpack.

"Oh, goodness. Here's her passport." Natalie studied the photo. "Not fair for someone to look that beautiful in a mug shot. Mine looks like I've been on a three-day drunk." She flipped through the passport. "Yasmine's been all over the world. London, Cyprus, Switzerland, Rio ... Golly."

"Try the other zipper pocket. The big one in the middle."

"Okay."

Natalie unzipped the central section of the backpack. Out came a long, sheer apple green scarf, embroidered in silver threads. "Ooh. This is what she was wearing when I met her at the airport. Isn't it pretty?"

"Wouldn't exactly keep you warm in the winter," he said with a grin. "What else you got?"

Natalie looped the scarf around her neck and peered into the bag. "Just a notebook. One of those things you write essays on in college. And a book. Looks like a Koran." She pulled it out. Her mouth fell open. "It's not a Koran."

"Then what—Holy moly, that's a Bible!"

~

Yasmine sat on her bed in a tiny cabin located in the dank, noisy bowels of the cruise boat, contemplating the sudden twist in her personal history. She should be frightened out of her mind.

Instead, possessed of nothing to call her own, she felt free.

No passport. No money. No clothes except her Elvis shirt and jeans. She'd even kicked off her sandals while running for the boat.

She watched her roommate, a young Russian woman who spoke practically no English—and certainly no Urdu—wearily strip off her black maid's uniform and fling herself onto the other bunk. The two beds, little more than cots, were so close together that one could barely stand up between them. A triangular closet with a skinny louvered door contained four drawers and two feet of hanging space. The two women would share a communal bath with six others in the staff section.

Yasmine was content.

Her new roommate, who called herself Oksana, rolled to her side to face Yasmine. It was broad daylight, barely afternoon according to Yasmine's watch, but Oksana had been on duty for ten hours already.

"Your shift when?" Oksana asked sleepily. Her eyes closed. She had outrageous Slavic cheekbones and blonde coloring.

"I do not know." Yasmine drew her feet up to examine her toes. The blisters across her instep were bleeding, the soles aching from stone bruises. She needed a pedicure. "The steward said he would bring me a schedule, along with my uniforms."

Oksana suddenly turned over on her back, eyes wide. "Do not give him in. Bad man."

Yasmine forgot about hiding her identity and switched to Russian. "Has he hurt you?"

Oksana sat up, all traces of sleep gone from her green eyes. She answered in Russian. "You speak my language! Oh, this is wonderful." She began to cry. "I miss my mother and my grandmother and my little boy and the village where I grew up. I came to the U.S. to get married, but I could not bring Misha right away. And then my husband beat me, so I left him to get a job, only I do not know how to do anything but clean—" The flood of words halted as Oksana crammed her fist against her mouth. "I am sorry. I do not know you, and I spill all this. How is it you know the Russian language?"

Yasmine scooted to the edge of the bed and took Oksana's trembling hands. "I translated in the American embassy in Islamabad, Pakistan. My Russian is simple, but I learned a little in college. Language is my gift." She smiled. "God gives good gifts."

Oksana's face twisted. "I do not know about that." She looked around, wrinkling her nose against the smell of diesel fuel that pervaded the cramped cabin.

"You will see." Yasmine jumped at a sharp knock on the door and squeezed Oksana's hands. "I will talk to the steward in the hallway. Do not worry."

She opened the door and found the man who had hired her yesterday blocking the narrow hallway. Dressed in a uniform of black slacks, a cheap white shirt, and a black military-style jacket, he carried a clipboard and a couple of black garments. "Yasmine." He looked her up and down with protruding ice-colored eyes. "I have brought your uniform and schedule. We will discuss it now."

Yasmine blocked his move toward the door. "I am sorry," she said softly. "My roommate is sleeping. If you will give me the schedule, I will study it." As she reached for the uniforms, she looked down at her bare feet. "Perhaps there are some shoes I could borrow?" Pride had come to an end.

"You'll bleed on the carpets. Go to Cook and ask for some Band-Aids." The steward frowned. "He'll tell you where the lost and found is. There should be a pair of shoes to fit you. What happened to yours?"

Yasmine's heart bumped. He couldn't know she had left everything behind in Memphis. He might put her off at the next stop, and she had to get to New Orleans. "They were not suitable for standing all day. My last job was a desk job." Both true statements.

He looked skeptical. "You will start work at four. Be in the kitchen ready to serve. If you have questions, Cook will instruct you."

It sounded to Yasmine as if the mysterious Cook was the person who actually ran the boat. She nodded. "Alright. Thank you." She backed toward the door.

He tried to peer past her into the room, but Yasmine quickly shut it in his face. Ugh. A voyeur.

Realizing Oksana was awake and watching her, she straightened her back and made herself smile. "See? I told you there was nothing to worry about."

TWELVE

It's no big deal, Dad." Natalie was still getting used to the sight of her father kicked back in Mom's overstuffed chair. For previously unknown reasons, it had stayed in the study all these years. Deb Tubberville, hard-nosed diva of prosthetic accounts, apparently had an unsuspected sentimental streak. Natalie, sitting on the ottoman at Dad's feet, waved a careless hand. "Matt doesn't even like me."

Dad snorted. "I find that hard to believe." He leaned forward to fix her with his Papa Bear glare. "Besides, your grandma always used to preach about the 'appearance of evil.' Maybe she had a point."

"As if Mrs. Dorothy's preaching ever deterred you from doing whatever you pleased." Mom turned from the computer, giving him an amused look over the top of her glasses. "You and I sowed our wild oats, so how can you lecture Natalie? I'm sure she'll be smarter than us and at least take precautions."

"Mom!" Natalie fanned her flaming face with the notebook in her lap. "I told you Matt and I aren't—and even if we were, I don't—because I believe you're supposed to wait until you get married."

Her mother looked offended and slightly guilty. "Well, of course that's all well and good, but it's not always possible to control your feelings. So *please*, sweetheart, don't go off with that boy without—"

"Deb, can't you see you're mortifying the poor girl?" Dad patted Natalie's shoulder. "She's serious about this religious stuff. It's *him* I don't trust. Is he coming by here to pick you up?"

"No, we're taking my car, so I'm picking him up at his apartment." Which, considering this humiliating conversation, was a very good thing. "Besides, you don't have to worry. The boat's docking tonight in Helena, Arkansas. There won't be any motel involved." She gave her father a pleading look. "So will you lay off?"

"Touchy, touchy."

Mercifully Mom found something less personal to pick on her about. "What happened to your sandals? Didn't you just buy those last weekend? You look like you ran a marathon in them."

"Our missing girl took off running, and I tried to catch her. She was faster than me." Natalie sighed. "Which is why we have to drive to Helena."

Dad looked at his watch. "What does that take? About two hours?"

Natalie shook her head. "Less than that. The boat's scheduled to dock at ten. I told Matt I'd pick him up after supper, and we'd get there in plenty of time." She stood up. "I'm going to go put on some jeans." She stuck out one blistered foot. "Learned my lesson about dressing for comfort on this job."

Mom patted her chest in mock disbelief. "Is the clothes horse coming in off the range?"

Natalie paused at the door of the study, wrinkling her nose. "Only temporarily."

In her room, she poked through a closet full of trendy skirts, feminine tops in a rainbow of colors, and slacks with "dry clean only" tags. *This is a sickness, Natalie Tubberville. You have serious garment issues.*

Trouble was, ever since middle school, Dad had bought her whatever she wanted. Probably felt guilty about not spending enough time with her. So every other weekend he'd take her shopping and whip out the credit card or send her to the mall with a wad of cash.

Which, for a fourteen-year-old with a shoe fetish, turned out to be a dangerous thing.

She pulled down a couple of long-sleeved T-shirts she rarely wore. Time to make a donation to the homeless shelter.

An hour or so later her cell rang as she was on her way to the car, staggering under an enormous pile of clothes. "Oh, fudgesicles." The phone kept ringing. "Hold on, let me put these in the trunk." Voice mail took over just as she fished it out of her purse. The clock above the message center indignantly flashed Matt's cell phone number. "Oh no! Six forty-five! How'd it get that late?"

"Where are you?" he demanded when she called him back. "Did you leave without me?"

"Of course not. I got a little—" she slammed the lid of the trunk—"sidetracked."

"Well, now we're going to have to hurry. Would you get over here?"

It was precisely sixteen minutes and twenty-one seconds later when she pulled up in front of the clock shop. Matt stood on the sidewalk, arms folded. He jerked open the passenger door and dropped into the open seat, whacking his head on the hard top.

"You could've put the top down." He sent her an irritated look, rubbing the rising knot on his temple.

She pulled out onto Beale Street. "I didn't want my hair to get blown around."

"We wouldn't want that to happen." He yanked the seatbelt across his middle and snapped the latch. "What have you been doing?"

Cleaning out my closet didn't sound like a very good answer. "Picking Daddy's brain about the Patel and Haq families. You said there's something odd about them. Daddy's been dealing with Abid for a couple of years now. I thought he might have some insight for us."

He was silent for a moment. "Just when you're having one of your blonde moments, you manage to surprise me." A grudging smile curled his mouth. "What did he say?"

She also wasn't going to bring up the "precautions" conversation. "In his opinion, Yasmine has no reason to run from the Haq marriage. They're wealthy and politically powerful, and Jarrar is considered a good catch. He's even what a lot of women would call good-looking."

Matt gave her a sideways look. "Do you think he's good-looking?"

"Not really." She mentally pictured the hooded dark eyes and thick black hair. "He's a little too macho-macho for me."

He laughed. "What does that mean?"

"I don't know." She shrugged. "Thick eyebrows, hairy chest, hairy arms ..."

"How do you know—"

"You can see it sticking up from the front of his shirt." How many embarrassing topics was she required to cover in one day? "Can we talk about something else?"

He just grinned and unbuttoned his top button. "Look, Mom, no hair."

"Would you please leave me alone? You're creeping me out."

"You're so much fun to needle." He relaxed against the seat. "Would you like to know what I found out about Rafiqah Akbar?"

"Oh yeah! The email. What's the deal? Has she seen Yasmine?"

"I doubt it. She finished her program in December and took a job in Washington State."

"How do you know?"

"Googled her name and came up with a list of new employees at a hospital there. It's definitely her."

"Wow. If we'd found her sooner, we might could've tracked Yasmine down by now. Now I guess it doesn't matter."

Matt shook his head. "It matters that Yasmine tried to get to a friend from school instead of her new fiancé. Why she would do that is at the root of what's going on."

"I guess you're right. When we catch up to her in Helena, we can ask her."

~

"I knew we should've turned left at Albuquerque." Matt grinned as Natalie's brows twitched together. "Well, it worked for Bugs Bunny. Are you sure you know where you're going?"

"I've driven this highway a bazillion times." She glanced at the GPS. "We'll be in Tunica in just a few minutes. Want to stop for some Fiddle Faddle and a root beer?"

"We don't have time. It's nearly eight o'clock, and there's still another sixty miles or so to—look out, that light's turning yellow."

"Didn't you ever watch *Star Man*? 'Green means go. Red means stop. Yellow means go very, very fast.'" Natalie stomped on the gas.

Matt held onto the dash and tried not to yelp.

Blue lights flared behind them.

"Natalie!"

"Oh, fudgesicles. It was yellow all the way." She hit the brakes.

But it was too late. The flashing lights drew closer.

Matt turned around to look. "I hope you practiced your eye-lash-batting this morning."

"I'm a former police officer. I do not play that game." Natalie pulled over into a gravel drive and grabbed her purse out from under her seat. "We'll just have to make up time on the other side."

"Now there's a fine idea," Matt muttered.

The brown sedan pulled to a stop behind them. Tunica County Sheriff's Office. Terrific. Natalie's former employer.

As the officer approached with the rolling swagger of law enforcement officials everywhere, Natalie rolled down the window and poked her head out. "Good evening, officer, I have no idea why you — Bradley! What are you doing here?"

Matt had a very bad feeling about this.

The deputy leaned down, planting his hands on thick thighs. Under the shadow of the stiff hat, all Matt could see was a square chin. "I'm working," a bassoon-like voice rumbled out. "I recognized your car, not to mention your driving habits. What are *you* doing here?"

Natalie glanced at Matt. "Just passing through. But I can't stay and talk. We're kind of in a hurry."

Matt could've predicted the guy's response.

Felschow peered through the window, past Natalie. "That your new boyfriend?"

"None of your business. If you didn't stop us for a legitimate reason, let us get back on the road."

So much for batting eyelashes.

Felschow stood up, towering over them. He pulled a flashlight off a clip on his belt and turned it on. "Your left taillight's out, Natalie. Maybe you should let me see your license and registration. Oh, and your insurance card."

Even in the dim light Matt could see the bright red spots on Natalie's cheekbones. "Come on, Bradley, you're not going to give me a ticket for a burned-out taillight."

"Oh really?" The deep voice remained polite. "Give me your license, Natalie."

"Don't be ridiculous. You're just mad because I've got another guy—"

"Natalie," Matt said quietly, "give him your license." He leaned forward to speak to the officer. "We've had a very tense day, you'll have to excuse her."

"What did she do—break a fingernail?" The deputy grinned a little. "When you've arrested two drunk drivers, confiscated a kilo of meth, and kept a husband from shooting his wife and himself, then you can talk about a tense day." The flashlight beam speared Natalie's face. "This is Mississippi, and we have inspection laws. You're not gonna talk your way out of a ticket."

Natalie started to object, but Matt had had enough. "Look, we're detectives working on a case. We haven't done anything wrong, so get that light out of her face, or I'll report you to the D.A."

"You break the law, you pay a fine." Felschow sent the light Matt's way. "Maybe you'd better step out of the car too. Let me see your ID." When Matt just stared at him in disbelief, Felschow's mouth curled. "I'm taking you both in. "

"For what?" Natalie demanded. "Bradley, this isn't funny!"

"Failure to comply with an officer's orders."

Natalie unzipped her purse. "Alright! I'll play along. For goodness' sake, here's my license." She threw it out the window. It hit Felschow's belt buckle with a little *clink*, then dropped to the ground. "Give me the ticket, then you can go tell your buddies at Krispy Kreme how you humiliated Natalie Tubberville. I hope it makes you feel better!"

Felschow leaned down to pick up the license. The smirk had disappeared, and Matt realized Natalie had injured the guy's pride. He was not playing around.

"Okay, now." Matt pulled out his wallet and flipped it open. "Here's my detective license. Let's just power this whole thing down a notch." He glanced at Natalie. "Come on, let's go along with the officer."

She gave him an uncertain look, but reached for the door latch.

Relieved, Matt jumped out and came around to hold Natalie's door while she climbed out.

The deputy, who had glanced at Matt's badge with little interest, pointed the flashlight at Natalie's feet, then took the beam up her shapely jeans-clad legs, and lingered on her T-shirt logo. "I'm in my own little world," he read it out loud. "You haven't changed a bit, Natalie."

Matt wanted to slug him.

"Oh yeah?" Natalie folded her arms. "I've quit letting people tell me what to think."

"Is that right?" Felschow flicked the flashlight toward the car. "Open the trunk."

Natalie huffed, but pushed the button on her key ring.

Felschow leaned into the Miata's tiny open trunk. He glanced over his shoulder. "Y'all stand right there and don't move."

"Talk about redundancy," Natalie muttered. "What did I ever see in him?"

"I was wondering the same thing," said Matt.

Bradley flashed the light around the trunk. "What is all this crap, Natalie? You could've at least put your clothes in a suitcase. Y'all going to Tunica to play the casinos? Which hotel you staying in?"

"See, that's your problem, Bradley. You never listened to a word I said to you, which means you don't have a clue who I really am. I don't gamble. I don't drink. I don't sleep around. I try to live my life to please God." Matt could feel Natalie vibrating. "I'm taking those clothes to a homeless shelter as soon as we get back to Memphis—which will be tonight. We're not staying at any hotel."

"If I didn't listen to a word you said, it's because you talk so dad-gum much it all starts to run together." Felschow slammed the lid of the trunk. "Give me your keys and get in the squad car. I'm taking you in for questioning."

Matt suddenly got fed up with this clown. "This is harassment. The girl dumped you. Get over it." He moved to get back in the car.

"Stop right there, Romeo," Felschow growled.

Matt looked at Natalie. "Has he always been such a drama queen?" He opened the car door. "Listen, Felschow, how about if I get in the car with you, and you let Natalie follow us to the station. I don't want to leave her car here on the side of the road."

Felschow hesitated for a moment, then shrugged. "Guess that's not a bad idea. But you go first, Natalie, and I'll follow. Don't try anything funny."

What was this, *Miami Vice*? Torn between aggravation and amusement, Matt touched Natalie gently between the shoulder blades. "I'll be right behind you."

"Okay." She looked up at him, biting her lip. "I'm sorry, Matt."

"It's not your fault." Well, except for her former unfortunate taste in boyfriends.

Felschow opened the back door of the squad car. "Get in."

Matt smiled at Natalie as he got into the car. "Be careful, Trouble. See you in a few."

She lifted her hand in response, then backed toward the Miata.

Felschow slammed the door in Matt's face, blocking his view of Natalie. The inside of the car reeked of cigarettes, vomit, and cleaning chemicals. No telling what kind of freaks and geeks had sat on this seat before him. Good thing Natalie hadn't been forced to join him. He hoped she wasn't too upset to drive. Until she'd run that yellow light, she'd proven to be a competent driver. Fast but careful. Given her mercurial temperament, he would've thought she'd be distractible or impatient.

The driver's door opened and Felschow flung himself behind the wheel. He waited until Natalie pulled out onto the highway, then followed.

The sliding Plexiglas window between the seats was cracked open. Felschow glanced at Matt in the rearview mirror. "If y'all ain't doing the casinos, where you going? Nothing else to do down this way."

"I told you—we're on a case." Matt saw no need to divulge anything beyond the basics to the guy. Not without a lawyer in the room.

"What kind of case? Natalie don't know how to do anything but answer the phone." Felschow snickered.

"At least she can speak English."

Felschow frowned. "Don't get smart with me."

"You asked for it."

"Look, bud, let's get one thing straight. Natalie's my girl, and I'm looking out for her."

Matt snorted. "Arresting a woman's a great way to warm her heart."

"I didn't arrest her—although I sure could've. She should be glad I was in a good mood."

"I think the shoe's on the other foot. Sexual harassment will get you in a lot of trouble these days."

"Sexual harassment? What's that little tease been saying about me?"

Matt knew he'd gone too far but suddenly didn't care. He leaned forward to put his face into the window opening. "She said you pressured her for sex and acted like a jerk when she said no. In my book, that's sexual harassment."

"Well, in my book, a guy being taken in for resisting arrest had better watch his mouth." Felschow reached back and slammed the window shut, nearly cutting off Matt's nose.

Deprived of the last word, Matt sat back, teeth gritted, to endure the rest of the ride into downtown Tunica. *Resisting arrest. Now what, Lord?*

THIRTEEN

Bradley took off his brown straw campaign hat as they came through the station doorway, glanced at Natalie, and sailed the hat toward the coat rack. It clanged against the metal tree and rolled to the dirty tile floor. Scowling, he picked it up and plopped it on a hook.

Natalie rolled her eyes. The first time she'd seen Bradley ring the coat rack, she'd been impressed. Sort of like Wyatt Earp twirling his guns before a showdown. But eventually she'd realized he was looking around for applause and sulking when he didn't get it.

The attraction wore off.

She stomped toward the desk that she had occupied until Friday two weeks ago. Maybe she'd clean out her drawers while she was here and not depend on Sheriff Luby to box everything up and mail it to her.

"Where do you think you're going?" Bradley jerked a thumb at the chairs in front of his desk. "Sit down here by your boyfriend while I fill out the paperwork."

Matt, looking righteously annoyed, stayed on his feet. "I was under the impression that law enforcement officials were supposed to treat citizens with respect."

"You're not a citizen, you Yankee playboy. Sit down." Bradley picked up a NASCAR mug full of stone-cold coffee and took a slurp.

Natalie marched over to stand beside Matt in sudden solidarity. "Matt isn't my boyfriend, and he's not a Yankee either. He's from Illinois. Since you were probably shooting spit wads during junior high social studies, that's in the Midwest, not New England. Where's Helen?" The night shift dispatcher's cookies had been the one thing that made her life in the sheriff's office tolerable.

"I don't know." Bradley rooted around a pile of files on his desk and unearthed the computer mouse. "Guess she went out to get a candy bar. She ain't as conscientious as you." He said it as if conscientiousness caused cancer.

"You can't leave the switchboard unmanned!" Natalie glanced at the phone. If it rang, she was going to answer it, whether she still worked here or not.

Bradley threw himself into his chair with a squeak of springs. "Yeah, I hear your daddy bought you a detective agency." He glanced at Matt. "This your sidekick?"

"It's *my* agency." Matt placed his hands flat on the only two square feet of clear space on Bradley's desk. "I'd appreciate it if you'd fill out whatever paperwork you have to complete and let us get back to work. We have to be in Helena, Arkansas, by—"

Natalie whacked him on the shoulder. "Matt! Shut up!"

It was too late. Bradley perked up. "By when? Y'all on a deadline crunch?"

Matt straightened. "Never mind."

"Bet there's a lot of money involved." Bradley smiled. "I could help."

Natalie glared at him. "No way!"

"I'm just saying. I could give you an escort across the river." Bradley laced his fingers over his belt. "The casino traffic is something fierce these days."

Matt's fists balled at his sides. "I think we can handle it."

"I was talking to Natalie." Bradley frowned. "*You're* not going anywhere until you produce bail."

"I'm calling a lawyer." Natalie headed for the phone on her erstwhile desk. "And when we get through with you, you're going to wish you'd been parked anyplace but Highway 61 tonight."

Bradley shrugged and used the computer mouse to pull up a misdemeanor report file. He looked around when Matt followed Natalie. "Hey, get back over here and sit down."

Matt ignored him and leaned close to Natalie. "Go on to Helena yourself and intercept Yasmine." His voice was low, urgent. "This is a pain, but we don't have any other choice."

"No, I've been thinking." She looked up into the multicolored eyes, trying to reassure him. "The boat won't leave until morning. Daddy'll have you out of here by then."

Matt chewed the inside of his cheek. "What if she leaves the boat in Helena? We'll lose her."

"Why in the world would she be going to Helena, Arkansas? More likely her ultimate destination's New Orleans."

"Natalie, we don't know anything about this girl. Nothing she's done has been logical."

"Well . . . I guess you could say that. A Muslim carrying around a Bible. I'm going to have to get really nosy and read that little notebook."

"I thought you were going to read it on the way here."

"How could I? I was driving!"

"You two stop arguing and get over here so I can book you!"

Natalie had forgotten all about Bradley. She waved an irritated hand at him. "Keep your shirt on." She stood on tiptoe and lowered her voice to a whisper. "If we don't go along with him a little bit, he'll make things worse. I need to stay out of jail so I can contact my dad and get you released." She squeezed his hands. "Don't worry. It'll be okay."

Matt just looked at her. Her reassurance would have been a lot more comforting if she hadn't been the sole reason he was in this mess.

*

Shortly after nine o'clock Yasmine stood on aching feet at the galley sink, washing the enormous pots in which Cook had boiled pounds and pounds of odd-looking little red potatoes. She had spent the afternoon trudging up and down the stairs between decks. The occasional glimpse of the rolling black river, the slow passing of wooded banks, reminded her of the *Adventures of Huckleberry Finn*, which she'd read in undergraduate school. By nightfall she had begun to sympathize with the slave Jim's longing for freedom. She also wondered if the captain had any intention of stopping before reaching the Gulf of Mexico.

Wherever that was.

At an ear-shattering whistle blast, she looked over her shoulder at Cook.

"Comin' up on Helena," he drawled around a toothpick. "We'll dock tonight and let the folks tour in the morning. Then we head on down to Vicksburg."

"Am I allowed to get off the boat?" Yasmine had not much idea of what her job entailed, other than following the orders of the mild-eyed, dark-skinned man who'd bandaged her feet and fed her crisp-fried catfish filets, creamy potato salad, and balls of fried cornbread which he called "hush puppies." Clearly she had landed in culinary heaven, even if she had to work for it.

"Long as your shift's over, you can do whatever you want. Just make sure you're back on board before we weigh anchor at eleven."

Yasmine hurriedly rinsed off a big cast iron frying pan. She would be off duty in a few minutes but had to get up at five a.m. to start setting the dining room tables for breakfast. She wouldn't be off again until three. By that time the boat would be headed downstream.

Maybe she should stay onboard. She was curious about the southern states where Zach had grown up, but Florida was her ultimate goal. She couldn't take a chance on getting left behind. Besides, Jarrar Haq and the detectives her father had hired would not give up chasing her. She had recognized the man following her at the barbecue festival as the one from the airport. Her fiancé's hired goon was infinitely more frightening than the two American detectives.

Biting her lip, she wiped the frying pan dry and hung it on its hook above the stove, then hung her towel on the dish drain. "Mr. Cook, may I be excused now? I'd like to check on my roommate."

"Lord, child, you don't have to ask me. It's eight o'clock straight-up." The cook's rubbery dark face softened as he made a little shooing motion. "You go on, get a good night's sleep. Everybody's first day's a hard one."

Out of habit Yasmine started to incline her head. Then she remembered she was in America. She smiled. *Freedom.* Freedom to talk about whatever mattered most to her, and freedom to go wherever she wanted. Even to a place called Pins Up Cola.

"See you in the morning," she said to Cook on the way out of the galley. "Good night."

She entered one of the narrow passageways that led to the female employees' sleeping quarters. The motion of the boat was so violent she had to slide her palm along the wall to keep her balance. Good thing she was quite a fine sailor. Twice she'd sailed on Mediterranean cruise ships with her family, and she'd loved yachting as a teenager.

A pang of regret surged through her. There might be no yachts or cruises in her future. Even if she found Zach, who was a navy man, he would not be allowed to take his wife on every tour of duty. He had warned her that navy wives were left alone on shore for long periods of time.

Yes, he had warned her, and then he'd left her. A sacrifice, he said, for her own good.

Bah. Men. Even the best of them could be stupid.

Halfway down the hall she halted with a jerk and flattened her back against the wall. Hewitt was standing outside the door of her room.

Dear God, oh my Father. Please let Oksana be gone. She's so afraid of him.

What was she going to do? What was that man doing here? How could she confront him alone like this?

Father, help me. Show me how to speak. Tell me what to say.

Almost against her will, courage eased the pounding of her heart.

She watched Hewitt test the doorknob. When it didn't open, he knocked. He rattled the doorknob again, violently. "Oksana, I know you're in there. Open the door. I want to talk to you."

Yasmine pushed away from the wall. "Oksana is not there." She prayed it was true. "Is something the matter?"

Hewitt wheeled. "Yes, something's the matter." He folded his arms, that intimidating stance she'd noticed in both Pakistani and American men. "She's late for her shift."

"Her next shift doesn't start until midnight." As a cocktail waitress in the bar at the center of the boat, Oksana worked crazy hours.

"Maybe I had the time wrong." Hewitt raked his gaze down Yasmine's figure. "I see you found some shoes. You know, that uniform doesn't do you justice. It's too baggy." He turned away, reluctantly. "Tell Oksana I want to see her before she starts her shift."

Shuddering with relief, Yasmine waited until Hewitt had disappeared into the darkness at the end of the passage before she unlocked the door. It was so swollen with age and moisture that she had to yank hard to get it open. The crew did not live in the best of quarters. Finally she went inside, slammed the door, and leaned back.

Oksana sat huddled at the head of her bed, knees drawn up under her chin. "He is gone?"

Yasmine nodded and inched her way across the tiny space between the door and the "closet." "I am glad I have a baggy uniform." She fell against the closet door when the boat lurched.

Oksana laughed and relaxed against the pillow propped against the wall. "That is the boat coming into the pier," she said in Russian. "I'm going to sneak out and find a beer. You want to come too?"

Yasmine paused in the act of slipping off her dress and looked over her shoulder. "You are kind. But Cook tells me some of the young people get together in his quarters and play cards and enjoy soft drinks. Maybe you join us?"

Oksana wrinkled her nose. "Maybe. I like beer."

"If I were you, I'd keep all my wits about me. People take advantage of you when you're drunk." She'd heard of women in America who lost their virginity, drove into light poles, and acted in innumerable other stupid ways.

Oksana was silent for a moment while Yasmine dressed in her jeans and T-shirt. She sat down on the bed to pull on her "new" tennis shoes and caught a glimpse of Oksana's thin, sharp face. Tears dripped down the Russian girl's cheeks.

Alarmed, she dropped her second shoe. "What is the matter, Oksana?"

"This is how I get in such the mess. I like the vodka and sign papers to come to America to get married." Oksana smeared her hand across her chin.

"Oh, no, I'm sorry to make you feel bad." Yasmine's heart hurt at the sight of her roommate's distress. On the other hand, one couldn't come to Christ without recognizing her need of him. She herself had been forced to do so. She picked up the shoe and looked down at it as she put it on and tied it. "I came to America to get married too."

Oksana gasped. "You did? Where is your husband?"

"I ran away before I met him." She lifted her shoulders. "I am a very scaredy-cat."

"I think you are the bravest woman I ever meet. I want to run away, but I afraid."

Yasmine's gaze flashed to the other girl, who stared at her with wide blue eyes. She smiled a little. "I think we have to be brave together. But first I need to tell you who takes care of me, and why I am not a jelly-puddle in the middle of the floor. Do you want to listen?"

Oksana's smile flashed like a beam of moonlight. "I like to have someone care for me too. I listen."

Yasmine wished she had not left her Bible in the park. She would have to repeat the words from memory. *Father, help me.*

⟳

"Matt, are you sure you don't want a fry? They're really good."

Matt looked up from Yasmine's notebook.

Natalie sat outside his holding cell off the sheriff's office on a folding chair, cheerful as a cricket. She'd talked Bradley the Badly into bringing her a basket of chicken fingers and fries from the local gas station, which she proceeded to drown in ketchup and poke through the bars despite Matt's assuring her his appetite had been left in Memphis.

"No thanks," he said absently. Trying to be productive, he'd spent the time waiting on Eddie to arrange bail flipping through the notebook. The last entry was the only one in English.

And it was a barn-burner.

"Listen to this:

The long flight from Pakistan has given me time to think. I have been reading the little Bible Zach gave me. I write in English because it makes me feel close to him. I have prayed, asking the Father why he allowed this to happen to me. I have read again the verses in Matthew 10 that Zach showed me: "Anyone who loves their father or mother more than me is not worthy of me; anyone who loves a son or daughter more than me is not worthy of me. Whoever does not take up their cross and follow me is not worthy of me. Whoever finds their life will lose it, and whoever loses their life for my sake will find it." Those are the verses Zach and I read together when I first became a Christian. I was afraid then, because I knew what Ammi and Abbi would say. But then he wrote the letter telling me to do my duty, and suddenly I am so confused. I know now what Jarrar Haq is. How could Zach urge me to marry this man? What does it mean? What action shall I take? How shall I lose my life?

Natalie swallowed the french fry Matt had refused, then wiped her mouth on a paper napkin. "Sounds like she was doing some heavy thinking. What does she mean about Haq? And who's this Zach person?"

"Someone she knew in Islamabad. A strong enough believer to give her a Bible." Matt leafed through the notebook. "There's nothing else here in English. If she became a Christian she probably had to be very careful of what she wrote down."

Natalie closed the Styrofoam container and stared at Matt. "This changes everything." Glancing over her shoulder at Felschow, who was sitting at his computer playing FreeCell, she lowered her voice. "Now we're not tracking down some random runaway bride. Yasmine's a sister in the Lord. And she may have a legitimate reason for not wanting to be found."

Matt stood up and covered the short distance to the cell door in one step. "We don't know that. Her family hired us to find her, and they obviously have her best interests at heart. We're not talking abuse here. She agreed to the marriage with Haq."

"Yeah, but it sounds like she found out something about him that makes him scary. She uses the word 'duty.' What if she's being coerced?"

"I don't know, Natalie. We don't know anything about this girl except what's in this notebook and what her family told us. Besides, all we have to do is locate her and let her know her family's worried about her. And make sure she's safe, of course." Matt grabbed the bars of the cell door. "We've got to find her. When's your dad coming?"

"As soon as he posts bail." Natalie pressed against the bars. She'd taken off her glasses to rub her eyes, leaving black smears. Little worry wrinkles pinched her brows together. "Matt ... I'm really sorry. If I hadn't antagonized Bradley, he probably would have let us go."

"It's not your fault the guy's a world-class sore loser." Matt leaned his head close. "But as far as unpleasant surprises go, I think we're even."

⌐

"Where are you?" Jarrar lit a cigarette, then tucked his lighter into his trousers pocket. He leaned over the balcony to watch the lights of downtown traffic pass. It was nearly midnight, but sleep was far away. His life had gone completely out of control with the arrival of Yasmine Patel. At the moment he quite hated her. He was looking forward to beating her.

It was a long moment before Feroz answered. "I am not sure. I am sitting outside a sheriff's office. The sign says 'Too-*nee*-kah County.'"

"I thought they were going to Helena, Arkansas. What happened?"

"I am not sure what law they broke, but they were stopped by a patrol car. The officer got out to talk to them; they got out, too, and then the woman drove her car into town while the man followed in the patrol car with the officer."

"Do you mean to tell me they are in jail?" What kind of idiots had his father-in-law hired?

"It is very strange," Feroz admitted. "I could not get too close, or they would have seen me. You said to keep a low profile."

"Yes, I want them to do the work, but stay close enough to keep tabs on them. You must get to Yasmine before they do. If she talks ..." Jarrar did not have to remind Feroz of the stakes. Feroz was a brother in their enterprise. Less valuable than Jarrar himself, to be sure, but he knew more than most.

"Jarrar, what if she slips away before we get to her? How can I stay with the detectives and look for her at the same time?"

"Clearly they know something we don't." Jarrar drew on his cigarette, letting the nicotine calm him. "Stay with them for now and call me in the morning with an update."

"I was not prepared to sleep in the car," Feroz grumbled.

"Sacrifices must be made," Jarrar said coldly. "You knew that at the beginning."

"Yes. I did." Feroz rang off.

Jarrar ground out his cigarette on the balcony rail. He opened the sliding glass door to the apartment and entered the blessed air conditioning. He did not care if Feroz was angry, and he certainly didn't care if he was uncomfortable. Each had his own part to play. Jarrar's part was planning — Feroz's was execution.

It was the way of things, and it was good. Allah be praised.

FOURTEEN

Around ten o'clock on Monday morning, Natalie sat in front of Bradley's desk, digging in her purse for a pen. She handed it to Matt as he took the release form from Bradley. His day's growth of beard made him look like he'd been locked up for drunk-and-disorderly. She smiled. "Cheer up. This is your 'Get Out of Jail Free' card."

Matt glowered at the Tunica County Sheriff's Department logo on the pen. "I doubt your dad would think it's free."

Last night Matt had loudly protested the five-hundred-dollar bail, but Natalie just shrugged and called Daddy. Fortunately, her father hadn't blinked an eye at the amount. "Pocket change, kiddo. Just find that girl. Oh, and get the taillight fixed."

Which of course she promised to do. She always had good intentions.

Looking rested and quite pleased with himself—he'd gone home, leaving a junior deputy to watch the two hardened criminals—Bradley sat back in his chair and propped his feet on the desk. "How about if I escort you folks out to the bridge? Wouldn't want you to get caught in that speed trap in Evansville."

"We'll manage." Matt signed the release with an angry scribble. "Come on, Trouble, let's blow this pop stand. We've got a boat to catch."

"You folks have a nice day." Bradley gave Natalie a flippant salute and took a slurp of the nasty black coffee for which the department was famous.

With admirable restraint Matt tossed the pen on the desk and stalked out the door.

Natalie followed, jingling the keys. "You want to drive?"

He stopped and glanced at her, a spark returning to his bloodshot eyes. "You serious?" By now he knew the Miata was Natalie's pride and joy.

"Unless you need a nap." She'd curled up on the lumpy couch in the employee break room and conked out immediately, leaving Matt to spend the night on the bunk in his cell.

"I'm wired for sound. Give me those keys."

Natalie settled down, watching Matt handle her car with confidence and skill. He was still tight-lipped, but at least he wasn't taking the whole fiasco out on her. In fact, he'd made the confrontation with Bradley almost fun, in spite of the circumstances. Matt wasn't really her boyfriend, but Bradley seemed to assume he was.

She sighed happily. It was going to be a good day.

Natalie took out Yasmine's journal and became engrossed in trying to decode the part of it written in whatever language the Pakistanis spoke. Urdu or Hindu or something. They'd passed the Evansville stoplight and waved at the nice police officer sitting in the gas station parking lot, when Matt snapped off the gardening call-in show blaring on the radio.

She glanced at him in surprise.

He was scowling as if planting fan leaf palms in north Mississippi was a capital offense. "Why'd you ever go out with that clown?"

"Huh?"

"You're obviously way out of his league. What were you thinking?" He drove with a wrist propped on top of the steering wheel, the seat as far back as it would go—he had really long legs. But the tension in his jaw belied his relaxed posture.

She shrugged. "I told you. I was looking for a Christian boyfriend, and I met him at church. Guess I was a little naïve. People in church aren't perfect."

"You *are* too trusting, Natalie. You should even be careful with me." He gave her an inscrutable glance, then quickly looked back at the road. "What I mean is, it's okay to make a mistake once. But you shouldn't go out with a guy who treats you like that over and over."

Natalie blinked. He sounded almost protective. "You want me to be honest? I thought I wasn't going to find anybody better. You should see some of the guys I dated before him."

He frowned. "Why? Why do girls do that?"

"I don't know. Maybe I never knew a man could be different. Even my dad had problems with fidelity. I think he genuinely loves my mother, and he's sorry he messed up so bad she booted him out. But he never had a true conviction that disrespecting her was wrong—at least until recently. Maybe." She pictured the way her father had looked at her mother yesterday. Tenderness and regret and maybe a certain amount of shame, all mixed in. "Anyway, he sure wasn't a good example when I was growing up." She sighed. "Matt, every woman wants to be loved exclusively. They'll put up with a lot of stuff if they think that's what they're getting."

He was silent for a long time. They passed a kudzu-infested stretch of road, a cement factory, and a soybean field. "Well, don't put up with it anymore," he finally said. "You're a valuable prize. There'll be somebody who deserves you one of these days."

Natalie's eyes watered. She cleared her throat. "That's a nice thing to say."

"It's the truth." He glanced at her. "You're a motor mouth and you drive too fast, but you've got a good heart."

At the backhanded compliment, she let out a huff of laughter. "You being the expert on romance. Why'd you take up with that girl from the café?"

His shoulders shifted. "She kind of ... came to the office and asked me out."

He sounded so sheepish, Natalie laughed. "Isn't the word 'no' in your vocabulary?"

"I tried. I didn't want to hurt her feelings." He glanced at her. "Plus I ... haven't had a date in a long time. I thought it would be fun and wouldn't hurt anything, yada yada." His cheekbones reddened. "Maybe I wanted to prove to myself that I haven't lost my touch."

"Lost your touch?" Natalie gaped at him. "Are you crazy?"

"It's a guy thing. You wouldn't understand."

"So this is a conquest issue? How Neanderthal is that!"

"Maybe so, but I'm being as honest as you were. Competition's hardwired into most men."

"Women are not game pieces!"

"I know that!" Matt rattled his hand against the steering wheel. "I'm trying to explain how it happens. Probably happened with your dad too—you said he's not a Christian. Without the influence of the Bible, when your mind's conditioned to what's on TV and movies and stuff, women start looking like trophies." He glanced at her and grimaced. "Don't look so disgusted. I know it's not right, but it's reality. I struggle with it too. I'm hoping it'll get easier as I get closer to God."

Natalie's stomach surged. Was that the source of the heat in Matt's eyes yesterday? He'd wanted to see if he could make her another notch in his belt?

"Okay, whatever." She knew in her head there weren't any perfect men. But she couldn't help being disappointed when they proved it.

"So how's your Urdu coming along?" he said, apparently trying to tease his way past the awkward silence.

"Let's put it this way. They're not going to hire me at the U.N. But I have run across Zach's name a couple of times before that entry in English. Look."

Matt glanced at her. "No, *you* look. I'll drive."

She turned a couple of pages. "Here it is again. And again. And—" She gasped. "Matt! There's a last name with it this time. I totally missed it before. Carothers—the guy's name is Zach Carothers!"

Matt swerved the car to the side of the road, nearly hitting a mailbox. "No way! Let me see." He jammed the gear shift to park and grabbed the notebook.

"Right there under that bunch of squiggles. See?" Natalie leaned over to point.

Matt stared at the words under her finger for a moment, then looked up at her, reluctant admiration in his expression. "I'd given up on finding this guy. Natalie Tubberville, you're stubborn as a mule, but you're a genius." He held out a hand for her to slap. "Way to go!"

She smiled at him, ridiculously pleased. "So now what do we do?"

"We go on to Helena and try to catch Yasmine. But on the way I'm calling Cole McGaughan. He'll have contacts to help us figure out who Carothers is. Someone attached to the embassy, probably an American serviceman or diplomat . . ." Matt put the car back in gear and pulled onto the highway. "If we can reach him, we'll have a big key to what Yasmine's up to."

⌐

"There's the boat!" Matt wheeled the car into the entrance to the riverboat landing. "Are your shoes on? We're going to jump out and run."

Natalie leaned forward, squinting against the bright morning sun. "Matt! They've pulled up the gangplank! Hurry!"

Road construction had slowed traffic down to a crawl as they crossed the Helena Bridge, Matt muttering under his breath all the way. It was now three minutes past eleven.

He glanced at her in frustration. Despite his reassurances, if they hadn't drawn Felschow's attention by running that yellow light outside Tunica, they wouldn't be in this fix. Natalie had been quiet since his dumb remark about women being trophies. He should've known she wouldn't understand. What good did it ever do to explain yourself to a woman? The safest course would've been to keep his mouth shut and fall back on charm.

Now he was going to look like an idiot again if he didn't figure out a way to get around the traffic. They couldn't miss that boat.

Ignoring the parking spaces—which were all full anyway—he slammed on the brakes. The car screeched to a halt beside the pier. Before it had even stopped rolling, Natalie jumped out.

Matt set the brake and yanked out the keys. He tore off after Natalie. She was right. The boat was chugging out into the river. He and Natalie pelted down the boardwalk pier jutting ten yards out into the water.

"Wait!" Natalie screamed. "Hold up! We need to talk to—"
She tripped and fell, landing heavily on her knees.

Matt ran another step or two. He stopped. There was no way they were going to catch the boat. It was already twenty yards out from the pier and slugging back out into the brown-black Mississippi. A row of tourists leaning against the deck railing waved at him.

He turned and walked back to Natalie.

She was sitting on the pier with her head down. "I knew I should've worn my tennis shoes. I fell, and I made Bradley mad, and Daddy was late getting the bail, and the traffic on the bridge was probably my fault too." She looked up at Matt and swiped a hand under red, teary eyes.

"Oh, for cripes sake." He couldn't help smiling. Talk about drama queens. He stepped behind her and grabbed her under the armpits, boosting her to her feet.

"Ouch!" She bent to dab at the blood seeping through two big rips in the knees of her jeans. She sighed. "These are my favorite jeans. They cost nearly a hundred dollars."

"Forget the denim." He crouched in front of her. "Let me see."

"But we missed the boat. Ouch!" she said again, flinching as he lifted one leg of her jeans.

Her shin and calf were smooth as pale silk. Swallowing, he gently cupped the back of her knee and examined the injury. It was about two inches square, more like a big strawberry than a cut. There were wood splinters jammed into the raw, reddened flesh. "I need some tweezers and antibiotic ointment. And a gauze pad and tape. We'd better find a pharmacy."

"But what about—ow! Be careful!—Yasmine?"

Matt got to his feet. "We'll catch up to her in Vicksburg." He slid his arm around Natalie's narrow waist. "Put your arm over my shoulder. We'll take it slow. Let's get you back to the car."

Natalie hobbled a couple of steps on her own, then sighed. "Oh, okay." She gave him a tentative look as she hooked her arm around his neck.

Snugged together side-by-side, Matt took most of her weight. She was so light he could have carried her. But maybe that wasn't such a good idea. Her feminine, summery scent was a little bit distracting.

They crept down the pier toward the car, silent, morose. Natalie sniffed now and then. He didn't know if she was more upset by losing sight of Yasmine or her tumble.

He squeezed her waist. "Cheer up. We'll catch up to her tonight."

She gasped a little.

"I'm sorry—want me to slow down?" He paused and looked down at her.

She looked away. "I'm okay." Her hand on his shoulder moved, and he could feel every imprint of her fingers through his shirt. "Never mind." They started walking again, and she chewed the side of her lip. "I guess I *am* trouble," she said on a sigh.

"Nah." He smiled. "Anybody ever call you that before me?"

"All the time, in middle school. 'Natalie Trouble-ville.'"

"Okay, then on behalf of every adolescent male in America, I apologize."

She laughed, and he felt better. So they'd have to extend the trip a little. Vicksburg was another four hours or so south by car. The boat would take a day. If they were lucky they'd have time to locate Zach Carothers. But this time they'd start early, take no chances on jealous deputy sheriffs or backed-up traffic.

Suddenly, inexplicably happy, he swooped to pick Natalie up, ignoring her squeak of surprise. "Come on, lady. Let's take care of those skinned knees and head south. We have a missing bride to find."

Natalie sprang for lunch at Chamoun's Rest Haven Restaurant—locally nicknamed the Khan on 61—outside Clarksdale, Mississippi. The city limits sign proclaimed Clarksdale a county seat home to a little more than twenty-thousand souls. She and Matt chose a window booth so they could keep an eye on the Miata. Outside the window, the flat, dusty Delta stretched for miles to the east, with only a few trees and a water tower to block the skyline. Behind them the late lunch crowd was a mixture of local farmers and professionals, blues enthusiasts in town for the museums and juke joints, and passersby like themselves in the mood for eclectic cuisine. The menu advertised Lebanese, Italian, and American fare. On the cash register, a stuffed camel toy sprawled under a sign that admonished, "No hookah smoking before 3:00 p.m."

"How are your knees feeling?" Matt took a big bite of kibbe and cabbage.

"Not too bad." Natalie busied herself twirling spaghetti around her fork. Truthfully, her knees still ached. She also wasn't going to mention the very carnal feelings that had sneaked up on her since he'd carried her to the car. Feet dangling, arms around his neck for balance, she'd been all too aware of the strong arms wrapped around her back and thighs. She knew she ought to keep a distance, and there had been an increasing amount of touching going on lately. She gingerly flexed one stinging knee. She was probably going to be black and blue for weeks. "Where'd you learn to do such a neat bandage?"

Matt washed down his food with sweet iced tea. "I played baseball all the way through high school, and I was a trainer for the football team."

"I played baseball too."

"You mean softball? So did my sisters."

"No, hardball. Little League."

He did a double take. "No kidding! I wouldn't have thought ..."

"You wouldn't have thought I have an athletic bone in my body." She shrugged. "I stank at fielding, but I was a great pitcher." A smile tugged at her mouth. "Coach used to tell me to get the ball across the plate and jump out of the way."

"Little League's competitive where I grew up. We lived way out in the sticks, and there wasn't much else to do. I would've had a college scholarship, but I blew out my shoulder in one of the last games."

"It felt pretty solid to me." The words were out before she thought. "I mean—"

Matt grinned. "And you just made my day." He teasingly flexed a bicep. "Always wanted to do that and never had an excuse."

To Natalie's relief, Matt's cell phone rang. He released her gaze and flipped the phone open. His expression clouded. "Mr. Haq. How are you?"

"Put him on speaker," Natalie whispered. "I want to hear."

Matt nodded. "Mr. Haq, I've got Ms. Tubberville with me. Is it okay if we put you on speakerphone?"

Haq's thick accent came through the phone. "Good afternoon, Miss Tubberville. I hope you are well."

"I'm good. Well, actually I've been better. But thanks for asking."

"I wish to obtain an update on the search for my fiancé. Please advise."

Wincing, Matt met Natalie's eyes. "We were just about to call you. We, uh ... had a little traffic problem and missed her."

"You missed her? How can this be?"

Natalie leaned back as their blue-haired waitress plopped two slices of coconut meringue pie on the table, along with a handwritten ticket. "Y'all have a nice day and come back to see us," she said and shuffled off to the kitchen.

Natalie dug into her dessert as Matt shoved aside his uneaten lunch and frowned at the pie. "I told her I wanted lemon."

"Yasmine brought you a lemon?" demanded Haq. "What is this stupidity?"

"No, not Yasmine." Matt grimaced at Natalie, who was laughing. "Natalie and I are in a diner in Clarksdale, Mississippi. We thought we'd catch her getting off the riverboat in Helena, but like I said, there was a delay. So we're going on to the next stop, which is Vicksburg."

"Why is she still on a riverboat, when she should be in Memphis? I do not understand this at all."

"I don't know, Haq. You tell me." Matt sounded a tad confrontational.

Natalie cautioned him with a look. "Look, Mr. Haq," she said, "I know you're worried. We are too. But at least on the boat she'll have food and a place to stay."

"How do you know she didn't get off the boat in Helena?"

Natalie frowned. "That's a good—" Matt chopped a hand across his throat. "I mean, there's no reason to think she did. We'll update you when we get to Vicksburg."

"I would appreciate that very much." Haq's tone softened. "Yasmine is unfamiliar with American ways and, I am sure, has no idea where she is going. As you say, I fear for her safety."

Maybe he wasn't as bad as Yasmine had made it sound. Natalie ignored the skeptical slant of Matt's eyebrows. "The cruise takes a whole day to get to Vicksburg," she said, "so don't look for us to call before this time tomorrow. Please be patient. Okay?"

Haq grunted. "I suppose I must. Good day." The connection ended.

Matt closed the phone. "What a jerk."

"Maybe he's worried about the woman he loves."

"He doesn't love her. He doesn't even know her."

"But they've corresponded over the last year or so. They probably know each other better than Bradley and I did. Love isn't all lust and heavy breathing."

Matt suddenly grinned. "Did you have lust and heavy breathing with Bradley the Badly?"

"Of course not. That was just a figure of speech." She made a face at him. "Anyway, back to Mr. Haq's question. How *do* we know she didn't get off the boat in Helena?"

"We don't." Matt shrugged. "But I think it's safe to say rural Arkansas isn't her destination. If we get to Vicksburg and find out she gave us the slip in Helena, we'll backtrack."

"This is a very frustrating business, isn't it?" Natalie crammed a forkful of meringue and coconut cream into her mouth.

"It can be." Matt shoved his slice of pie over to her side of the table. "I hate coconut."

"Oh, goody." Natalie sighed happily. "There are definite perks to the job."

FIFTEEN

You think playing pinball is a sin?" Matt hovered, ready to jump in if Natalie needed help. Since she'd just lit up half the Motel 6 arcade with Luke Skywalker's light saber and nailed a couple thousand points, that wasn't likely. The Death Star, hovering just above Chewbacca's hairy head, blinked malignantly in the background.

"I don't think so." Tongue between her teeth, Natalie pulled the spring and let loose another ball. It bounced off R2-D2's feet and set off an explosion of bells and whistles. She worked the flippers, racking up points, and still managed to talk. "But just in case, I won't tell if you won't tell."

Matt folded his arms and watched her, entertained. He'd called to tell her Cole had found an American named Zach Carothers attached to the embassy in Islamabad, apparently with ties to NCIS. Natalie wanted to come down to the lobby and discuss it, and they wound up in the arcade.

Pinball in the middle of the night. Nothing about this girl was normal.

She was dressed in a pair of flamingo-colored knit shorts, green rubber flip-flops, and a black *Wicked* T-shirt. The back of it read, "Defy Gravity." Her hair was pushed back with a polka-dot headband, and she didn't have on a scrap of makeup. Though he'd have cut out his tongue before using it out loud, the word "adorable" came to mind.

He shifted to lean an elbow against the side of the machine. "What were you doing up at this time of night?"

"Reading." She glanced at him from under her lashes. In their natural state they were a soft dark brown, with bronze tips that matched the freckles sprinkled across her nose. There was something innocent and alluring in that scrubbed-for-the-night look.

Back up the truck, Hogan. You got her down here to keep your mind occupied, remember? Not to take it down dangerous trails.

"Reading what? The newspaper? The *Farmer's Almanac*? *Vogue*?"

"Actually, I'm a John Grisham fan. I like courtroom drama." Her last ball dribbled off C-3PO's shoulder. She stuck out her bottom lip. "Oh, fudgesicles."

"My turn, Pinball Wizard." Matt traded places with Natalie. He put a couple more quarters in the machine and released his first ball. "Once you've testified in a case that drags on for weeks, you'll discover the real thing isn't so much fun."

"So what were *you* doing? I had a good nap this afternoon while you drove. I would have thought you'd be dead on your feet."

"Just channel-surfing. I'm kind of a night owl. Cole told me I should hunt up good company when I get lonesome. Keeps me out of trouble."

"What kind of trouble?"

"You know ... trouble." He didn't want to say it out loud. "I used to have some bad habits, and I'm still kind of new at avoiding them. My parents go to bed with the chickens, or I would've called my dad. Didn't figure you'd mind ..." When he glanced at her and lost his concentration, the ball caromed into the dead pocket. Red zeroes on the scoreboard glared at him. Probably what she thought of him. "I can't believe that."

Natalie grimaced in sympathy. "Try again. You'll catch up."

He grinned at her before sending another ball zooming up the chute. "You don't have a competitive bone in your body, do you?"

She laughed. "I don't like to hurt other people's feelings if I can help it."

He sobered. "Is that why you came down here tonight? You didn't want to hurt my feelings? Feel free to go back to your book."

"I'd rather talk than read any day." She clapped her hands when he navigated a difficult shot, making the ball bing-bong several times in a high-point area. "Way to go!"

Cheered by her glowing smile, he tried to concentrate. "How come you're so good at this?"

"I used to travel with my dad sometimes during the summers. After his sales calls were done, we'd hang out in arcades and play pinball." She patted the top of the glass. "*Star Wars* has always been my favorite." She laughed. "When I was little, I used to twist my hair up in those Princess Leia side knots and wear my mom's bathrobe around the house."

Matt laughed and lost control of his last ball. Shaking his head, he let her have the machine. "I can picture it. You're sort of the smart-mouth princess type."

"What does that mean?"

"From a well-off family—Daddy's girl and all that—deciding to go into law enforcement. Takes some guts."

"All I need is for somebody to tell me I can't do something, and I'm dead set on it. For example, I wanted to run for student body president in college, but everybody said I didn't have a chance unless I was backed by the Greek system. I was a resident assistant in my dorm, didn't do the sorority thing." She grinned. "I was the first female to hold the position since 1980."

"Big Woman on Campus, huh?"

She shrugged. "Well, I make friends easily, and my parents always encouraged me to go after anything I wanted to do." A gusty sigh lifted her shoulders. "But law enforcement's a hard, cold mountain to climb. The boys' club expects you to prove yourself. I couldn't ever seem to get past the glass ceiling." Her ball went out of play and she stared at the flashing lights. "That's the reason I was so excited about going into business on my own." She slid him a guarded look. "I'm pretty surprised you were willing to give me a chance."

For once, Matt thought about his answer before blurting out whatever was on his mind. The only reason he'd given her a chance was because he'd been forced to. "You're gonna make a fine detective, Natalie. You're smart, you use your instincts, and you're good at getting people to talk to you. But I want control of my own agency again."

She turned to lean back on the machine. "I know," she sighed. "I'm kinda tired, Matt. We'd better try to get some sleep before we head to the river in the morning."

Yeah, she definitely thought he was a loser. "Okay. Even though you beat the stuffing out of me, I'll walk you to your room." He offered his elbow.

"Chivalry lives." She smiled and hooked her arm through his.

They headed outside and up the stairwell to the second floor. His room was on the opposite end of the hall from hers, but he turned with her to make sure she made it inside okay. In front of her door, she released his arm and fished in the pocket of her shorts for her key card.

Tension suddenly hooked his stomach. How many times had he stood in front of a woman's door, expecting to be invited inside? How many times had he teased until he got the invitation and then took whatever was offered without one thought for the emotional consequences? That wasn't going to happen here, of course, but how did he know what was going on in her head?

"Natalie, I'm sorry about this situation." He stuffed his hands in his pockets to keep from touching her face. "I don't want to hurt you."

She looked up, eyes wary. "Is that on the menu?"

"I'm no good at friendships with women." He looked away. "Whatever happens with this case and our ... our deal, I wish you the best."

"Matt, what's the matter? You didn't call me up in the middle of the night just to play pinball."

Matt opened and shut his mouth a couple of times.

His phone rang, startling them both. "Who'd be calling this time of night?" He looked at his phone "That's weird." The number was blocked. He flipped open the phone. "Matt Hogan here."

"Mr. Hogan, this is Agent Zach Carothers. I'm sorry to disturb you so late, but I'm on the other side of the world. I didn't think you'd want to wait."

He looked at Natalie to see if she'd heard. She was wide-eyed, grinning. "No problem, Agent Carothers. Give me a second to find a better place to talk. We're out in the open here."

"Come on in my room," Natalie said, fumbling to unlock her door.

Matt followed her inside and sat down in a chair while Natalie perched on the bed. "Okay, we're a little more sheltered. I'm really surprised to hear from you so quickly."

"Who's with you?"

"My partner, Natalie Tubberville. She knows everything."

"Okay." Carothers sounded hesitant. "What I'm going to tell you is sensitive. But first, tell me about Yasmine. Is she alright?"

"Judging by her ability to run when necessary and keep us off her trail, she's in good shape," Matt said ruefully. "Right now she's on a riverboat cruise headed to Vicksburg, Mississippi. We think."

"Then she's already married?"

"No. She absconded at the airport four days ago. We've been running her down ever since."

"Good Lord. Haq will kill her."

Matt nearly fell out of his chair. "What?"

"Listen, Hogan, this is all on the q.t., you understand?"

"S-sure. Of course."

"We've been watching Haq for a year or so, suspecting his involvement in arms trading with Al-Qaeda. Trying to nail him is how I met Yasmine. I didn't plan on ..." Carothers cleared his throat. "Yasmine wasn't what I expected. When she became a Christian I knew she was in real danger. But the only way we could catch this guy red-handed was to let him go a little longer. To keep him from getting suspicious I encouraged Yasmine to go through with the wedding, thinking I'd—thinking I could get to her before it was a done deal."

"But she must've realized something was up and decided to take things into her own hands," Matt guessed.

"Yeah." Carothers sighed. "Didn't realize she had that much nerve."

"She's got plenty of nerve," Natalie interrupted. Clearly she was hearing the whole conversation.

"Listen, Hogan, you've got to get to her before Haq does. He is completely ruthless. If she embarrasses him ... But be careful. We don't want him to know we're on to him. I'll wrap things up here tomorrow, then fly into Pensacola."

"Pensacola? I thought NCIS was in Virginia."

"My office is at the NAS down there. You won't be able to reach me, but I'll call you when I get to the States."

"Alright. Anything else?"

"Just—find Yasmine," Carothers said. "I care about her a great deal."

"You got it, man."

Matt closed the phone and looked at Natalie. "Can you believe that?"

She was wide-eyed. "I am so not trained for this."

"Surely they've got agents looking for her too."

"But we're the last ones who saw her. And Haq's going to keep bugging us until we find her."

New fear slugged Matt in the chest. "I can't believe I dragged you into this. I wish I had a way to get you home."

"Are you kidding me? This is the most exciting thing that ever happened to me."

"Natalie, this isn't a pinball game. This is international terrorism!"

"Which is why we need the armor of God all over us." She bounced off the bed and sat down cross-legged in front of Matt. "I'll start, you finish."

"Finish what?"

"Praying." She looked up at him like he was a moron. "We should have done this a long time ago."

His mouth opened. Then closed. She was absolutely right, and he was a spiritual kindergartener not to have thought of it. "Good idea." He bowed his head.

"Dear Lord, thank you for being with us," Natalie began. "Matt and I want to bring you our problems and needs and ask you to give us wisdom. Please keep Yasmine safe until we can catch up to her, and help us do that quickly. I pray you'll frustrate Jarrar Haq and keep him from hurting anybody else. Please give Zach a safe trip back to the States."

She paused, and Matt waited for a moment to be sure she was finished. He rarely prayed in front of anybody else. But for some reason it felt perfectly natural with Natalie. He cleared his throat. "Uh, ditto." He hesitated. Didn't that sound enlightened? But he was talking to God, not Natalie. "I mean, I agree, Lord. We really need direction bad. You know what we need, and you have us in your hand. Yasmine and Zach are a brother and sister in Christ, so I ask you to cover them and meet their needs too. Help us support and love each another in one spirit. Thank you for what you're going to do for us and in us. Thank you for your love."

He finished, out of breath, smacked down by powerful emotions that rarely had time to catch up to him. After a moment, he looked up and found Natalie staring at him with tears dripping off her chin.

"What's wrong?"

She picked up the hem of her T-shirt and wiped her chin. "That was lovely."

He stared at her. "I've got to get out of here," he finally muttered and bolted out of the room.

At the door to his room, he looked over his shoulder. Natalie was standing in her doorway looking at him. He lifted a hand and waited until she'd disappeared. Inside his own room, he dropped into a chair and slid down onto his spine.

"Hogan, you are certifiable. This is not high school. And you're talking to yourself instead of God." He slid his hands across the top of his head. "Lord, I wish I knew what you're up to. Would you help us find Yasmine Patel and get this whole thing behind us?"

His gaze fell on the Gideon Bible stacked on top of a Book of Mormon and a Koran on the nightstand. There was also a *Watchtower* publication. Take your spiritual pick. No wonder people got confused.

He reached for the Bible and opened it randomly. Ecclesiastes 5:4: "When you make a vow to God, do not delay to fulfill it. He has no pleasure in fools; fulfill your vow."

Oh wow. Did that mean the vow about fasting from women? That would include Natalie.

No more flirting?

But maybe that hadn't been a real vow. He'd just been sticking his toe in the water. But what if God took him seriously? Wouldn't that be par for the course if he'd just met the woman he could actually spend the rest of his life with?

➤

"Remember, this is not my fault." Natalie leaned over Matt's shoulder, peering deep into the bowels of the Miata's engine. "You're the one who left the dome light on last night."

She couldn't see his face, but the set of his shoulders made it clear he was restraining a good deal of polluted verbiage. "Yeah, but *somebody* left her purse in the car and sent somebody else out in the dark to get it. And after *that* somebody looked all over the car, the *first* somebody remembered she'd locked it in the trunk." He frowned at her over his shoulder. "And *you're* the one who doesn't own a set of jumper cables."

"I do so," she protested. "I loaned them to Nick, and he forgot to give them back."

"Well, there ya go. Vindication." He stood up and looked around the hotel parking lot. "Look for a guy in a truck. Somebody's bound to have a set of—look, flag that guy down. Hurry!"

Natalie bolted into the center aisle of the lot, waving her arms. "Hey! Stop, mister!" The driver of a minivan slammed on the brakes to keep from hitting her.

"Not that one!" shouted Matt. "The SUV over there with his brake lights on. Catch him before he backs out."

"Oh. Okay." Natalie smiled apologetically at the grandpa behind the wheel of the van and ran for the SUV. She banged on the driver's window. "Hello! We need help!"

The window rolled down. A mustachioed man wearing a red Dupont cap and matching jacket gaped at her. "What's the matter, miss? Somebody stealing your car?"

"No, we just need to borrow a set of jumper cables."

Dupont Man grinned. "Almost sent 'em off with my wife this morning. You're in luck."

"I wouldn't exactly say that," Natalie muttered, looking at her watch. She and Matt had both overslept, ten o'clock had come and gone, and it was going to be a close call getting to the riverboat landing on time. The boat would be in port for most of the day, but she and Matt wanted to meet it in order to catch Yasmine before she disembarked.

Mr. Dupont got out of the truck. "My name's Donald Wolf," he drawled, giving a hike to a belt buckle roughly the size of the Talladega Speedway.

"I'm Natalie. Nice to meet you. My friend Matt and I are on our way to catch a riverboat coming in from Memphis." She looked at her watch again. "We're ... kind of in a hurry."

"A hurry, huh?" His eyes twinkled under heavy brows. "Well, let's get a look at where you're at before I move my car." He commenced a limping stroll across the parking lot, indicating with a jerk of his head that she should follow. "I'm headed over to the racetrack. You ever been to a NASCAR event? It's a lot of fun. My wife lets me shake loose a couple times a year if I don't overdo the hunting in the winter."

Natalie adjusted her gait to keep from outrunning him. "Sounds like fun. I've never been to a car race."

"You're joking." Donald Wolf stared at this sacrilege. "Y'all come get in the car right now and I'll take you."

"Thanks, but we're in the middle of—hey, Matt!" She waved as Matt came out from under the hood of her car. "This is Mr. Wolf. He's going to jump us off."

"Great." Matt approached to shake hands. "Matt Hogan. Thanks for the rescue. Somebody forgot to turn out the dome light last night." He glanced at Natalie as if it were her fault.

She opened her mouth to defend herself, then noticed Matt's red ears. What good would it do to strip his masculinity in front of their Good Samaritan?

Rolling her eyes, she backed off to let the men discuss positive and negative charges. Mr. Wolf limped back to his SUV and moved it closer to the Miata. They realized the Miata's hood faced the wrong way, which meant putting the car in neutral and pushing it to the middle of the lane. A few minutes later, Matt got behind the wheel of the Miata and cranked it. It purred to life.

Natalie cheered. "Now we're cookin' with gas!"

Matt got out to shake hands with Mr. Wolf after he disconnected the jumper cables. "Thanks, man. If you're ever in need of investigative services, be sure and look us up." Matt handed over his business card.

"Goll-ee. Sure will." Hitching the belt buckle northward again, he stowed his cables in the back of the SUV and rumbled out of the parking lot.

Natalie snatched open the driver's door. "Come on! We've got to get out of here if we want to catch Yasmine."

"I think we're cursed." Cracking his knuckles, Matt took a frustrated turn across Vicksburg's deserted concrete flood levee.

Not only had the battery failure delayed them, but they found the boat had docked an hour and a half before the brochure indicated.

Now the *Delta Queen* floated in lonely splendor out on the river, her calliope silent, half a dozen American flags on her top deck flapping in a desultory breeze. All passengers had departed for a frolicsome day of touring antebellum mansions, making a pilgrimage through the National Military Park, and pigging out on southern cuisine. Two crew members crawled like circus performers over the enormous red paddle wheels at the stern of the boat, scrubbing them with long-handled brooms. Otherwise, all was still.

Natalie stood at the foot of the levee clutching Yasmine's backpack—which she'd insisted on bringing because Yasmine "might need it." Natalie turned to look at Matt. "We missed her again. Now what do we do?"

"We get on that boat and talk to people. See if anybody knows where she is."

"Maybe she's still on board."

"Why would she be? She knows we're trailing her." Matt walked down the sloping levee to join Natalie. "Bottom line, we don't know if she's coming back, or if this was her destination. Come on. Let's see if they'll let us look for her."

He hurried onto the gangplank. Natalie stood a moment before taking a deep breath and tiptoeing behind him, staring uneasily at the unruffled brown river. When he stopped abruptly halfway across, she bumped into him and lost her balance. With a little squeal she grabbed his arm.

He looked down at her, amused. "What's the matter?"

"Water—" she gulped—"it makes me really nervous."

"I didn't think you were scared of anything."

"Well, now you know."

He smiled, but let her stick close as they covered the remaining distance to the boat's front deck.

The temperature had warmed to the mid-seventies, the breeze taking humidity from the river and flinging it into their faces. The boat loomed, white and glistening like a wedding cake, her upper three decks ringed by white balcony railings. The wheelhouse bulged on top like a knotted forehead.

Matt was beginning to think nobody would challenge their entrance onto the boat, but the door to the lower cabin was blocked by a yellow-painted chain.

A voice came out of the darkness beyond the chain. "'Morning, folks. Can I see your ticket?"

Matt took off his sunglasses and peered into the cabin. A shadowy, knobby-kneed figure sat in a folding chair tipped back on two legs against the far wall. He had on a limp canvas cap and khaki uniform-style shorts.

"We don't have a ticket. We just want to talk to one of your passengers."

"Everybody's gone ashore." Mr. Knobby Knees clumped his chair onto the deck and rose. "Did this person know you were coming?"

"Not exactly." By now Matt's eyes had adjusted to the dimmer light inside the cabin. The man's nametag said "Hewitt—*Delta Queen* Steward." He was on the shrimpy side, and his khaki shirt was open one button too far. *Ego alert.* "We don't mind waiting."

"You can't come on board unless you have a ticket."

Matt looked at Natalie. "Okay, look, we're detectives from Memphis. We want to talk to a woman who got on the boat there. Her name's Yasmine Patel."

"Yasmine? What did she do?"

Natalie took a breath. "Then you know her?"

"Maybe." Hewitt looked cagey. "Why are you looking for her?"

"Her family's worried about her. They hired us to find her."

"Runaway, huh?" Hewitt's expression was avidly curious. "She doesn't look like a minor. The family got money?"

Natalie scowled at him. "Mr. Hewitt, we're not telling you anything else until we know if Yasmine's safe. Is she on the boat or not?"

Hewitt shrugged. "And I'm not telling *you* anything else unless you pay for a tour. My time's valuable."

Matt reluctantly pulled out his wallet. This trip was racking up business expenses right and left. After getting burned by George Field, he'd become a lot more cautious. "I'll need a receipt." He handed the steward a twenty, which disappeared in his pocket.

"You can get one at the ticket office when you get back on shore." Hewitt unhooked the chain across the doorway.

Resigned to being shafted, Matt exchanged glances with Natalie as Hewitt picked up the radio on his belt and called a staff member to take his place at the passenger entrance. Momentarily a young man dressed in a waiter's uniform arrived and made himself comfortable in the folding chair.

Hewitt nodded at Matt. "Okay, let's go. I'll show you the dining room first."

"Do we have to do this?" Natalie muttered as they followed the steward around the outside deck, where they skirted lounge chairs and plastic tables bolted to the floor.

"Play along. We'll find out what he knows and take it from there."

Matt stuck close to Natalie as they entered a large, well-lit dining room. Fine white cloths covered the tables; brass chandeliers hung from the low ceiling. A thick red carpet complemented two walls full of framed black-and-white photographs of river scenes from bygone days. Antique cutlasses, swords, and guns decorated the third wall, and on the far side of the room a row of windows looked out on the river.

"This is really nice," Natalie said with apparent sincerity.

"Yeah, if your AARP membership has kicked in," Matt muttered.

"Our seven-day cruise makes a great anniversary celebration." Hewitt glanced at Natalie, then gave Matt a significant look.

Natalie shook her head. "Mr. Hewitt, we're not married, and we're not interested in a cruise, so let's just cut to the chase. What do you know about Yasmine Patel?"

Hewitt peered at her from under that ridiculous cap. "Is her family offering a reward?"

"As a matter of fact, they are." Matt didn't like this guy's looks, but he was all they had to work with. "But we have to actually talk to her before they'll cough up the moolah. So where is she?"

"She isn't on duty right now." Hewitt shrugged. "She talked about going on shore to buy a pair of shoes. Her afternoon shift starts at noon, which is when we cast off. If she comes back early, I can let her know you're here. You can wait for her in the lounge, if you want."

Matt frowned. When something sounded too good to be true, it usually was.

But Natalie pounced. "That would be fabulous! Thank you so much!"

"My pleasure." Hewitt led the way out of the dining room and down a passageway to the left. They wound up in a small, comfortable lounge with a bar set up on the far side. It was deserted. The steward seated Matt and Natalie at a high, round table and hovered with a hand significantly extended. Matt sighed and filled it with a five. Hewitt smiled. "The waitress will be right with you. Oksana!" He turned, snapping his fingers. "Where are you?"

A small, pale-faced young woman with a blonde ponytail, wearing a short black skirt and a white polo, hurried through a doorway behind the bar. "I am here."

"Come serve these people." Hewitt gestured peremptorily. "They're waiting to talk to Yasmine."

The girl's eyes widened. "Yasmine! Why?"

"She's a runaway," Hewitt said flatly. He turned to Matt. "Oksana and Yasmine are sharing a cabin."

"Is that right?" Natalie smiled at the girl. "Do you know where she is?"

"I'm not sure ..." Oksana glanced at her boss.

He scowled. "If you know where she is, you'd better—" He stopped when the radio crackled.

A deep drawling voice boomed, "When's the delivery truck supposed to get here, Hewitt? I can't make sweet potato casserole without sweet potatoes."

Hewitt held the radio to his mouth. "Keep your shirt on. I'll check on it." He grimaced at Matt. "You folks'll have to excuse me. Oksana will fix you up with a drink and tell you more about Yasmine. Talk slow—she's Russian." He backed toward the doorway. "But you gotta be off the boat by noon." He hurried out of the lounge, muttering into the radio.

Oksana sent a scared look from Matt to Natalie. "Why do you want to talk to Yasmine? She is good girl."

"I'm sure she is," said Natalie. "But we're kind of in a pickle. We've missed Yasmine a couple of times already, and we've *got* to talk to her today before the boat leaves. Did you know her family is looking for her?"

"I do not know 'pickle.'" Oksana's eyes shuttered. "Why her family is looking for her?"

"Never mind the pickle." Natalie elbowed Matt, and he covered his grin. "She was supposed to get married. Do you know why she left Memphis without telling her family where she was going?"

"I sorry. My English is bad." Oksana clutched her order pad so tightly, her fingernails were white.

Matt had a feeling the Russian girl understood far more than she let on. "Yasmine's family has lots of money. They'll pay for information to get her back."

Oksana frowned. "I no sell my friends."

"I don't blame you." Natalie gave Matt a scorching look. "Ignore that bobo." She patted one of Oksana's thin hands. "Do you know anything about Yasmine's faith in God? Do you think that's why she's running from her fiancé?"

Oksana looked confused. "You mean Jesus? Yasmine tell me about how I can know him." A smile lit her face, making her quite beautiful. "So I do. I know him now."

Matt and Natalie exchanged glances. He let out a whistle. Their Pakistani former-Muslim was now making converts.

"That's great, Oksana," he said. "We're Christians too. So would you mind telling us where Yasmine went this morning? Or maybe when she'll be back?"

Oksana turned a pair of clear green eyes on him. "She is still on boat."

Natalie slid off her bar stool. "Oh my gosh! Why didn't you say so. Where is she?"

"She is counting cans in food pantry."

Matt exchanged glances with Natalie. She looked as confused as he was. "Hewitt said she's off duty. Something about going to buy a pair of shoes."

Oksana waved a hand. "That—that bobo. He does not know anything."

This time Matt did grin. "Can you go get her for us? We'd really like to talk to her."

"I take you to her. Come." Oksana whirled and was halfway across the room before Matt could get off his stool.

"I guess we're going to the pantry," said Natalie.

He and Natalie trailed the Russian girl through the doorway from which she'd entered the lounge and saw her clattering down a set of narrow metal stairs. Following, they found themselves in a compact galley. Oksana was peering at them from the other side of an open doorway on the opposite side of the room.

"Here is pantry. Come." She ducked out of sight.

Matt shrugged and followed, Natalie at his heels. Alice and the rabbit hole came to mind, but they had little choice. The pantry was basically a large walk-in closet lined with shelves, with several six-foot freestanding bins blocking the view of the back wall. Oksana was nowhere in sight.

"Oksana?" Matt peered around the closest metal bin. "Yasmine?"

Oksana's voice came from the left, behind a shelf. "She is at the back of the room. She has a sneeze and cannot hear good."

"She has a sneeze?" Natalie laughed. "Oh. A cold. Poor kid." She wandered toward the end of the row of shelves. "Yasmine!" she yelled. "Where are you?"

Matt followed.

And then he heard the door slam behind him. And the click of a lock.

CHAPTER
SIXTEEN

Yasmine! There you are! I was beginning to think you were not coming back."

Yasmine, trudging down the levee in her beautiful new sneakers, looked up to find her roommate pelting toward her as if pursued by killer bees. Oksana kept jabbering in nearly incoherent Russian.

It had been a long walk to the closest strip mall and back, and Yasmine's feet were sore in spite of the new shoes. She had passed the time mentally replaying the book she'd borrowed last night from the ship's library—lost in a long-ago, faraway world where rich, handsome Rhett Butler wooed spoiled Southern belle Scarlett O'Hara and refused to let her run all over him. Yasmine would never talk to a man the way Scarlett did.

On the other hand, she had lately behaved with quite a bit of impropriety and scandal of her own ...

"Of course I'm here." She looked at Oksana in surprise as her roommate snatched her hands. "For goodness' sake. What is wrong?"

"You can't get back on the boat! The man and woman looking for you—I have locked them in the pantry."

Yasmine's knees buckled. "A man and woman? Looking for me? Oksana, what have you done?"

Oksana shook her head, clearly at sea.

Oh, goodness. In her agitation, Yasmine had answered in Urdu rather than Russian. Switching languages, she squeezed Oksana's hands. "I am sorry. Who is looking for me? And why on earth did you lock them in the pantry?"

"They asked questions about you. They said you ran away, and they offered me money to tell where you are." Oksana's wide eyes filled with tears. "I didn't give you away, but I lied. I said you were counting cans and locked them in. This is a bad thing, but I didn't know what else to do!"

Yasmine felt the blood drain from her face. Her family must be spending a great deal of money to find her. Poor dear Ammi would be frantic.

"It is okay." She tried a smile, though it wobbled at the corners. *Think, Yasmine. What to do?*

She couldn't go back to the boat now. She would have to find another way to get to Zach. Her idea of American geography was admittedly vague, but she knew that she must go south, then east. Zach's base was in a place called Pins-Up-Cola, somewhere on the Gulf of Mexico. New Orleans was also on the Gulf of Mexico, presumably near her destination. But if she couldn't go downriver on the *Delta Queen*, she would look for another mode of transportation.

"Oksana, I do not know how to thank you for warning me. I must go now." Yasmine flung her arms around the Russian girl. "I will pray for you every day, and you must do the same for me."

"Oh! Oh! Why is this happening?" Oksana returned the hug. "I never had a friend like you."

"We are more than friends. We are sisters in Christ." Oksana's tears made Yasmine's eyes water as well. "And we will see one another again." Yasmine gave a shaky laugh. "Give me a few minutes to get away, then you must let my pursuers out of the closet!"

Oksana stepped away from Yasmine, wiping her eyes. "God be with you, my friend."

"And you."

Yasmine backed away, turned, and ran up the concrete slope. She passed a row of behemoth-sized buses the Americans called "arvees" parked at the top of the levee.

"Jewel!" came a man's crisp baritone. "Bring me that road atlas in the console, would you, hon? I need to figure out the best way to get to the Confederate Memorial Park."

"Now, Curtis, you know you promised me a cruise." The sweet but firm female voice drifted from the other side of the arvee. "I'm not spending the next two days driving around, gawking at statues of dead Yankees."

"I'm just saying. We can spend the rest of the day here and take the cruise tomorrow."

Yasmine peered from behind an arvee a few rows down. A tiny gray-haired woman in white calf-length pants stepped around the side of the vehicle and approached her husband. He lay halfway under the arvee, apparently working on something.

Jewel dropped a spiral-bound book on his chest. "You said we could do the dinner cruise."

And that was when Yasmine spotted Jarrar Haq's henchman crossing the gangplank onto the *Delta Queen*. He had followed her all the way from Memphis!

Unreasonable terror clawed its way up her back. Darting from behind her hiding place, she ducked between the rows of arvees until she reached the woman named Jewel's petite figure.

"Please, ma'am," she said, panting in fear. "I am in danger. May I hide in your arvee?"

◞

Hoarse from nearly an hour of shouting, Natalie leaned on the end of a shelf. "I am not believing we fell for this."

"That door must be solid steel." Matt sat on the floor in front of the door, clutching his shoulder.

"I told you it was silly to try to shove it open. Who do you think you are, Rambo?"

"Well, excuse me for trying to get us out of here." Wincing, Matt rolled his neck. "Who would've thought that little Russian girl would have the guts to do something like this?"

"She knows where Yasmine is. I bet she went to warn her not to come back."

"This is insane. All we have to do to get our money is pin her down and talk to her for a few minutes. Then we could go back to her dad and say, 'Your daughter's a grownup and she doesn't want to get married. Find another way to seal your business alliances.' But no. I'm stuck in a pantry with—" He stopped and looked at her guiltily.

"With what? Go ahead and say it, Matt." Natalie folded her arms. "How is this my fault?"

"I didn't say it was your fault."

"No, but you're thinking it loud and clear." She looked at her watch. "How long do you think it'll be before somebody comes looking for us?"

"Eventually the kitchen crew will let us out. Until then, nobody knows we're here, except Oksana." His voice was tense. After a moment's silence, he let out a breath. "I'm sorry, Natalie. I know this isn't your fault. I'm frustrated with myself."

"It's okay. I am too." She wandered around. The shelves were very close together, the aisles only a couple of feet wide. Good thing she didn't have claustrophobia on top of the water issue.

Matt cut a glance at Natalie. "Sit down, kid, you're making me noivous."

She put her hands on her hips. "Serves you right." But she hauled a ten-pound sack of dried beans onto the floor and perched on it. "The real deal," she said, stretching out her legs and wincing at the pain in her knees.

Matt noticed. "How're your Band-Aids holding up?"

"I'm okay." She didn't want him feeling sorry for her. She'd been enough of a whiny-baby crossing the gangplank.

"Let me know if—"

"I'm fine, Matt. Thanks."

They sat quietly for a while. Natalie felt her head begin to bob. It had been a long day. All the adrenaline of the day seemed to have seeped out her toes.

"Natalie."

She jerked her head off her chest. "Huh?"

"You're going to get a crick in your neck. Come on over here by me."

His voice was soft, cajoling, and she was so sleepy. "Okay, but you'll have to move over."

"Get the light, will you?" Matt moved to lean against the door, bracing the elbow of his injured arm in the opposite hand.

Natalie hit the light switch, then wedged herself between Matt and the closest shelf. She leaned her head against the wall. She was almost asleep when Matt shifted to put his arm around her, muttering something that sounded like, "I give up." He pulled her against him, tucking her under his arm.

Too tired to protest, she leaned into him, closing her eyes. "You smell good."

He laughed softly. "Thanks, kiddo. Go back to sleep."

"I'll probably dream about Big Macs. I'm hungry."

"Me too." As if to prove it, his stomach growled. "I don't guess you have a can opener on you?"

She shook her head. "All this food and no way to get to it."

"No justice in this world." Something softly touched the top of Natalie's head. Maybe his chin, maybe his lips.

She smiled and drifted off.

Matt pressed the LED button on his watch again. Its green glow softly lit the top of Natalie's head.

The last two hours, spent locked in a dark closet with a woman he not only enjoyed looking at, but whose mental and emotional processes fascinated and charmed him, had been an excruciating exercise in self-restraint. With Natalie tucked against him, his imagination kicked into overdrive.

He'd slept for a few minutes, but the injured shoulder kept waking him up, so he finally gave up and sat there praying. For Natalie. For himself. For Yasmine and whatever her problem was.

The Lord sure had peculiar ways of getting a guy's attention.

Speaking of getting people's attention, maybe they should stand up and yell or bang on the door again. Maybe somebody would pass by and rescue them.

Natalie sighed in her sleep, and he stayed put.

He'd always been restless, impatient. Reluctant to wait and listen. Surveillance was the part of his job that drove him crazy. Yeah, that and watching people cheat on one another. If he hadn't seen his parents stay together for nearly forty years, he wouldn't have believed people could commit for life.

Was he capable of loving one woman exclusively? What if he couldn't? Honoring his commitment to stay mentally pure was turning out to be harder than expected.

Natalie stirred, rubbing her cheek against the Polo insignia on his shirt. His heartbeat picked up. A sliver of light seeped under the door, and he could trace the outline of her brow and the glasses which had slid down her nose. He took them off.

Her lips curved. "Thanks," she mumbled, rubbing a fist into her eyes. "Forgot 'em. Bugging me."

He tucked the glasses into the front of his shirt. "No problem." Actually, it was a big problem. The desire to kiss her was setting him on fire. He was going to move away. Right now. Right after he touched her cheek. After he lifted her chin. After he pressed the pad of his thumb against her lower lip and bent down to kiss it. After ... whatever.

It was too late. She made a little humming sound and kissed him back, sweetly, without reservation.

"Matt, I think I'm falling in love you," she said against his lips. "I tried not to, but I couldn't help it."

Cold-water fear jerked him away from her. "What?"

"I said—"

He put his hand over her mouth. Too fast. Too much too soon. "You don't mean that. You don't know me, I don't know you, and you'll be sorry you said it, the second we get out of this d-doggone pantry."

Natalie stiffened and shoved his hand away. "I'm already sorry! Why did you kiss me if you don't ... You've been looking at me like—"

"Yeah, but that doesn't mean ... For crying out loud, it was just a kiss."

The second it came out of his mouth, he knew it was the wrong thing to say. He also knew it wasn't true. That had been way more than a kiss. It was a prelude to forever. At the moment, however, he had no idea what to do about it. His skin was clammy with terror.

"You're just like the rest of them. Worse!" She scrambled to her feet and stood over him, looking like a kitten that someone had squirted with a water pistol. "At least Bradley was honest about what he wanted."

"Come on, Natalie, I don't want sex, if that's what you're talking about. I kissed you because you're cute and kind of funny, and it seemed like you wouldn't mind. If I'm not mistaken, you *didn't* mind."

"That's beside the point," she said through her teeth.

As far as he was concerned, it was exactly the point. But he could see she was in no condition to be reasonable. He put up his hands. "Okay, whatever. You stay on your side of the pantry, I'll stay on mine, and maybe somebody will get us out of here before we strangle one another."

"Fine." She backed against the door.

"Fine." He moved back to the opposite shelf, which was all of two feet away.

They glared at one another.

Suddenly the door behind her opened from the outside. Oksana the Evil stood there. "Sorry sorry sorry. You come out now. But fast. Boat is leaving."

⟿

"Leaving?" Restraining a shriek, Natalie leaped for the doorway, nearly mowing Oksana down.

She could hear Matt clattering behind her up the metal stairway to the first deck. She burst onto the open foredeck and ran to the railing.

The gangplank had been retracted. A smooth, widening expanse of brown Mississippi River stretched between the boat and the levee.

"Matt! What are we going to do?" She whirled and found him right behind her. He was bent double, hands on his thighs, gasping.

With laughter.

"Of all the harebrained, idiotic—" He stood up and wiped his eyes. "I bet Yasmine's on shore somewhere, probably thumbing her nose." He closed the distance between them and slung his arm around her neck. "We, my dear Watson, have been had."

"How do you figure? She couldn't have planned this. *We* didn't know we were coming on board, so how could *she* have known?" Natalie shoved Matt's arm away. "It's just a bizarre coincidence."

Matt just grinned at her. "Bizarre is right. Look, unless you want to go swimming and drown in that current, we're stuck on the Love Boat until it reaches New Orleans. Might as well relax."

"Love Boat!" Considering his recent behavior, Natalie failed to see the humor. "I'm going to find the captain. Maybe he'll turn the boat around and take us back." She turned to look at the rapidly vanishing Vicksburg shoreline. The boat had already chugged quite a way downriver.

"Knock yourself out." Matt leaned over the rail. "I'm going to enjoy the cruise."

Natalie glared at his back. "What's the matter with you? Don't you want to find Yasmine? Don't you want that reward?"

He looked over his shoulder. "Come on, it's just a matter of time. We'll eventually find her. She can't run forever."

"Oh! You are impossible." Natalie retraced her steps down to the lower deck. They were so far away from Vicksburg by now that even if they turned and went back, Yasmine would be long gone. The only consolation was that the Pakistani girl was clearly headed south. Maybe Natalie could make friends with Oksana and get her to part with more detailed information about Yasmine's goals.

Or maybe something else would occur to her. Matt didn't seem to be worried about the kink in their plans.

Love Boat. Good grief. How could he kiss her like that, say she was cute and funny—or was that *funny-looking?*—then claim it didn't mean anything? He was a cad, just like Bradley. A piggish, good-looking, protective gentleman with the best belly-laugh she'd ever heard.

And he kissed like the guy in that old movie where John Cusack stood outside the girl's window holding a boombox over his head. What was that song? She couldn't think of it, with "Dixie" still screaming from the calliope speakers over her head.

Oh, phooey on him. She used to fall for a good kisser, but not anymore.

She was holding out for John Cusack.

⌒

"You two are stowaways." Hewitt had pounced on Matt and Natalie shortly after they finally located Oksana in the lounge. The steward was stiff with outrage. "I can have you put in jail."

"Been there, done that." Matt put a brotherly arm around Natalie. He was giving up on this fasting thing. As much as they'd been thrown together, he might as well.

Natalie didn't seem to notice. She looked down her nose at Hewitt. "You can't put us in jail. It wasn't our fault."

"Mr. Hewitt, I lock them in pantry," Oksana whispered, twisting the rag in her hand.

Hewitt's head whipped around. "What do you mean, girl? Are you out of your Siberian mind?"

"I am from Ukraine, not Siberia." Oksana's mouth firmed. "I lock them in because they chase my friend."

Hewitt looked at Natalie. "You mean Yasmine? Where is she, anyway?"

Oksana ducked her head.

"She never came back from the stop in Vicksburg." Matt speared Oksana with a look. "Isn't that right, Oksana?"

"I do not know."

She was lying. Matt picked up a handful of cocktail peanuts from a bowl on the bar and crammed them in his mouth. He couldn't shake the truth out of her. He glanced at Natalie.

She took the hint. "Oksana, listen. What Yasmine doesn't know is that we don't want to hurt her. We wouldn't even try to make her go back to her fiancé if she doesn't want to go. We just want to talk to her and make sure she's okay. Her mother and father are worried about her, because she's never done anything like this. What if someone besides Matt and me is after her?"

Oksana chewed on her lower lip. "I do not talk to Hewitt."

Matt caught the threat in the steward's chilly gaze. Whoa. Something else going on under the surface here. He stood up, moved closer to Oksana. "Come on, let's go through the buffet and sit down." He intercepted Hewitt's protest. "Don't worry, I've got a credit card. We'll pay our way."

"Oksana's working." Hewitt grabbed her arm.

Oksana seemed to take courage from Matt and Natalie's support. "My shift is over." She jerked away from Hewitt's hand and exited the lounge like a queen on a Mardi Gras float.

Matt grinned at Natalie as they followed Oksana to the dining room. "I think you made an ally."

"I hope so, because I'm starving."

In the dining room doorway, Natalie peered over Matt's shoulder, groaning. The buffet line snaked around the room and every table was full.

"Is okay," said Oksana. "Follow me." She led the way straight into the kitchen.

A tall black chef tending a Dutch oven full of sweet potatoes looked around and frowned at the invasion of his domain.

"Cook, these are my new friends—" Oksana blinked at Natalie. "I do not know names."

"I'm Natalie." She pointed at Matt. "He's Matt."

Oksana wilted onto a stool and put her hands over her face, her bravado disappearing like air out of a slashed tire. "Now I lose my job! Hewitt will throw me back in river like fish."

"Oksana, you don't have to let the guy treat you that way." Natalie put her hands on her hips and stared at Matt. "Tell her!"

Matt shrugged. "Of course you don't. You can sue the pants off him for sexual harassment."

"Sue? I do not know this word. And I want him keep pants on!"

Matt snorted. "On second thought, I guess you do. Just tell him to take a hike when he bugs you. Be firm, like Natalie." His gaze held hers.

"You—you—" Natalie whirled to address the chef. "Have you got anything to eat? We've been locked in your pantry all morning and we're starved."

"I got a key lime pie in the cooler over there. Help yourself." The chef continued to stir his potatoes. "Not gonna ask what you all were doing in the pantry. Um-mm. Nope. Not any of my business."

Natalie's eyes widened as Matt grinned. "Shut up, Matthew!" She stuck her head inside the stainless steel cooler and emerged with a meringue-topped pie. "Cook, this looks wonderful. Thanks for sharing. The pantry thing was just a misunderstanding."

The chef whacked his spoon against the side of the pot. "Friend of Oksana's is a friend of mine. Y'all new employees?"

"Not exactly. It's a long story. You got any plates and utensils, or do we scoop it out with our fingers?"

Oksana jumped to her feet. "I get plates. Sit." She took the pie from Natalie, set it on a counter, and proceeded to serve them each a big slice of the fluffy dessert.

Leaning against a counter, Matt scooped a forkful into his mouth and closed his eyes in ecstasy. "Tootie would kill for this recipe."

"And I'd gladly sit in a closet for another day if I had one of these waiting on me." Natalie sighed. "Pie for lunch. I'm in Disneyland." She licked a puff of meringue off her upper lip.

Distracted, Matt jabbed his fork into his chin. "Ow! I mean, yeah. So, does anybody know how long this egg crate takes to get to the Big Easy? Days? Months?"

The cook turned off the burner and dumped the potatoes into a strainer in the sink. Fragrant steam misted the galley. "Today's Tuesday. We cruise tonight, all day tomorrow, and roll into New Orleans Thursday morning."

"Oh, brother." Natalie's face was priceless. "Matt, where are we going to sleep?"

He shrugged. "Stowaway quarters in the pantry, I guess."

"Ha ha. Very funny." Natalie made a face.

"Yasmine is gone," Oksana said reluctantly. "You can stay with me." She smiled faintly at Matt. "*You* stay in the pantry."

The cook looked over his shoulder. "There's an extra cot in my room."

"Thanks, man." Matt nodded. "We'll work for our passage. Don't have anything else to do." This was working out pretty well after all. Natalie could pump Oksana for information, and he could work on the cook, who had apparently been Yasmine's direct supervisor.

Sometimes the zig-zag path was the best way to get where you were going.

CHAPTER
SEVENTEEN

D on't worry, honey, I'll get my cruise on the next trip. Won't I, Curtis?" Jewel scowled at the five red dice scattered on the table. "Farkle. Your turn."

Yasmine scooped up the dice. Curtis had been in the driver's seat of the monster motor home for the last three hours, while Jewel taught Yasmine to play a rather brainless game called "Alabama Farkle." The only difference, Jewel informed her, between Mississippi and Alabama Farkle was the color of the dice.

Not that Yasmine would know. She'd never played a dice game in her life. There was something faintly risqué about it, though she couldn't for the life of her figure out why. There was certainly no money involved.

She held the wooden cubes in her palm and regarded her hostess. "Why are you so kind to me?"

Jewel's brown eyes nearly disappeared as she smiled. "If my granddaughter was out on the road, I'd want somebody to take her in. This world is full of fruits, nuts, and flakes, don't you know. I couldn't enjoy a cruise knowing you were hitchhiking your way south."

Yasmine glanced over her shoulder at Curtis. "But the war memorial park . . . I wouldn't mind if you'd stayed—"

"I don't want to hear another word about it." Jewel patted her hand. "Curtis has been through that park half a dozen times. Besides, Barbara—that's our eldest—was all in an uproar because we were gonna miss Jessica's graduation party. She's graduating from Alabama tomorrow."

Yasmine blinked against sudden tears. It sounded like the Hardys had a lovely, close family. She missed her own—Abbi, Ammi, Liba . . . Pictures flickered across her mind like the postcards taped to the walls of the Hardys' motor home. She thought of Jewel's fit of laughter when she'd had to explain to Yasmine that an "arvee" was actually a recreational vehicle, shortened to RV. *RV.* The things Yasmine didn't know. Her melancholy faded as she smiled at the older woman and rolled the dice.

God had been good to her, rescuing her time after time. No matter what Muslims in the Middle East thought, most Americans were kind and generous. At least the ones she had encountered.

"You said your home is near Pensacola." Another misspelling she'd been carrying around in her head. Though he had spoken of it, Zach had never written the name of his base on paper. "When will we get there?"

"To Satsuma? We'll stay tonight and tomorrow night in Tuscaloosa at the RV park, then go home on Thursday. We'll figure out a way to get you to the naval base. It's just another hour and a half across the state line."

Yasmine nodded. In two, maybe three days, she would see Zach. After the adventures of the last few days, she could hardly believe it.

"Do you have a picture of your young man?" Jewel studied Yasmine's throw. "You've got two thousand points there. I'd stop and go with that."

Yasmine shook her head as she handed over the dice. "He would never let me take his picture. He said it was dangerous."

Jewel looked up from recording Yasmine's score. "Dangerous? Is he in some kind of special service?"

"I do not know." Yasmine's stomach dropped as another thought occurred to her. "Maybe he didn't even tell me his real name."

Curtis turned off the radio, which had been blaring George Strait. "What's your boy's name?"

"Zach. Zach Carothers."

Jewel nodded. "That's a nice name. Sounds solid and dependable."

"Yes, that is a good description." Yasmine smiled. "He is a good man. I will keep praying. God has listened to me. I know he will help me find Zach." And Zach would find a way to protect her family from Jarrar Haq and his arms brokering deals.

⌒

Oksana was a tough nut to crack. Twenty-four hours on the same boat, in the same room, working the same job, and the girl had yet to share one crumb of information about Yasmine. The boat would dock in New Orleans in the morning, and neither Natalie nor Matt had the first idea where to look for their quarry.

Natalie stuck her head out of the bathroom door, looked both ways, and darted down the short passageway to the room she was sharing with Oksana. Supposedly only women were quartered on this side of the boat, but you never knew when that slug Hewitt might appear. Natalie wouldn't go so far as to call him a stalker, but the guy definitely had an eye for pretty girls. She could totally understand why Oksana was jumpy.

Inside the tiny cabin, she removed the towel from her wet hair and hung it on the open slatted door of the closet. She'd had to put on the same jeans and shirt she'd been wearing since Sunday—three days ago, she could hardly believe it—but at least Oksana had been willing to loan her a pair of clean underwear so she could wash the pair she'd had on. Lack of luggage was a serious handicap.

Didn't seem to bother Matt. He'd borrowed a pair of shorts and a T-shirt from somebody and seemed to be happy as a clam. In fact, Matt did whatever Hewitt told him with a cheerful attitude that made Natalie want to clock him.

Absently finger-combing her hair, she settled on the hard bed. The cook had kept her running most of the day. Now she had nearly an hour to relax before going back to the kitchen for a late supper with the rest of the staff.

Thank goodness she'd brought Yasmine's backpack onto the boat. She took it from behind the pillow and pulled out the Bible. What a blessing to have it.

She'd been reading for about fifteen minutes, engrossed in First Corinthians, when Oksana's slight figure slipped through the door.

The Russian girl flung herself onto the bed, flat on her back. "Ooh. That bobo. I shove him overboard and feed him to the fish!"

Natalie closed the Bible on her finger. "Wow. That was vehement."

Oksana looked at her. "I do not know this word, but I am very, very angry. I get away from bad husband, but now I am in badder pickle."

Natalie smiled. Oksana had picked up quite a bit of American slang. "I think you should look for another job. You're not in a position to sue the little slimeball, unfortunately. What do you mean 'bad husband'?" Oksana looked barely sixteen years old. They must marry young in Russia.

Oksana looked away. "I do not know any other job."

"Oksana. *What* bad husband? Are you some kind of a slave?" She'd heard that women in communist countries often sold themselves to get out of desperate poverty.

Oksana sat up. "Slave? No. But I come to U.S. to get married, like Yasmine, and I find out my husband not so nice as his emails. He has children he doesn't tell me about, and he will not pay to bring my son here."

"You have a son?" Natalie blinked. "But you look so young! How old is he?"

"Misha is six. I am twenty-two." Oksana blushed. "He is born without father. I am bad woman." She raised her chin. "But Yasmine says I am new in Christ, so is okay for me being mother without husband."

"She's absolutely right." Natalie slid her legs over the side of the bed and leaned toward Oksana. "I certainly wouldn't condemn you. You should've seen *me* before the Lord got ahold of me."

"You say you are Christian." Oksana glanced at the Bible in Natalie's hand. "Maybe I like to believe you. Maybe I need another friend."

Natalie felt tears sting her eyes. "I need a friend too." *Thank you, Lord*. Hewitt, nasty as he was, had frightened Oksana into being open with Natalie. "And you definitely ought to stay away from that creep Hewitt. Don't worry, Matt's watching out for you."

"Matt is your boyfriend? He is nice man." Oksana fluttered her fingers. "And hot."

"I'm sure he'd be happy to hear you think so, but he's not my boyfriend." She thought of the kiss in the closet and her humiliating unrequited confession. "He's my business partner. But we're friends. Sort of."

"But he looks at you as if ..." Oksana wrinkled her nose. "I truly do not understand American men."

"That makes two of us." Natalie laughed. "I have an idea. When we get to New Orleans, why don't you leave this dead-end job and come work with me and Matt. I'm sure we need a—a secretary or something."

Oksana's eyes widened. "Truly? Truly, truly? You are not pulling my foot?"

"Well ... I have to check with Matt first. But we're a lot more likely to be able to afford a secretary if we find Yasmine and collect on her daddy's money. Come on, you're not selling her out," she hastened to add when Oksana's brow clouded. "I told you, we won't send her back where she doesn't want to go. Just tell me where she went when she left the boat."

Oksana withdrew, leaning back against the wall of the cabin. "I think about it. I pray about it."

"Okay, Oksana. You pray." Natalie sighed. At least that was a step in the right direction.

⌐

"What do you mean, we have a new secretary?" Matt, leaning on the forward rail as the *Delta Queen* chugged into the New Orleans harbor, turned to stare down at Natalie. "The girl can't even speak English!"

"It's a little mangled, but—"

"And I refuse to hire somebody who calls me 'bobo.'"

Natalie looked guilty. "I guess that's my fault. I'll tell her not to do it anymore."

Matt jammed his sunglasses on. The sun was blinding this morning, and his eyes hurt. He'd been awake half the night listening to Cook snore like a cement mixer. Would he ever be glad to get off this canoe. Running into Natalie every time he turned around had been torture.

He looked down at her again. Her fine, sunny hair blew in the wind like a fairy cap, and her freckles had multiplied over the last day and a half. He found himself wanting to kiss her worried mouth.

Instead he grunted and pretended to scan the ramshackle New Orleans skyline. "Yeah, and people always do exactly what you say."

"Why are you so crabby this morning? I got Oksana to tell me Yasmine's going to Pensacola."

Matt sighed. It wasn't her fault he was sleep deprived. On second thought, it kind of was her fault. But she didn't need to know that. "Yes, you did. You're Super Sleuth, Natalie. I salute you." He touched his forehead with a couple of fingers.

Maybe he sounded more sarcastic than he intended. She bit her lip. The one that tasted like strawberries. "I'm sorry. I just wanted to warn you that Oksana's going to meet us in Memphis after she finishes this cruise. I'll go say goodbye to Cook."

Matt felt it when she was gone. He looked down at the water churning under the blunt prow of the boat like chocolate milk in a blender. His thoughts tumbled just as violently. *Lord, I'm not ready. What if she's not the right one? I don't want the responsibility.*

He listened, but heard nothing except the cheerful, circus-like hoot of the calliope. *Oh, I wish I was in the land of cotton! Old times there are not forgotten — Look away! Look away! Look away, Dixieland . . .*

Had God looked away from him? Doubt took him by the throat. He'd put up a front of confidence for Natalie, but this case had turned out to be just as frustrating and confusing as the one involving George Field.

So they were headed for Pensacola. Fine. But Pensacola was a big place. And it was a long way off from New Orleans. After renting a car, they'd have to call somebody to take care of Natalie's Miata left in Vicksburg—probably Eddie, who was going to be none too thrilled with Matt's lack of management skills—and try to get a hold of Yasmine's family again. They weren't going to be happy either.

Lord, what a mess. And now Natalie had taken on a Russian mail-order bride as a secretary for a business that was about as stable as a house made out of popsicle sticks.

Looking out at approaching Lake Pontchartrain, Matt felt a smile tug at his mouth. Hanging out with Natalie Tubberville was anything but dull.

⌐

"I will be on my way to Mobile in thirty minutes." Jarrar let a Wilson Air parking attendant affix a hang tag to the Lexus's rearview mirror, then handed him the keys. Not having Feroz here to handle the details of travel was inconvenient, but necessary.

Now that his business was satisfactorily concluded, and he knew where to find Yasmine, he was going to go after her himself. He knew exactly how to convince her that her best interests lay in a speedy marriage.

⌐

"I know we're in a hurry, but I've got to have some clean—" Natalie caught herself just short of mentioning her unmentionables—"clothes."

She stood in line with Matt at a po'boy kiosk in the New Orleans Riverwalk. The smell of fried shrimp and sourdough bread, grilled sausage and onions was turning her stomach wrong-side out. People milled around them in thick droves, accents from all parts of the country, all parts of the world. The atmosphere, even in post-Katrina non-Mardi Gras season, proclaimed the local philosophy—let the good times roll.

Natalie wished it were that simple.

Matt glanced at her as he handed a credit card to the cashier. "Hang in there, we're in the home stretch." He took the tray with their food and headed for a table. "I'm going to find an electronics store so I can charge our cell phones. Then I'll call a rental car company, while you go buy whatever clothes you need, and we'll meet back up."

"Okay. Did you get a hold of my dad before your phone battery went dead?"

"Yeah." Matt's expression said Daddy had given him a hard time. "He and your mother are going after the Miata."

Natalie stopped in the act of squirting cocktail sauce on her sandwich. "My *mother*?"

"That's what he said. Are you sure those two aren't, you know, getting a little action going again? They spend an awful lot of time together for divorced people."

"I know." Natalie shook her head. "I don't have the nerve to ask my mom about it. My sister thinks I'm crazy. She says they're haggling over child support issues. But you know, Nina and Nick will be out of college in a year or so, and all that will be a moot point. I wish my parents had a relationship with Christ. You can't talk to people about biblical marriage if they don't believe cohabiting is wrong." She grimaced. "Right before you and I left for Helena, they gave me a lecture about safe sex."

Matt choked on his po'boy, and Natalie whacked him on the back. He got control of his voice. "They seriously thought you and I—Are they *insane*?"

Natalie sighed. "That's what I'm saying. They don't think it's wrong or dangerous for two healthy unmarried people to, quote, have a good time. Just told me to be careful. It's like I'm the grownup in our family."

He sat silent for so long she thought he wasn't going to reply. Then, "You think it's possible to be pure after you've ... let the horse out of the barn?"

Natalie looked up from the pickle she'd been trying to spear with a plastic fork. Matt's expression was intense. He really wanted to know what she thought. "I have to believe that, Matt. I'm not saying it's easy, but I can't live in guilt the rest of my life." She searched his eyes. "Can you?"

"I don't want to." He pressed his lips together. "Hey, look at that hairdo."

She followed his gaze to a street musician putting together a saxophone a few yards away in front of an airbrush T-shirt shop. The guy's long dreadlocks, twisted with shells and yarn, flopped around as he bent to open the case and throw in a couple of dollar bills as seed money.

"Wonder if he's any good." Evidently the heart-to-heart was over. She sighed and stuck the pickle in her mouth, puckering at the sour taste.

Laissez les bons temps rouler.

⌁

I–10 through Louisiana was patchy, and huge stretches through Mississippi were under construction. Matt let Natalie drive to Mobile while he spent the time making phone calls. Cole McGaughan was the first person on his list. Turned out the McGaughans were home from Montgomery on sabbatical, so Cole insisted Matt and Natalie stop off at their home.

Located in midtown Mobile, it was a quiet old neighborhood, many of the houses marked by historical plaques beside the doors. The unpretentious brick bungalow had a small yard dwarfed by a huge oak dripping with Spanish moss, a couple of pecan trees, and a magnolia in full bloom. The grass was a blinding emerald green. Matt told Natalie to park on the street; they waved at a lady watering her flowers next door as they got out of the car.

Matt hadn't seen his friends in several months; Laurel came to the door at his knock, and he grabbed her up in a bear hug.

"Hey, watch it, you'll squish the bambino," Cole protested from behind her. He gently nudged his wife aside and shook hands with Matt, giving him a whack on the shoulder. "Welcome back to the Coast. Is this Natalie?"

Matt watched Cole take in Natalie's smiling face. Instinctive recognition, incipient friendship. He relaxed. Laurel ushered in the guests with her usual graciousness. The judge was, as always, glowing with natural beauty, but the bulge in the front of her maternity top gave her a sort of sleepy earthiness that rather took Matt aback. The dark red hair was pulled up into a ponytail, her strong-boned face devoid of makeup.

"Sorry for the way I look." She wrinkled her nose. "Just woke up from a nap. The baby saps all my extra energy." She laid a hand on her belly.

Natalie looked fascinated. "We shouldn't have barged in on you, but Matt said—"

"Matt knows I'd take his arm off if he passed through here without stopping." Cole grinned at his friend.

"What is that noise?" Matt looked around. "Sounds like wolves have surrounded the house."

"Oh, that's just Colonel," said Laurel, gesturing for everybody to sit down. "We put him outside, not knowing if Natalie's afraid of dogs, and he's mad because Charles Wallace—that's our cat, Natalie—got to stay in."

"I love dogs!" Natalie sat beside Matt on the sofa.

He shook his head. "Colonel's not a dog, he's an animated pogo stick."

Laurel laughed. "Come outside, Natalie, and I'll introduce you while the men catch up. We can grab a glass of iced tea on the way through the kitchen."

Natalie bounced off the sofa. "Sounds great."

As the women left the room, Matt stretched out his legs, while Cole propped his feet on a floral ottoman. After a few minutes discussing the Patel case and catching up on the baseball playoffs, Cole went for the jugular.

"So tell me about Natalie."

Matt tried for nonchalant. "She's a nice kid."

Cole snorted. "Yeah, yeah. You just spent a week on the road together. Went to jail for her. Took a senior citizen cruise with her. She's not your usual play-toy. What's the story?"

Matt crumbled. He leaned his forearms on his knees and studied his fingers. "Man, I don't know. You never know what's going to come out of her mouth. She's already said the 'L' word."

Cole blinked. "To you?"

"Yes, to me!" He looked at Cole from under his brows and found his friend grinning. "Is that so hard to believe?"

"No, no. I just figured if that ever happened, you'd be on a plane to the next state. I take it you didn't say it back."

"Of course I didn't. She took me completely off guard. By the time I got my tongue unglued from the roof of my mouth, she was on her feet shouting at me." Matt ran a hand around the back of his neck and shuddered. "It was awful."

"I bet." Cole was laughing now. "You unmitigated goober."

"And the course of true love went so smoothly for you two. As I recall, you couldn't even get a legitimate annulment."

"Well, it all turned out okay in the end." Cole fingered his wedding ring. Sympathy softened his expression. "It's worth the hassle, man."

"Is it really?" Matt ducked his head. "That's what worries me. I'm pretty happy right now. Why should I take on a complicated relationship?"

Cole shook his head. "Only you know the answer to that question. I'd say don't get married unless you can't imagine life without her. I'll be praying for you."

"I'd appreciate it." Matt sighed. "And while you're at it, remember the Patel thing. The thought of Natalie involved with terrorists scares the bejeebers out of me."

CHAPTER
EIGHTEEN

Yasmine could have found a faster way to get to Pensacola, but a more entertaining cultural experience than traveling with Curtis and Jewel Hardy would be hard to imagine. Rural Mississippi and Alabama came alive with tales of Indian uprisings (Jewel explained that this did not mean immigrants from Bombay), battles between Damyankees and Brave Confederates, and the social habits of reclusive writers. Curtis insisted on stopping at every flea market and estate sale along every county road, in a quest for weapons and tools. Jewel was into produce and flowers.

As soon as they crossed the Alabama state line, a Crimson Tide flag went up on a short flagpole extending from the rear of the Winnebego. Never mind that Curtis finished high school in Citronelle, went straight into the navy, and then entered his father's dairy business. Anyone who lived in the state of Alabama had an obligation to declare loyalty to either Auburn or Alabama (the university). Curtis had always liked The Bear—a former football coach still held in religious esteem by alumni and fans—so he went for Bama. Therefore so did Jewel.

Therefore so did their children. Barbara, the eldest daughter, spent a couple of years at a local Baptist college, where she met her husband and dropped out after two years. The middle daughter married a boy who wanted in on the dairy industry, and the youngest, a son, followed his father's tradition of military service. He was killed in Desert Storm.

Yasmine learned all this family history as they traveled, playing endless games of Farkle, singing silly songs and hymns that Jewel's mother had taught her, and stopping every hour or two whenever the urge for ice cream, plow disks, or peaches struck. Yasmine almost—almost—forgot about being followed by Jarrar Haq.

But she couldn't forget Zach. As she watched the graduation ceremony, she imagined Zach walking across that big coliseum stage, shaking the hand of Dean So-and-So, and receiving his diploma. Later she sat in a nylon-webbed lawn chair beside the RV, eating slices of cantaloupe out of a paper bowl, and pictured him camping with his family. Roasting marshmallows over an open fire, teasing girl cousins with frogs and lizards, maybe chasing a dog through the woods or jumping fully clothed into a pond. This was the way he'd grown up.

For the first time, she wondered what would happen after she finally reunited with him. Maybe he loved her—surely he loved her. But an enormous cultural chasm stretched between them. How was she going to fit into his world?

On Thursday evening they drew up under the Hardys' covered RV port. They had reached Satsuma, Alabama—just an hour and a half from Zach's base. Terror and anticipation clawed her stomach.

Quietly she helped Jewel and Curtis unload the vehicle. Jewel seemed to realize how tired Yasmine was and kindly showed her to a quaintly furnished bedroom.

"Here you go, hon. You stay here as long as you want. Bathroom's two doors down on the right." Jewel opened the closet and twitched through a few garments. "Jessica left some things last time she was here. Borrow whatever you need, okay?"

Yasmine nodded and looked around. A quilt, pieced to resemble interlocked wedding rings, covered a high double bed; two more handmade quilts were folded on top of a cedar chest at its foot. The furniture was old and heavy, stained a dark mahogany, and a blue rag rug lay upon a pine floor. A wall of shelves housed nearly a hundred or so dolls, all of them staring at Yasmine with blank eyes. The room had a faint odor of lilac.

"Mrs. Hardy?" Yasmine timidly called after her hostess.

Jewel appeared in the doorway of the family room. "Yes, sweetheart?"

"Could I borrow your phone and call my sister? I will pay you—"

"Oh, for goodness' sake, child. I should've thought of that a long time ago. You can use my cell phone and it won't cost us a thing. I'll be right back." Jewel bustled to the kitchen and came back a moment later, digging in her purse for the cell phone. "Here. I'll be in the kitchen. Take your time."

Yasmine sat down on the bed with the phone in shaking hands. Should she really call Liba? Her sister had a phone, but Ammi closely monitored its use.

The longing to hear a familiar voice overcame her fear. She pushed the numbers for Liba's cell phone. *Please, Lord, let her be alone.* The phone rang once, twice.

"Hello?" Liba sounded hesitant. She wouldn't have recognized this number.

Yasmine couldn't get out a word at first.

"Hello?" Liba said again, sounding impatient.

"Liba! It's me." She started to cry.

⌐

"So Matt actually lived here with you for a while?" Natalie sat on the back stoop with Laurel. She petted the squirmy, panting, slobbering Colonel, whose eclectic parentage had blessed him with shaggy brown hair, long ears, and squatty legs on a muscular body. He was so ugly he was cute.

"Not exactly." Laurel grabbed the dog to keep him from slurping Natalie's face. "Matt lived here last fall, house-sitting while we were in Montgomery. He was pretty broke when George Field went down. You don't get paychecks from crooks."

Natalie absently scratched Colonel behind the ears. "No wonder he took my dad on as a partner."

"Your dad's a detective too?"

"Ha. He can't find his car keys half the time. But he's a great salesman and has a talent for making money. He needed a tax shelter. So when he ran across Matt's ad on a business website, he bought in." Natalie scratched under Colonel's collar. "Turns out Daddy planned all along to give me a share—he's very generous with me and the twins. I just wish he'd told Matt right from the beginning."

"So Matt didn't know he was getting a real partner?"

"No. And he was plenty resentful." Looking up, she found sympathy in the judge's deep brown eyes. Natalie suddenly realized she had a golden opportunity for wise counsel. "Laurel, you know Matt. Is he ever going to forgive me for barging in on his space? Or should I back off and find some other way to do what I've always dreamed of doing?"

Laurel hesitated. "Emotions aren't always trustworthy. But sometimes a cold, clinical decision isn't best either. What's the wise and loving thing to do—for Matt?"

The way the question was put stung Natalie. "For Matt? What about me?"

"What about you? Do you want what you want at his expense? Because if you do, that's not love."

"How do you know ..." Natalie swallowed. She'd thought she was covering her feelings. "It's insane to think you love someone you've only known for a week."

"I wouldn't have advised it." Laurel smiled. "But if you want to give this thing a chance to grow, you'd better be careful. At the very least, Matt's your brother in Christ, and he deserves to be treated as such."

"Whoa. What does that mean? I thought I was doing that."

"Among other things, love isn't self-seeking. It always protects, trusts, hopes, and perseveres."

"First Corinthians. I was just reading that the other night on the boat. Are you telling me you always give in to Cole, no matter what he wants?"

Laurel raised her brows. "Do I look like a pushover to you? Of course not. The *wise* thing, the *loving* thing." She looked at her linked fingers a moment, then smiled at Natalie. "You and I just met. But you asked, right?"

Natalie nodded.

"Okay, then." Laurel leaned forward. "You've got several things going on here. One is your career, another is your love life. But the most critical issue is your and Matt's relationship to God. If that's not right, you don't have a chance at a happy marriage."

Natalie winced. "I knew that. Deep down I know that. But I get so impatient, waiting on him!"

"Waiting on who? God or Matt?" Laurel's eyes lit.

"Both!" Natalie gave a weak laugh. "Matt kissed me the other day, and you'd have thought he'd jumped off a cliff he was so scared. Me and my big mouth—I blurted out that I was feeling something for him, and that made it worse."

"I bet. Most men will go with the path of least resistance, just because it's easy. But they're not satisfied if the challenge is gone. They want security, admiration, and respect, but they also want to lead. If I were you, I'd relax and give him a little more room. Make him take responsibility for his part of the relationship." Laurel tipped her head. "That will probably take care of the career thing too. Once he sees that you're not hounding him, not trying to take his agency away—you're just trying to help him succeed—I bet you'll be his best friend."

"That's what I want." Natalie blinked against watery eyes. "More than anything. Why didn't I see that?"

"Love is blind," Laurel sighed, "not to mention deaf and dumb." She winked and patted her swollen belly. "But it sure is fun."

⌒

Matt sat across from Natalie at Laurel's elegantly appointed dining table, diligently avoiding her gaze. The problem was, she didn't seem to be aware of it. She was engrossed in making Cole laugh at her conversation with Silky O'Sullivan's goat.

Laurel smiled. "You two have had some adventures."

"We've met a lot of great people." Natalie reached for the roll basket. "Eaten some amazing food."

"Spent the night in jail. Went three days without a bath." Matt made a face. "Welcome to the glamorous world of investigation."

"At one time you were talking about getting out of the business." Cole touched Laurel's shoulder as he got up to stack plates. "Keep your seat, babe, I'll get dessert."

Matt looked away from Natalie's questioning gaze. "Depends on how this case works out. Nat and I have a deal. If she finds our heiress first, she gets a full partnership. In that case, I sell her my share. If I find her, Natalie sells to me."

Cole paused in the kitchen doorway, eyebrows raised. "What happens if you never find Yasmine? Is there a deadline?"

"Yeah, the wedding date. The first of June." Matt stared at Natalie's downcast face. He'd brought up the issue on the way to Mobile and knew she wasn't happy with it. But he couldn't keep working with her day after day and maintain this weird friendship. And he wasn't quite willing to turn it into something else.

Fortunately, his cell phone rang before he could commit further acts of verbal hari-kari. He checked the ID. "Eddie! Where are you?"

"The office." Eddie's stentorian voice blared loud enough for everyone at the table to hear. "What in the world's going on down there? I didn't buy your company so you could run off with my daughter. You're supposed to be working on a case."

"We *are* working on the case. We're making progress. Yasmine's headed to Pensacola, and we're right behind her." Matt glanced at Natalie, whose eyes were wary.

"You should have caught her by now. I'm getting phone calls from Abid Patel five or six times a day, not to mention harassment by the fiancé—Haq. Poor fellow's beside himself."

"Haq's been calling you?" Matt glanced at Natalie. Carothers's warning to keep his mouth shut came to mind. "Eddie, there's something not right about that guy."

"I don't blame him for being upset. You were supposed to find the Patel girl before she left Memphis. This thing has gotten completely out of hand. Natalie said there would be no hotels involved. Now I find out you've been on a cruise!"

"Just a minute, Eddie." Matt covered the phone with his hand. Natalie was frowning, and Laurel's expression was a study in curiosity and amusement. "Excuse me, I'm going out to the screen porch to finish this call." He rose and tossed his napkin on the table. Reaching the porch, he shut the door behind him, but didn't feel like sitting. He took a deep breath and uncovered the phone. "Alright, Eddie, calm down. The only reason Nat and I went on the cruise is because a Russian cocktail waitress locked us in the kitchen pantry."

Eddie's voice rose. "Is that supposed to make me feel better?"

Matt paced the length of the porch, skirting the huge bulk of Laurel's Siamese, Charles Wallace, who appeared to be asserting his right of primogenitor. "Okay, well, we were only in there a couple of hours before she let us out. And Natalie was asleep part of the time."

"What happened the rest of the time?"

"Well, I ..." He'd kissed her and humiliated her. *Next subject.* "Like I said, we weren't in there for long. Then Natalie stayed with the Russian girl, and I bunked with the cook. On the complete opposite end of the boat," he added desperately. "Once we got to New Orleans we headed straight for the rental company and came here. Pretty much, that's it."

"I want to know, what are your intentions toward my daughter?"

Matt scowled at Charles Wallace, who blinked up at him sleepily. "I don't have any intentions whatsoever. Anyway, this whole thing was your idea. It's a little late to squawk."

"No, it was not my idea. I told Deb I didn't trust you. Are you in love with Natalie?"

"Why do people keep asking me that?" Did he have some kind of tattoo on his forehead that said *Natalie Tubberville's Ball and Chain*? "That's personal."

"One day when you have a little girl—if I let you live that long—you'll understand. Let me just say this. If you break her heart, this partnership is over." Eddie paused for effect. "You got that?"

Matt shoved the swing with his foot. "I got it. Now *you* listen to me, Eddie. I appreciate your fatherly concern, but what's between me and Natalie is just that—between us. It has nothing to do with business transactions. When I gave my life to God, he took it and shook me inside out. Maybe you can't understand that, but trust me, he's capable of straightening me out. I'm listening to *him* for the go-ahead. My career is his, too, which is something I should have realized a long time ago. If he takes this one away, he's got a better one somewhere else." He found himself smiling. This felt pretty good. Right and true. "So thanks for checking on us, but I recommend you work on your own marriage. Nat and I'll figure this thing out."

Matt paused, waiting to be blown away.

He could hear Deb's voice in the background. "He's right, Eddie. Natalie's a grown woman. It's time to treat her like one."

Great. Natalie's mother had heard this humiliating conversation too.

Fortunately, Eddie seemed to have lost some steam. "Okay, well. I'm just saying. Watch your step, mister."

Matt sighed. "We're spending the night with my friend Cole McGaughan and his wife—that would be Supreme Court Chief Justice McGaughan." He clearly enunciated every word of Laurel's title.

"That right?" Eddie sounded slightly mollified.

"That's right. Look, Eddie, I've got to go. We're in the middle of dinner here. I'll call you with an update when we get to Pensacola. And I'll call Haq to reassure him."

Eddie hung up, and Matt walked back into the dining room. He grimaced at Natalie. "I wish I'd known your father's a maniac before I took his money."

Around ten o'clock that night Natalie went out to the car for Yasmine's notebook and brought it inside. Laurel had gone to bed, but Matt and Cole were still up, flipping through the news channels.

She handed the black hardback composition book to Cole. "Here's the journal we found in Yasmine's backpack."

He flipped through it. "What language is this? Urdu?"

Matt nodded. "We think so. There's a tiny section in English, which is how we found out she's a Christian. We need to get the rest translated, but there hasn't been time or opportunity so far."

Cole handed the book back to Natalie. "I have a friend, a professor at the university, who could probably translate it for you. He's from Pakistan."

"That would be awesome."

"I'll call him in the morning." Cole stood up. "Natalie, Laurel showed you the guest room, right? Matt's going to bunk on the futon in the attic." He gestured toward a pile of pillows and blankets Laurel had left on the coffee table. "Y'all know where the bathroom is. Make yourselves at home and let us know if you need anything else." With a smile he wandered off down the hall, leaving Natalie staring uneasily at Matt.

She backed toward the guest room. "Well. Good night. I'm sorry about my dad. He's a freak."

"No. Actually, if I were him, I'd say some of the same things."

"What did he say?"

"Just threatened to break my legs if you shed a tear." He grinned a little.

"Don't worry. It's all good." She ducked through the doorway, then stuck her head back around. He was standing there looking at her, as if expecting her to reappear. "Good night, Matt."

"'Night, Natalie. Sleep well."

She brushed her teeth, put on a T-shirt she'd borrowed from Laurel, and climbed into the antique four-poster. Then the tears came.

But it didn't matter, because Daddy couldn't see.

NINETEEN

Friday morning Natalie woke up sneezing. She pushed a fluffy white tail out of her face and sat up. Through itchy, streaming eyes she met the disdainful gaze of a big, blue-eyed Siamese cat. "Charles Wallace. How'd you get in here?"

A glance at the door standing ajar answered that question. Dabbing her eyes with the sleeve of her T-shirt, she retrieved her jeans from the floor. A trip to the guest bathroom to brush her teeth and comb her hair helped some, but she stared at her red, swollen face in the mirror with disgust. If she didn't find some Benadryl, her whole head was going to burst.

Rubbing her eyes, she wandered into the kitchen, from whence the smell of coffee and bacon wafted like ambrosia. Matt and Cole sat on opposite sides of the breakfast table situated under a sunny window, each engrossed in the newspaper.

"Morning," she said, yawning. "Anybody got an antihistamine handy?"

Both men looked up. Cole jumped to his feet. "Uh-oh. Looks like Charles Wallace got loose. I'm so sorry, Natalie." He hurried to a cabinet near the stove and came back with a package of tablets. "There's OJ in the refrigerator. Glasses beside the sink."

"He's a beautiful sweet guy," Natalie said, helping herself to the orange juice. "But I've never been able to tolerate cat hair."

Matt frowned. "You should've said something. You don't look so good."

Sighing, she snitched a strip of bacon and a muffin off the stove, then sat at the table. "Usually if I keep my hands away from my eyes I'm okay. But he had his, um, tail, right in my face."

Cole laughed. "He used to sleep with Laurel until I came along and booted him out. She's still in bed. This last trimester's been hard on her."

Natalie watched Matt's face. He was a study in conflict. Curiosity, embarrassment at the intimate topic, and maybe a twinge of envy. *Envy?*

She made herself look away. "The baby's due in June?"

Cole nodded. "She'll take a maternity leave and go back to Montgomery in August." He grinned a little. "We didn't exactly plan to start our family this soon, but ... well, I'm glad." His cell phone rang. He looked at the ID and answered quickly. "Dr. Kasuri. Thanks for calling back." He listened for a moment. "Yeah, what we need is a translator. If I bring you this thing, have you got time to take a look at it?" He paused. "Well, as soon as possible. Before lunch? Great. We'll bring it over to you. We can be there in twenty minutes."

"Twenty minutes?" Natalie jumped to her feet. "My face still looks like a birthday balloon."

Cole looked unconcerned. "Dr. Kasuri is about seventy years old, and he's been teaching political science for forty years. He's seen it all." He got up and pushed his chair in. "Let me see if Laurel wants to go."

Matt gave Natalie a brotherly pat on the hand. "Not so much a balloon as ..." He squinted at her. "You kind of remind me of my sister's Cabbage Patch doll."

She put her hands over her face. Nothing like putting on the beauty queen act for the man you were falling in love with.

⸾

Dr. Kasuri's office was in a long, skinny brick building near the Student Center on the University of South Alabama campus. The three of them—Matt, Natalie, and Cole—barely fit in the tiny space between the professor's desk and the door. Matt was glad Laurel elected to stay home. She and the baby would never have squeezed in.

While the professor pored over the notebook, scribbling notes on a legal pad, Matt glanced at Natalie. He'd tried to convince her to stay home with Laurel, but she'd insisted on coming. Eyes a bit glazed from the medicine, she sat on her hands, eagerly leaning forward in her chair. Fortunately, some of the swelling had gone down.

"This young lady has a most engaging style, even in such a personal piece," said the elderly but dapper professor. His Americanized accent still sang with the slightly British lilt of his heritage. "She has been trained well. Most of her comments involve her anxiety over leaving Pakistan, leaving her friends, abandoning a satisfying job—for marriage to a stranger." He tapped the pen against his cheek.

"Honestly," said Natalie, "I don't know how she could do it. Couldn't she just say *no*? I mean, she had her own money, right?"

"Family honor is much more compelling in Pakistan than here, even in wealthy families like the Patels." Dr. Kasuri smiled. "Parents have tremendous influence on their children's career choices and on whom they choose to marry."

"Yeah, we know that," said Matt. "What else has she got to say?"

"I assume you saw the section in English, where she mentions the Bible, a gift from a man named Zach." The professor, who according to Cole was Muslim, looked faintly disapproving. "I do not understand this nonsense about finding and losing lives. But it sounds as if she was considering flouting her parents' wishes."

Matt nodded. "Natalie and I read it. Do you think she's a Christian?"

"I would certainly say she has abandoned the Muslim faith. There is more of that kind of language in the Urdu portions of the journal. She quotes sections of biblical text about abiding in Christ, identification with his sacrifice, and the possibility of suffering persecution of her own." The professor's expression held a certain amount of reluctant admiration. "She is no doubt sincere in her new faith. She had quite a bit to lose."

"Good for her," said Natalie stoutly. "I've never had to really give up anything for my faith. I've always wondered how I'd stand a test like that."

Dr. Kasuri turned the legal pad around on the desk. "Here is the last entry in the journal. Her 'test,' as you call it, was a difficult one."

Matt, seated between Natalie and Cole, held the pad so they could read over his shoulder.

I think about Zach's home in a place called Texas. He grew up there in a large Christian family that loved to travel together. Disney World. The Mississippi River. The Gulf of

Mexico. Yellowstone Park, which he visited as a teenager. The Great Lakes where he was stationed for boot camp. The Florida beach, where he attended college and trained before his deployment to the Middle East. How could I not fall in love with this handsome, educated, gentle man?

Hearing about his faith was like a light being turned on in my heart. The Muslim faith I'd grown up with became a closet of fearful darkness I longed to leave behind. I embraced Zach's Jesus with great joy. He became my Savior and my Lord. I grieve over my family's bondage to their god of anger and fear. I pray they will someday understand and forgive my treason and come to know the Lord. I was horrified when my father visited the capital two months ago and informed me that I was scheduled—scheduled!—to be married this summer to Jarrar Haq. For Abbi, this was a real coup, since the Haqs wield tremendous influence over the oil industry. I suspect the marriage alliance is Abbi's way of assuring familial preference. But I could not sacrifice my faith and my loyalty on the altar of some lucrative business deal. Prepared to swallow my shame and beg Zach to take me with him, I contacted the American ambassador. But I discovered that my sweetheart had suddenly been called away, leaving me only the note.

Heartsick, I hid it. How could I tell my parents I wished to refuse their choice for me—alone, without Zach's stalwart presence? I am no courageous American girl. I have been brought up to revere and obey my parents. Like a woman under anesthesia, I went through the motions of wedding preparations. I was not to meet my fiancé until the day of the wedding, which will take place in Memphis, Tennessee. The irony of the fulfillment of my dream of visiting the United States strikes me cold.

Matt looked up. "That's all?"

Dr. Kasuri spread his hands. "She stops abruptly as though interrupted. Maybe that is when the plane landed."

Natalie took the paper and peered at it as though she might see an invisible message. "She mentioned a note from Zach. I wonder what happened to it."

"You're a woman. What would you do with something like that?" Matt glanced at her curiously.

"I'm not the kind of girl men write love notes to." She shrugged. "But I suppose if it were me, I'd keep it on my person."

Cole pulled his lip. "If she did, we're out of luck. But what if she put it somewhere else? Where'd you find this notebook?"

"In the backpack." Natalie lifted the backpack in her lap. "Along with the Bible and that scarf-like thing the women wear over their heads."

"A *dupatta*," supplied the professor.

"Yeah, that." Natalie unzipped the bag. "And this wallet. It's got her passport, a credit card, and a little American and Pakistani money."

"We've each looked through it several times," said Matt.

The little office was quiet. The professor sat back, a little quirk between his eyes. "There is one thing I do not understand. In the next-to-last entry there is a phrase I skipped, not knowing how to translate it."

"Really? That's weird." Matt reached for the notebook to turn it around. "Show me." Like he was going to be able to read Urdu when a native with a PhD couldn't.

Dr. Kasuri tapped a series of words with a neatly trimmed fingernail. "Here. 'Pins up cola.' It sounds like an American phrase, doesn't it?"

"Sure does." Matt frowned, unenlightened.

"Pins up cola. Piinnsss-uupppp-coooolaaa ... Pinsup—" Natalie laughed. "Pensacola. That's where Yasmine's headed—at least, according to Oksana. Maybe she's hoping to meet Zach at the base."

Cole nodded. "She may already be there. She's got a pretty good head-start on you."

"Maybe. We haven't heard back from Carothers." Matt stood up, retrieving Yasmine's notebook and ripping the sheet containing the professor's translation off the legal pad. "Let's go."

⌒

"I wish I could come with you guys, but I've got an article due to the *Journal* this afternoon." Cole stood in the doorway with Laurel. "Keep us posted, okay?"

"Will do." Matt shook hands with Cole. Praise the Lord for good friends like these.

Natalie hugged Laurel. "Pray for us. And tell Charles Wallace I'm bringing my mask next time he wants to sleep with me."

Laurel laughed. "I'm glad you're feeling better."

Natalie's cell phone rang. She checked the ID and snatched it open. "Liba!"

"Put her on speaker," Matt commanded.

Natalie punched the speaker button. "Liba, I'm here with Matt. How are you?"

"I am ..." Yasmine's sister took an audible breath. "I have to hurry. My mother does not know I am calling you."

"Why? What's the matter?"

"It's Yasmine. She called me last night."

"Last night!" Matt grabbed the phone. "And you're just now letting us know?"

"I had to think about what to do. My sister is in trouble."

"What kind of trouble? Where is she?"

"She is in Japan. A village called Satsuma."

"Japan!" Natalie looked dumbfounded. "How'd she get to Japan?"

Laurel burst into laughter, and Cole snickered.

"What's so funny?" Matt demanded.

"Satsuma's not in—" Laurel hiccupped, laughed some more, and got control of her giggles. "It's not in Japan. It's right here in Mobile County, about fifteen miles up the interstate."

Natalie had to smile. "Liba, what else did she say? How did she get there? Did she say why she ran away?"

"She is frightened. And homesick. But in many ways she does not sound like my sister. I do not tell my mother because Yasmine will break her heart. She says she has become Christian and does not want to marry Jarrar Haq." Liba paused, then blurted, "How can she do this to our family?"

"I knew it," Natalie muttered.

"She couldn't have gotten this far alone," said Matt, frowning. "Who is she with?"

"She traveled with an elderly man and woman with a name something like Curtis and Jule Hardy. They bring her to their village and let her stay in a room with many dolls and quilts. She would not tell me anything else. Just that she would not come home."

Natalie shook her head. "Why not?"

"You do not understand my father. He will cut her off. It is a very serious thing to renounce Islam. Even if she repents, he will make her to marry Jarrar Haq." Liba hesitated. "She says she will never see me again, and is sorry to hurt Ammi and Abbi. She asked me to tell no one that she called, and I promised. But I—" Liba's voice broke—"I lied."

Matt could hear the girl crying on the other end of the line. "Hey, don't do that! You did the right thing. We'll find her and make sure she's okay—"

"You do not understand," Liba said again. "My father loves me, but he will punish me when he finds out I didn't tell him immediately. But I worry about Yasmine, and I had to tell someone. Please find her, but don't tell my father she has broken our faith. The Haqs will be so angry and insulted. Make her change her mind!"

Natalie bit her lip. "I don't know, Liba," she stalled.

Matt took a breath. "We'll handle it. Don't worry. Can I call you at this number?"

"No, my mother is coming. I have to go. I will call you again when I get a chance."

"Wait!" Matt clutched the phone hard. "Give me the number Yasmine called from."

"I am so stupid—I should have—goodbye," Liba whispered hastily, and the phone went dead.

Words Matt hadn't needed in a long time burned his tongue. Somehow he managed to keep control. Laurel's laughter had disappeared. Cole was frowning.

Natalie tried to pry the phone out of Matt's hand. "We have to find her right now! How do you get to Satsuma?"

"Wait. Just hold your horses." Giving up the phone, Matt held up a hand. "First we call this Curtis and Jule, whoever they are, and get their address. We can't just start knocking on doors in Satsuma."

"Oh. Yeah, of course." Natalie put a hand to her forehead. "Laurel, could we borrow your phone book?"

"Come on in. I'll get it." Cole stepped into the kitchen and came back with a huge phone book, which he plunked on the coffee table. "Hardy, right?"

"I think that's what she said." Matt leaned over Cole's shoulder. "Good night, there are a million of them."

"Yeah, and three of them are Curtis. Popular name. Wait, here's one that's Curtis and Jewel. That's 'Jule' in South Alabama lingo." Cole winked at Laurel. "I'm getting pretty fluent."

"Let's call and make sure they're the right ones." Matt took out his phone.

It rang four times and went to voice mail. "This is Jewel. We can't come to the phone right now. Please leave a message or call later. Bye."

Disappointment crushed Matt for a split second. But the Lord was in control. The recorder clicked on. "My name's Matt Hogan," he said. "I'm a friend of Yasmine Patel, whom I believe is staying with you. We think she's in great danger, and we have a message for her from her friend Zach. I'd appreciate it if you'd have her call us back." Matt left his and Natalie's phone numbers, ended the call, and looked at Natalie. "I think I should go ahead to Pensacola, since she's so far ahead of us. You drive up to Satsuma, see if Yasmine's still there, and call me."

"Good idea. Except we're short on cars."

"She can borrow mine," Cole offered. "I'm working at home today."

"Thanks, man." Matt absently hugged Natalie. "Looks like God's answering prayer."

Yasmine had grown up in Karachi, a coastal city which some claimed to be the second largest city in the world in terms of population. She had gone to school in England and lived and worked two years in the capital city of Islamabad, a bustling metropolis. In comparison, Mobile, Alabama, was a little tidewater village.

But riding a public bus in this enormous foreign country—knowing that Jarrar Haq could still overtake her before she reached Zach—left her feeling exposed, her nerve endings raw.

How long had she been on the bus? Jewel had bought her a ticket and seen her off at the station in Mobile—it seemed like an hour ago. Wasn't that how long the trip to the base should take?

The bus, stopping several times along the way, took a route along a wide tree-lined boulevard, crossed a bridge, twisted around an interstate connection, then dipped through a long, dark tunnel. On the other side, daylight flared, blinding her. The bus started across a long, six-lane bridge.

Then she saw a sign that made her heart leap with relief: *Battleship Parkway*. Evidently she had reached her destination, the naval base, without realizing how far she had come. And there was the battleship. It loomed off in the distance to the right of the causeway, a hulking gray-steel beauty.

The bus slowed and took the exit ramp.

Her heart pounded. She was almost there.

The bus traveled a half mile or so, and she saw the ship, the USS *Alabama*. Surely there should be more than one, if this was a naval base. At the entrance a fighter jet hovered on top of a pole like a green dragonfly. More small jets lined an airfield, with a submarine poised on the far side of the ship. To her surprise, nobody stopped the bus as it entered a broad parking lot and stopped behind several cars and an RV or two. Shouldn't there be a security checkpoint at a gate? If American military security was this lax, no wonder they were having trouble in the Middle East.

She sat for a moment, afraid to get off. After a couple of other people exited, she followed them toward a small building sitting at the end of the parking lot. "Gift Shop," the sign said.

Gift shop?

Yasmine approached a young woman tending a computerized cash register. "Excuse me. I'm trying to find Lieutenant Zach Carothers. He's stationed here at the air station. Do you know how I can find—"

The young woman cut her off with a look of utter confusion. "Air station? Ma'am, this is a museum."

"A museum? But there's a ship ..." Yasmine stopped, feeling foolish. "Museum?"

"This is a World War II battleship and submarine." The girl laughed. "The only lieutenants here are mannequins dressed up in 1940s gear."

Yasmine grabbed for her dignity. "Then could you tell me where I could find Pensacola Naval Air Station?"

"Oh, wow. You *are* lost. You're nowhere near Pensacola. It's almost an hour away. Get back on the causeway, take the exit to I–10 east, and head over to Florida. When you get to Pensacola, you'll take the ..."

The instructions jumbled in Yasmine's brain. She stared at the young woman, seeing only numbers and bridges and vast expanses of water. If she'd been at home in Karachi or Islamabad—or even England, where she'd gone to boarding school—there would have been no problem. But here, in this enormous country of mile-long tunnels and rivers so wide one could not see across them, fear filled her with nausea. She had gotten off the bus too soon.

The young woman finally stopped talking. "See? It's easy." She smiled, a perfect specimen of American orthodontics.

Yasmine produced an answering smile from somewhere. "Yes. Thank you." She turned and ran back through the gift shop.

The bus was gone. She stared at the towering turrets of the battleship. It represented Zach. It also reminded her that she was alone and utterly out of place. *Oh, Lord. What do I do?*

Suddenly she longed for a familiar face, or at least a familiar voice. She could not call Liba again. Her sister, she sensed, was on the verge of giving her up.

She slipped her hand into the pocket of the jeans she'd borrowed from Jewel's granddaughter and found the dollar Jewel had given her, along with a scrap of paper containing the Hardys' phone number. Jewel would tell her what to do. Or at least reassure her that she was not alone. All she had to do was find a pay phone.

She trudged back inside the museum gift shop and approached the young woman behind the cash register. "Excuse me, please," she said timidly, "but could you direct me to a pay phone?"

"Car trouble?" asked the girl sympathetically.

"No, I ..." How humiliating to admit that she had no car, but had been stranded due to her own stupidity. "Well, yes. I need to call my friend to pick me up." Jewel would insist on driving all the way to rescue her, when of course the dear lady had many more important things to do. Stupid, Yasmine.

"Here," said the clerk. "Just use the store phone. Dial nine to get out. It's local, right?"

"Satsuma," Yasmine admitted, her stomach knotting. "I do not—"

"Oh, that's local." The girl smiled. "Go right ahead." She turned the phone in Yasmine's direction and politely moved to the other end of the counter to give her privacy.

Sick with embarrassment, Yasmine picked up the receiver. She dialed nine and then Jewel's number. The phone rang twice in her ear before Jewel's gentle voice answered. "Hello?"

Yasmine deliberately firmed her voice. "Jewel? It is Yasmine."

"Yasmine? Are you in Pensacola already?"

"No, I am at the battleship museum."

"What on earth are you doing at the battleship? Never mind. I'm so glad you called, because there's somebody here who wants to talk to you. Will you promise to stay where you are and not run off?"

A shiver went through Yasmine. "Who is it?"

"Wait just a minute, honey. Hold on. Here she is."

Yasmine clutched the phone. "Jewel?"

But Jewel was gone. A young female voice came through the speaker. "Yasmine? Please don't hang up. This is Natalie Tubberville. I really need to talk to you."

TWENTY

Natalie sat in a gingham-cushioned kitchen chair in Jewel Hardy's kitchen, heart pounding like a jackhammer. She had actually heard Yasmine's voice. Yasmine sounded a little like her sister Liba, a lot like her mother, and wholly scared out of her mind.

And no wonder, being chased all over the South by strangers.

Natalie waited, hardly daring to move. There was no answer for so long she was afraid Yasmine had hung up.

At last there was a sharp breath. "Please, I beg you, do not tell my father where I am."

Natalie felt tears spring to her eyes. "I'm not doing anything until I talk to you in person. Where are you?"

"I am stuck." The soft voice sounded forlorn. "I need to talk to Mrs. Hardy."

"Oh, Yasmine, I'll come get you. Please tell me where you are."

"No! I am not going back to my—no!"

"Listen to me." Natalie strove for calm. "I know you're a Christian. I found your backpack, and I have your notebook and Bible."

This time tears splintered Yasmine's voice. "I want them back. Please."

"Of course. But listen, I'm a believer in Jesus too. I think I know why you're running away, but you don't have to. Nobody can make you marry somebody you don't want to. This is America, remember?"

"But I am not an American citizen. I must do what my father says." The broken voice took on a note of stubbornness. "But not if he cannot find me."

Natalie looked at Jewel, who seemed to have heard every word. The elderly woman's deep-set eyes swam with compassion. "I'm on your side. So is Jewel." Natalie made up her mind. "Will you let us come help you? I think you need a friend."

Yasmine was sobbing in earnest now. "Maybe. I need to think. Okay. I stay, you come. But don't tell my father. Don't tell *anyone*."

Matt made it to the Pensacola Naval Air Station in just under an hour. He would love to have made the drive across the bay bridge in Natalie's open-topped Miata. Instead he was stuck in a compact sedan with cloth seats and an AM radio.

He had to grin at himself. Riding shotgun with Natalie had spoiled him.

He'd gotten spoiled by her company, period. Maybe she came at an investigation sideways and backwards, but she always managed to get there. He'd bet she would pull something useful out of Jewel Hardy.

The naval base began with a long, winding drive through flat, palm-lined Florida sand. The Gulf of Mexico stretched like water in a lead-colored bathtub on one side, a golf course with jewel-like greens on the other. After passing a series of barracks and warehouses, the secured entrance appeared under huge iron letters.

Matt stopped at the gate and rolled down his window.

A uniformed guard stepped out of his little booth. "Morning, sir." He leaned on Matt's open window. "Need to know your business."

Matt handed over his card. "I'm going to NCIS. Judge Laurel McGaughan called ahead for me, I believe."

The guard's tired face lifted slightly. "She did. I have a pass for you." He reached into the booth for a ticket, which he handed to Matt. "Bring that back to me on your way out."

"Yes, sir." Matt touched a finger to his brow and drove through.

A few minutes later he sat in an office facing a young officer with "Digman" on his nametag. In a khaki uniform with a bunch of colored ribbons on his collar and across his shirt pocket, he was Navy from the top of his close-clipped hair to the tips of his shiny shoes.

Feeling positively slovenly, Matt took the chair offered by the petty officer. Laurel had pulled rank to get him this far. He'd better act confident, even if he felt like an eight-year-old in the principal's office.

Matt straightened his spine. "I'd like to speak to Special Agent Zachary Carothers, who was stationed in Pakistan just three weeks ago. Do you know him?"

Digman, who had about as much expression as the coffee mug on his desk, regarded Matt with hooded eyes for nearly thirty seconds. Finally he picked up a pen and tapped it on the blotter. "I don't think so. What's your business with him?"

Matt understood the game. *I tell you a little, you tell me nothing, eventually I give you the whole spiel, and maybe we get somewhere.* "Carothers has connected with the daughter of a well-placed Pakistani oil baron. She's trying to find him."

"Connected? How?"

"I believe they're engaged to be married. And her father's not happy about it."

"What does this have to do with NCIS?"

Matt tried to decide how much he could make up and get away with it. Then he remembered he wasn't supposed to make things up anymore. He cleared his throat. "Look, I talked to Carothers Tuesday night. He was in contact with the girl while she was a translator at the American embassy in Islamabad. She came to the U.S. last week with the intention of marrying the son of the Pakistani Commerce Chairman but disappeared in the airport. Her father and fiancé hired me to locate her. I've tracked her this far. I'd like to talk to Carothers and see what he knows about her."

Digman glanced at his watch. "Wait here, Mr. Hogan. I'll be right back." Without waiting for an answer, he disappeared through his office door.

Matt slouched in the chair and clasped his hands across his stomach. Hurry up and wait. The story of his life.

Some five minutes later, the petty officer opened the door sharply. He stood with his hands behind his back, feet shoulder-width apart. "Special Agent Phillips will see you now."

"Wow. Okay." Matt leaped to his feet.

Digman gave Matt a cool look. "I'll need to hold your cell phone, sir."

"Why?"

"Security." No other explanation was offered.

Matt shrugged and handed over his cell phone.

"Thank you, sir." The petty officer moved aside.

Matt had no idea what was going on, or how this little dance was going to help him find Yasmine. He passed Digman with a nod and entered the office. The two agents in the room, both dressed in civvies, stood as Matt entered the room. The one behind the desk was clearly the Agent in Charge. He looked like someone who rarely heard the word "no."

The younger agent offered a hand to Matt. There was nothing familiar about the strong, clean features, but Matt still had a feeling he should know him. The guy wasn't tall, but his shoulders were broad and muscular; extreme intelligence and a glint of humor lit the dark gray eyes. Matt instantly liked him.

"Mr. Hogan," said Phillips, indicating that Matt should sit in one of the two leather chairs opposite his desk. "This is Special Agent Carothers. I believe you have spoken with him by phone."

Matt smiled, relieved. "Absolutely. Nice to meet you, Carothers. Thanks for seeing me."

"My pleasure. It's good to get back on solid ground." Carothers took the empty chair and deferred to his superior.

Phillips steepled his fingers. "Mr. Hogan, we understand you have current information about a young woman named Yasmine Patel. We'd like for you to tell us what you know about her."

Matt looked at Carothers. The young agent's gaze was steady, if a bit guarded. Yet there was a hint of eagerness in his expression. "I think what I have to say may be … personal, as well as related to national defense."

Carothers's smile was dry. "I'm afraid lately those two things are all mixed up. Feel free to go ahead."

Matt started with Natalie's aborted pick-up at the airport, continued through interviews with the Patel and Haq families, and wound up at Liba's phone call and the translation of the notebook.

Carothers straightened. "May I see the journal?"

Matt flicked the cover of the book in his lap. "A lot of it's written in Urdu. We had to have it translated." When Carothers gave him a look, he handed it over.

The young agent read in silence for several minutes. As he reached the end, his tanned cheeks reddened. He looked up at Matt. "I didn't know she felt this strongly. I thought it was just me."

Phillips frowned. "Were you having a love affair with this woman?"

"No sir. Not exactly." Carothers looked down. "We're both Christians, sir, and everything stayed very ... platonic. I have the greatest respect for Yasmine. My assignment was to investigate her father and his dealings with the Haq family. But eventually ... well, you'd have to meet her to understand, sir."

"I'd like that." Unexpected humor slid into Phillips's expression. "But it appears Miss Patel has been misplaced."

"My partner and I are certain she was headed this way," said Matt. "You can tell from the journal that she was obsessed with what she called 'Pins Up Cola.' Carothers, I think she was determined to get to you, even though she couldn't have known you'd actually be here."

Carothers frowned. "Her father's going to make it hard on her. He's probably outraged that she ran away. And the Haqs—" He looked at Phillips.

"Speak freely, Carothers."

Carothers shrugged. "Yasmine's family's Muslim. They'd arranged her marriage to Haq, even though he's been here in the States for nearly a year. *His* family is a powerful political entity, with control over oil transportation—imports and exports. So the engagement was in the nature of a political and business merger. For Yasmine to back out against her parents' wishes is not only a breach of honor, but a torpedo in the side of her father's financial hopes." Carothers leaned forward, his bony face intent. "But Haq himself is the most dangerous thing about this situation. What I've learned about him in the last month makes many of the terrorists we deal with look like a bunch of flying monkeys."

Matt felt the hair rise on his arms. "What do you mean?"

Carothers clamped his lips together. "I had to let Yasmine go to keep Haq pacified. Now that she's here ..." He glanced at his superior. "I need to find her, sir."

⌐

Natalie could understand how Yasmine got confused. The Interstate exchange where I–165 met I–10 at Water Street was a snarl of bridges, tunnels, and underpasses, with conflicting signage that would give the most seasoned truck driver a headache. Natalie, at least, had the advantage of familiarity with the English language and the American interstate system.

Eventually she made it to the USS *Alabama* exit. Veering off the causeway, she entered Battleship Park and parked in the lot next to the battleship. Shaking her head, she got out of the car. Yasmine must have been severely shaken up to have taken this for a military ops base.

She opened the door of the gift shop and looked around. On a Friday morning it was fairly deserted. Most school field trips had been taken long ago, and the summer tourist season wouldn't start for another few weeks. She approached the ticket counter, where a gray-haired woman wearing a navy polo embroidered with the battleship insignia sat reading a magazine.

Natalie greeted her and got down to business. "I'm looking for a dark-haired young woman about my age. She has a Middle Eastern accent ..."

"Oh, yes." The woman jerked a thumb over her shoulder. "She's in the café. Just walk through that door."

Natalie pushed open the glass door, savoring a little shiver of anticipation. She was halfway afraid Yasmine might have slipped away again. But the woman she'd been chasing for over a week sat at a table, sipping at a straw stuck in a can of Sprite. Natalie stopped for a moment and closed her eyes in thankful prayer.

She approached Yasmine with a great deal more caution than she'd exhibited in the Memphis airport. "Yasmine? Remember me?"

Yasmine, tense as a drawn bow, set the soda can on the table. "Hello, Natalie."

Natalie's emotions cartwheeled. Relief. Joy. A smidge of resentment at the struggle she'd endured just to land in the same room with Yasmine. She smiled, pulled out a chair, and sat across from her erstwhile quarry. "How are you?"

Yasmine sighed. "I am very tired. And confused. And—" She smiled wryly. "And a little scared of what you will do."

Natalie spread her hands. "Why? I just want to help. Your father asked my dad to pick you up from the airport. Now that I know why you ran away—" She halted abruptly. "Yasmine, you're a grown woman, you're in America, and nobody can make you go back to your family if you don't want to."

Yasmine looked as if she might blurt something out. She pressed her lips together.

"Why didn't you tell them you're afraid of Haq?"

Silence.

Natalie sighed. "Does your family know you're a Christian?"

Yasmine hung her head. "No." Her voice was a whisper. "I am afraid to tell. And I am ashamed that I am afraid."

"Dr. Kasuri said it's a very serious thing for a Muslim to convert to Christianity."

"Who is this Dr. Kasuri?"

"Never mind. Will they really cut you out of the family once they know you're a Christian?"

"I do not know. Probably." Yasmine hunched her shoulders, pain tightening her face. "I cannot go back to them anyway. So I suppose it does not matter."

Natalie could tell that it mattered very much. "I'm so sorry, Yasmine." She fumbled for direction. "Matt and I talked to Zach the other night. He seems like a wonderful man, and he's very worried about you."

"You talked to Zach?" Yasmine's expression lightened. "Is he well? Can you help me get to him?"

"He said he would be flying back to the States—into Pensacola, in fact—yesterday. Of course I'll take you there."

"Oh!" Yasmine lit up as if her personal sun had risen. "You are so kind. The good God has listened to me."

"Matt's over in Pensacola right now, trying to locate him." Natalie flipped open her cell phone. "Let's see what he's up to."

⟶

Matt cooled his heels in the NCIS outer office while Carothers made arrangements to go in search of Haq. Unable to sit still, he got up and yanked a Dixie cup out of the dispenser next to the water cooler. He filled it, tossed it back in one swallow, and poured another.

Digman, clicking away on the computer behind his desk, gave Matt a sour look. "I could probably find you a bigger glass, sir."

"No, thanks. I'm just bored. How much longer do you think—" His cell phone rang. Natalie's number chased across the display. "Hey, Nat. What's up?"

"You're never going to believe who's sitting across from me."

"Who?"

"Yasmine."

"No way!"

"Yep. Matt, she's really nice—"

"I'm sure she is. Just don't let her get away again. I've got news too. I found Zach Carothers."

"Really? So do you want us to come to you, or what?"

"Sit tight. Where are you, anyhow?"

"In the gift shop of the battleship *Alabama*. You know—the one off the causeway?"

"I passed right by there on my way to Pensacola. It's a little hard to miss." He paused. "What are you doing there?"

"It's a long story. I'll fill you in later. Right now Yasmine wants to talk to Zach."

"He's not here. He's gone to finalize some paperwork. I'll have him call as soon as I can."

"Wonderful. Matt . . ." Silence pulsed for a moment.

"What?" Something in him fluttered at her pause, and he held his breath, although he wasn't sure why.

"Never mind." The phone clicked in his ear.

He looked at the phone. Most of the time Natalie couldn't keep her mouth shut. Yet the minute he *wanted* her to say something, she went mum as an oyster.

He met Digman's curious gaze and grimaced. "My partner. We don't communicate too well sometimes."

CHAPTER
TWENTY-ONE

Natalie closed the phone and released a big sigh. To Yasmine, her new friend's smile seemed forced.

"Matt said for us not to leave," said Natalie. "He and Zach are coming here."

"I can hardly believe it!" Yasmine tweaked the front of her T-shirt. "I wish I had my beautiful clothes back."

"Yasmine, you could wear a flour sack and look like a super-model." Natalie's eyes twinkled. "We have a little while. Tell me how you met Zach."

Yasmine felt herself blush. She had kept her love story close inside for so long, it felt strange to share it with anyone but her journal. "I was very sheltered, as most Pakistani young women are. The only men I knew well were my father and my Uncle Rais. I spent my teenage years in an English boarding school." She spread her hands. "Then a bit of freedom came when I worked in the embassy in Islamabad."

"You were a translator, right?"

Yasmine nodded. "I was in the market looking for dinner one evening after work, when some American sailors accosted me. An officer chased them away and escorted me home to my apartment. He was so kind and respectful and spoke perfect Urdu. We met again in the market—accidentally once, then more and more often by assignation. He was so different from my male relatives. He listened to me as if my opinion mattered. He told me about his home. I'd always dreamed of visiting America."

"I always wanted to travel too." Natalie smiled.

"It was very strange, my feelings when the plane landed—as you say in America, 'conflicted,' yes? When I saw you waiting for me, I asked myself hard questions. How could I disappoint such friendliness? How could I do this thing—abandon my family forever, for an American I'd known for only three months? Lose your life, I remind myself."

"That verse means a lot to me too." Natalie hesitated. "Although, I have to admit I've probably never experienced the reality of it the way you have. I mean, my parents aren't Christians either, but at least they haven't disowned me."

The confession warmed Yasmine. "Anyway, I did it—sent you away for coffee and I ran for the exit."

"You left your clothes and everything. I saw the guys in the electrical van drive away with you."

"Joey and Leland. Angels sent by God."

Natalie laughed. "In a really good disguise. Never would have guessed you'd agree to go to a dive like Porky's."

"I normally would not," Yasmine agreed. "But I had no choice. And I wasn't there long. There was a big bearded man standing near the door—"

"That would be Dean."

"Yes, Dean. He very kindly called a cab for me."

Natalie raised a skeptical eyebrow. "I don't know that *kind* is exactly the word I'd associate with Big Dean." She pushed back her chair. "We've got nearly an hour before the guys will get back across the bay. Come on, let's buy a ticket and wander around the ship while we wait. I've always wanted to see this thing."

Yasmine shrugged and followed Natalie back into the welcome center/gift shop. She needed something to take her mind off her impatience to see Zach.

Tickets in hand, she and Natalie tromped across the metal gangway onto the *Alabama*. Yasmine stared up at the battleship, squinting against the midmorning sun. A flock of seagulls dodged in screaming circles around its gun turrets, turning the morning to playtime. The ship, nearly twenty stories high, dwarfed her with its bulk and strength. It represented Zach. His service, his loyalty. Now that she was about to be reunited with him, her fear of Jarrar Haq lessened.

A plaque posted beside the first hatch said the ship had been built in 1942 and saw service during World War II from 1943–1945. Yasmine had little concept of American naval history except what she'd studied in school. All she knew was that the ship was big, cold, and ruthlessly neat, with what seemed like miles of gray iron and steel stretching in every direction. Natalie led the way through a succession of cabins on the first deck, pointing out the displays set up to represent what the ship would have looked like in its heyday. Fascinating to note the antique machinery—a manual typewriter on a metal desk, radios, radar, and teletype machines. Miraculous that *anybody* could win a war with such equipment.

Clambering behind Natalie up a set of spiral stairs that led from one deck to another, Yasmine found her thoughts wandering from the sailors who had manned this ship over sixty years ago to the man whose influence had brought her here. A knot of nerves returned to claw her stomach. It had been two months since she'd seen or heard from Zach. Did she really know him? He was an American naval officer—an agent, she suspected from the mysterious nature of his assignments. How could she be sure that what he'd told her was truth?

"Hey, Yasmine? You coming?"

Startled, she looked up to find Natalie staring down at her from the top of the stairs. Halfway up, a hand on the rail, she'd been caught in a brown study. "Oh, my—I am sorry. I was thinking about ..." Natalie wouldn't care. "Nothing."

Natalie's green eyes softened. "Are you tired? We could find a place to sit for a few minutes. I think there's a lounge type place up here somewhere."

"No, no. Thank you. I am well." Yasmine pushed her apprehension away and continued the noisy climb up the narrow stairs. When Zach arrived, everything would be fine.

They emerged at the top in an empty, echoing metal shaft with low ceilings and uneven floors. It felt like a torpedo shaft. A couple of turns through connecting corridors brought them to a row of cell-like rooms with glass windows. The rooms had been appointed as officer's quarters with a narrow bunk and tiny desk taking up all the floor space. A mannequin dressed in a World War II uniform sat in the desk chair, poring over a letter.

Yasmine stared at the dummy's pensive profile, her eyes filling with tears. She jumped when Natalie touched her arm.

"You'll see him in just a little while," Natalie said softly.

"I'm not—" Yasmine sighed. Why was she pretending? "What if I misunderstood him? What if I have come all this way for nothing?"

Natalie looked troubled. "There's always a risk, I suppose." She glanced away. "I'm not the best at figuring out a man's intentions."

Yasmine walked up to the glass and pressed her hands against it. The mannequin, intent on his letter, ignored her. "I found a note in my Bible after Zach left Islamabad. He said he wanted me to be happy with a man of my own culture. He knew that my family would put me out if they thought I had been converted by the influence of an American Christian. At first I thought he was being noble because he really loved me. But what if he was using me for information?"

"Information? What kind of information?"

Yasmine laid her forehead against the window. She couldn't pinpoint when it had occurred to her. The events of the last eight days had stripped away naïveté until suspicion warred with the desire to believe in the man she loved. Zach had asked many questions about the Haq family. She might be in more trouble than she'd thought. Jarrar's family belonged to a politically conservative sect. Their loyalties were distinctly Muslim. What if Yasmine, tied to the Haqs, was suspected of aiding Al-Qaeda?

"I would like to know this also, Yasmine," said a dark, accented voice behind her. "What information have you shared with our American friends?"

Yasmine turned with a jerk, flattening herself against the window. Jarrar Haq, dressed in an impeccable Italian suit, leaned against a metal pole riveted to the ceiling and floor in the center of the chamber.

Words would not come. All she could do was suck in a huge, gasping breath.

Natalie whirled. "What are you doing here, you sneak? You scared the bejeebers out of me."

He shook his head, a faintly supercilious smile on his lips. "My, how ladylike you are. And what a sleuth. It has not been difficult to keep up with Yasmine at all."

Natalie scowled. "You've been following us? Why?"

Jarrar's thick brows rose. "Why do you think? I want my fiancée."

Yasmine didn't like the black glitter in Jarrar's eyes. Her voice returned with her anger. "And now that you have found me, I tell you to your face that I have decided not to marry you. I gain much courage while I travel the South alone. I meet people who have a stick up for themselves. I discover I am not just Abbi's little girl." She lifted her chin. "I am sorry to disappoint you, Jarrar. You have come all this way for nothing."

Haq pushed away from the pole. "Oh, no. I never do anything for nothing. You promised to be my bride. Your father will make sure you are."

"I am not going back to my father." Said aloud, the words had a bald finality. Yasmine swallowed and committed herself to exile. "I am a Christian."

"You do not know what you are saying." He smiled indulgently. "Allah will forgive you when you are married to a good Muslim."

"Like *you*? You are not a good anything, I think. I am an adult. I have made up my mind." Yasmine caught Natalie's eye. "We should be going. It has been nearly an hour since — "

"Yes, we should really be going," said Natalie, taking Yasmine's arm. "I'm tired of this place anyway. My feet hurt from climbing all those stairs."

"You will come with me." Haq nodded toward the stairs. "I have made arrangements."

Yasmine drew strength from Natalie's arm in hers. "I told you, Natalie and I are not going anywhere with you."

"I am responsible for your well-being." Haq made a peremptory gesture. "I have a car. I will take you back to your father." He held out a well-shaped, almost feminine hand. "Give me your cell phone. Now."

Yasmine's heart thudded hard, but she pretended a bravado she did not feel. "I left everything in Memphis."

Haq frowned. "You are lying. Give it to me or I will search you."

He would make good on the threat. Yasmine's skin tightened in revulsion. She reached into the backpack Natalie had returned to her and withdrew her cell phone. She handed it to Haq. "It is dead anyway."

He looked at Natalie. "Give me yours too."

Natalie was shaking so hard Yasmine could feel the tremors, but she squeezed Yasmine's arm in a comforting way. "No way, you jerk. If I scream, there'll be people down here in seconds."

Haq folded his arms and spoke to Yasmine in Urdu. "There is a pistol in the inside pocket of my jacket. You will make sure your friend does not scream." He paused, glanced at Natalie, then back at Yasmine. His tone remained soft and courteous. "I have your father's permission to move the date of the wedding up. I promise I will be a good husband to you, Yasmine. We should hurry."

Yasmine dragged in a breath and answered in her native tongue. "Move the wedding up? Are you insane?"

Jarrar smiled and said gently, "No one will get hurt if you both come with me, but you should know that I have connections that will greatly affect your family's ability to return to Pakistan should you decide to cross me."

Yasmine closed her eyes. *Father God*, she prayed, thoughts stuttering, *I am terrified. For me, for Natalie, for my family. You have brought me safe this far. I know you can handle this madman. But what should I do?*

Though she heard no audible voice, she had a sense that she should cooperate, at least outwardly. With the blood roaring in her ears, she opened her eyes and looked at Natalie. Her eyes were closed. She was probably in prayer too.

For where two or three come together . . .

She squeezed Natalie's arm. "I have changed my mind. We will go with him."

Natalie blinked. "W-what? Where is he taking us?"

Does that matter? Yasmine thought in despair. "I am not sure, but it will be alright. I will make sure he does not hurt you."

"But what about you? Yasmine, you can't—"

"I said it will be alright." Yasmine sharpened her voice. "Please, Natalie, do not make it harder on me."

Natalie's mouth opened; she shook her head, but couldn't seem to verbalize her outrage.

"I will have your cell phone now," Haq said to Natalie in English.

"I beg your—"

"Natalie, let him have your phone," said Yasmine. "It is for your protection."

Scowling, Natalie reached into her purse. "Here." She threw the cell phone at Haq.

Catching it, he gave her a thoughtful look. "Thank you. Please to come with me."

Yasmine dragged Natalie toward the stairs. The good God would help them somehow.

He had to.

⌒

Natalie stumbled across the parking lot with Yasmine and her psycho terrorist fiancé. Ridiculous that she was in a park full of American military vessels and aircraft, full of tourists and museum curators and other workers, and yet she could not stop the chain of events. She kept straining to watch for Matt pulling up. Unless he was speeding, he wouldn't arrive for another twenty minutes. And he wasn't the speedster of their dynamic duo.

No, Natalie was the one who always jumped head-first into trouble.

Haq's demeanor was suave, courteous—well, if you discounted that ridiculous demand that she surrender her cell phone—and therefore infinitely chilling.

He had clearly made some sort of threat to motivate Yasmine to insist on accompanying Haq to his car. For eight days Yasmine had run, just as hard as she could go, away from this man and his marriage proposal. Now she walked along beside him, if not exactly blithely, then at least with serene resignation.

Haq approached a long, sleek black sedan parked at the back side of the parking lot. A uniformed driver sat in the front reading a newspaper. Haq opened the rear door and politely gestured for the women to get in. "Please," he said, though clearly it was a command and not a request.

Natalie gave him a fulminating look as she slid into the car after Yasmine.

He smiled slightly, shut the door, and went around to get into the front passenger seat. He turned and said something to Yasmine in that liquid language she presumed was Urdu.

Yasmine wetted her lips and responded briefly.

Haq then said in English to Natalie, "Yasmine's parents charged me with the task of making sure she returns safely to Memphis." He clicked his tongue. "I believe they did not quite trust the ability of you and your partner to accomplish the task. The fact that you allowed her to leave Memphis at all was not a good recommendation. This has become quite an expensive venture."

At this point, Natalie decided, it would probably be more dangerous to let him know she was aware of his real motives. "First of all," she said, "*you're* not the one footing the bill, so you have no room to complain. Second, Matt and I have done exactly what we said we would. We found Yasmine, safe and unharmed."

"I assure you I had no intention of hurting your feelings, Miss Tubberville. Please forgive me." The guy was smooth as glass.

Natalie turned her head away. Since she wasn't familiar with the city of Mobile, she looked out the tinted window, trying to figure out where they were headed. They'd already skimmed back across the causeway, through the tunnel and into downtown. A left turn took them down an oak-tree-lined avenue into an increasingly depressed area where tiny shotgun houses and subsidized apartment projects moldered amongst turn-of-the-twentieth-century mansions. Eventually the mansions gave way to dilapidated rentals and commercial wrecks held together by graffiti and burglar bars.

Just when it seemed the road might disappear into the Gulf, it jackknifed off to the right. The sedan swung into an industrial complex of warehouses, brick and aluminum office buildings, and airplane hangars.

"Where are we?" Natalie whispered to Yasmine.

Haq spoke over his shoulder, intent on every sound the women made. "I have arranged a plane to take us to Memphis."

"Hey!" Natalie sat up indignantly. "I'm not leaving my car and my partner here. Turn this school bus right around and take me back where you found me."

"I am sorry," Haq said calmly, "but Yasmine and I are in a hurry. There is no time. You will have to accompany us."

"Natalie, please don't leave me alone," Yasmine murmured.

Natalie felt Yasmine's small hand reach for hers. It was ice cold. On second thought, she wasn't letting Yasmine out of her sight unless she had to. Not when she'd traveled over five hundred miles by land and sea — okay, well, river — to find her. She gripped Yasmine's hand. "Don't worry, Yasmine. I'm hanging with you."

Yasmine's mute smile trembled.

The car executed several more turns and pulled through a gate in a chain-link fence around a private airfield. The driver stopped in a parking lot beside a hangar with several small prop planes parked nearby.

Natalie got up the nerve to address Haq. "Which one of those is yours?"

"My private jet will arrive soon."

The guy had a private jet? He must be pulling in money from somewhere.

The driver got out and opened the door for Natalie and Yasmine. He hadn't said a word during the whole trip from the battleship to the airfield. Presumably he didn't speak English. Now he addressed Haq gruffly in Urdu.

Haq answered, then the driver slid back into the car, put it in reverse, and drove out of the parking lot the way he'd come. Natalie didn't know him from Adam's housecat, but she suddenly felt bereft. Crazy.

Haq looked at Yasmine. "Come, we go inside." He approached the hangar, held open a door marked "office," then waited with perfect courtesy for Yasmine and Natalie to enter.

Natalie stopped just inside the door. The windowless room contained a metal desk, one small rolling chair, and two file cabinets. Something wasn't right. But she had no idea what to do. Haq had not threatened her with a weapon, but a contained menace tightened his expression. Nothing like this had ever happened in Tunica County. The worst she'd had to deal with were drunk gambling addicts and parents who abandoned their children in parked cars.

She glanced at Yasmine. "Are you sure you want to do this?"

Yasmine nodded without looking at Natalie. Her hands were clenched in a knot at her waist.

"Wait here," said Haq. He walked out the door and shut it behind him with a solid *clump*.

Natalie heard a deadbolt click. Her knees buckled. "Yasmine, why are you going along with that man? He's a terrorist!"

Yasmine's face bled out to chalk. "I didn't — didn't know until it was too late," she stammered. "I'm sure my parents don't know. They would never do this to me. Zach asked me questions. About Jarrar. How I came to know him. What he wrote to me. I thought it was natural jealousy." Tears spurted from her eyes, which were squeezed shut. Her mouth twisted. "I am such a fool."

Natalie sank against the edge of the desk for support. "But Yasmine, why did you make me come? Why are we here? We could have gotten away while we were at the battleship. There were people all around!"

"He has a gun. Hidden in his coat. I do not think he would hurt me, at least not now, but he might have hurt you. And he threatened my parents and my sister. He knows where they are." Yasmine mopped her face on the sleeve of her T-shirt. "He is very dangerous. Al-Qaeda, maybe. Natalie, I am so sorry." She began to sob.

Natalie walked to the door and tried the knob. Of course it was locked. She whirled. "Stop crying, Yasmine. We're going to figure out how to get out of here."

TWENTY-TWO

They bought tickets for a battleship tour?" Incredulous, Matt stared at the woman behind the gift shop ticket counter. "I told her to wait for us here!"

Carothers looked equally mystified. "Are you sure it was Yasmine and Natalie?"

The woman shrugged. "I heard the little blonde say they had nearly an hour to kill, so they might as well do something educational."

"That would be Natalie." Matt pinched the bridge of his nose. "Of all the—"

"Do you know how big that ship is?" Carothers's voice rose. "We could spend the day searching and still miss them. And I doubt if her cell phone will work inside it."

Matt growled in frustration. "Let me at least try." He unclipped his phone from his belt. After a couple of failed calls, he slapped the phone shut and put it away. "We'll have to wait. Maybe she'll call me and check in."

Carothers took a tense turn up and down an aisle full of World War II memorabilia. "I'm worried about Yasmine."

Matt watched him. "I know you're into classified stuff, man. But if I'm going to be any help, I think you'd better explain more about what we've gotten ourselves into. Who is this Haq guy?"

Carothers looked around. Besides the lady behind the cash register, who was busy counting credit card receipts, a large group of homeschoolers on a field trip cruised the aisles. "Come on out-side." Once they were out in the parking lot, Carothers stopped and folded his arms. "Alright. You know Haq is the son of the Pakistani Federal Minister for Commerce, right?"

Matt nodded.

"We've been watching him for some time, because of some shipments—supposedly oil transfers—that went to weird places. After he moved to the States, our guys collected Intel that suggested he's an arms broker. But whatever he bought apparently cost more than he could pay. He showed signs of needing cash. Hence the sudden arranged marriage to Yasmine."

"You think her dad was going to settle *that* much money on her now?"

"By Muslim law, the dowry goes to the girl from the groom—for her maintenance. But when the bride's father is as rich as Abid Patel, it often goes the other way. And Abid's daughters mean everything to him."

"Did you know this when you first met Yasmine?" Matt couldn't help the question.

Carothers thrust his hands behind his back and stood straight as a flag mast. He met Matt's gaze fiercely. "I knew. And believe me, I'm a cynical guy. I was prepared to hold her in contempt." His expression lightened. "But you'd have to meet her. She's nobody's spoiled princess."

Matt nodded. "I'm looking forward to it." Curiosity pulled him back to the original topic. "So Haq's dealing in arms, and NCIS sent you all the way to Pakistan to chat up his fiancé?"

"That wasn't my only mission, and I can't go into details. But yeah, Yasmine was definitely a person of interest. See, the marriage would serve the double function of sealing the relationship between her father and Haq's—a merger of interests, if you will—as well as supplying funds for an Al-Qaeda stinger missile deal." Carothers's expression was grim. "I arranged an accidental introduction to Yasmine, and we hit it off. She was interested in my faith because she'd had a Christian roommate in boarding school. I spent a lot of time talking to her about the Lord. Once she became a believer—" he reddened—"it didn't take me long to fall in love with her."

Matt looked down. "Kind of hits you over the head, doesn't it?"

"I take it you know the feeling."

"Maybe." Matt sighed. "I'm not used to feeling responsible for somebody else. It's making me nuts." He shrugged. "But I'm discovering there are some things a whole lot more important than your own comfort and convenience."

⌒

Natalie walked restlessly around the room, circling the desk, rattling the drawers of the file cabinets. They were all locked. There was a closet door, which was also locked. She looked at Yasmine, sitting on the floor propped against the wall. "You remember when you had Oksana lock me and Matt in your cabin?"

"I did not tell her to do that." Yasmine made a face. "Although I thought it was a good idea at the time."

"Well, this is what it felt like."

Yasmine hunched her shoulders. "I am sorry." She looked up into Natalie's eyes. "I am sorry about many things. I wish I had trusted you when I first got off the plane."

"You had no way of knowing I'd be on your side." Natalie sighed. In Yasmine's place she might have done the same thing. "Did you suspect Haq was a criminal before you got engaged to him?"

Yasmine shook her head. "You have to understand—in the Middle East, many people think of men like Jarrar as heroes. They are protected. His father is a high-ranking official in my country. My parents were honored to be connected to the Haq family."

"So you didn't know for sure, until he told you he had the—the gun?" Natalie still couldn't believe she was being held hostage by an international arms dealer. This was so not in her career plan.

"Remember, I did not know him except through our parents' introduction and email. I began to see hints of fanaticism as we corresponded. Couple that with Zach's questions ... Once I suspected, I was afraid for my family." She sighed. "But as you say, that is a river under the bridge."

"You're right." In spite of the queasiness of her stomach, Natalie had to smile. "Now we have to figure out how to get out of here. I wish I hadn't had to give up my cell phone." She started opening desk drawers. Everything else had been locked, but one had to try. The lap drawer, to her surprise, slid out to reveal a couple of army-issue ballpoint pens that looked like they'd been there since the Korean War. A handful of paper clips rattled in a tray beside some rubber bands and a Band-Aid.

Nothing useful.

She jerked open the file drawer on the left, but found it empty, as well as the two small top drawers. Hesitating, she almost didn't open the remaining deep drawer on the right. She finally shrugged and yanked on the handle. Curiosity was a disease.

And might just be their salvation. Under a pile of yellowed file folders squatted an ugly black seventies-style phone. Its cord was neatly folded and tied with a bread tie.

Natalie barely restrained a whoop of victory. They had to stay quiet. Haq might have left a guard outside the door. "Yasmine!" she whispered. "Help me look for a phone jack." She hefted the old phone. Solid plastic and stainless steel, it weighed about five pounds. "Good grief," she muttered, "how did people survive the seventies?"

"I've seen those in the villages outside Karachi." Yasmine obediently got to her feet and started searching the walls.

"When I was little my grandmother had one in the attic that my cousins and I used to play with." Natalie put the clunky receiver experimentally to her ear. "This one probably got left here in case of hurricane emergencies."

"Hurricanes?" Yasmine looked around nervously, as if expecting a typhoon any moment.

Natalie smiled. "The season doesn't start until late summer. Oh, look, here's an outlet behind the desk. Help me move it out a little."

The two of them managed to shove the desk—which, also being standard military issue, weighed roughly the equivalent of a cement truck—away from the wall, enough to allow Natalie to squeeze her hand into the space. She jimmied the cord into the phone jack with a soft click and hopped onto the desk with the phone in her lap. "Here we go. Pray, girlfriend." She held the receiver to her ear again—and got a dial tone. She gave Yasmine a thumbs-up. "Hallelujah. We're cookin' with gas."

"I do not understand. You make dinner with the telephone?"

Natalie stifled her laughter by stuffing her fist against her mouth. "It's a figure of speech. It means we're in business." She shook her head at Yasmine's confused look. "Never mind. Let's try Matt." She laboriously dialed his cell phone number. "Whoever owns this office is going to love their next phone bill. Matt's cell is long distance."

"But he and Zach are in Mobile, yes?"

"I didn't mean *they're* long distance. Just the phone." Natalie listened. The phone rang twice, three times. If she had to leave a voice mail, she was going to—

"Matt Hogan here."

Natalie nearly fell off the desk in her relief. She held her voice down with an effort. "Matt! It's Natalie."

"I didn't recognize the number, almost didn't answer it. Where *are* you?" He sounded irritated.

"Honestly, I have no idea. Jarrar Haq has Yasmine and me locked in some little office in a warehouse complex. It's near an airfield, I think close to downtown. It didn't take us long to get here."

"What? How'd that happen? What's he doing here in Mobile?"

"Apparently he's been following us all the way." Her composure, which she'd been holding onto by a fine thread, suddenly shredded. "Matt, Yasmine said he's got a g-gun, and we're really scared, so you've got to come get us out of here before he takes us who-knows-where—"

"Okay, calm down, sweetheart," he said, his voice every bit as tense as hers. "Of course we'll come get you. You must be at Brookley. Does he have a plane already?"

"I don't think so. He said his private jet would arrive soon. He told us to wait here, locked the door, and left. He took our cell phones, but we found this old rotary phone in a desk drawer."

"Thank God for that." Matt's voice directed away from the receiver. "You hear that, Carothers? How fast can we get to Brookley?"

Natalie heard a muffled conversation between Matt and a man with a deep, calm voice. An authoritative voice. She looked at Yasmine, whose eyes had gone wide.

The Pakistani girl jumped to her feet. "That is Zach! Oh, may I talk to him?"

But Matt came back on the line. "We'll be there in about ten minutes, fifteen tops. Don't hang up until you have to. We'll want as many details about the warehouse location as you can give us."

Natalie clutched the heavy black receiver. "Okay." Her throat closed. "Matt, hurry. I don't want to go anywhere with this guy. Yasmine thinks he's h-hooked up with Al-Qaeda somehow."

"I'm coming for you, Nat. Remember, don't hang up unless you hear Haq coming back."

Natalie hung on and listened to Matt breathe. It was the most reassuring sound she'd ever heard.

⟶

Matt left the rental car in the battleship parking lot and rode with Carothers in his SUV. He kept Natalie on the phone as long as he could. She managed to keep her voice cheerful, though she had to be scared silly. Abruptly, however, as they reached the tunnel, the call failed. As they exited the tunnel and turned south on Broad Street with little regard for speed limit, Matt waited, hoping she'd call back. He couldn't ring her and risk alerting Haq with the sound of the phone.

Nothing. It was as if she'd been swallowed whole.

Frustrated, he squeezed the phone in his palm. "I lost Natalie, Carothers. Now how are we going to find them?"

"Shouldn't be a problem." Carothers swung the vehicle confidently through the maze of warehouses toward the air traffic control tower. "I took a few flying lessons from a private company here at Brookley before I joined the navy, so I'm familiar with the layout. The tower will have the location of Haq's jet, and they'll have his flight plan."

"Okay. That'll work." Matt tried to relax. The thought of Natalie in the hands of a man who had no qualms about selling missiles to terrorists—and might even be one himself—froze him to the marrow. His life had never felt so completely out of control, even in the middle of the George Field debacle.

It occurred to him that a truly spiritual man would be praying. But he hardly knew what to say except *God, help.*

Maybe that would be enough.

⌐

After losing contact with Matt's voice, Natalie dropped the receiver into its big black cradle and stared at Yasmine.

Yasmine twisted her hands. "What should we do now?"

"Well, we could sit here like helpless twits and wait for somebody to come rescue us." Natalie set the phone on the desk. "Or we could figure out something ourselves."

"Figure out what? We are locked in."

"I think we should start by praying. You know, together." Natalie held out her hands, palm up. "Want to?"

"Oh, I do." Yasmine took a shy step toward Natalie. "But not out loud. I do not know how ..."

"There's not any 'how' to it. Talk to God like a friend." Natalie smiled. "You're already a witness. Look how you helped Oksana."

"I did, didn't I?" Yasmine lit up. "She is my sister now."

"That's right. And so are we. Sisters, I mean." Natalie reached for Yasmine's hands. "So when we pray together, God's right here with us."

"Does he always give you what you want?" Yasmine looked curious. "I mean, when you pray with somebody else?"

Natalie considered her answer carefully. She had the feeling whatever she said to Yasmine would be taken to heart and believed no matter what. "I wouldn't say that, exactly. But he gives what he knows is best. And when we pray, he knows we're serious about doing his will. He gives us strength to do the right thing. He says if we need wisdom, all we have to do is ask."

"How will we know what he says?"

"Gosh, Yasmine, you ask good questions, but I'm no expert." Natalie shrugged. "All I know is that we pray and listen. Something will happen."

Yasmine tipped her head. "Okay. I am confused, but I will pray with you. And I will listen."

"Cool." Natalie closed her eyes. "Dear Lord, I know you see Yasmine and me, and you know our problem. We sure do love you, but we're pretty scared. So please help us know what to do. Do we wait here for Matt and Zach to come get us? But what if we wait too long, and these thugs haul us off in Haq's plane?" She swallowed, dampening her panic. "Yasmine doesn't want to marry him. So we need you to keep that from happening."

Natalie paused, but Yasmine didn't say anything, just squeezed her hands.

Natalie thought about Matt's prayer at the hotel in Vicksburg. She wished she had half his faith. It was good to know he was her brother in Christ, and he was coming to get her—even if he wasn't quite in love with her. "Thank you, Lord for providing that phone. Thank you for Matt and Zach. Please keep them safe. Amen." She looked up at Yasmine, who was smiling as if they were eating watermelon at a Sunday school picnic instead of trying to figure out how to get out of a locked office.

Personally, she felt like throwing up. Maybe that would stop Haq from hauling her and Yasmine off. She could see the headlines: "Victim barfs her way out of captivity."

Um, no.

If only they had a weapon. All they had was a set of office furniture, a pair of flip-flops, and a twenty-pound telephone.

Natalie dredged through her memory for TV episodes involving escapes. Nothing came to mind. She picked up the phone receiver. Maybe she could try Matt again. But he was on his way. There was nothing else he could do for her, and he'd only tell her not to do something stupid.

She started to replace the phone, but something about its solid weight in her hand made her look at Yasmine. "I'm feeling really gross," she said experimentally.

"You feel ... large?" Yasmine wrinkled her nose. "This is a German word I know."

"No, not that kind of gross." Natalie grinned. "Gross as in 'not well.' You know, ill." She held her stomach, which truthfully enough was still queasy, even after the prayer. "I need to go to the restroom."

Yasmine looked around helplessly. "I am so sorry."

"We're going to have to make a bunch of noise and get somebody to check on us. Maybe Haq left someone out there."

"Maybe." Yasmine's brow furrowed. "Jarrar will be angry if we attract attention."

"I don't care. I've got to—" she put her hand to her mouth— "you know," she mumbled.

"Okay. I try." Yasmine took a deep breath and walked up to the solid oak door, whacking it with the flat of one tiny hand. "Jarrar!" she shouted. "Hello—is anybody out there?"

There was no immediate answer.

Natalie unplugged the phone receiver's cord at its base. As weapons went, this one was on the bizarre side. But it was all they had. Clutching it tightly, she edged toward the door. She flattened herself against the wall, ignoring Yasmine's wide-eyed confusion. "Try again," Natalie whispered.

"But—"

"I'm feeling *extremely* gross," Natalie said grimly.

Yasmine shrugged and banged on the door again. Several times. Finally she took off her shoe and hammered enthusiastically. "Somebody please come. My friend is very ill!" Her look at Natalie implied the infirmity might be of the mental variety, but she continued to shout and pound on the door.

Just when Natalie was about to drop the heavy receiver in disgust, an irritated and thickly accented male voice growled through the door, "What is the matter? Stop that immediately."

"You have to let us out," demanded Yasmine. "My friend does not feel well. I am afraid she is going to—to—"

"Vomit," Natalie supplied with ghoulish glee.

"Yes, vomit," Yasmine echoed. "She needs to go to the restroom."

"Shut up," said Mr. Cranky Pants. "Jarrar does not like noise."

"Then he should tell you to open this door." Yasmine's voice was as imperious as Queen Elizabeth in a press interview. "What is your name?"

The guard sounded startled. "Feroz."

"Do you know that Miss Tubberville's father is a dignitary of great importance? She is not to be treated this way."

Silence.

Natalie tensed. They might have made their situation worse. What if the angry guard decided to tie them up and gag them? He probably had a gun. What self-respecting terrorist henchman came on the job without a weapon of some sort?

Then the lock clicked. Natalie's heart took a pogo bounce into her throat. She lifted the phone receiver, holding it so tightly it should have melted in her hand. "Back up," she mouthed to Yasmine.

Yasmine obeyed, eyes like saucers, cheeks pale as antique lace. Her lips moved in prayer.

The door thrust open. Natalie struck.

She'd had enough self-defense training to aim carefully. The back of the receiver chopped the tall, muscular guard at the base of his throat, where the gag reflex was the strongest. When he grabbed his throat, she clocked him in the temple.

He went down in a noiseless heap—Goliath felled by a couple of female Davids with a conversation piece.

Yasmine clapped her hands over her mouth. "Oh, my," she whispered.

Natalie was shaking. She made herself think. "Where's the key?"

"It is in his hand." Yasmine recovered from her shock enough to bend down and gingerly remove the key from the guard's slack ham-sized fist. She looked down at him dubiously. "He is very ... gross." She grinned at Natalie.

"Yasmine! You made a joke." Smiling, Natalie dropped the phone and peered outside the door. The hangar was empty, its broad doorway open to reveal a bright, sunny May afternoon. "I don't see your fiancé anywhere."

Yasmine's grin disappeared. "Jarrar is no longer my fiancé."

"Okay, sorry." Natalie put her hands on her hips. "We're gonna have to drag him into the room and lock him in—quick, before he wakes up. You game?"

"This is not a game, Natalie. But I will help."

Shaking her head, Natalie walked around to grab one of the guy's ankles. "You get the other leg. Here we go."

By dint of huffing and puffing and pulling, they managed to tow their captor into the office without rousing him. Natalie took the phone—you couldn't be too careful—and turned the deadbolt. "We've got to hurry." She pocketed the key. "Haq could come back any minute."

The two women slipped quietly along the inside wall of the hangar, heading for the open doorway.

"Where are we going?" whispered Yasmine.

"To find anybody who can get us out of here—preferably a security officer."

"What if we see Jarrar?"

"We'll cross that river under the bridge when we come to it."

TWENTY-THREE

Playing sidekick to a federal agent was pretty cool. If Natalie and Yasmine hadn't been in danger, Matt would have enjoyed busting into the control tower and demanding the location of Jarrar Haq's private jet, as well as a copy of his flight plan.

As it was, his stomach twisted as he and Carothers, armed with the requested information, sped through the industrial complex. They entered the airfield and arrived at Hangar 12C, where a small Learjet waited, already running, steps resting on the tarmac. With a screech of tires, Carothers stopped the SUV in front of the jet and got out, gun drawn. Matt followed, armed with a small 9mm Glock. He prayed he wouldn't have to use it.

Natalie was in that building, locked in an office, probably scared out of her mind. The urge to protect her was feral, violent. The job had always been just an entertaining way to spend his time and make a buck. Now ...

Now he wanted to destroy the man who threatened her.

He let Carothers take the lead, staying behind the protection of the vehicle until it was clear they weren't going to be fired on. In fact, there seemed not to be a soul around, either in the hangar or near the jet. Matt watched Carothers's expression evolve from quiet aggression through stillness to a sort of deflated confusion.

The agent stood up, frowning, holding his firearm in position. "You think they sent us to the wrong hangar?"

Matt shook his head. "I don't know, man. Not likely the control tower would get that wrong." He got to his feet. "Let's take a look around to be sure."

"Alright. I'll check the jet first. Cover me." Carothers held his gun steady and proceeded cautiously toward the plane. After a glance at Matt, he ascended the steps.

Raising his gun, Matt watched the open doorway. Carothers reached the top, paused, then stepped into the plane. Ten seconds passed, thirty, then a whole minute. Matt waited, hardly aware of holding his breath.

Carothers appeared again, gun lowered to his side. "Nobody home," he called.

"You're joking." Matt moved away from the car, lowering his own gun. "Where are they?"

"The flight plan has them taking off at 1:40. It's five minutes past that." Carothers shrugged, then clattered down to the tarmac. "Let's look in the hangar. Maybe there's been some kind of delay."

Tension hooked Matt's shoulders again as he and Carothers stalked toward the wide-open hangar. He would have expected, at the least, an attendant running around somewhere.

As they ducked close to the building, just outside the opening, Matt began to hear faint sounds of conversation. Heart hammering, he peered into the empty hangar. On the right was a closed metal door marked "Office."

"What the heck?" muttered Carothers. Gesturing for Matt to follow, he entered the hangar. He approached the office. "Federal agent!" he shouted, raising his gun. "Open this door."

The noise inside the office halted. After a moment, the door burst open. "Matt!" Natalie's bright face appeared. "I was just about to call you!" She suddenly took in Carothers's gun aimed at her chest. She frowned. "Maybe you'd better put that thing down before somebody gets hurt."

All Matt's tension drained out of his toes, leaving him light-headed with relief. "What's going on around here?" he shouted. "Are you crazy? Where's Yasmine? Where's Haq? I thought you were being held hostage!"

"I was. Yasmine's right here. Homeland Security took Haq and Feroz into custody. We have to go straighten everything out and get debriefed and all that stuff, as soon as—" She looked over her shoulder and stepped aside. "He's right here, Yasmine. Come on."

A small, dark-haired young woman catapulted out of the office and launched herself at Carothers, who caught her in his arms, staggering but laughing. "Whoa, lady. Let me get rid of this weapon." He awkwardly holstered the gun in his underarm clip, then proceeded to kiss Yasmine with blind concentration. She flung her arms around his neck and kissed him back.

Matt stared at them for a bemused moment, then looked at Natalie. She was smiling like a proud mama.

"What are you doing here?" he demanded. "Are you going to tell me what's going on?"

Natalie shrugged. "We decided we didn't want to wait to be rescued. So we conned the guard into opening the door, bonked him over the head with the telephone receiver, and went to find some help." She paused. "It really wasn't such a big deal."

She didn't need to be rescued. Translation: she didn't need him after all. He was surprised at how strongly that twisted his gut.

"We?" He stalked toward her. "This was your idea, wasn't it? You *never* do what you're told, Natalie Tubberville. Do you have any idea what a dangerous situation you were in? You could've been killed. Or worse."

She looked confused. "What's worse than being killed? We were afraid Haq would haul us off before you could get here. The least you could say is 'Good job, Natalie.'" She took a step backward. "What's the matter with you?"

Matt glanced at Carothers and Yasmine, billing and cooing in a corner. No intervention there. Frustrated, he looked back at Natalie.

"You win," he said. He tore his gaze away, looking down at the gun as he released the firing mechanism, unloaded it, and stuffed it in his pants pocket. "You found her first."

"Yeah, but that wasn't . . ."

He could feel her gaze, sense her uncertainty. He made himself smile at her, cool and neutral. "I told you before, and I meant it. You're a first-class detective. You win the finder's fee, and that gets you controlling interest in the agency." He held out a hand. "Congratulations, partner."

TWENTY-FOUR

Dread roiled in Yasmine's stomach as she walked through the lobby of the Peabody Hotel Saturday morning. The strength of Zach's shoulder above hers was comforting beyond measure. There was no way to predict how Abbi was going to react when he saw her. Maybe he would at least tolerate her presence and allow her to talk to Ammi.

Zach reached out and hooked his pinky through hers; the gentle, slight touch stopped the tears about to escape from her eyes. Whatever happened, she had him.

But oh, how she wanted her parents' acceptance.

She and Zach got on the elevator and rode up to the fifth floor. The beautiful old hotel reminded her of places she'd stayed in Europe. Maybe it was the quiet hush imposed by thick carpet; maybe it was the rich paneling. In any case, by the time she reached her parents' room, a sense of supernatural calm had descended. She knew it had less to do with the man beside her and her surroundings than the presence of the Holy Spirit.

"Yasmine."

She looked up at Zach, whose somber blue eyes searched her face.

"Whatever they say to you, remember you belong to God. And we belong to each other."

Her lips trembled toward a smile. "Yes. I know." She stood on tiptoe to kiss his cheek. "Thank you." Raising a hand, she knocked timidly on the door.

It opened. Ammi stood there, one hand clutching the doorknob. She looked as if she might open her arms, but after a moment, stepped back. Her lips trembled.

Dread sank like a stone in Yasmine's stomach. "Ammi, I missed you. I am sorry to make you worry."

Her mother laid her beautiful hand across her lips. "Is it true? Have you taken on the infidel religion?" Ammi looked at Zach, a challenging, resentful glare.

Yasmine gulped. The dreaded question had come. "It has nothing to do with Zach. I love him, yes, but I have accepted Jesus as my Lord—because he is truth. He is the way. He is my life."

"Yasmine—"

"No, listen, Ammi. You will not change my mind about that. I should be sorry—yes, so *very* sorry to lose your and Abbi's regard. But I must follow the Lord Jesus now."

Ammi's tears began to flow. "Your father is heartbroken. The marriage—"

"Ammi, you can't seriously regret the fact that I won't be marrying a criminal like Jarrar Haq!"

"No—of course not. But we both want to see you settled with a good husband to care for you. Otherwise you remain a woman alone."

Yasmine started to speak, but she felt Zach's large, gentle hand cupping her shoulder. "Mrs. Patel, may I speak with you and your husband?"

Ammi stared at him, reluctantly, fiercely. "I don't know what you have to say to us."

"Please." Zach's voice was respectful but firm.

Ammi looked down. "Oh, I suppose. Come with me."

Taking courage from Zach's presence, Yasmine followed her mother into the beautifully furnished living area of the suite. She stopped when she saw her father seated on the edge of a brocade wing chair. His posture and expression were every bit as stiff as his portrait hanging in their home in Karachi.

Then her sister appeared in a doorway to the left. "Yasmine!" Liba flung herself at her.

Yasmine, distracted by her father's stoic face, hugged Liba with all her might. Tears, always near the surface, overflowed. Maybe it was her imagination that her little sister seemed to tower over her now. It had been nearly a year since they'd seen one another. "Liba, oh Liba. I missed you so much. Why did you tell where I was? How could you, when I asked you not to? But I love you anyway, bad girl."

Liba was sobbing. "I missed you too. I couldn't let you run away and never see us again." She drew back, holding Yasmine's shoulders. "Why did you? Don't you love us anymore?"

"I told you. I have become a believer in the Christian God. In Jesus his Son. I didn't mean to hurt you, but I didn't know what else to do." Yasmine smeared her tears away with a tissue she pulled from her jeans pocket. "Besides, I knew Jarrar was hiding something. I had to find Zach and get his help." She looked over her shoulder. Zach stood quietly at the door to the entryway, watching the reunion. His eyes smiled at her. Encouraged, she turned to her father. "Abbi, I want you to meet Zach Carothers. He saved my life."

Her father jerked to his feet, outrage in every line of his face and body. "*Saved your life?* He is the one who takes you away from us."

Yasmine straightened, moving away from Liba to stand beside Zach and proudly take his arm. "Zach is a good man, Abbi. Would you have me married to a terrorist who sells weapons designed to kill innocent people?" When her father didn't answer, only staring at her stubbornly, Yasmine sighed. "I know you do not want to sanction my marriage to a Christian, but it is going to happen whether—"

"Yasmine," Zach said gently. "I would like to say something to both your parents."

She looked up at him. Confidence and love radiated from his eyes. She swallowed. "Alright."

Zach stood tall, but respect restrained his tone. "Mr. and Mrs. Patel, I did share my faith with Yasmine, but she made her own decision to follow Christ. No one can do that for another person. You can't make her Muslim either. But I want you to know that even if you choose not to see either of us again—and that would put a considerable damper on our happiness—you can know that I'll take good care of your daughter. I love her in the way Christ loved his church, and that is enough to give my life for her." He paused, looked down at Yasmine. Tears stood in his eyes, unexpected in this strong man she loved so much. "If there's any way you could allow her to remain part of your family, I'd be grateful," he said simply.

Abbi pressed his lips together in silence.

Father, Yasmine prayed, looking at her sister, who stood with her knuckles pressed to her mouth, *let me not lose my family.*

"Abid." Yasmine's mother cleared her throat. "I think we must move into the twenty-first century. It is very common for modern young people of different faiths and cultures to intermarry." Her voice faltered. "I do not want to lose my baby again! Please, Abid." She buried her face in her hands and began to cry.

Helpless, Yasmine watched her father's face tighten in resentment and confusion. He stared at his wife and shook his head. "Is it the modern way for a man not to be the ruler of his family? Have we come to this, that a rebellious young woman demands acceptance after she flouts her father's authority?" He folded his arms. "I do not agree with this."

Liba fell to the carpet in a heap of grief. Ammi began to sob as if Yasmine had died.

Perhaps she had. Yasmine lifted her hands to her father. "But Abbi, I love you so."

"You are not my daughter." He stared at her, eyes stone cold. "You will please leave."

She would have fallen if Zach had not taken her hand. She clutched him like an old woman and backed toward the door. "Ammi ..." Zach waited, not pulling her, simply moving with her like a rock of comfort. "Liba, I love you."

Liba wailed, and Yasmine moved toward her. Her father stepped between them.

She let Zach hold her up as they left the suite.

Ah, Jesus, you are truly my father, she thought in despair.

⌒

"I can't believe he disowned her!" Natalie, pressing her recovered cell phone to her ear, sat in the wooden rocking chair in Cole and Laurel's living room. It was the only piece of furniture in the house not dusted with cat hair. She eyed Charles Wallace, perched on top of the armoire in the corner. "Poor Yasmine ..."

"Abid was furious she became a Christian," her father boomed. "But it looks like he's going to come through with the finder's fee after all. You two hardboiled detectives are going to be rolling in the dough." He chuckled. "How about that?"

"That—that's great." Natalie shoved the rocker into violent motion. In the dining room she could hear Matt talking and laughing with the McGaughans. They weren't leaving her out on purpose, but she didn't feel part of their triumvirate of friendship. After that disappointing congratulatory handshake in the hangar, Matt's attitude toward her had been casual to the point of rudeness. He'd all but held up a sign that said, "Back off, Barbie."

"What's the matter, sissy?" demanded Dad. "Now that the excitement's died down, you can get back to Memphis, find a new office for the agency, maybe work on some marketing and publicity. I knew you and Hogan would make good partners."

Natalie felt her throat close. After everything they'd been through, the thought of working with Matt on such brotherly terms was more than she could stand. "I don't know, Dad," she blurted. "I'm thinking about going back to Tunica."

"Are you nuts? You hated Tunica."

"No, I—I just needed a break. Now that I know how to handle Bradley, I'll be fine. He won't intimidate me anymore."

"Natalie—"

"Gotta run, Dad. I'll call you on my way home, and we'll talk about it some more."

"Okay, but—wait a minute, peanut, I called you for another reason. Your mom and I wanted to tell you something."

"What is it?" Natalie was afraid she sounded desperate. The tears were close to the surface again.

"Well—humph. You know how much I've always loved your mother, even when we were having problems." He paused, blew out a loud breath.

Speechless, Natalie waited. She could hear her mother in the background. "Just tell her, Eddie."

"Tell me what?"

Dad hemmed and hawed. "We, well, we went to the justice of the peace and got remarried yesterday."

"You got *remarried*? Without telling Nick and Nina and me? *Now* who's crazy?" Natalie clutched the phone. The whole world was spinning out of control.

Her mother's voice came again, louder. She'd confiscated the phone. "I told him we should wait, but he thought it would be romantic to elope and have a honeymoon here at the Peabody, like we did the first time." Mom sounded giggly, of all things. "We'll have a reception or something later. Please be happy for us, Nat."

"Of course I'm happy for you." Natalie couldn't help smiling, though her head ached from the effort of controlling her emotions. "This is wonderful, Mom, truly. I'll throw you a party. But I have to go, okay? I'll see you and Dad next week."

"Alright, baby. I love you."

"I love you, too, Mom—and Dad. Give him a kiss for me."

She closed the phone.

Her parents had remarried. How perfectly screwy.

But nice. She grimaced at Charles Wallace. If only her own love life had had such a happily ever after.

⌒

Matt woke up Sunday morning with the feeling that something was wrong.

Messed-up, down-the-toilet wrong.

He sat up on the attic futon and cast off the sheet Laurel had insisted he bring up with him. The temperature was close to eighty up here, and he was sweating like a pig, but that couldn't quite explain this feeling of general malaise.

Guilt. He mentally poked around, trying to figure out where it came from and decided it must be lack of prayer and Bible study.

Yeah, that was it.

Nothing to do with Natalie's expression when he'd reached out and grabbed her hand yesterday, shaking it like a fraternity brother. No, not even that close. Like an acquaintance who'd won a raffle in a gas station.

Okay, so he was a classic chicken in the love department. He wasn't going to take any chance on her finding out what a loser he was and throwing it in his face. He'd never been any good at holding onto relationships, and the thought of laying himself out there to a woman like her—a woman who followed God with all her heart even when it was painful and embarrassing—

Well, it put him in a sweat.

He rolled off the futon and yanked on his shirt and pants—the same khakis and polo he'd been wearing for the last couple of days. Cole had offered to loan him some clothes, but since McGaughan was well-nigh gigantic, Matt had declined. He couldn't wait to get back to Memphis and his closet full of clothes. Back to Tootie and Ringo and the clock shop. Maybe he'd get home in time to attend church at the mission chapel tonight. A man needed to go to church when he was confused.

At least that was one thing he'd learned on this crazy adventure.

He checked his watch as he tromped down the attic stairs. Seven o'clock. Laurel would probably be cooking breakfast before getting dressed for church. She was a true southern hostess, with a gift for creating beautiful food.

He didn't even know if Natalie knew how to cook anything besides French toast. The man who married her would be taking his chances.

Matt stopped, three steps from the bottom of the stairs. The thought of anybody walking off with Natalie—anybody except *him*—made him break out in a fresh sweat. He wasn't sure he was ready to get married, but losing her wasn't an option either.

Abruptly he sat down. *Holy smoke.* He was in love with Natalie.

"Hogan, you feeling alright?" Cole had wandered through the hallway and paused at the foot of the stairs. "I told Laurel we should put a fan up there or something—"

"I'm fine." He plowed his hands through his hair. "I'm just losing my mind."

"Oh, is that all?" Cole sounded amused. "Natalie must be too. She left around five o'clock this morning. Said she had some loose ends to tie up before she moves."

"What? Moves where?"

"I'm disappointed in you, man. You must have reverted to type. I thought she was a keeper."

"What are you talking about?"

McGaughan stuck his hands in his pockets. "I tried to tell her to be patient, that you're not a complete jerk all the time, but when she started crying I gave up. You'll have to dig yourself out on your own this time."

"I'm not a jerk at all! Why would she say that?" Matt lurched to his feet. "You let her leave without me?"

"How was I going to stop her? You've got a lot to learn about women. I bet you never even told her you love her."

"I'm not saying that unless I mean it."

"Oh, really?" Cole raised his brows. "That sounds noble. But let me explain something on your kindergarten level. Making yourself vulnerable to a woman takes a lot more courage than chasing crooks. Letting her hold you accountable for your spiritual growth, taking responsibility for guarding your relationship. I never took you for a coward, Hogan. Guess I was wrong."

Matt watched Cole saunter into the living room, whistling. He would have gone after him, except for the fact that he had nothing to say in his own defense.

He *was* a coward, and he didn't deserve Natalie.

Natalie hit Germantown shortly after noon—having driven straight through with only one stop for gas and a restroom break—and set to packing like a woman possessed. It took longer than she'd anticipated. Turned out she'd left things pretty much in a wreck, with clothes and shoes and books scattered all over the bed, floor, desk, chair. There was even a pair of fishnet hose flung across the curtain rod.

But by five o'clock she had all her possessions stuffed into a mesh laundry sack, two suitcases, and a hanging bag. She could leave in the morning, after she'd had a chance to talk to Mom—assuming her mother actually planned to come home. Natalie wouldn't be surprised if her parents elected to stay another week on their impromptu honeymoon.

The house was silent as a tomb; even Tinkerbell had gone to visit Nina for the weekend. Restless, Natalie turned on the TV, clicked through several mindless programs, and decided she didn't even have the patience for a rerun of *What Not to Wear*, her favorite show. By six she was starving; a scavenger hunt through the refrigerator produced a carton of blueberry yogurt and a Granny Smith apple. Grimacing, she ate them standing at the kitchen sink.

Eventually it occurred to her that since it was Sunday she should probably go to church. The mission chapel—she could offer to play piano again. Grabbing her purse, she hopped in the car and drove over to Beale Street.

When she got there, however, the doors were locked up tight. She peered in, hands on the glass. What kind of mission didn't have church on Sunday night?

Probably one run by people who had a life.

She turned and slumped against the front door. She could walk over to the mission itself, hang out with David and Alison and the baby. And Keturah. Or . . .

She looked across the street, down the next block. At seven o'clock the Jailhouse Rock Clock Shop sign already glowed in orange neon, though it was still full daylight. She could walk down and say hello to Tootie. Matt was still in Mobile, hanging out with his friends. Her friends too. Cole had been very sweet to her this morning, blinking sleepily at her from the kitchen doorway after she dropped the tea kettle and made so much noise the dog started howling in the backyard. He'd tried to get her to stay and talk to Matt about her feelings.

Matt could go jump in a lake. She didn't want to work with him anymore. The big jerk.

She hadn't thought about him all day. Well, not much. Every time those twinkling hazel eyes appeared in her brain, she'd blinked really hard to make them go away. It almost worked.

So there was no reason she couldn't stop by to see Tootie, as long as she was on this side of town. People. She needed people around. Sane people who said what they meant and meant what they said.

Leaving her car parked in front of the mission, she crossed the street and marched down the cracked sidewalk. A few tourists hung around outside the bars and cafés and clubs, reminding her of her first venture down Beale Street looking for Yasmine. Sometime she would have to duck into Silky's and say hi to Wilson and Conrad and Ray. And Killian the goat.

She grinned. In spite of everything, she'd had an adventure she'd be able to tell her grandchildren about. Assuming she ever let another male within ten feet of her.

The law office beside Matt's apartment was locked up tight, but a lamp glowed in Tootie's front window. Natalie pushed the doorbell and waited. She probably should have called first.

Before she could turn around and head back to her car, the door opened abruptly.

"Natalie!" Tootie backed up, a welcoming grin softening her severe expression. "How's the blanket coming?"

"Blanket? Oh, the blanket." Natalie laughed. "Haven't had time to work on it since Matt and I left for—" Reminded of her partner's shallow interpersonal skills, she looked away for a moment before making herself smile at Tootie. "You know we found Yasmine?"

"Matt called to tell me he's staying in Mobile another night. He mentioned it. Come on in, I was just making a cup of tea." Tootie gave Natalie a searching look over her shoulder as she opened the door of her apartment. "He sounded a little depressed but wouldn't tell me what's wrong."

"He's probably just mad because I won our bet." Natalie tried to drum up triumph. "He doesn't like to lose to a girl."

"He doesn't like to lose period. Come talk to me while I make the tea."

Ringo, snoozing on the sofa, picked up his head as the women passed through the living room. He jumped down to follow hopefully. "You've had your supper, Ringo," Tootie told the waddling little dog. "Lie down."

Ringo sighed and flopped onto the rug in front of the refrigerator. Natalie bent to pet him as Tootie buzzed around the kitchen. "Well, I'm not sure I can work with a sore loser. I've packed up to go back to Tunica."

"Oh, that's mature." Tootie gave her a dry look. "What does Matt say about that?"

"He—he doesn't know. I didn't make up my mind until I got home. Here, I mean."

"This is home, isn't it?"

"It's where I grew up. But I've got to be independent. I wanted to prove I could be a detective, and I did. So I'll just keep working until the sheriff promotes me. I gave up too soon."

Tootie didn't say anything, just shook her gray head, turned off the whistling tea kettle, and poured boiling water into a porcelain teapot.

Natalie stood up. "What are you thinking?"

"Matthew says I'm too free with my opinions."

"I suspect you don't usually let that bother you." Natalie wandered to the breakfast table and sat down. "Come on, Tootie. My mom's not available, and I need some advice. You probably know Matt as well as anybody. Do you think I'm giving up on *him* too soon? I l-like him better than any guy I've ever known, but I'm not going to throw myself at him again."

"Again?" Tootie's eyebrows climbed. She set the teapot and cups on the table.

"Well, it was sort of mutual." Natalie sighed. "But he made it clear yesterday he doesn't want to go beyond friendship and a little, um, making out."

Tootie put her hands on her hips. "You young people. You don't know what to do with real emotions, so you jump right into the physical stuff way too soon."

"I know, I know!" Natalie groaned. "So help me!"

Tootie sat down and covered Natalie's hands with her slightly arthritic ones. "It's like knitting a blanket, sweet cheeks. One stitch at a time."

CHAPTER
TWENTY-FIVE

As he ladled himself another cup of punch, Matt yanked at the knot of his tie and looked around the crowded dance floor. Why Natalie had picked a banquet room at the Peabody for Eddie and Deb's second wedding reception was beyond him. Baby back ribs at the Rendezvous would have been more appropriate to this rowdy party. Nick, in charge of hiring the DJ, had come up with a fellow college student with an apparent hearing loss, and Eddie and Deb made sure drinks at all levels of alcoholic content flowed free. Matt was working on a headache.

He was considering asking Natalie to dance just to relieve the tension.

As if that would help. He'd called her several times over the last two weeks. But would she give him the time of day? Oh no. She was polite. She was interested in the investigation they'd taken on for the Memphis PD. She denied she'd seriously thought about moving back to Tunica.

"Where'd you get an idea like that?" she'd laughed when he mentioned it the Monday she showed up at his office for work. "Cole misunderstood me."

And she categorically refused to talk about what made her pack up and leave Mobile that Sunday morning without him.

"Don't take everything so seriously, Matt. We have work to do."

And she was good at the work. She'd learned how to run an Internet background check with efficiency and thoroughness. She was a genius at getting police officers to talk to her off the record. And her marketing skills were unmatched.

There she was now, over on the other side of the room—one arm hooked through her father's, the other around her mother's waist—talking to some aunt or other. They were a good-looking family, Matt would have to admit.

Okay, *Natalie* looked beautiful tonight. She wore a green spaghetti-strap dress with a flirty hem that ended just above her knees, from which, he noticed, the scabs had finally disappeared. She had on a pair of skinny high heels that were barely more than a bunch of black straps around her pretty feet. Some of her hair was kind of bunched on top in a little flowery clip, and it made her look sophisticated and very un-Natalie-like.

He *really* wanted to dance with her.

He tossed back his punch and plowed through the crowd toward her.

The aunt wandered off as Deb smiled at Matt, radiant. "Matt! Are you having a good time?" she asked.

At least Matt thought that was what she said. All he could hear was a deafening rendition of "Geek in the Pink."

He nodded, then looked at Natalie. She was staring at her polished toes. "Would you like to dance?"

She didn't even look up.

Irritated, he glanced at Eddie, who grinned and cupped his ear.

Oh. Matt touched Natalie's shoulder, electrified by its silken warmth.

She flinched and looked up at him. "What?"

"Dance?" he shouted.

She looked confused. He noticed she didn't have on her glasses. She probably couldn't see *or* hear him.

Winking at Deb, he disengaged Natalie's hand from Eddie's elbow and tugged her toward a relatively abandoned corner. By the time they got there an old Eric Clapton ballad was playing. Without further attempt to talk, he pulled her into his arms.

Of course she resisted. At first.

But within a few seconds he had her left hand in his right, and his left hand lay at the back of her waist. She relaxed and moved with him.

They swayed that way until Matt was sure he'd won some kind of skirmish in this incomprehensible war of emotions. He had no idea what to say to her, but maybe if he kept moving she would eventually break down and tell him what he'd done wrong.

Then the song ended. He stepped back.

Holy smoke, she was crying.

❧

"What's the matter?" Matt's voice cracked in the sudden emptiness after the music stopped.

Natalie hastily swiped her fingers under her eyes and looked around. Thank goodness nobody was looking at them, so she gave him a teetering little smile, the best one she could produce. Dancing with him, being held casually in his arms with his chin against her temple, was exquisite torture. "Nothing. Thanks, Matt. I've got to go—"

"Oh no you don't." He slid in front of her so that she had to stop or run over him. Which would have been a pleasure, except he was too big and solid. She could feel his eyes burning on her face. "Come here." He pulled her through a door into a hallway outside the banquet room. It was blessedly quiet.

They stared at one another. Every sensation gathered on Natalie's skin until she felt like she'd run headlong into a cactus.

Matt was the first to show signs of life. He gave her a little grin, so that his dimples slashed his cheeks. "Can you hear me now?"

She picked at her bracelet. "What do you want?"

He sobered. "I want to know what *you* want." His voice sounded strained. "The paperwork on the partnership will be finalized next week. We've got cases coming in. Your dad's happy. Your mom's happy. Heck, *I'm* happy. Everybody but you ..."

Natalie shrugged. "What makes you think I'm not happy?"

"I don't know. I can't explain it. Ever since we got back from Mobile, you've been so ... so weird. Why are you acting like this?"

She looked up at him in despair. He was asking all the questions, without volunteering his own feelings, and she couldn't answer honestly without sounding like a pathetic twerp. "I'm just tired, Matt. It's been a long day."

"You need to relax. Let's dance again."

She backed away. "I'm in charge of the party. I've got to get back inside and mingle."

"Not yet. Please, Natalie." He sounded wistful.

One stitch at a time. She waited for him to say something else, but he just looked at her sort of helplessly. She swallowed. "I have to go." She stepped around him.

"Hold on." This time he took her by the upper arms. She could feel the weight of his hands, hard and masculine and urgent. "Nat, come on. I've been trying to figure out the right time and place, but it never comes. The right words, they just disappear." He glanced at the door, through which another rock song could be heard booming. "At least we're well chaperoned. I know you worry about stuff like that."

She looked up at him in disbelief. "Now's a fine time to think of that!"

"There are probably a lot of things I haven't thought about enough." He sighed, rubbing his thumbs against her bare shoulders. "I've dragged you all over Mississippi and insulted you and kissed you and treated you like my little sister until it's no wonder you want to haul off and slap me."

Shivering, she backed toward the door. "I didn't say I wanted to slap you."

"It's all over your face." He followed, catching her hands in his. "Or something is. Maybe I'm misreading. Anyway, I wanted to tell you I'm sorry for taking you for granted. And that I'm really glad we're partners because ... because I can't do without you now."

Natalie felt the metal door behind her. There was no place else to go. The feel of Matt's fingers threaded through hers took every coherent thought out of her head. "What?"

He was a very affectionate person, she reminded herself, staring at the little polo guy on his shirt. He'd kissed her on the forehead several times, plus that electrifying occasion in the pantry. He liked girls, and she happened to be female. He didn't mean anything personal.

Her gaze moved to the tanned opening of his unbuttoned shirt. She wanted to kiss him there. But probably that would not be a good idea.

"I said, I can't function without you." He almost sounded angry.

She looked up at him and found his eyes blazing into hers.

"Natalie, you are the most irritating, beautiful, brilliant woman I've ever met. You challenge me and make me a better man, because you don't let me slide by with mediocre. I'm pretty sure God gave you to me on purpose."

"Matt—"

"No, wait. One day I'll let you do all the talking, since that's what you're good at, but I need to say this before I lose my nerve." He smiled then, lifting her hands against his chest. "I want to do this right. Your dad said I should give you time to make up your mind—but if you think you could give me a chance, I'd be the happiest man in the world."

Natalie blinked up at him as relief and joy rushed through every nerve ending in her body. She thought she understood him, but she'd better make sure. "I've already told you I don't want more than a fifty-fifty share of the agency. Daddy agreed—"

Matt's expression fell. "I'm not talking business. I'm handing my heart over to you. I've never done this before, so I probably didn't say it right, but I'm falling in love with you. I want to court you. I want to pick you up and take you out on dates and hang around with your family and maybe ... maybe duck into a closet every now and then."

It was her turn to frown. "Then you *don't* want to be business partners?"

"Of course I do! Lord, no wonder I've spent the last few weeks whacked out of my mind. I want the whole stinkin' enchilada!"

They stared at one another until Natalie began to laugh. "Boy, that was romantic."

Finally Matt cracked a smile. "I told you I was messed up. Okay, it's your turn to say something."

"I don't know what to say."

"Well, that's a first." He put his mouth next to her ear. "I'll give you a hint. How about something like 'I feel the same way, Matt,' or 'Shut up and kiss me, Matt'?"

"I feel the same way, Matt," she breathed. "Shut up and kiss me."

He did.

Fireworks

Elizabeth White

Susannah is out to prove that pyrotechnics genius Quinn Baldwin is responsible for a million-dollar fireworks catastrophe during a Mardi Gras ball.

With her faithful black Lab, Monty, she moves to the charming backwater city of Mobile, Alabama, to uncover the truth. But this world-traveled military brat with a string of letters behind her name finds herself wholly unprepared to navigate the cultural quagmires of the Deep South.

Captivated by the warmth and joy of her new circle of friends, Susannah struggles to keep from falling for a subject who refuses to be anything but a man of integrity, compassion, and lethal southern charm. *Fireworks* offers a glimpse into the heart of the South and a cynical young woman's first encounter with Christ-like love.

Softcover: 978-0-310-27390-5

Pick up a copy today at your favorite bookstore!

Fair Game

Elizabeth White

Jana Cutrere's homecoming to Vancleave, Mississippi, is anything but dull. Before she's even reached town, the beautiful young widow hits a stray cow, loses her son in the woods, rescues an injured fawn, and comes face to face with Grant Gonzales, her first high school crush.

Grant recently returned to town himself amid hushed controversy. His only plan: leave the corporate world behind and open a hunting reserve. Seeing Jana again ignites old memories … and a painful past. Tensions boil over when he learns exactly why she returned. Jana plans to convince her grandfather to develop a wildlife rescue center — dead center on the prime hunting property he promised to sell to Grant!

With deadlines drawing near for the sale of the property and no decision from her grandfather, can Jana trust God with her and Grant's future, or will explosive emotions and diametrically opposing views tear them apart?

Softcover: 978-0-310-26225-1

Pick up a copy today at your favorite bookstore!

ZONDERVAN®
.com

Off the Record

Elizabeth White

Judge Laurel Kincade has it all—brains, beauty, and an aristocratic Old South family to back her up. A political rising star, she's ready to announce her candidacy for chief justice of the Alabama Supreme Court.

Journalist Cole McGaughan has ambitions too. Working as a religion writer for the New York *Daily Journal*, he longs to become a political reporter. Then his old friend Matt Hogan, a private investigator, calls with a tip. The lovely young judge may be hiding a secret that could derail her campaign. Would Cole like to be the one to break the story?

Cole sees a clear road to his goal, but there's a problem. Laurel's history is entangled with his own, and he must decide if the story that could make his career is worth the price he'd have to pay. Can Cole and Laurel find forgiveness and turn their hidden past into a hopeful future—and somehow keep it all off the record?

Softcover: 978-0-310-27304-2

Pick up a copy today at your favorite bookstore!

Share Your Thoughts

With the Author: Your comments will be forwarded to
the author when you send them to *zauthor@zondervan.com*.

With Zondervan: Submit your review of this book
by writing to *zreview@zondervan.com*.

Free Online Resources at
www.zondervan.com/hello

 Zondervan AuthorTracker: Be notified whenever your
favorite authors publish new books, go on tour, or post
an update about what's happening in their lives.

 Daily Bible Verses and Devotions: Enrich your life
with daily Bible verses or devotions that help you start
every morning focused on God.

 Free Email Publications: Sign up for newsletters on
fiction, Christian living, church ministry, parenting, and
more.

 Zondervan Bible Search: Find and compare
Bible passages in a variety of translations at
www.zondervanbiblesearch.com.

 Other Benefits: Register yourself to receive online
benefits like coupons and special offers, or to participate
in research.